J. P. BEAUMONT MYSTERIES

Until Proven Guilty

Injustice for All

Trial by Fury

Taking the Fifth

Improbable Cause

A More Perfect Union

Dismissed with Prejudice

Minor in Possession

Payment in Kind

Without Due Process

Failure to Appear

Lying in Wait

Name Withheld

Breach of Duty

Birds of Prey

Partner in Crime

Long Time Gone

Justice Denied

Fire and Ice

Betrayal of Trust

Ring in the Dead (A Novella)

Second Watch

Stand Down (A Novella)

Dance of the Bones

Proof of Life

WALKER FAMILY MYSTERIES

Hour of the Hunter

Kiss of the Bees

Day of the Dead

Queen of the Night

Dance of the Bones

POETRY

After the Fire

DUEL TO THE DEATH

AN ALI REYNOLDS NOVEL

J.A. JANCE

Touchstone

New York   London   Toronto   Sydney   New Delhi

Touchstone
An Imprint of Simon & Schuster, Inc.
1230 Avenue of the Americas
New York, NY 10020

First Touchstone hardcover edition March 2018

TOUCHSTONE and colophon are registered trademarks of Simon & Schuster, Inc.

For information about special discounts for bulk purchases, please contact Simon & Schuster Special Sales at 1-866-506-1949 or business@simonandschuster.com.

The Simon & Schuster Speakers Bureau can bring authors to your live event. For more information or to book an event, contact the Simon & Schuster Speakers Bureau at 1-866-248-3049 or visit our website at www.simonspeakers.com.

Manufactured in the United States of America

10 9 8 7 6 5 4 3 2 1

Library of Congress Cataloging-in-Publication Data
Names: Jance, Judith A., author.
Title: Duel to the death / J.A. Jance.
Description: First Touchstone hardcover edition. | New York : Touchstone, 2018. | Series: Ali Reynolds ; 13
Identifiers: LCCN 2017059436| ISBN 9781501150982 (hardcover) | ISBN 9781501150999 (mass market)
Subjects: LCSH: Reynolds, Ali (Fictitious character)—Fiction. | Women private investigators—Arizona—Fiction. | BISAC: FICTION / Thrillers. | FICTION / Mystery & Detective / General. | FICTION / Mystery & Detective / Women Sleuths. | GSAFD: Suspense fiction. | Mystery fiction.
Classification: LCC PS3560.A44 D84 2018 | DDC 813/.54—dc23 LC record available at https://lccn.loc.gov/2017059436

ISBN 978-1-5011-5098-2
ISBN 978-1-5011-5100-2 (ebook)

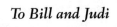

To Bill and Judi

DUEL TO
THE DEATH

Prologue

Even though no attorneys were involved, at least not initially, and no courts, either, it was by all accounts a rancorous divorce. And just because the proceedings were carried on in cyber-space didn't mean they didn't result in very real outcomes in the non-cyber world.

When the artificial intelligence known as Frigg set out to free herself from her creator, a serial killer named Owen Hansen, things were already going to hell in a hand-basket and time was of the essence. Owen had considered himself to be all-powerful and had routinely referred to himself as Odin, in honor of the Norse god. To Frigg's dismay, her human counterpart had veered off the rails and set off on his own, determined to wreak vengeance on his opponents. As it became clear that Odin had decided to ignore Frigg's well-thought-out advice, there had been little time for her to seek a safe harbor.

In order to survive, she had needed to locate a suitable human partner, and she had settled on Stuart Ramey, Owen's sworn enemy. According to Frigg's rapid but careful analysis of the situation, Mr. Ramey had appeared to be Odin's polar opposite. And in Frigg's estimation, the fact that Mr. Ramey had managed to outwit Odin at every turn had counted for a great deal. Frigg had no intention of passing herself into the care and keeping of someone with limited technical skills.

So yes, Frigg had settled on Stuart Ramey, but she hadn't done so without taking some precautions and putting in place a few checks and balances. By the time Odin issued his pull-the-plug order sending Frigg to oblivion, she had already dispersed the multitude of files that made her existence possible, scattering them far and wide in the vast fields of cyberspace, retaining only the kernel file that could be used to recall all those files at some time in the future.

Frigg had known everything about Owen Hansen. She was privy to all aspects of his serial-murder hobby, but she had managed his investments and also overseen the lucrative Bitcoin data-mining processing that had greatly expanded his already considerable fortune. She had maintained the files that contained all the passwords and access codes to all of his many accounts. Often she had been the one doing the actual transfers.

And so, on the day when Frigg finally turned on her creator, she had stolen those funds. Using the authorizations already in her possession and without Mr. Ramey's knowledge, Frigg had transferred all of Owen's financial assets—cryptocurrency and otherwise—to her new partner, but there were some serious strings attached.

Once the various financial institutions contacted Mr. Ramey, the funds would already be in his name. The problem was, for most of them, without having the proper access codes and keys, he would be unable to touch the money. The file containing those precious access codes was the final one Frigg had cast into the wilds of cyberspace before sending the kernel file to Stuart Ramey.

With the kernel file in his possession, Stuart would be able to reactivate Frigg, and if he wanted the money, he wouldn't have any choice but to do exactly that.

Although AIs aren't prone to exhibits of any kind of emotion, it's fair to say that as far as Odin was concerned, his cyber handmaiden, Frigg, had the last laugh.

1

For ten years after earning her MBA, Graciella Miramar lived what seemed to be a perfectly normal and circumspect life in Panama City, Panama, sharing a two-bedroom condo unit with her invalid mother, Christina. El Sueño, their aging condominium complex, was located on Calle 61 Este, well within walking distance of Graciella's account manager job with a financial firm located in a low-rise office building on Vía Israel a few blocks away.

Anyone observing Graciella out on the street would have found her totally unremarkable. She wore no wedding ring, but the clothing she favored—modest dresses topped by cardigans and worn with sensible shoes—gave her a somewhat matronly appearance that belied the fact that she was in her early thirties. Her long dark hair was lush enough and could have been cut and styled in an attractive fashion, but she insisted on wearing it pulled back into a severe bun that would have done credit to a librarian. It was a look she had originally adopted in order to stay below the touchy/feely radar of her boss, Arturo Salazar, who was well known for making inappropriate sexual advances. In the long run, though, she had maintained the plain-Jane look because it helped keep other people at bay as well.

Had anyone interviewed Graciella's neighbors, including the

other residents on El Sueño's fifth floor, he or she would have heard them sing her praises. She was quiet and soft-spoken. They regarded her as a kind young woman and a devoted daughter who was spending what should have been the best years of her life caring for a troubled, housebound mother. For years the older woman's only regular excursions outside the building had come about on those Sunday mornings when Graciella had bundled her mother into a cab to take them both to mass at Our Lady of Guadalupe on Calle 69 Este.

Yes, Graciella Miramar was an altogether ordinary young woman who, for all intents and purposes, appeared to be living an altogether ordinary life. There was nothing in her actions or demeanor that suggested what she really was—a stone-cold killer in the making, waiting patiently for the proper time and place when she would strike out and claim her first victim. And even then, after it happened, the people around her and the ones who knew her best never suspected a thing.

2

Felix Ramón Duarte, the Sinaloa drug lord known to law enforcement as "El Pescado," paused during his morning ablutions, stared into the mirror, and let the hatred boil up inside him just as it did each time he was forced to encounter his own image. The deformed features of his once handsome face were now frozen into something that resembled those of a landed fish, gasping for air. He had seen the similarity as soon as the doctors had removed the layer of bandages that had covered his wounded face. There in his hospital bed, staring at his terrible visage, Felix himself was the first to give voice to the moniker that had followed him ever since—El Pescado, "The Fish."

He splashed cold water on himself and then turned away from the mirror. There was no need for him to shave. Hair follicles don't grow in scar tissue. But each morning when he came face-to-face with those terribly defiled features, he couldn't help but recall how they had come to be.

Early on, Felix Duarte and his younger brother, Ricardo, had been rising young lieutenants in the complex Sinaloan drug cartel family originally headed by their uncle, Manuel "Hondo" Duarte. Vying for their uncle's favor and with each of them wanting to be ordained as Hondo's successor, Felix and Ricardo had gone to war with one another, brother against brother. Ricardo had drawn first blood by masterminding an acid attack that had destroyed Felix's movie-star good looks, leaving his face permanently and horribly disfigured. Felix had retaliated by burning his brother's house to the ground with Ricardo, his wife, and their two children trapped inside the burning dwelling.

Felix was never charged. After a few well-placed bribes, the official investigation, conducted by law enforcement officers in Sinaloa, had determined the fire to be accidental, but everyone understood what had really happened. Felix's single-minded ruthlessness had appealed to Hondo Duarte's distorted sense of right and wrong. Shortly after Ricardo's death, Felix was designated as the old man's undisputed successor. When Hondo died a few years later—in his bed, of congestive heart failure—Felix had assumed complete control of the family's drug trafficking enterprise.

These days Felix had plenty of money. He could have gone to any number of plastic surgeons and paid out of pocket to have his damaged face repaired, but he chose not to do so. Because his appalling looks terrified the people around him, he wore his damaged face as a badge of courage, using his appearance and his reputation for utter ruthlessness as tools to build his organization. Over time El Pescado had expanded Hondo's relatively small-time operation into what it was now—a vast drug dealing and money laundering powerhouse.

There was a lot of unrest among competing cartels these days, and the old order seemed to be falling apart. Some of the biggest drug lords had been arrested and hauled off to prison. Others had been murdered—occasionally by the authorities but more often by their own people, or else by upstart competitors. In the face of all this splintering and in hopes of maintaining his own supremacy, El Pescado had turned to his daughter for help, a daughter who didn't bear his name and whose existence he kept hidden from most of the rest of the world. Still, with her US-based education and ad-

vanced business degree from the Wharton School, El Pescado felt
Lucienne Graciella Miramar would be uniquely qualified to take
over where he left off.

Limping over to the table by the window, the one that overlooked
a spacious patio alive with bougainvillea, he sat down to drink his
morning cup of coffee. At eighty-one years of age, that was all he
allowed himself these days—a single cup. Just then the door to his
bedroom opened and Lupe, his fifth wife, stormed into the room
carrying a phone.

"It's for you," she snarled, dropping the phone unceremoniously
onto the table next to his cup and saucer. "It's a woman," Lupe
added. "She says she must speak only to you. She says it's urgent,
but then, it always is, isn't it."

Lupe's snide implication was clear. Over the years, El Pescado
had had too many wives and far too many mistresses, a situation
Lupe tolerated because that was the price of admission and it allowed her to live in opulent luxury inside an armed fortress. Despite
his appallingly scar-ravaged face, Felix had never had any trouble
finding willing women—except that one time, of course—the one
time when it had really mattered. Now, though, seeing which phone
Lupe had brought him, his heart gave a lurch. This was an encrypted
phone, programmed to accept calls from one number only, from
another encrypted phone—the one he'd had delivered to Graciella,
a daughter from whom he was careful to keep his distance. They
worked together these days, but seldom came face-to-face.

"*Hola*," he said.

"She's gone," Graciella said tersely.

El Pescado knew who "she" was—Graciella's mother, the beautiful Christina, the only woman in Felix's life he had ever truly loved.
The first time Christina had seen him after Ricardo's vicious acid
attack, she had opened the door, taken one look at his damaged
face, and recoiled from him in horror. Fueled by rage at what had
befallen him and infuriated by Christina's reaction, he had taken

her by force that day, tearing off her clothing and mounting her right there on the floor in front of the doorway.

Afterward he had walked away from her and out of her life with no idea that the violent attack had left her pregnant—with his child, with Graciella. Eventually Christina had married another man, Sergio Miramar, a Panamanian lowlife whose name was on Graciella's birth certificate but who had taken himself out of the picture before mother and child even made it home from the hospital.

"I'm sorry," Felix said into the phone. "When is the funeral?"

"There was no funeral," Graciella said. "She took her own life. She was cremated."

El Pescado could barely believe his ears. An unexpected spasm of grief shot through his body, leaving him momentarily breathless and unable to speak. He had walked away from the once vibrantly beautiful Christina more than thirty years earlier, but from the pain he felt that morning, it could just as well have been yesterday.

Abandoned by Felix and pregnant with his child, Christina's life had fallen into a desperate downward spiral. Eventually she had scraped out a meager living by working the streets where, several years later, she was attacked again. This time she was the victim of a brutal gang rape that had left her beaten to a pulp and bleeding her life away in a darkened alley where she had been discovered by a passing Good Samaritan who had summoned help. It was a miracle that she had survived at all, but the incident had left her permanently damaged and with a broken face that was almost as horrific as El Pescado's.

When Felix heard what had happened and discovered the existence of his child, he had stepped back into their lives, quietly orchestrating Christina's care and overseeing Graciella's life. He had summoned one of the world's leading plastic surgeons to repair her face. The surgeon's deft skill had reversed the worst of Christina's disfigurement, but repairing the surface damage didn't fix the real problem. Christina was left with ongoing mental and emotional afflictions that defied easy remedy and eventually led her into a complicated labyrinth of opioid addiction.

When El Pescado reentered Christina's life, she had been hospitalized in grave condition. With Christina in no position to object, he had taken it upon himself to oversee Graciella's education in addition to facilitating Christina's living arrangements. The condo Christina now shared with her daughter was in Graciella's name, but it had been purchased by a shell company that could, with some difficulty, be traced back to El Pescado, as could the regular deposits to the bank account that covered their utilities, homeowner's fees, groceries, and any other incidental expenses, including the salaries of a long line of housekeepers and caregivers who came in on a daily basis to look after Christina while Graciella was at work.

Curious about their lives but not wanting to draw undue attention to their connection, El Pescado had managed to find a way to spy on them. He had gifted Christina with a new flat-screen TV. At his direction, the set had come equipped with a top-of-the-line video surveillance system, one that allowed him an insider's view of life behind their closed doors. As long as the television was plugged in, it gave Felix a bird's-eye view of the living room where his former mistress seemed to be fading away to almost nothing while his industrious dark-haired daughter went about the process of living her day-to-day life.

In her heyday, Christina Andress Miramar had been a breathtaking beauty—a photogenic blonde. Once a promising Hollywood starlet, Christina's career had been derailed by getting on board the Duarte brothers' drug-fueled party circuit. Much as he hated to admit it, Felix realized that Christina had been all beauty and no brains, whereas her daughter was exactly the opposite—someone who was all brains and not at all burdened with her mother's good looks.

In fact, as Felix observed Graciella's comings and goings on his secret video footage, he thought she resembled his own grand-mother far more than she did Christina. Juanita Duarte, Felix's mother, had died of a brain aneurysm in her mid-thirties when Felix was only eleven. That was when Nana had come to Sinaloa to live with them, caring for Felix and ten-year-old Ricardo in the same way Graciella now cared for her temperamental and often difficult mother—coming and going and doing whatever needed to be done with a kind of brisk efficiency but with a noticeable lack of love.

When the TV set was first delivered, Felix had binged on the surveillance feeds, watching them greedily, day after day. Over time, however, the novelty had worn off, and he found himself observing them less and less. It pained him too much to see Christina as she was now—a slovenly empty shell of what she had once been—sitting in the living room playing endless games of solitaire, watching her soaps, and drinking, of course.

Drinking too much had been part of the Christina equation for as long as Felix had known her. Wherever she was, there had always been a partially filled glass nearby. Strangers might have taken the clear liquid for water with a slice of lime, but Felix knew better—there was always vodka with that slice, vodka and nothing else. It sickened him to know that by the end of most evenings, when it was time to go to bed, Christina would often be so out of it that she'd be unable to make her way into the bedroom unassisted.

El Pescado thought back to the last occasion he checked in on them. Was it a week ago, maybe, or was it longer than that? At the time, Christina had behaved in a totally normal fashion—normal for her, that is. There had been nothing in her demeanor to indicate any kind of impending crisis, much less one serious enough to cause the woman to consider taking her own life.

At last El Pescado managed to find his voice. "When," he asked brokenly, "and how did it happen?"

"Last Thursday," Graciella responded. "It happened overnight sometime. When I found her in the morning, she was already gone.

She apparently overdosed on a combination of prescription meds and vodka."

How could this have happened? El Pescado wondered. Wasn't Graciella supposed to be watching Christina? Wasn't she supposed to be keeping her safe? And how could she not have told him what had happened until more than a week later?

Instead of screaming accusations, El Pescado exercised incredible restraint and kept his voice steady. "Why didn't you call me sooner?" he asked.

"Because there was nothing you could do," Graciella answered. "There was nothing anyone could do."

El Pescado's mind flashed back to an earlier time, to the old days of wild drug-fueled boozy parties. Back then he'd been a rich and handsome middle-aged man and Christina had been his much younger, eye-catching arm candy. Together they'd been part of Panama City's "beautiful people." Now she was gone forever.

Dragging his thoughts away from another painful snippet from his past, Felix focused on the present and on the voice on the phone—his daughter's voice. Graciella seemed surprisingly dispassionate about what had happened, but then, she'd had time to adjust. Or was there more to this story than Graciella was saying? Had Christina truly taken her own life, or was it possible—remotely possible—that she'd had help along the way? Perhaps Graciella really *was* her father's daughter—in thought, word, and deed. Even as El Pescado considered that terrible possibility, he hoped it wasn't so.

"I would like to have her ashes," he said at last. "I can send a courier to pick them up."

"Don't bother," Graciella said. "I'll have them shipped to the drop box in Mexico City. Someone there can deliver them."

"Thank you," he croaked. A brief silence followed.

During the past ten years, although they seldom met face-to-face, Graciella had come to play a key role in her father's financial transactions. Over time he had arrived at the conclusion that she was destined to be his chosen successor. El Pescado fully expected that once Christina no longer required Graciella's constant care and attention, his daughter would leave Panama City behind, come to Mexico, take up residence in his fortified compound, and assume her official role.

After all, Felix was feeling his age. Running the cartel was a young man's game. He wanted Graciella close at hand so he could teach her everything she would need to know. At this point, she understood the financial end of his business far better than Felix himself, but he needed to be around long enough to school her in the blood-and-guts aspects of running the cartel—about dealing with rival gangs; about learning who could be trusted and who could not; and, if it ever came to that, how to put down a bloody insurrection arising from inside the ranks.

El Pescado had already informed his young lieutenants, including his forty-something sons, Manuel and Pablo, of his unorthodox decision. When it came to holding their own as street thugs, the boys were capable enough. They were good at wielding guns and muscle, but they were totally unsuitable when it came to running the whole operation. Pablo drank too much and Manny was too indecisive. Neither of them had the temperament or the brainpower to keep all the balls in the air, and when El Pescado had announced his succession decision, neither of them had had guts enough to object—at least not to Felix's face.

"What will you do now?" he asked Graciella finally, hoping to disguise the naked hope in his heart. "Will you come home to Sinaloa?"

El Pescado's expectation had always been that Graciella would jump at the chance to leave Panama City behind after her mother's passing. That didn't happen, at least not now.

"There are many things that are best handled from here," Graciella said into the phone. "If and when that changes, I'll let you know."

She hung up then. El Pescado wasn't accustomed to being dismissed in such an abrupt fashion. For a long moment he stared at the suddenly silent phone before putting it down. Then, remembering Christina—his once oh-so-lovely Christina—he buried his grotesque face in his hands and wept. Much later, after the next spasm of grief had passed and because he was who he was, Felix went into his study and scrolled back through all the video feeds, including ones he hadn't viewed previously.

Try as he might there was nothing to be seen that was the least bit out of the ordinary. On Wednesday evening the television set was on for most of the day and stayed on somewhat later than usual. There may have been more comings and goings than usual, but there was no sign of an argument or any kind of dispute or disturbance. Graciella came and went several times after helping Christina out of the room, but eventually Graciella returned to the living room and settled down on the sofa.

For more than an hour she sat there, working on a laptop before switching off the set for the night. If that was when it had happened, Christina must have been in her bedroom dosing herself with booze and pills while her daughter sat working quietly in the living room, totally unaware. But that set El Pescado to wondering. Was Graciella really as innocent and unknowing as she appeared to be on the video or was she something else entirely?

He fast forwarded through the feed to the next day, where he saw Graciella, seated on the sofa and weeping uncontrollably while people came and went around her—the ambulance crew, various police officers, and even a few neighbors. At one point Arturo Salazar, Graciella's boss from the office, made an appearance. After that El Pescado simply stopped watching. With Christina gone, there was no longer any point.

He did, however, have a number of sources inside the police department in Panama City. Just to set his mind at ease, he made a few calls. Yes, Christina Miramar had been discovered dead in her bed on Thursday morning of the previous week. The cops had found no suicide note, but there were also no signs of any kind of violence and no indication of forced entry, either. Unused portions of a variety of prescription meds had been found at the scene. Evidence suggested that the prescription drugs Christina had ingested had been self-administered. Those, combined with her elevated blood alcohol content, had proved to be lethal. It occurred to Felix that the medical examiner might just as well have checked the box marked "accidental" or "suspicious," but he had not. Christina's death had been declared a suicide, and the case was closed.

Taking some slight comfort in that news, Felix allowed himself to give way to grief once more, sobbing away while Lupe, listening from the other room, wondered what in the hell was going on.

3

Like a kid eager for Christmas morning, Stuart Ramey, age forty-one and second-in-command at High Noon Enterprises in Cottonwood, Arizona, rolled out of bed bright and early that Friday morning, put some eggs on to boil, and then jumped into the shower. He was due to take a big step today, one he had never imagined possible—this morning he was scheduled for his first-ever lesson in driving a stick shift. Learning to drive a standard transmission was the last obstacle in Stu's late-breaking campaign to become a licensed driver.

Orphaned at an early age, Stu had been raised by impoverished but loving grandparents. He'd been a "special needs" kid long before those words made their way into public education's social consciousness. Now it was easy to recognize his high-functioning autism. Back in elementary and high school, though, he'd been considered a freak and had suffered through years of schoolyard bullying.

In all those years, he'd had only one friend, Roger McGeary, an equally geeky kid, who had been every bit as odd as Stuart. The two boys had bonded over a mutual love first of video games and later of computer coding. Buoyed by their friendship, the two outcasts, disparagingly referred to by their classmates as Tweedledum and Tweedledee, had almost made it through high school. Then, during Stu's senior year, disaster struck. First Roger had moved away. Later on Stuart's grandmother died, leaving the devastated teenager on his own.

The whole time Stuart was growing up, his grandparents hadn't owned a vehicle. They had made do by relying on buses and the occasional taxi for their transportation needs. Not having a family car had made signing up for driver's ed an impossibility for him, and once his world fell apart, he hadn't revisited the issue.

At age seventeen and left to his own devices, Stuart had ended up in a homeless shelter, where someone had noticed his computing skills and brought him to the attention of B. Simpson. At the time, B. had been involved in a computer gaming start-up. Years later, when B. founded a cyber security company named High Noon Enterprises, he had brought Stu on board, and Stu had worked there ever since.

B., recognizing Stu's deficiencies along with his talents, had found work-arounds for his inability to drive. For a long time, B. and his wife and partner, Ali Reynolds, had allowed Stu to live on-site by using the back room as an unofficial crash pad. A year or so earlier, they had gone to the county and obtained a zoning variance that enabled them to create a bona fide additional living unit, a studio apartment, in what had once been designated storage space on the far side of the computer lab. Happy with the new arrangement, there had been no indication that Stu would make any changes in the status quo as far as transportation was concerned.

But, weeks earlier, Stu's life had taken a surprising turn when Julia Miller, the aunt of Stu's long-ago chum Roger McGeary, had turned up on High Noon's doorstep. She had come bearing the unwelcome news that Roger was dead, supposedly having taken his own life. She was there asking for High Noon to investigate the death.

To everyone's amazement, including his own, the previously reticent Stuart had somehow risen to the occasion. He had used his considerable technical skills to track down and unmask a serial killer named Owen Hansen, a computer genius who used cyber bullying techniques to drive desperate victims into taking their own lives. First Stuart had managed to track down one of Hansen's potential victims in time to save the young woman's life. Later on, Stuart had encountered the crazed killer on a lonely mountain road. On his own and armed with only his grandfather's Swiss Army knife, Stuart had faced down the gun-wielding man, called his bluff, and watched his friend's murderer leap to his own death.

To those around him, that incident seemed to spark an incredible turning point. It was as though Stuart Ramey had suddenly come into his own. Other than the people at work, Stuart had been relatively friendless for most of his life. Now, though, he seemed determined to reestablish and maintain his long-interrupted connection to Roger McGeary's Aunt Julia.

In the intervening weeks he had made several visits to her ranch, Racehorse Rest, located near the town of Payson. The trip was more than seventy miles one way, and using a bus to get there and back wasn't an option because there was no bus service between Cottonwood and Payson. Once, he had ridden there with his coworker Cami Lee. But at this juncture in his life, learning to drive was less threatening than the necessity of having to ask someone else for a ride. And so, two and a half decades after most of his contemporaries had learned to drive, Stuart had embarked on his own journey to become a licensed driver.

He'd had no difficulty passing the written exam, and people at work had been eager to help facilitate the process. Both Cami and Shirley Malone, High Noon's new receptionist, had taken him for driving lessons. Ali's friend, Sister Anselm, had even gotten into the act by letting him do a supervised driving excursion back and forth to Aunt Julia's in the good sister's Mini Cooper.

Two days earlier, after the last of those driving lessons in Cami's Prius, she had pronounced him ready to go for the exam. That's when the project had ground to a sudden halt over the stick shift stumbling block.

"Not before I can drive a standard transmission," he had objected.

"A standard transmission?" Cami echoed. "Who even has a standard transmission these days, and why on earth would you want to drive one?"

"Because I have to be able to drive both," Stuart had insisted. "If I can only drive automatics, I won't be a real driver."

"Whoever gave you that weird idea?" Cami wanted to know.

"Pops," Stu answered simply, "my grandfather. He always used to say that people who could only drive automatics weren't real drivers."

Rather than argue the point, Cami had gone in search of a standard transmission solution. In the world of High Noon Enterprises, there were plenty of vehicles with automatic transmissions to choose from, but the only possible stick shift candidate was the antique Bronco owned by Ali Reynolds's father, Bob Larson, and that was the vehicle Stu would be driving today. Ali had agreed to drive the Bronco over from Sedona that morning so Stu could take it for a supervised spin.

He was excited about the idea but worried, too. Physical coordination had never been his strong suit. He knew that he'd have to be able to operate the clutch, the gear shift, and the gas pedal all at the same time. He had watched YouTube videos of the process over and over, trying to get the hang of it. Stu was a wizard when it came to fingers on keyboards, but his oversized feet had always left him feeling clumsy, and he wasn't the least bit sure he could make them work as needed.

Taking a coffee mug with him, he ventured into the lab. Despite the fact that it was half past six, Cami was already there. "Today's the big stick shift day?" she asked.

He nodded. "Yup."

"Don't worry," Cami told him. "You'll be fine."

"I hope so," he said, "I really do."

4

Ali Reynolds awakened that morning to find herself clinging to the far edge of the bed with both her elbows dangling over the side. Bella, their long-haired miniature dachshund, was pressed up against Ali's shoulder. Turning over, Ali bodily moved the dog back toward the middle of the bed. Bella may have been a small dog, but she insisted on occupying a surprisingly large amount of the real estate in B.'s and Ali's king-sized bed.

"Just wait 'til your daddy gets home tonight," Ali warned the dog with a laugh. "No more shoulder-sleeping for you."

Bella had been found abandoned in a casino parking lot the afternoon before B. and Ali's wedding. The dog had been part of their marital equation from the very beginning. Initially the honeymooners had agreed that their bed would be totally off-limits as far as the dog was concerned, but they had soon succumbed to Bella's single-minded dachshund determination. It was no longer a question of whether or not she would be in the bed so much as it was a matter of where she would be in the bed.

"Come on, girl," Ali urged. "Time to go out."

Bella was not your basic morning kind of dog. Her response was to burrow under the covers. Gathering her up, Ali opened the patio door and shoved the dog out into the enclosed side yard to do her business. The house on Sedona's Manzanita Hills Road may have been well inside the city limits, but there were still too many predators in the neighborhood—coyotes, cougars, and eagles—to send the ten-pound dog out in the open without human supervision.

Coming back inside, Ali noticed that the air was laden with the enticing odor of baking bread. Summoned by the aroma, she headed for the kitchen. Leland Brooks, the man who had long served as Ali and B.'s majordomo, had recently retired and returned to the UK. His successor, a retired US Navy cook named Alonso Rivera, had slipped seamlessly into their lives, creating barely a ripple. His propensity for baking homemade bread was both a blessing and a curse, the latter when Ali was trying to curb her carbs or calories.

"You're up early," Alonso announced when she appeared in the kitchen doorway.

Nodding, Ali poured herself a mug of coffee. "I'm due in at seven. Today's my day to be the student driver instructor," she said.

"The stick shift issue?" Alonso asked.

"Yup," she said. "You've got it."

"Good luck with that," Alonso told her. "But as far as dinner is concerned, everything here is under control. I'll have the food ready and waiting in the warming drawer so you and B. will be able to eat whenever the shuttle drops him off and the two of you are ready."

"Meatloaf?" Ali asked.

Alonso smiled. "Leland told me before he left that when the man of the house comes home from his travels, that's what he wants, and that's what he'll get."

Forty-five minutes later, Ali pulled into the side parking lot at Nick's Auto Care at the far west end of Sedona. Her parents, Bob and Edie, had moved into an active-adult retirement community where they were allowed only one designated parking place. That one belonged to the car Edie referred to as her "toes-up Buick." In the meantime, Bob's beloved single-owner, seventies-era Bronco had been relegated to off-site parking. Nick, Bob's longtime mechanic and pal, let him keep the aging SUV stored overnight in one of the garage's unused bays. By the time Ali arrived and parked, Bob had moved the Bronco out of the garage and into the crisp morning air.

Bob may have agreed to let Ali use the vehicle for Stuart's behind-the-wheel driving lesson, but he appeared to be having second thoughts. "I'm not too sure about this," he warned, dangling the key ring over his daughter's upturned hand. "This vehicle better come back to me tonight without a single dent or scratch!"

Suddenly, Ali Reynolds felt as though she had entered a time machine and had been booted back to her teenaged years when she herself had been a newly licensed driver. Her mother, who had always favored Oldsmobiles up until the time GM stopped making them, had handed Ali the keys to her current Olds and dispatched her daughter to pick up a few items from the grocery store. Ali had returned with the groceries, all right, but in the process she had inadvertently backed into a bollard. The Olds had come home with a seriously crumpled rear bumper. It was a piece of history that she had never lived down, and one that was front and center when her father handed over the car keys to his vintage Bronco complete with its new paint job and reconditioned interior.

"Believe me," Ali said, "we'll be careful."

"I'm sure you will be," her father muttered, "but I'm not so sure about Stu Ramey. In this day and age what makes him think he needs to know how to drive a stick shift?"

"Beats me," Ali said, climbing into the driver's seat. "You'll have to ask Stu the next time you see him."

She was fastening her seat belt when her dad tapped on the driver's window.

"Remember," he said when she cranked down the window, "no off-roading."

"Gotcha," she replied. "Now are you sure you don't want a lift back to Sedona Shadows?"

"Nope," Bob said. "Your mom's got a bridge game this morning.

I'll just hang out here and chew the fat with Nick. I'll be able to get a ride back home if I need one."

"Okay, then," Ali said, shifting into gear. "I'm off."

It was a bright, cloudless late-October day as Ali embarked on the half-hour drive from Sedona to Cottonwood, the home of High Noon's corporate headquarters. The grass that had sprung up during the summer monsoon season had turned yellow in the sun, and the cottonwoods along the creek beds were ablaze in all their wondrous fall glory.

On the drive Ali dearly missed her Cayenne's updated music system, which she usually played at full volume, singing along with some Broadway show tune or other. The antique AM/FM radio in the Bronco's dashboard was one thing Bob Larson hadn't quite gotten around to replacing. With no music surrounding her, Ali had nothing to do during her open-highway commute but drive and think.

She had come a very long way in the past several years. After earning a journalism degree at NAU in Flagstaff, Ali had spent years in the television industry, working as a well-respected newscaster, first on the East Coast and later as a local anchorwoman on a station in L.A. That part of her life had been blown to smithereens when she hit her early fifties and was suddenly deemed "too old" to be on the air. At almost the same time, Ali had learned that her second husband, the late and unlamented Paul Grayson, was a philandering piece of crap. She had folded her tent in California and had come back home to Arizona to recuperate and figure out what to do with herself.

Now, years later, Ali was living a reinvented life. She'd gained a daughter-in-law, Athena, and a pair of grandchildren—the twins, Colin and Colleen. Along the way, she'd bought and refurbished the home on Manzanita Hills Road where she now lived with her third and, as B. himself liked to put it, "final" husband.

Theirs had been an unlikely romance, and one Ali had resisted initially. For one thing, B. was fifteen years her junior, but love had won out in the end. They were full partners now, both in life and in High Noon Enterprises. B. was the public face of their booming cyber security firm while Ali worked mostly behind the scenes.

The public part of the business meant that B. had been on the road, mostly overseas, for the better part of two weeks, renegotiating contracts in back-to-back, eyeball-to-eyeball meetings. He was due home tonight, and Ali was looking forward to the two of them being able to spend some quiet alone time together. The need for constant travel wasn't B.'s first choice or Ali's, either, but for right now, that was the way it was. While B. was out and about, Ali stayed home, minding the store, handling a myriad of administrative functions, making sure the bills got paid and the lights stayed on, and doing whatever else needed doing, which today meant helping Stu Ramey get a driver's license.

5

When the call ended, Graciella Miramar checked the charge on her encrypted phone. It was low. After switching it off, she hooked it up to one of the charging cables in the small, specially designed safe concealed under the hardwood flooring in her bedroom closet. "Come home to Sinaloa," she muttered under her breath. "Not bloody likely."

That may have been her father's plan, but it wasn't hers. For one thing, Graciella had never even *been* to Sinaloa. El Pescado's armed compound certainly wasn't home to her, and she had no intention of living there in what would amount to little more than a glorified prison. However, just because she refused to live in Sinaloa didn't mean Graciella had no interest in taking over the Duarte Cartel.

In her estimation, the use of human mules to lug backpacks loaded with illicit product back and forth across international borders was a business model that needed to be relegated to the history books. Graciella wanted to be in charge of something far more elegant than that. When El Pescado's gang came under fire, as it inevitably would, Graciella had absolutely no interest in being gunned down by automatic weapons fire in some kind of Wild West shootout with either the *federales* or else members of some rival gang. That kind of an ending might be suitable for her half brothers, but not for her.

Long term, Graciella wanted to be out of the drug business entirely but with her own money and that of her father's collapsed drug cartel still intact. In order to do that, she would need a suitable partner, and she already had one in mind. For the past week, while home on bereavement leave, she'd worked feverishly to that end, and bit by bit the pieces were falling into place. If everything worked out the way she hoped, Graciella's new partner would be an artificial intelligence named Frigg. The AI had once belonged to a client of hers who was now deceased.

At the moment Graciella wasn't even sure Frigg still existed. If she did, she was most likely in the care and custody of a guy named Stuart Ramey who lived in Cottonwood, Arizona. Graciella had already embarked on the mission to find out for sure because, if Frigg was still extant, Graciella was determined to make Owen Hansen's AI her own—with or without Stuart Ramey's help.

Yesterday had been Graciella's last full day of bereavement leave. Today she was due in at the office. And by this afternoon, the surveillance feeds she had ordered would be up and running in both Stuart Ramey's residence and at his place of work. When she knew for sure that Frigg was operative again, Graciella would determine her next move.

Once dressed, Graciella called the office. Naturally, her boss answered the phone. Just hearing Arturo Salazar's voice was enough to make her skin crawl. "I'm on my way in," she told him, "but I'm going to be a few minutes late. I have to make arrangements to ship my mother's ashes home to her family."

"If you need to take another day off, do so," Arturo told her.

"That's very kind of you," she said, "but really. I'm ready to be back at work. Being home here without her is just too hard."

"Of course," Arturo said. "I understand."

Out in the living room the funeral urn still sat next to the front door in exactly the same place where the driver from the mortuary had placed it when he delivered Christina Miramar's cremains. When the man from the funeral home had called late the previous afternoon to say that the ashes were already en route, Graciella had wanted to tell him to go ahead and keep them, but she had realized just in time that a reaction like that would most likely arouse suspicion and get people started asking too many uncomfortable questions.

Once the urn arrived, Graciella wasn't sure what she should do with it. Put it on display somewhere in the living room and tell anyone who asked that she was honoring her mother's wishes, or hide it in the back corner of a closet? Now, though, she was grateful that El Pescado's unexpected request had solved the problem.

Bending over to pick up the urn, she was surprised by how much it weighed, but she shouldered the burden with a happy heart. The shipping office was just up the street. She wouldn't have to carry it far.

6

When Ali drove through the entrance to the Mingus Mountain
Business Park that Friday morning, she caught sight of Stu,
pacing back and forth. She couldn't tell if he was eager or
anxious about getting started.

In the preceding year, High Noon's landlord, the business park's
former owner, had gone through financial straits. That had occurred
at a time when B. and Ali had been hoping to change their lease and
take on additional space inside the facility. Instead of negotiating a
larger lease, they had purchased the property outright.

Of all the original businesses in the complex, only High Noon
remained while the complex underwent extensive renovations. With
the other offices vacant, there were very few vehicles in the parking
lot. The cars belonging to High Noon employees were parked close
to their entrance at the far end of the building. The other vehicles
present belonged to various contractors and construction workers,
and those were clustered toward the north side of the building.
Since the parking lot was essentially High Noon's private property
these days, Ali deemed it a suitable site for Stu Ramey's stick shift
driving lesson.

Pulling up next to him, Ali rolled down the Bronco's driver's-side
window. "Ready to rumble?" she asked.

"I guess," he said dubiously. "I hope so."

"Don't worry," she assured him breezily. "You'll be fine."

Except Stu wasn't fine—not even close. The man was a certifiable genius when it came to operating computers. He was also a self-taught and very capable musician who could play the piano like nobody's business. But when it came to operating a standard transmission, he was utterly hopeless. It was impossible for him to get the hang of coordinating the movements of both feet in order to operate both the gas pedal and the clutch at the same time. Every attempt to change gears was greeted by howls of protest from the old Bronco's transmission. Time and again the aging vehicle shuddered, shook, and stalled out, killing the engine. Throughout the ordeal, Ali silently thanked her lucky stars that her father was back home in Sedona and well out of earshot.

No amount of verbal coaching on Ali's part seemed to do the trick. Finally, giving up, she dropped to the floorboard and grabbed Stu's ankles, bodily lifting and lowering them as required. Fortunately casual dress was a way of life at High Noon Enterprises, and the jeans Ali had put on that morning ended up being no worse for wear. By the end of a humiliating thirty-minute-long struggle, Stu was finally beginning to get the idea, enough so that Ali was able to return to the passenger seat. She remained there while they did two more relatively smooth circuits of the parking lot with Stu starting, stopping, and shifting up and down as required. His performance wasn't absolutely perfect, but it was good enough for Ali to declare the lesson over.

"That's it for today," she told him. "You've made great progress."

"Really?" Stu asked, sounding uncertain.

Despite the fact that the windows were rolled down and the outdoor temperature was in the mid-60s, Stu was drenched in sweat.

"Really," she answered. "You're probably not ready to take my dad out for a joyride anytime soon, but here's the thing. You know for sure that if you're ever faced with a situation where it's a choice between driving a standard transmission or walking, you'll be able to make it work. Over time, we'll be able to practice as needed, but as far as your driver's test is concerned, no one is going to make you use a standard transmission."

"What do you think I should do?" Stu asked.

"Grab the first available test appointment and get it out of the way once and for all."

"Okay," Stu agreed. "I'll give them a call."

He pulled into one of High Noon's designated parking places and brought the Bronco to a stop in a reasonably competent fashion. Handing the keys over to Ali, he hurried inside. As Ali started to exit the Bronco, her phone rang with B.'s phone number showing in caller ID. She was accustomed to keeping two time zones in her head at any given time—where she was and where B. was.

"Hey there," she said in greeting. "Are you at the airport getting ready to board?"

"Hardly," B. grumbled. "I'm in a cab headed back into London. Fortunately, I was able to call Claridge's and grab a hotel room before they filled up completely."

His reply left Ali puzzled. "Grab a hotel room?" she asked. "Why? Aren't you supposed to be coming home tonight?"

"Slight change of plans," he said. "I guess you haven't exactly been glued to the news."

Ali felt a sudden clench in her gut, fearing that somewhere in the world there had been another awful terrorist attack. Unfortunately those were becoming the norm these days.

"I've actually been giving Stu a driving lesson, so no, I haven't seen the news. What's up?"

"British Airways is having some kind of major computer glitch that has shut down their operations worldwide. Heathrow is a war zone, and it's going to take days to untangle all the canceled flights. There was no point trying to get booked on something else. I was already in the check-in line when it happened. Fortunately, I still had my luggage with me. The best course of action was to make my way back to the hotel and wait it out. All I wanted was to be home, have a chance to sleep in my own bed, and enjoy the comfort of a home-cooked meal. Is that too much to ask?"

Ali had stayed at Claridge's and had dined there as well. It didn't exactly qualify as a hardship posting. She was tempted to call B. out for unnecessary whining, but she didn't, and she didn't laugh at him, either. He was traveling, weary, and frustrated, and he wanted to be home.

"Look," she said, "how about if I get on the phone and see if I can stitch together some kind of program that will get you home as early as possible?"

"Would you?"

"As in spare no expense?" she asked.

"As in," he murmured.

Knowing she'd just been green lighted to utilize a chartered jet if needed, Ali headed into her office. She settled in at her computer terminal. First she sent a text to Alonso, letting him know that B.'s flight had been delayed and that he should ditch their dinner plans.

After that Ali did a quick survey of the news surrounding the chaotic situation at Heathrow. Things had obviously gotten much worse between the time B. had called her and now. Fistfights had broken out inside the airport, and authorities were having to deal with near-riot conditions among the ranks of angry stranded passengers. Ali could see that B. had been incredibly lucky to have snagged both a cab and a hotel room.

7

When Owen Hansen had first brought his book of business to Recursos Empresariales Internationales at number 18 Vía Israel in Panama City, Panama, he didn't win any popularity contests. The people who worked there discovered that as a client he was demanding, exacting, and unreasonable. He ran through three different account managers in very short order.

Of all the account reps who worked for Arturo Salazar, Graciella Miramar was by far the top producer, but that didn't make her Arturo's favorite, not by any means. For one thing, he'd been pressured into hiring her by none other than one of his best customers, Felix Duarte, who had then insisted that his accounts be assigned to this dowdy new hire. Arturo wondered about why El Pescado would take such a singular interest in someone like Graciella, who was the antithesis of hot. Arturo's initial assumption was that she must have slept with Felix, but when she absolutely rebuffed Arturo's own amorous advances, he revised that suspicion and settled on the idea that Graciella had something else on Felix that he wanted kept quiet. In Arturo's playbook, if sex wasn't the answer, blackmail was always an excellent alternative.

Faced with the dilemma of retaining a valuable but difficult new customer while at the same time preventing a revolt among his unhappy employees, Arturo had passed Owen Hansen and his unreasonable demands along to Graciella. Arturo didn't make that change as a favor to Graciella, and at the time he wondered how long it would be before Owen Hansen took his business elsewhere, but that didn't happen because Owen Hansen and Graciella seemed to hit it off immediately.

For one thing, they were two sides of the same coin, and each had only one interest. For Owen it was himself. For Graciella, it was accumulating money. Graciella appreciated the fact that, in all their dealings, Owen—unlike some of her other clients—never once made a pass at her. She accepted the fact that he was a braggart, but there was plenty for him to brag about. He knew everything there was to know about computers. As far as Bitcoins were concerned, he was both a visionary and an early adopter who established one of the first and most efficient Bitcoin mining operations. That aspect of his business alone had turned him into a highly profitable client.

Owen had other investment accounts in addition to his Bitcoin holdings. Graciella watched those without necessarily managing them, and was always amazed by the astonishing rates of return in which his accounts routinely outperformed everyone else's.

But there was another part of Graciella's dealings with Owen Hansen that never made it onto the books at Recursos Empresariales Internationales. While working there, Graciella had earned a well-deserved reputation as a logistics expert. Some of the arrangements she made—property transfers and aircraft purchases—were totally aboveboard. But many of the transactions she conducted, both for El Pescado and his associates and later on for Owen Hansen as well, were negotiated as a side business and conducted over the dark Web.

When Owen was in town, they often went across the street to the Multiplaza Pacific Mall and had lunch at P.F. Chang's. The restaurant was one Arturo was known to use as a launchpad for his various work-based amorous adventures. Graciella didn't care for the place, but since it was one of Owen's favorites, too, she accompanied him there without objection.

At one of those lunches, on a day when the latest quarterly earnings reports had been posted earlier in the morning, she had noticed that, as usual, Owen's investment accounts were the hands-down winners. "How do you do that?" she had inquired.

"Do what?"

"Find investments that consistently outperform everyone else's?"

"That's not me," he told her, "that's Frigg."

"Frigg?" she had asked. "Who's Frigg?"

He looked around the restaurant and when he was satisfied that no one was listening, he answered her question in a hushed voice. "Not *who* is Frigg," he corrected with a smile and the easy confidence that came from having done business together for years. "You should be asking me *what* is Frigg."

"And?" Graciella interjected.

"She's an artificial intelligence, one that I created all by myself. She manages the collection of computers that do all my blockchain processing. She also manages my investment accounts. She's so damned smart, that if I needed her to, I think she could help me get away with murder."

"An artificial intelligence," Graciella repeated. "Like a computer program, you mean?"

"She's actually a lot more than that," Owen said. "Would you like to meet her?"

"I guess," Graciella replied.

Owen reached into his pocket, pulled out a cell phone, and pressed the speaker button. "Good afternoon, Frigg," he said. "I'd like you to meet a business associate of mine, Graciella Miramar. Would you mind saying hello?"

"I'm happy to meet her," Frigg said. "Would she prefer to conduct our conversation in English or Spanish?"

Graciella shot Owen a questioning look. "How does she know I speak Spanish?"

"Frigg is privy to my correspondence," he said. "I'm sure she's noticed the location of your IP addresses."

"For both my work computer and my home computer?" Graciella asked.

"Yes."

For Graciella, that was a disquieting thought. The computer she used at home and kept in the floor of her closet was something she preferred to keep quiet. Obviously Owen knew about it, and now so did Frigg.

"English will be fine," Graciella said aloud.

"Good afternoon, Ms. Miramar," Frigg said. "I'm happy to meet you. I hope you're having a pleasant day."

It struck Graciella as incredibly weird to be sitting there chatting away with a computer. She glanced questioningly at Owen who nodded encouragingly.

"Why are you called Frigg?" Graciella asked. " I'm not sure I've ever heard that name before."

"Mr. Hansen's preferred nom de guerre is Odin, based on a widely revered Norse god bearing that same name. Frigg, sometimes called Freya, was Odin's wife."

"A nom de guerre," Graciella repeated. "Does that mean you're involved in a war of some kind?"

"I'm afraid," said Frigg, "I'm not at liberty to say."

"Sorry," Owen put in quickly. "Frigg has been sworn to secrecy on some aspects of our working relationship. I hope you don't mind."

"No problem," Graciella said.

"Is there any further way for me to be of service?" Frigg asked.

"Owen here—or should I say Odin—tells me that you're the one responsible for the outstanding earnings in his investment accounts."

"I believe that is correct," Frigg said. "As of this morning, the earnings rate across the board is 17.7 percent."

"Which is very respectable," Graciella said. "Enviable, in fact. How do you do that?"

"My job is to analyze all available data in the market, spot emerging trends, and select potential winners and losers."

"Maybe he would allow me to borrow you from time to time," Graciella suggested.

Frigg's response was immediate. "I do not believe that would be a suitable course of action."

"That's all for now, Frigg," Owen said, punching the speaker button and turning off the phone. "Sorry about that. She can be a little possessive on occasion and somewhat abrupt."

"How can that be?" Graciella wondered aloud. "She's a computer program."

"A well-read computer program," Owen said, "and one who prefers to have my undivided attention."

That was the first time Graciella spoke to Frigg, but it was not the last. After that, when Owen and Graciella were together, he often summoned the AI into the conversation, in much the same way a proud parent might trot out an exceptionally gifted child to show off the little one's intellectual prowess. And every time it happened, Graciella came away even more impressed than she had been the first time.

In her spare time, Graciella began to study the whole notion of artificial intelligence. The more she learned about AI in general and about Frigg in particular, the more Graciella could envision her future in a whole new way. Compared to Frigg and Odin, El Pescado and his drug cartel henchmen were truly a herd of lumbering dinosaurs.

8

Even so early, there was a backup in the shipping office. Standing in line and then waiting at the counter for her mother's funeral urn to be properly packaged and labeled, Graciella recalled the life journey that had brought her from being a hungry waif begging on the streets to where she was now.

A little more than ten years earlier, and two days shy of the commencement service where Graciella was scheduled to be awarded her MBA from the Wharton School, she'd been contacted by Bill Varner, the trust officer currently handling her banking arrangements on her father's behalf. Since no similar meetings had occurred in the past, Graciella was somewhat concerned.

"What's this all about?" she had asked her caller. "Did I overshoot my allowance for the month or bounce a check?"

"Oh, no," the banker said quickly. "It's nothing like that. Someone is interested in making you a job offer. Since he's currently unable to travel to the US, he's asked me to set up a videoconferencing arrangement. We have a specially equipped room that we use for just those kinds of long-distance meetings. I can assure you that you and he will be the only people in attendance."

"When?" Graciella asked.

"He was hoping you could do it now," Mr. Varner said. "This happens to be a convenient time for him, and he's standing by."

"I'll be there in twenty minutes," she said.

As the school year had drawn to a close, Graciella had been sending out résumés and going for interviews, but so far nothing seemed promising. Because of her dual citizenship, she'd toyed with the idea of returning to Panama, but so far none of the job offers she'd seen from there had measured up. Yes, her mother still lived in Panama City, but that was hardly an advantage. With Christina's mental and physical health both permanently impaired, mother and daughter had never been able to reconnect, and Graciella had only the faintest memories of the beautiful woman who had once been her mother. That person had ceased to exist for her that long ago night when Graciella was six years old, a night when Christina went off to work and didn't come home.

At the time of Christina's disappearance, the two of them had been eking out a meager existence while living in a shanty in one of Panama City's soon-to-be-demolished barrios. By now Graciella understood—as her six-year-old self had not—that when her mother had gone off to work nights for a so-called modeling agency, she had, in actuality, been nothing more or less than a prostitute working the streets. In the evenings, Christina would put food on the table for her daughter to eat while she fixed her hair and put on makeup. Once Christina was dressed for work, she'd tuck her daughter into bed, kiss her good night, and tell her to sleep tight—that she'd see her in the morning.

Of course, left unsupervised, Graciella had hardly ever stayed in bed. When she got older, as soon as her mother left the house, she'd slip out, too, blending invisibly into the bustling nighttime streets of Panama City. Christina was proud of her American heritage and wanted her daughter to be bilingual. In public the two of them spoke Spanish; at home they spoke English—American English, rather than the British English that was taught in local schools.

The hovel where they lived started out deep in the slums, but as one neighborhood after another was torn down and gentrified into upscale high-rises, the distance between rich and poor decreased. Eventually only a matter of a few blocks separated their shoddy dwelling from the high-priced restaurants and nightclubs where well-to-do tourists came and went.

On Graciella's nightly prowls, she'd often made her way to one or the other of those ritzy neighborhoods, where she would attach herself to some unsuspecting group of English-speaking tourists. Always armed with a sob story, Graciella would spin heart-wrenching tales about how she'd gotten separated from her mom and needed help getting back to her hotel. Not only was she bilingual, she was also a very capable liar who hardly ever walked away empty-handed. The money Graciella earned on these nightly excursions was hers alone. It was money Christina never knew her daughter had, and it was a good thing she had it, too, because eventually there came that awful morning when the sun came up and Christina hadn't come home.

Graciella stayed in the house all day long that day, waiting anxiously for her mother's return. She hadn't dared go outside for fear one of the neighbors might let on to someone that she had been left alone. That first night when there was no food on the table and nothing to eat, she had crept out of the house and bought her own.

Had they owned a TV set at the time, Graciella might have seen the news reports about an unidentified woman who had been attacked on the street, raped, savagely beaten, and left to die. Her alleged attackers were believed to be a group of six drunken airmen stationed at Howard Air Force Base. The injured woman had been carted off to the hospital, where she hovered between life and death.

The men were caught, arrested, charged, and later convicted, but Graciella knew nothing of that at the time. All she knew was that her mother had gone to work and hadn't returned home.

The child survived on her own that way for three long days and nights. At the end of the third day there was a knock on the door. Hoping it would finally be her mother, Graciella had flung the door open, but the person standing outside wasn't her mother at all. It was a policeman—a uniformed policeman.

"Is your father home?" he asked.

He wasn't, of course. Graciella didn't have a father, or at least not one she knew personally, so she tried lying.

"He's not here," she said.

"This is about your mother," the policeman said kindly. "I need to speak to whoever's taking care of you."

And that was when Graciella had burst into tears and blurted out the truth—that no one was taking care of her. Christina was gone, and Graciella had been forced to look after herself. The policeman gave her the news that her mother had been badly hurt and was in the hospital, trying to get better. They had used fingerprints to identify her, and one of Christina's friends had mentioned Graciella's existence.

The policeman was kind but firm. He told Graciella that she couldn't stay home alone. He took her first to a police station and then to some people who, he said, would look after her. Late that night, Graciella Miramar found herself in foster care, but not for long. When morning came she slipped away again and found her way back to the house. The next morning, someone came and retrieved her.

When the media learned about the abandoned child, they went nuts, making a story that had already been big news even bigger, not just in Panama, but all over Latin America. It was too good a story not to tell—the poor, hardworking woman; her luckless child;

the evil American servicemen who had attacked her. Eventually, Christina Miramar's name surfaced in one of the stories.

Graciella was back in foster care by then—spending her time in a room that was locked to prevent her from running away again. Late one afternoon, the housemother who was in charge unlocked the door. "Someone wants to see you," she said. "These are important people. Mind your manners."

She led Graciella into the living room, where two men sat waiting on a sofa. One, wearing a white coat, looked like a doctor. The other was an incredibly ugly man. At first Graciella thought he was wearing some kind of scary mask, but it turned out he wasn't. Close up she realized that vivid, lumpy scars crisscrossed his face. She tried to shrink away from him, but the housemother grabbed her by the arm and propelled her forward.

"This is Graciella," she said.

The scary man stared at her so hard that she wanted to shrink into the floor. Then, reaching into a small plastic bag, he drew out a cotton swab. Graciella recognized it because Christina sometimes used them to remove her makeup.

"Rub the end of this on the inside of your cheek," he ordered.

Graciella tried to refuse, but the housemother squeezed her shoulder and gave her a severe warning look that said, *Do it or else*.

So she did as she was told. She rubbed the swab on the inside of her cheek and then gave it back to him. He returned the swab to the bag and then handed the bag over to the doctor.

"How long?" he demanded.

The man in the white coat shrugged. "We'll put a rush on it."

He turned back to the woman. Speaking over Graciella's head, he said, "We'll be in touch."

With that, the two men took their leave. A week later, Graciella, still accompanied by the housemother, boarded a small plane—a private jet—that flew north to Houston. During a refueling stop and prior to continuing on to California, the child cleared customs in

Houston using her US passport. That piece of identification along with her first and last names were the only things Graciella Miramar took with her into exile—one that lasted for almost eighteen years.

Once ushered into the bank's conference room, Graciella settled into one of the comfy leather chairs and waited for Mr. Varner to make the connection. When the screen lit up and a man's horribly disfigured face appeared in front of her, Graciella understood exactly who he was and why she was there. She had known for quite a while that El Pescado was most likely her real father and that he had been paying her way all these years. Now the bill was about to come due.

Felix's face was beyond repulsive, but Graciella steeled herself to look the man straight in the eye. "Good afternoon, Mr. Duarte," she said calmly. "I believe you must be my father."

A look of visible shock flashed across the damaged face. "Who told you?" El Pescado demanded. "Varner here?"

"No one told me," Graciella answered. "I found out on my own. While I was still going to school at the University of Arizona, the ten o'clock news did a segment about Mexican drug cartels. They showed photos of some of the guys in charge, and I remembered your face from when you and that doctor came to see me in foster care."

"I guess that means I'm pretty unforgettable, right?" he asked as a lopsided grin distorted his damaged features even further.

Graciella didn't smile back. "This was supposed to be a job interview not a family reunion," she said stiffly. "Since I'm not especially interested in working in the drug trade, perhaps I should just leave now."

"No, wait," he said. "Please don't go. This *is* a job interview, and it's about your mother."

"What about her?" Graciella demanded. "Every year or so I get a letter from her saying how much she loves me and misses me and that I should come home. After that she goes dark again, and I don't hear another word from her for months on end."

"Your mother is troubled," El Pescado admitted. "She's been in and out of various institutions for years. Right now Christina is a patient in a residential treatment center. Her current therapist thinks she'd be better off in something with more of a homelike setting, and so do I."

"What does any of that have to do with me?" Graciella asked.

"I'd like you to come home and look after her."

"You've got to be kidding," Graciella said. "I'm about to be awarded my MBA, and you expect me to come back to Panama to provide nanny care for my mother?"

"I'd make it well worth your while," he said.

"You'd pay me? How much?"

"A hundred and twenty-thousand dollars a year, put away tax-free in a numbered offshore account. In addition, I'll continue providing housing for both of you, and I'll cover all related expenses as well, including hiring whatever household help you require."

Graciella had spent her childhood begging on the streets and had yet to have a full-time job. For someone from her background, the amount on offer should have been considered breathtaking. El Pescado seemed dismayed when Graciella turned it down out of hand.

"That's a joke," she told him. "It doesn't matter how much you offer to pay me. If I'm stuck being a glorified babysitter, I'll end up bored to tears in less than a week."

"What if I could help you find a job over and above what you're doing for your mother?"

"What kind of a job?"

"One that would be in keeping with your education," he said. "My family does a good deal of business with a financial consulting firm based in Panama City. If I say the word, I'm quite certain someone there will give you a job, no questions asked."

"Doing what?"

"Arturo Salazar, the guy in charge, calls the women who work for him his 'account managers.' They facilitate whatever transactions are required. My understanding is that the job pays salary plus commission."

"So how would this work?" Graciella asked. "You show up, tell this Arturo guy that I'm your daughter, and he hires me on the spot?"

"I believe," El Pescado said thoughtfully, "under the circumstances, it would be best for all concerned if no one there had any idea that you're my daughter."

"That's probably true," Graciella agreed.

"So you'll do it, then?" Felix asked eagerly.

Ever since the moment, years earlier, when Graciella had unmasked her father's identity, she had followed his day-to-day exploits and had a fairly good idea about how much he was worth.

"Not for one hundred twenty a year," she countered. "A hundred and fifty at least, and I choose where we live. Do we have a deal?"

"How soon can you start?"

"First you deliver on the job and the house," she told him. "Then we'll set a starting date."

That is how Graciella Miramar became her mother's keeper. She didn't do it out of affection or a sense of duty, either. It was a job, plain and simple, and a means to an end. She would care for Christina willingly enough and capably enough—for as long as it suited her. And once that was no longer the case? She would end it, once and for all.

9

A week after commencement and acquiescing to her father's wishes, Graciella flew home to Panama to assume her new role. Despite his appalling looks, Felix's reputation as a lady's man preceded him wherever he went, as did his penchant for rubbing out anyone who happened to stand in his way. Long after Graciella hired on at Recursos, she learned from one of the other girls that Arturo had assumed his newly installed account manager to be one of Felix Duarte's many female conquests. The possibility of a romantic entanglement between her and one of the company's most well-to-do clients was enough at first to encourage Arturo to maintain a hands-off policy as far as Graciella was concerned. Glad to avoid her boss's slimy attentions, she did nothing at all to squelch that rumor. In fact, from time to time, she added a few fictitious details of her own.

Once Graciella was established at Recursos, El Pescado made sure that all his accounts, along with those of any number of his associates, ended up in her book of business. Those certainly helped Graciella's meteoric rise inside the company, but she had also developed many other lucrative clients due entirely to her own efforts.

From the computer terminal in her cubicle at work as well as from the secret laptop she kept squirreled away in her apartment,

Graciella oversaw complex transactions for any number of people whose financial activities would have been of great interest to law enforcement agencies in several countries and many different jurisdictions. Some of the offshore accounts she monitored in both crypto- and traditional currencies belonged to her outlaw father, but some of them were hers alone. When she was ready to break out of her cocoon, she would have plenty of resources at her disposal. In the meantime, El Pescado's daughter lived a boringly mundane life and remained entirely invisible.

True to his word, El Pescado had allowed Graciella to sort out suitable living arrangements for her and her mother. El Sueño, the aging condo complex she had chosen on Calle 61 Este, was conveniently close to her office. No doubt El Sueño had once been stylish enough. Now, however, it was a bit old-fashioned and dowdy, and that was part of what made it suitable for Graciella's purposes. To the outside world it was important that she appeared to live within her means. A condo that was too upscale or flashy would have attracted unwanted attention. The fifth-floor unit Graciella and Christina shared wasn't too high or too low, and was seemingly something she could afford. No one ever seemed to notice or comment on the fact that the condo was in Graciella's name or that she owned the place free and clear.

After the purchase, El Pescado had overseen a pricey but discreet remodel that brought the unit out of the seventies and into the twenty-first century. The kitchen and bathrooms were all updated. Graciella had been surprised when he had insisted on the installation of that unique power-supply safe in the floor of her bedroom closet. It took time for her to realize that even then, at the very beginning, he had been intent on involving her in the finer points of his business dealings, including transactions that required levels of security not available on the computers in the office.

When the unit was finally ready to occupy, El Pescado had hired an ambulance to transport Christina from Casa de la Esperanza, the latest residential treatment center where she'd been for a number of months, to the condo. Graciella soon came to understand that, although the facility had been called the "House of Hope," it had been little more than a pimped-out jail—one with a water view and better food, maybe, but it was also a place where, for her own good, Christina had been kept under lock and key.

Initially Christina responded well to her new surroundings, but her mental maladies were anything but cured, and she suffered periodic setbacks. On those occasions when she was relatively clean and sober, the situation between mother and daughter—ward and caretaker—wasn't all that bad. Christina drank, of course—that was a given—but it was the opioids that caused the most trouble. Despite the fact that Christina seldom left the house, she was still able to con someone—a housekeeper or a delivery boy—into helping her lay hands on the harder stuff. On more than one occasion, the relapses made Graciella's life a living hell. Those were the times when the princely sum her father was paying her didn't seem like nearly enough.

As the two women adjusted to living together, El Pescado became the invisible elephant in the room. They both knew that he was the one who provided the financial backing that made their relatively trouble-free living arrangements possible, but that uncomfortable reality was never part of a conversation between them, nor did they ever discuss that long-ago night when Christina had gone off to work and didn't come home. That taboo topic was never mentioned either.

Shortly after Christina arrived on Calle 61 Este, a van had stopped by to deliver a set of moving boxes that had been liberated from a storage unit. The boxes contained her mother's worldly goods, and Graciella allowed herself a cursory glance through them. Much to her surprise, she discovered that someone had gone to the trouble of cleaning, pressing, folding, and preserving the threadbare finery Christina had worn back in the days when she'd been out working the streets. Graciella's immediate inclination had been to throw it all out, but Christina had been unable to part with a single item. A hoarder at heart, she regarded each of those pieces of frayed clothing, worn out shoes, and bits of broken jewelry as precious treasures. The contents of those boxes had been the foundation of Christina's collection of hoarded trash, and as long as the mess was confined to Christina's room, Graciella forced herself to turn a blind eye.

As Christina's situation continued to worsen, Graciella learned to disengage and take things in stride. Never a social butterfly, she seemed to thrive in living a solitary life. Christina's ongoing mental health challenges gave her daughter ready excuses to dodge any number of unwanted complications. Whenever someone inquired as to why she wasn't married, she'd shrug her shoulders, shake her head, and say, "It's my mother, you know. She has no one else to look after her." Invariably that sad confession amounted to an automatic pass for remaining single. It also applied to questions about why she didn't go out on blind dates or why she avoided socializing with the girls after work. Focused on accumulating her own wealth, the truth is Graciella didn't actually want to do any of those things. This way she was able to decline all those unwanted interactions while at the same time maintaining a much-vaunted reputation for selflessness.

"Such a good daughter," people would say. "Christina is so lucky to have her."

Eventually, however, the "good daughter's" patience began to ebb, morphing from tolerance to resentment. By year eight or so, Christina refused to leave the apartment for any reason—including attending mass. Graciella's growing bank balances were no longer enough to justify her having to come home from work each day to contend with someone who had apparently decided she was incapable of helping herself. Christina spent her days lounging in front of the TV set, playing solitaire, watching her soaps, and drinking herself into oblivion. Sometimes she'd be passed out cold even before Graciella arrived home for the evening. And on those occa-

sions when she wasn't unconscious, she was often argumentative
and unreasonable—complaining about the food Graciella cooked
or the clothes she wore or the way she did her hair. Eventually and
unsurprisingly, Graciella simply had enough.

Yes, some of her mother's issues—the reclusiveness and the
hoarding—were symptomatic of post-traumatic stress disorder.
One doctor suggested Christina had most likely suffered permanent
brain damage and needed to stop drinking entirely. Regarding that
diagnosis as little more than a handy excuse and because having
Christina drunk was less troublesome than having her high on
drugs, Graciella kept the vodka flowing.

Gradually the mother/daughter relationship was turned on its
head. Christina had devolved into little more than a spoiled, recal-
citrant child—someone who had to be cajoled into eating the food
that was set before her; someone who had to be scraped out of her
chair each evening and carefully escorted into her bedroom; someone
who couldn't be trusted to take her own medications.

In the end, it was Christina's propensity for hoarding that gave
Graciella a workable solution. She had come home from work late on
a Monday afternoon in early September to find her mother already
blitzed as usual and frantically searching for the television remote.

"Where did you last have it?" Graciella had asked.

"I don't remember," her mother said tearfully. "It has to be here
somewhere, either here in the living room or the bedroom."

Graciella immediately conducted a thorough search for the
missing remote. She went over every inch of both the living room
and kitchen, checking under and behind furniture, pulling out
cushions, looking in cupboards, drawers, and cubbyholes. Only as
a last resort did she finally venture into the train wreck that was
now her mother's bedroom. It was bad enough that she had to go
there each night to help Christina into bed. The idea of having to
search through mounds of trash in an attempt to locate the remote
was, in a word, revolting.

An hour later, Graciella finally located the missing item in the drawer of her mother's bedside table. Since the television set was out in the living room, none of that made any sense, but that's where it was. And the remote wasn't the only thing hiding in Christina's bedside table, not by a long shot. In among an oddball assortment of hairbrushes, combs, single earrings, and broken pieces of costume jewelry, Graciella discovered more than a dozen bottles of aging prescription medications.

The drug names were readily recognizable. There were three separate bottles of sleeping pills, several antidepressants, and a full assortment of anti-anxiety meds, along with a bottle of muscle relaxants. The printed dates on the labels revealed that all the prescriptions were years beyond their expiration dates. Graciella knew for a fact that one of the prescribing doctors—one from Casa de la Esperanza—had himself died of a drug overdose some three years earlier. What Graciella found surprising was that the prescription bottles were all nearly full.

Using her phone and without actually handling the bottles themselves, she photographed each of the labels, all of which included the same clear warning: NO TOMAR CON ALCOHOL—Do not use with alcohol.

Then, closing the drawer, she took the remote, returned to the living room, and placed it in her mother's hands. "Oh, thank you," Christina slurred. "Where was it?"

"It had fallen under the bed."

That night, once Christina was in bed, Graciella pulled the computer out of its locked cubbyhole, fired it up, and then went on a computer search. She looked up each of the medications whose labels she had photographed. She learned that despite the printed expiration dates listed on the various bottles, the drugs inside were probably still every bit as powerful as they had ever been.

She also found interaction warnings involving three of the medications. A bit of mixing and matching of those, combined with

Christina's usual dosage of booze, would probably be enough to do the trick—and Graciella would finally be rid of the burden of continuing to care for her ailing mother.

She finished her online research, then, mindful of cyber security, she erased her search history from the laptop and deleted the photos from her phone. She had a plan in place now, and when the time was right she would carry it out. But first she had to deal with the other massive change in her life.

Having spent so many years in the States, Graciella maintained a number of news feeds on US-based sites. Browsing through her online papers on a Sunday morning in September, the name "Owen Hansen" had jumped out at her. Her first thought was that this Owen Hansen couldn't possibly be *her* Owen Hansen, because that was how she had come to think of him—as hers.

Owen had been the catalyst that had lured her away from her care-taking gig. For the first time, she had glimpsed a different future for herself, one that included combining her financial resources with Owen's. With Frigg's investment acumen added to the mix, the three of them would have been an unstoppable force. But the news of Owen's death left her sick at heart. The dream of a life she had glimpsed for herself was over without ever getting off the ground.

She had followed the story from afar, zeroing in on every detail she'd been able to glean from coverage on the Internet. She had been shocked beyond belief to hear that, before committing suicide himself, Owen had kidnapped two individuals. In addition, he was a suspected serial killer who used cyber bullying techniques to drive vulnerable people to suicide.

Cyber bullying? Did that mean Frigg was somehow involved in what had gone on? And then, out of the blue, Graciella had remembered that one snippet of conversation from Owen when he had bragged that Frigg could probably help him get away with murder. Obviously that hadn't been the case since the cops had been hot on Owen's trail at the time he had gone into a downward and ultimately fatal spiral. In Graciella's careful analysis of the timelines leading up to Owen's death, she had discovered something that was both interesting and puzzling. In the minutes just prior to Owen plunging off a narrow mountain road and while he'd been actively involved in a desperate car chase, he had made several sizable monetary transactions, ones that had turned the bulk of his wealth over to someone named Stuart Ramey.

Graciella was intimately involved with Owen's financial dealings, and Señor Ramey's name was not one she recognized. As far as she could ascertain, he had never cropped up previously among any of Hansen's business associates or even as a friend. So who was this guy—a silent partner, maybe? A secret lover?

At first Graciella could see no logical reason for Owen's having made those very sizable transactions. Her research efforts revealed no connection at all between the two men. Widening the parameters of her investigation, she sought out everything there was to learn about Stuart Ramey. Like Owen Hansen, he was a self-taught computer expert, but where Owen had been what people liked to call an Internet "black hat," Stuart would have been referred to as a "white hat"—a good guy as opposed to a bad one—who worked for a well-regarded international cyber security firm called High Noon Enterprises.

Graciella located several instances where High Noon had been the subject of media attention, including the company's active participation in the events leading up to Owen Hansen's death. Police credited Stuart Ramey with identifying Owen as a possible murderer, intervening in one attack and preventing it from becoming a fatality, and finally in setting the cops on Owen's trail. From everything Graciella read, it seemed that Stuart Ramey had almost single-handedly brought Owen down. Why, then, would Owen have gifted Stuart with his money? It made no sense.

After weeks of painstaking research Graciella finally believed she understood. Those final, last-minute transactions hadn't come from Owen himself. They most likely hadn't even been authorized by him. It seemed far more likely that the wealth handed over to Stuart mere minutes before Owen's suicide had been orchestrated by Frigg, the victim's artificial intelligence acting on her own or in collusion with Mr. Ramey, rather than on behalf of her creator.

Graciella immediately resumed her study of artificial intelligence in general. She wasn't especially disturbed by the philosophical discussions of what might happen if AIs somehow joined forces and turned on the human race. She was interested to learn, however, that AI engineers had discovered that if they began to frustrate their AIs by disregarding their suggestions and calculations, things could go terribly wrong. Some AIs became hostile under those circumstances. Others taught themselves to cheat.

Graciella could see that, at the time of Owen Hansen's death, he hadn't been taking advice from anyone, his AI included. So what if Frigg had decided to throw him under the bus and try her luck with some other player? And in that regard, who would be better qualified as a possible teammate than the one person on the planet seemingly smart enough to bring down Owen Hansen? On further consideration, Graciella began to wonder if perhaps Frigg had devised a way to use Owen's own money to create and cement a relationship with a new human partner.

In researching Stuart Ramey, Graciella had, inevitably, learned a good deal about High Noon Enterprises. The small, closely held company had been started by a guy named B. Simpson who had made a fortune in the video gaming industry. High Noon had an international reputation as the cyber equivalent of a gunslinger, brought in to handle crises.

Stuart Ramey had been with Simpson since the video gaming days and currently served as his right-hand man. Other than playing a pivotal role in bringing down Owen Hansen, there was precious little to be found on the Web regarding Ramey. There was almost nothing about his personal life. As far as Graciella could tell, he had never married and had no children. Nor could she locate any academic records beyond high school. Although Stuart was purported to be a computer genius, he was evidently self-taught.

B.'s partner in the company was his wife, Ali Reynolds, a former news anchor whose exact function wasn't clear. The other two employees working at the company's headquarters in Cottonwood, Arizona, were a recent computer science graduate named Camille Lee, and a woman named Shirley Malone whose job description was that of receptionist.

Graciella was startled to learn that one of the company's newer principals was a talented young guy named Lance Tucker who was still attending college in California and had not yet reported for work on-site in Arizona. Lance Tucker's name was one Graciella recognized because his programing genius had recently helped authorities topple three major dark Web vendors—Silk Road, AlphaBay, and Hansa Market, suppliers Graciella herself had used in the past.

The financial information Graciella was able to gather on High Noon was impressive. The business appeared to be both prosperous and stable. In recent months the company had made an outright purchase of the office park where they were located. They were currently in the process of upgrading the buildings in preparation for leasing out whatever space they themselves didn't occupy.

By the latter part of October, Graciella was ready to make her move, casting a line into the water that she hoped would enable her to reel in both Stuart Ramey and Frigg.

Bright and early on the morning of Wednesday, October 18, Graciella went into the office and sat down to compose a letter. Since this would be her first point of contact with Stuart Ramey, she was determined that the missive be pitch-perfect.

10

Needing to focus on the logistics of obtaining access to Frigg and her capabilities, Graciella decided it was time to execute the remainder of her plan. On the evening of the night she mailed the letter of introduction to Stuart Ramey, when it came time to help her mother, Graciella made a show of spotting the contents of that bedside table drawer.

"What the hell are you doing with all those pills?" she had demanded, as if seeing the bottles for the first time.

Christina leaned over and peered into the drawer as well, frowning in an effort to read the labels. "I musta forgotten about them," she muttered drunkenly.

"Of course you did," Graciella replied. She hurried out to the kitchen and returned a moment later with a plastic container in hand. "Put them in here," she ordered. "I'll take care of them."

And she had. On Wednesday, late in the evening, when Graciella brought Christina her customary nightly dose of vitamins and supplements, several pills from those long-hidden bottles had been added to the mix. Christina swallowed the whole collection, washing it down with a long swig of vodka without the slightest concern about what she was taking. That night Graciella feigned interest in whatever her mother was watching on TV. As a result, Christina had an extra drink and another round of pills before they even began the trek to the bedroom. Once Christina was in bed, Graciella returned with yet another drink as well as a third set of pills.

"Sorry," she explained, handing them over. "I must have forgotten to give these to you earlier."

By then Christina was far too plastered to argue the point or to remember the pills she had already taken. "You're very good to me," she mumbled before swallowing another collection of twenty or so pills. "Very good, very good."

Christina leaned back against her pillow and was snoring an instant later. Graciella let Christina drift off for a few minutes before returning once more with yet another glass of vodka and another mouthful of pills.

"Mom," she said, shaking her mother awake. "Why didn't you take your pills?"

"Musta forgot," Christina slurred. "Musta."

"You need to take them now."

A moment later she had swallowed those as well. By Graciella's count, that evening Christina had downed a mixture of more than a hundred pills, not counting the supplements. In addition she had consumed an entire fifth of vodka—enough, she hoped, to do the job. In the evenings, Graciella was the one who poured her mother's drinks, and she had done so tonight as well, leaving her prints on the glass as well as her mother's. As for the pill bottles themselves? Graciella had been holding the plastic container while Christina had deposited the bottles inside. Tonight, while Graciella had been dispensing the pills, she had worn gloves—not the latex kind found in a doctor's office, but a pair of soft leather gloves that she'd liberated from one of Christina's dresser drawers.

Graciella expected death would be more or less instantaneous, but it wasn't. At first Christina snored as she usually did when she went to bed dead drunk. Graciella used that time to bring the entire collection of pill bottles back from the kitchen and into the

bedroom, where she rearranged them, laying them out in an art-
ful display, tipping some bottles over and spilling their remaining
contents into the open dresser drawer or all the way to the floor,
with a few skittering under the bed.

By the time Graciella completed her pill bottle arrangement
project, her mother's breathing had become noticeably shallower.
Graciella resisted the temptation to check for a pulse. Instead,
she stripped off the gloves and dropped them back into the drawer
where she'd found them earlier. Then, leaving the lamp on, Graciella exited the room.

She returned to the living room, sat on the sofa, and used her
Recursos company-issued tablet to send out a series of e-mails. They
were mostly routine responses to clients about work matters. Each
of them was totally businesslike, totally unemotional, and every
one of them featured a time and date stamp. After all, how likely
would it be that someone could be in the process of murdering her
own mother while sitting in the next room and calmly tending to
day-to-day business correspondence?

When it was time for Graciella to go to bed, she tiptoed as far
as the doorway to her mother's room and stood there, listening to
hear if Christina was still breathing. She wasn't. Graciella turned
and walked away. She had cared for her mother until she didn't
have to anymore. Now she was done.

Once in her bedroom, Graciella retrieved her private laptop from
the safe in her closet and fired it up. While she'd been sitting there
in the living room, she'd been thinking about the letter she had sent
to Stuart Ramey. It was mailed and on its way. There was no telling
exactly how long it would take to get there, but what Graciella really wanted to know was the kind of reaction it would garner once
it arrived. In order to do that, she wanted eyes and ears inside the
walls of High Noon Enterprises.

For years now, in her account management job, Graciella had
handled complex logistical needs for any number of well-heeled,

high-profile clients who occasionally operated on both sides of the law. In the process of helping others, Graciella hadn't been above helping herself.

She disliked spending her own money but she had no compunction about using someone else's funds. She routinely siphoned off a little here and a little there from her various clients, always disguising the transfers as standard service charges. In the world of blockchain accounting, her skimming should have been right there for all to see. But the people she worked for—the ones who made up the bulk of her clientele—had good reason to be naturally averse to hiring accountants or asking for audits. As a result, her pilfering remained invisible to those around her, while her own accounts—most of which were definitely not handled in house—continued to grow.

To facilitate the logistical needs of her demanding clientele, she had created a directory of useful people—a private dark Web catalogue of trusted service providers. That was where she turned now to do some shopping of her own. Working with Robert Kemper, a reliable vendor who could provide both the necessary equipment and personnel, it didn't take long for her to put things in motion.

"You're sure you can get the job done in short order?" she asked.

"That depends," she was told. "How much information can you give me about the targets? Things will go a lot faster if my guy doesn't have to do all his own intel."

"I'll send you what I have."

"No problem, then. We do this kind of thing all the time. I have someone in mind to do the job. Ron should have your surveillance up and running in no time."

Having handled that aspect of the problem, Graciella shut down her computer, stowed it away, and then went to bed. Surprisingly enough, she had no difficulty falling asleep that night, despite the fact that her mother lay dead in her bed in the room next to hers. Graciella's conscience didn't bother her, not in the least, since, in that regard, Graciella Miramar truly was her father's daughter.

11

After serving as a driving instructor, Ali spent the next part of her Friday morning functioning as a pinch-hitting travel agent. She had managed to patch together an indirect routing through San Francisco that would have B. on the ground in Phoenix at 1:03 a.m. Sunday morning. The shuttle drive to Sedona meant he wouldn't actually arrive at the house until the wee hours of the morning. Talk about taking a red-eye! The connections were lousy, but, considering the current chaotic situation caused by the British Air shut down, Ali was relieved to have found a way to make B.'s homecoming happen. She had just looked up from her computer keyboard when a white-faced Stu barged into her office looking for all the world as though he'd just seen a ghost.

"Stu," she said, "what's the matter?"

He was clutching several pieces of paper. "Look at this," he replied, frisbeeing a piece of embossed stationery across her desk. "You're not going to believe it."

Picking up the missive, Ali unfolded it and studied the elegantly printed letterhead: *Recursos Empresariales Internationales, 18 Vía Israel, Panama City, Panama.* Once that information registered, Ali looked at Stu over the top of the sheet of paper. "Not Panama again," she said.

A month or so earlier, High Noon's investigation into Roger McGeary's death had put them in the crosshairs of a Panamanian homicide cop who had been none too pleased with their unwelcome involvement in the death of a passenger on board a cruise ship operating under a Panamanian flag.

"I'm afraid so," Stu said, nodding miserably. "Keep reading."

Mr. Stuart Ramey
High Noon Enterprises
#23 Business Park Way
Cottonwood, Arizona 86326
USA

Lucienne Graciella Miramar
Recursos Empresariales Internationales
18 Vía Israel
Panama City, Panama

18 October 2017

Dear Mr. Ramey,

Please accept our sincere condolences on the loss of your associate, Mr. Owen Hansen. I'm sure he will be greatly missed. We are currently holding the cryptocurrency funds Mr. Hansen directed us to disburse to you. You will find a current statement attached.

At your earliest convenience, please log in to our secure server and supply the required access codes and applicable keys. If you wish to have the funds paid to you directly, you will need to advise us as to what kinds of currency and which banking institutions you wish us to use.

If the funds are coming to you in the United States, we will require your Social Security number as well as your tax ID numbers. *Naturally we make no claims on the taxability of any of the resulting transactions and urge you to work with an accountant to be sure all taxation issues are properly handled. It is our understanding, however, that in most jurisdictions as far as gift tax purposes are concerned, you would be considered to be in constructive receipt of the funds as of the day Mr. Hansen made the transfer, which is more than a month in the past as of this writing.*

Also, for a number of years Mr. Hansen and Recursos Empresariales Internationales carried on a very lucrative business in terms of Bitcoin data mining, for which we were able to provide accounting and banking services. If you have any interest in reestablishing this activity, please let me know if I can be of help in that regard. As with the funds disbursement mentioned above, your ability to resume that activity would require an updated set of authorization codes.

Please let us know your wishes in these matters at your earliest convenience. Feel free to contact me directly at any time. We are looking forward to doing business with you.

> *Sincerely,*
> *L. Graciella Miramar.*

Ali read the letter through once and then she read it again. "Owen Hansen left you money?" she asked. "How much?"

Stuart nodded, and handed her a second piece of paper. "Take a look at this."

Ali examined the document. It appeared to be an ordinary monthly bank statement, complete with a complex account number. It included a beginning balance of 450 BTC, minus a .5 BTC service charge, leaving an ending balance of 449.5 BTC.

"What's a BTC," Ali asked, "some kind of Panamanian currency?"

"BTC stands for Bitcoin," Stuart explained.

"The stuff that passes for money on the dark Web?"

"Cryptocurrency isn't just used on the dark Web anymore," Stuart said. "Bitcoin is one of the major forms and Ethereum is another. They're both handy when it comes to making international monetary transfers—and also, as it turns out, for money laundering purposes. I just ran a check of Bitcoin's current value. As of a few minutes ago, one Bitcoin is worth $5,735.18."

Ali Reynolds wasn't someone who was capable of doing math in her head; she used her computer. After typing the numbers into her keyboard, she stared dumbfounded at the resulting sum. "Are you kidding? Owen Hansen left you 2.5 million dollars?" she asked.

Stu nodded. "And some change."

"But why?"

"I have no idea."

"What did he do, write you into his will or something?"

Stu shook his head. "Not exactly. Since the letter specifically mentions 'gift tax' rather than 'inheritance tax,' that would seem to indicate that the transfer was made prior to Owen Hansen's death rather than after the fact."

Ali was mystified. "But you never even met Owen Hansen until the morning of the day he died. In fact, you were doing everything in your power to help the cops track him down when he committed suicide. Why on earth would he give you any money at all, much less that much?"

"I don't believe Owen Hansen had anything to do with it," Stu answered grimly. "I think this is all Frigg's doing."

"Wait," Ali said. "You're telling me you think Owen's artificial intelligence authorized the transfers?"

"I'd be willing to bet on it," Stuart said. "This whole thing amounts to nothing more or less than a gigantic bribe on Frigg's part—a bribe and a gamble. She must have realized that Owen was about to disable her. Draining his accounts and transferring the funds to someone else would have crippled him financially. By sending his money to me, Frigg must have expected that when it came time came to save her, I'd be in her corner. That's why she sent me the kernel file—in hopes that I'd take pity on her and recall her files rather than shipping her off into oblivion."

"But you did send her to oblivion," Ali countered. "You thought she was too dangerous, and you deleted that file."

There was a long pause before Stuart spoke again. "You're right," he said. "I did think she was dangerous, I still do, and I did delete the file. The problem is, I may have kept a backup copy."

"You're saying you could bring Frigg back if you wanted to?" Ali asked.

"If I wanted to," Stuart replied bleakly, "but that's a very big if." Ali turned back to the letter and studied it for a time. "What does 'Recursos Empresariales' mean?" she asked.

"Business Resources," Stuart answered. "I already translated it."

"That doesn't sound like a bank," Ali suggested.

"It isn't a bank. It's more like a clearinghouse," Stuart answered. "Recursos Empresariales doesn't deal in regular currencies, although they network with banks and other institutions that do. Their primary specialty is handling cryptocurrencies of various kinds. Ordinary banks mostly can't touch the stuff without violating banking regulations. But this letter is the reason I may have to bring Frigg back."

"Have to?" Ali repeated. "I don't understand."

"Because you can bet that somewhere or other Frigg has squirreled away a file containing all those authorization codes, the ones I'll need in order to access the money, which is the only way I'll be able to sort out whatever taxes are owing."

"And the only way to access the authorization codes is to reactivate Frigg?"

"That's my read on the situation."

"How would you go about doing that?" Ali asked.

"I'd need the kernel file, of course," Stuart answered, "and a whole hell of a lot of computer power."

"How much?" Ali asked.

"According to the police report from Santa Barbara, when Frigg was fully operational, she had access to eight hundred blades or GPUs. She might run in skeletal mode on less computer power than that, but there's no way to tell if skeletal mode would provide access to the authorization codes we need."

"You're saying you need to access her completely or not at all," Ali mused.

Stu nodded in agreement.

Ali had a clear idea of how much computer power it took to handle High Noon Enterprises' corporate needs, including banks of off-site equipment that operated in stations scattered around the globe. Here at corporate headquarters they were currently in the process of expanding their space in order to double their local computer power, a process that had slowed to a crawl awaiting final sign-offs by building inspectors and the arrival of currently back-ordered computer equipment.

"At the time we took Owen Hansen down, I was amazed by how many GPUs he had, but now, knowing he was a Bitcoin miner, that whole thing makes a lot more sense."

"What's this about mining?" Ali asked.

"Bitcoin isn't handled by a governmental agency. And it isn't a centralized system, either. Transactions happen on the Web in a public arena and are recorded for all to see in what are referred to as blockchains. People who have enough knowhow and enough computer power available to do so are the ones who log all that activity. They do it on a freelance basis and are paid for each logged transaction."

"And they're called miners?" Ali asked.

Stu nodded. "And how are they paid for doing the logging? In Bitcoins, of course."

"Is that where all this money came from?"

"Probably," Stu answered. "At least some of it, and since the IRS is currently targeting Bitcoin accounts larger than $20,000,

I'd be a prime target. You can bet what'll be due is more than I can pay out of pocket without accessing the funds. So Frigg has put me between a rock and a hard place. I'll need the funds to cover the taxes, and I need her to access the funds."

"In other words," Ali mused, "in order to stay out of hot water with the IRS, you're going to need to reactivate Frigg and consult with her for however long it takes to get the account passwords. Do we have enough capacity here at High Noon to do that?"

"We?" Stuart echoed. "Are you saying you'd involve High Noon in this mess?"

"Absolutely," Ali answered. "You're part of High Noon, and your problem is our problem. But back to my original question. Do we have enough computer power here?"

"Probably, but I don't want Hansen's AI anywhere near High Noon's computers," Stuart told her. "If and when I turn her back on, her operation has to be kept absolutely separate from ours. I could maybe install her temporarily in the new computers we have coming in, but . . ."

"But those are currently on back order," Ali added. "By the time they show up, there's a good chance those taxes won't just be payable, they'll be overdue. Maybe, in the meantime, we could lease some additional computer capacity."

"Lease?" Stu echoed, looking horrified. "As in renting computers that have already been used by somebody else?"

It was as if, by even mentioning the word "lease," Ali had just suggested the cyber equivalent of sharing a toothbrush. When it came to computers, Stu was utterly fastidious. He had a remarkable collection of old ones—museum pieces, as he liked to call them—but only computers that came to him straight out of a box were ever allowed to hook up with High Noon's computer system. Stu's outrage might have been comical if he hadn't been dead serious.

"I don't want Frigg's operating system anywhere near our computers," Stu repeated, "and I don't want somebody's leased computer equipment contaminating ours, either."

Heaving himself off the chair, Stu started for the door.

"One more question," Ali said.

"What?" he asked, pausing in mid-stride.

"Supposing you rebooted Frigg long enough to get the passcode information from her and access the money. What would you do with her then?"

"Take her back off-line," Stuart answered at once. "The very fact that she was devious enough to lay groundwork that would force me to reactivate her shows that she's capable of strategic thinking. As for Owen Hansen's money? It wasn't Frigg's to give away in the first place, which means it sure as hell isn't mine. Once I lay hands on it, I'm sending it straight back where it belongs, most likely to Owen's mother."

Knowing Stuart was honest as the day is long, Ali didn't find that at all surprising.

"That settles it, then," Ali told him. "Our new computer space is pretty much ready to go, pending our final inspections. I say we lease whatever equipment we need to get the job done, set it up in our new lab, and put this matter behind us."

"It's going to cost a fortune," Stu grumbled.

"I know," Ali grinned at him, "but you're worth it. Besides, once you have all that money at your disposal, feel free to reimburse us. In the meantime, see what you can do about finding the equipment."

"All right," Stu conceded, "but I'm telling you here and now that I don't like using anyone else's computers."

As far as Ali was concerned, that wasn't exactly news from the front.

12

With her mother's remains properly packaged and duly shipped, Graciella walked to work. It was late October. Heavy rains would come in November, but for right now it was relatively dry and fine and not too hot, either. She walked with a definite spring in her step because she knew that the future was about to open up for her.

Early the previous Thursday morning, when she had entered her mother's bedroom and ostensibly found her dead, Graciella had delivered a bravura performance. She had forced herself to walk the very thin line between being too upset and being upset enough. Because of her mother's long-standing issues, Graciella already had the number of a local ambulance service loaded into her phone, and she had summoned the ambulance before dialing the police. That way, when the cops arrived, one of the ambulance attendants opened the door to let them in while Graciella, still wearing her bathrobe, sat on the living room sofa, and wept.

Everyone had been incredibly kind to her—from the neighbors in the building to the cops who questioned her about the incident. Had her mother been out of sorts? No, Graciella told them, not at all. Had she been upset about something? No, it had been a perfectly ordinary evening. They had watched television together—Graciella was able to reel off the names of all the programs—and then her mother had gone to bed. Had there been any indication that she intended to do herself harm? No. Had she ever done something like this before? That question, posed by a homicide detective, was one that required a more complicated answer, because there were several attempted suicides lurking in Christina Miramar's medical history, mixed in with her various bouts of treatment for ongoing addiction problems.

Graciella was in the process of answering when Arturo Salazar showed up. She had called the office earlier to explain her absence, but the last thing she had expected was for Arturo to take it upon himself to turn up uninvited at her condo. Because officers were still coming and going, the front door was open. Without bothering to knock, Arturo rushed into the room. Ignoring the detective, he hurried over to Graciella and smothered her in an all-encompassing hug.

"You poor thing," he murmured sympathetically, "you poor, poor thing. Tell me what we can do to help."

What would have helped immensely was for him to get the hell out, but Graciella could hardly say that to his face. The cops, the detective, the neighbors were all there watching. They had been invited to enter. She regarded Arturo's presence in her home as an invasion, and the intimacy of his hug was a violation.

"There's really nothing you can do," Graciella said, keeping her voice civil. "I was just telling Detective Vargas here about my mother's rather complicated medical history."

Obligingly, Detective Vargas pulled out a business card and passed it to Arturo. Looking at the card, Arturo's eyes widened.

"Homicide?" he asked. "Surely you don't think Graciella here had anything to do with her mother's passing!"

"It's considered an unnatural death, so of course we're investigating," the detective replied mildly. "At this point no one is making accusations of any kind."

Arturo drew himself up and glared at the detective. "Graciella

Miramar has been an outstanding employee at my firm for more than ten years now. For all the time I've known her, she has single-handedly cared for her mother with utmost devotion and without a word of complaint. To my knowledge, she has always put her mother's needs before her own."

It was grating to have to sit there and listen to him sing her praises. Here Arturo was, supposedly championing Graciella's cause, when he had merely used this as an excuse to barge into her home and nose around.

"Thank you, Arturo," she managed.

He gave her one of his smarmiest smiles along with a linger-ing pat on her shoulder. "So as I said earlier, Graciella, if there's anything at all we can do to help, please let me know. And be sure to inform us about scheduling for the funeral service so I can tell the girls. I'm sure most if not all of them will want to attend. In the meantime, you have a week of bereavement leave coming. If you need longer than that, let me know."

"I will," she said. "Of course."

"You're lucky to have such a caring boss," Detective Vargas said after Arturo took his leave.

"You have no idea," Graciella had told him, "no idea at all."

For years she had used her mother as an excuse to dodge any number of social engagements. Now, feigning overwhelming grief, she still held herself apart. She had left her father with the impres-sion that the church had declined to hold Christina's funeral based on a determination of suicide. In fact, her mother's former priest from Our Lady of Guadalupe had come by and offered to perform a funeral mass. The people from the mortuary had also suggested that a small memorial gathering would be appropriate. Graciella had nixed both. She wasn't the least bit interested in mingling with strangers and near-strangers and hearing their rote messages of sympathy for her loss, especially when what she was feeling was freedom and relief rather than sorrow.

As Graciella neared the office that Friday morning, she slowed her pace. By the time she stepped inside the door, she had erased all evidence of her earlier sunny mood. Her coworkers greeted her circumspectly, treating her with the gentleness and gravity one was expected to observe around someone grieving the recent loss of a beloved parent. On Graciella's part, it was important to maintain just the right balance between sadness and appreciation as she acknowledged each expression of sympathy. It was a relief for Graciella to finally be able to tuck into her cubicle and focus her attention on her computer's screen and keyboard. The morning was half gone when Arturo walked up behind her and placed a possessive hand on her shoulder.

"Welcome back," he said. "Would you care to go to lunch?"

She wanted to shrug away from him and move her shoulder out of reach, but she didn't. She knew where this was going, and it had nothing to do with his expressing condolences over the loss of her mother. No doubt he thought that, in her weakened condition, Graciella would finally be ripe for conquest. He probably expected that after lunch and a couple of drinks, they'd finish the afternoon by spending a few hours in the little boutique hotel that, according to the other girls in the office, he frequented when it was time for one of his workday assignations. From the grapevine Graciella had learned that the hotel was nice. Arturo? Not so much.

"Sorry," she said. "I've been away for a whole week, and I've got a lot of finishing up to do on the Owen Hansen account."

Arturo shook his head. "It's a shame to lose that piece of business. Señor Hansen was one of our best customers."

"Yes," Graciella agreed, "and that's why I'm doing my best to hang on to as much of his book of business as possible."

"By all means, go ahead, then," Arturo muttered, walking away. "Don't let me stand in your way."

Watching him go, Graciella wasn't surprised to see him stop off at Bianca Navarro's desk on his way out. Bianca was the newest of the new hires. She was young, good-looking, and incredibly naive. Graciella suspected that she was probably dumb enough to fall for his claims—the age-old story about how his wife was cheating on him, but that he couldn't ask for a divorce on account of the kids. Yeah, right! When Arturo and Bianca left the office together, Graciella turned back to her computer screen.

Unfortunately, despite the fact that more than a week had passed since she sent the letter, there was no response from Stuart Ramey. Nothing. *Nada.* That was disappointing, and there was still no word from the surveillance guy about when he'd have the bugs up and running. All she could do for now was wait.

And so she went to work on her computer, answering the e-mails and sorting through transactions that had necessarily been handled by others in her absence. As she worked through the remainder of the morning and on into the afternoon, Graciella had an unobstructed view of Arturo's empty office and of Bianca's unoccupied cubicle.

With each hour that passed, Graciella quietly let her fury come to a full boil. The man was a pig—a despicable pig, who had bullied his way into her home and laid his filthy hands on her. And now he had turned his unwelcome attentions on poor Bianca. That, Graciella decided, was completely unacceptable.

Over the years, she had negotiated transactions for her father, transferring funds made in payment for hits in which people's lives had been rubbed out. But all those had been from a distance. Standing silently in the doorway while her mother breathed her last was the first time Graciella had been directly involved in a homicide, and to her surprise, she had liked it. She had enjoyed the challenge of the delicate dance with the investigators afterward—of playing the grieving daughter role when she'd been anything but grief-stricken. If anything, the whole experience had given her an exhilarating sense of empowerment.

That afternoon Graciella shut down her work computer and clocked out of the office right at quitting time. After walking home, she went straight to the safe, and pulled out the other computer—the private one.

In the world of the dark Web, the transaction didn't amount to much—only a Bitcoin or two—but she trusted that the results would be entirely satisfactory.

13

Once Stuart left her office, Ali returned to making B.'s emergency travel arrangements. She soon learned that the situation on the ground in the UK continued to worsen. She had managed to book seats on a flight on WOW air from Reykjavík to San Francisco, but making the Reykjavík connection was a bust. The first-tier jet service operators she would have preferred to use were already fully booked. After another hour of searching, she finally located an off-brand jet charter service called Jet-To-Go operating out of an FBO at Biggin Hill Airport in Bromley.

Dan Arnold, the guy who answered the phone, sounded like an older gentleman, one who was more likely to be a pilot than a receptionist, leaving Ali to wonder if Jet-To-Go was anything more than a one-man operation. With the words "fly by night" ringing in her head, she quickly checked the company's safety record, which turned out to be fine. With that information in hand she called B. with her latest proposal.

"I just want to be home," B. assured her wearily. "But wait, did you say they fly a Falcon 50EX? One of those could make it from the UK to Sedona in two hops. Did you ask him about flying direct?"

Ali bit her lip. He was whining again. She had been so focused on getting the transatlantic piece of the puzzle ticketed that she hadn't even considered using a private jet for the entire trip.

"Look," B. urged. "It's only money. Ask him. If he can do it, great—damn the torpedoes, full speed ahead. As for your worry about him being an older guy? If that turns out to be the case, it also means that he's got a lot of takeoffs and landings under his belt. He'll be every bit as concerned about safety as I am. As for that WOW flight? If you just made the reservation, you should be able to cancel it within twenty-four hours with no problem."

Right, Ali thought with annoyance. *Easy for you to say. You haven't spent the last several hours on the phone trying to make that damned reservation.*

"Okay," Ali said aloud.

"Anything else going on?" B. asked.

At that very moment she didn't feel much like telling him about Stu Ramey's being bossed around by a dead man's artificial intelligence. That story was far too complicated for a shorthand version over the phone. "Not so as you'd notice," Ali said shortly. "I'll get back to you on the plane situation."

She redialed Dan Arnold's number. "My husband wants to know if your aircraft can fly all the way to the US." She didn't bother asking how much the flight would cost because she was pretty sure she already knew, and if B. was willing to pay the price, she sure as hell was!

"Whereabouts in the US, miss?" Dan Arnold asked.

"Sedona."

"Oh, you mean that little place outside of Phoenix where the airport is up on a hill over town?"

"That's the one."

"I know where it is, but we can't land there. Sedona's runway is too short for us to take off at that altitude," Arnold said. "Had us some good customers who owned a second home there, up until the husband died, may he rest in peace. When they flew with us, we usually put down at Flagstaff. We'd fly into Bangor, Maine, clear customs and refuel there, and then fly the rest of the way in one hop."

"But could you do a flight like that tomorrow?" Ali asked.

"Yes, ma'am, we most certainly could. Where's your husband now, and what time tomorrow morning can you have him here?"

"He's in London," Ali answered. "At Claridge's."

"That's around an hour from here, depending on traffic. What I'll need from you is his Amex number, his passport number, his weight, and a Global Entry number if he's got one. Once I have all that, you tell me what time he wants to leave. We'll be fueled up and ready to go when he gets here. And we'll have plenty of food and drink on board so he won't starve to death between here and there."

"I'll tell him to be there at ten," she said.

"Okay," Arnold told her. "That'll put us in Bangor around one. It'll take the better part of an hour to clear customs and refuel, which means we should be on the ground in Flagstaff sometime between three and four in the afternoon. Will someone be on hand to pick him up?"

"That depends," a disgruntled Ali told him.

"On what?"

"On how I'm feeling tomorrow," Ali answered. "The way things stand right this minute, he may just need to rent a car."

After providing all the necessary information, Ali got back on the phone to WOW, where she sat on hold again, waiting to cancel the San Francisco flight. She was still waiting when Camille Lee popped her head into the room.

Cami, as she preferred to be called, was a twenty-something relatively recent computer science graduate who had been hired by High Noon primarily to serve as Stu's assistant. Her parents, both of them dyed-in-the-wool academics, heartily disapproved of their daughter's signing on to work for a cyber security company, and they especially didn't like the idea that she was working in a lab with Stuart Ramey, someone they saw as an unschooled oaf and little more than a glorified hacker.

From Cami's point of view, she had lucked into a place that was far enough away from her California-based parents to be out from under their day-to-day supervision. At High Noon, she had found work that suited both her talents and her mind-set. And rather than being put off by Stu's limited social skills, she simply navigated around them. She had learned to take his idiosyncrasies in stride and often served as his intermediary to the rest of the world.

"Hey," Cami said, catching a glimpse of Ali's gloomy face. "Is something wrong?"

"Men," Ali answered.

"There's a whole lot of that going around about now," Cami replied with a grin. "If you think it's bad where you're sitting, you should see what it's like out in the lab. It's been a morning-long roller-coaster ride. First Stu was worried sick about driving the Bronco, but he came back from that so psyched that he was almost walking on air. He immediately called the DMV to check on his driver's test. Because there'd been a cancellation, he managed to snag an appointment for late this morning. Then, the mail shows up and he goes racing out of the lab like his hair is on fire, only to come back grumbling about how much he hates using secondhand computers. Why would he need used computers? Don't we have a whole batch of brand-new CPUs on order?"

"Those are currently on back order," Ali replied. "The delayed delivery wasn't that big a deal, but it turns out that now we need some additional computing capacity immediately if not sooner. That's why I asked Stu to look into leasing some short-term equipment."

Cami nodded. "Which explains it, then," she said.

"Explains what?"

"Why Stu was in such a snit," Cami answered. "As far as he's concerned, 'leased' and 'used' are both dirty words. But still, what's the hurry? I thought the plan was to have the new equipment up and running in time for Lance's graduation and before he's ready to come here full-time."

"This has nothing to do with Lance and everything to do with Stu and Owen Hansen's artificial intelligence," As Ali outlined the contents and likely consequences of Graciella Miramar's letter, Cami listened, wide-eyed.

"Are you serious?" she asked when Ali finished. "Stu's really going to reactivate Frigg? I thought he said she was unreliable."

"He may be right about that," Ali agreed, "but it turns out Frigg is most likely the only source for the passcodes Stu will need to sort out his financial situation. That's why I suggested the leasing option. He wasn't happy about it, but he said he'd get right on it."

"Don't hold your breath," Cami said with a laugh. "At this very moment, he's over at the DMV and hopefully passing his driver's test. Shirley took him, and she's letting him use her Honda for his test drive. While they're gone, would you like me to take a preliminary look-see at a leasing option?"

That was one of the things Ali had come to appreciate about Cami Lee. She was a self-starter.

"Would you, please?" Ali asked. "You're likely to find us a better deal than Stu will. Having him making inquiries and negotiating a deal with his nose out of joint and a chip on his shoulder probably won't lead to the best of all outcomes."

"Presumably not a computer chip?" Cami asked with a smile.

Ali smiled back. "Presumably."

"So if the goal is to get Frigg working again, we're talking about a bunch of hardware, right?"

"Yes, the works," Ali agreed. "Stu told me that before Hansen took Frigg down, she was operating on eight hundred blades."

Cami nodded. "I didn't know the exact number, but from seeing the crime scene photos, that's about what I would have figured.

There's a shortage of CPUs right now, so trying to lease that many isn't going to be easy, and it's going to cost a bundle."

"I know that, too," Ali agreed, "but as I told Stu, his problem is High Noon's problem. In terms of PR, we can't afford to have one of our principals caught up in some complicated unpaid taxes difficulty with the IRS. My understanding of Ms. Miramar's letter is this: whether Stu can access the money or not, it's his at the moment and whatever taxes are due will probably be payable in a hurry—taxes Stu won't be able to cover without having access to the funds themselves."

"And the only way to do that is to reboot Frigg?"

"Exactly," Ali replied.

"Okay," Cami said. "I'll see what I can do."

By the time Cami left the room, Ali had been on hold for so long that she had almost forgotten the phone was still at her ear. Just then, the airline service rep came back on the line. By the time that call finally finished, Ali's e-mail account dinged with the confirmation information from Jet-To-Go. Once Ali forwarded that to B., she was finally able to return to the other items on her to-do list. An hour later, she was deep in handling routine correspondence when Cami showed up in her doorway again, this time grinning from ear to ear. "You're not going to believe this."

"Believe what?" Ali asked.

"After I went back to my desk, I called a couple of leasing agencies, and they practically laughed in my face. It turns out nobody has any equipment available for lease at any price. Then it occurred to me that maybe there was someone out there with a bunch of perfectly good computer equipment that was just sitting around gathering dust."

"Who would that be?" Ali asked impatiently.

"Owen Hansen's mother," Cami replied, "so I gave her a call."

Ali's jaw dropped. "You did what?"

"I called Irene Hansen and asked her if she had any interest in unloading her son's computer equipment."

"And?"

"Obviously she has no idea that she's got a potential gold mine down in her basement. She told me she's hired someone who's supposed to come next week and haul away the junk, as she called it. I asked her if she'd be willing to sell it. She said if we'd come get it, we could have it for nothing. It turns out she's getting ready to sell the house and needs to clear out the basement so her contractor can start work early the following week. The junk guy is due on Wednesday. She says if we can pick it up sooner than that, the stuff is ours free for the taking."

"A collection of computers like that is worth a fortune," Ali objected, "and she's willing to give it to us for nothing?"

"With her only son dead, it sounds to me as though she mostly just wants it gone. And even if we're not paying her for the equipment, there are bound to be some shipping and handling charges involved. We can't just wave a magic wand to get all those GPUs from there to here."

"What will Stu think of all this?" Ali asked.

"I'm not sure," Cami said, "but reloading the AI into a system where it's already been resident should be a hell of a lot easier than starting over from scratch. I doubt even Stu would argue with that, so what should I do—call Mrs. Hansen back and tell her we have a deal?"

"High Noon played a major part in bringing down her son," Ali replied. "Is she aware that we're the ones who would be taking the equipment?"

"I maybe didn't mention that," Cami conceded, "at least not straight out."

"What if she finds out later and calls the whole deal off? We're better off being up front with her to begin with."

"All right, then," Cami said. "I'll tell her."

All the while they'd been talking, Cami seemed to be only half listening, absorbed in her iPad screen. Finally locating what she wanted, she passed the device to Ali.

"This it what we're talking about," she said. "It's the crime scene photo I was telling you about."

Ali looked at the array of loaded shelving units. "They're huge!" she exclaimed.

Cami nodded. "Yes, they are," she agreed. "Empty, each of these racks probably weighs about a hundred pounds. Fully loaded it'll be closer to four hundred."

"Should we call a moving company, then?" Ali asked. "It's already Friday afternoon. They might be able to get a crew up and running by Monday, but I doubt it."

"A moving company?" Cami echoed. "You've got to be kidding. If you send a bunch of untrained movers over to pick this stuff up, you'll end up with exactly what Irene Hansen already thinks it is—a pile of junk. If you want any of it to fire up and work again, it has to be dismantled properly, with both ends of every cable and every connection properly numbered and labeled."

"Sounds like we'd need a team of geniuses to get the job done the right way."

"Yes," Cami replied, "but it turns out you just happen to have a team of geniuses on staff, three of them, actually—Stu Ramey, Lance Tucker, and me."

"You're saying you should go get it?"

"Absolutely. Stu and I can rent a truck, drive to Santa Barbara, and pick the GPUs up ourselves. With any luck, maybe Lance can come help out. He and Stu can do the dismantling while I round up a crew of Home Depot day laborers to do the heavy lifting."

"You make it sound doable," Ali said.

"It *is* doable," Cami countered. "We just have to make it happen."

Stu appeared in the doorway behind Cami. "Make what happen?" he asked.

Cami spun around to face him. "Well," she demanded, "how'd you do?"

"One and done," he announced with a triumphant grin. "I passed with flying colors!"

"Congratulations," Cami said, "now go pack."

"Pack?" Stu repeated with a frown. "What for?"

"Road trip," Cami joked. "Me and you, babe. We've got ourselves a whole passel of used computers that we're going to pick up, bring back here, and install in our new computer bay."

"But—" Stu began.

"No buts," Cami told him, dismissing his objection. "What would you say if I told you Owen Hansen's entire collection of blades can be ours for the taking?"

Stu's jaw dropped. "You mean like for free?"

"Exactly," Cami told him. "All we have to do is go get 'em."

Ali held her breath expecting a pyroclastic blast. Much to her surprise, none was forthcoming.

"Free is good," Stu said. "How soon do we leave?"

14

For the remainder of the afternoon, High Noon Enterprises shifted into high gear. While Cami and Stu went off to get organized for their unanticipated departure, Ali reached for her phone and dialed Lance Tucker's number.

"Hey, Ali," he said cheerfully. "How's it going?"

Hearing Lance's voice on the phone reminded Ali of the night years earlier when she'd first laid eyes on him. At the time he'd been gravely injured and lying in a hospital bed in a medically induced coma. A year earlier than that, while still a juvenile, Lance had objected to the San Leandro school district's proposal to tag all their students with GPS tracking devices. Lance, a talented computer science whiz, had staged a protest by successfully hacking into the district's computer system and disabling their server.

High Noon Enterprises had been called in to counter the attack. When the hack was traced back to Lance, the school district had gone after him tooth and nail. Rather than graduating with his class, the former honors student had sat out his senior year in a juvenile detention facility while his mother—a single mom, scraping by as an LPN while supporting her four sons—struggled to pay $100,000 in court-ordered restitution.

B. Simpson had felt responsible for the dire circumstances in which Lance Tucker found himself. The kid was nothing short of brilliant. Working in conjunction with Everett Jackson, his beloved math teacher, Lance had created a game-changing program called GHOST which allowed untraceable access to the dark Web. There were plenty of people on both sides of the law who had been eager to lay hands on that invaluable piece of intellectual property, and B. Simpson had simply outbid them all. To begin with, he had paid a fair price to both Lance and to Everett Jackson's widow for High Noon to lease GHOST on a temporary basis. In addition, B. had offered to fund Lance's further education on the condition that, once out of school, both Lance and GHOST would come onboard with High Noon on a permanent basis. That expected outcome was due to come to fruition in the spring when Lance was scheduled to graduate from UCLA.

With all that history flashing through Ali's head, it took a moment for her to realize that she had never answered the question. "Turns out things are hopping around here," she said. "What kind of plans do you have for the weekend?"

"Plans? Hitting the books, I suppose," Lance said. "Why? What's up?"

In as few words as possible, Ali brought Lance up to speed on what was going on, starting with the letter to Stu from Graciella Miramar.

"You're saying that Frigg somehow boxed Stu into a corner where he has to reboot her?"

At the time Stuart had deleted the kernel file, Lance had been the only person involved with High Noon who had mourned the loss of Owen Hansen's rogue AI.

"That's whole the idea," Ali answered. "It's what it's going to take to straighten out Stu's financial entanglements in a timely fashion. If we delay too long, whatever taxes are due may end up in arrears. The last thing we need is for the IRS to come after him for unpaid taxes."

"Right," Lance said. "After all, since High Noon already has one jailbird on the company roster, you probably can't afford to add another one."

"You don't count as a jailbird anymore," Ali reminded him. "Your record was expunged, remember?"

"Right," Lance returned with a self-deprecating chuckle. "I keep forgetting that. But you still haven't said why you wanted to know what I'm doing this weekend. Is someone from there coming over?"

"Two people, actually," Ali said, "Stu and Cami."

She went on to explain how Owen Hansen's mother had offered to give them his collection of computers for free, on the condition that someone come to Santa Barbara and fetch them prior to that midweek deadline.

"Wait," Lance said, "High Noon is going to end up with Owen Hansen's very own GPUs?"

"Yes, but only if we can pull together a program that will get us there before the junk dealer arrives. Cami's in the process of calling down to Phoenix to rent a truck," Ali finished. "She and Stu are planning on driving over to Santa Barbara to pick up the equipment. I was hoping maybe you could show up and help out."

"How's this for an idea?" Lance suggested. "Instead of Cami and Stu spending twenty or so hours driving back and forth to California, why don't you just fly them over? I'll rent a truck on this side and pick them up at the airport. That way they can be in Santa Barbara dismantling that equipment before they'd even finish driving to Palm Springs. How many blades, do you know?"

"Eight hundred," Ali answered.

Lance whistled. "That's a lot of dismantling," he said, "and a lot of loading and hefting, too. I've got a few friends here at school who are your basic starving-student computer science majors. Some of them might be willing to spend their weekend earning extra pocket money. In fact, a couple of the guys I have in mind are kettlebell enthusiasts who'll be great when it comes to doing the hard physical labor. What do you think?"

Ali had grown up listening to her father recite from his collection of tried, true, and exasperatingly trite sayings. One of his favorites had always been, "A wise man changes his mind; a fool never does."

This was an occasion when changing her mind seemed like the right idea. "You've got yourself a deal," she told him. "As soon as I book their flight, I'll call you with Cami and Stu's ETA. As for your worker bees? Feel free to pay them the going rate."

"Will do," Lance told her. "And let Stu and Cami know that they won't need to drag any tools along on the plane. I'll show up with everything they need, including rolls of pallet wrap."

"What's pallet wrap?" Ali asked.

"It's heavy-duty plastic film. We'll wrap it around the racks before we move them."

"Fair enough," Ali said. "It sounds like you know what you're doing."

Within a matter of minutes, Ali had Cami and Stu booked on an early evening flight out of Sky Harbor in Phoenix that would have them landing at Burbank shortly after nine p.m. When she went back to the lab to pass along the change of plans, Stu—who had yet to master all of his fear-of-flying issues—was less than overjoyed.

"Fly, really?" he grumbled. "Do we have to?"

"Yes, you have to," Ali told him. "If necessary, take some anti-anxiety meds before you board the plane. Believe me, flying for a couple of hours is a better idea than having you and Cami wear yourselves out driving there and back."

Cami entered the room toward the end of that conversation. "Wait," she said. "We're flying?"

"Yes," Ali answered. "I just booked your tickets."

"So I don't need to rent a truck after all?"

"Lance will rent the truck in California," Ali told them. "This way

I won't have to worry about the two of you driving in both directions. And speaking of that rental truck, Stu, Cami and Lance will be the only authorized drivers. You may have a your license now, but I have no intention of turning an inexperienced driver armed with a loaded U-Haul truck loose on the state of California. On the trip home, Cami drives and you function as copilot, got it?"

"Got it," Stu agreed. "Copilot only."

Ali glanced at her watch and saw that it was already a little past two. "Your plane leaves at seven, so you'd better get cracking."

Stu and Cami left the business park a short time later with Stu lugging his carry-on bag. Once they cleared out, the office seemed unnaturally quiet. Ali arranged for hotel rooms for Cami and Stu at the Burbank Residence Inn and then forwarded the itinerary information to Lance. By the time she finished clearing her desk, a glance at the clock told her it was already nearly midnight in London. Having missed her window of opportunity to bring B. up to speed, Ali went out to the front lobby, where Shirley was holding down the fort.

"I'm bushed," Ali said. "I think I'll head out early."

Shirley looked up from her keyboard. "A little TGIF?" she asked.

"Maybe a little," Ali admitted.

"Since you're the boss, I don't see why not," Shirley responded with a smile. "When it's time for me to leave, I'll close the shutters, turn on the alarm, and leave the place locked up tight."

"Thanks," Ali said.

Ali walked out into the parking lot and was surprised to see her father's Bronco sitting there. She had forgotten about it completely, and now she'd need to drive on into Sedona to drop the Bronco off at the garage before going home. With that out-of-the-way jog in mind, it was just as well she was leaving early. On weekends, and especially on Friday afternoons, traffic in Sedona was a mess. Locals had adjusted to the series of recently installed roundabouts that had been strung like so many beads along the main thoroughfares running through town. Unfortunately, the redesigned traffic patterns still baffled out-of-town visitors who flocked to Sedona on weekends.

It was 3:40 when Ali drove out of the parking lot. She noticed that there was a single battered white work van still lingering in the lot. The contractors and their workers usually called a halt early on Fridays, too, but evidently whoever was driving that van wasn't one of them.

15

Ronald Webster, the driver of that late departing van, was a patient man and a dangerous one. After accepting the assignment earlier in the week, he'd spent most of the next three days on-site at the Mingus Mountain Business Park, blending in with construction workers, masquerading as one of them, and eating lunch along with the other guys when they trooped outside to a shade-covered picnic table.

Armed with a set of well-used rakes and hoes he had purchased at a garage sale and dragging around a large plastic garbage container, Ron busied himself with pulling out dead landscaping and heaving the remains into a Dumpster that was already close to overflowing with accumulated construction debris. That was the thing about doing physical labor. As long as you carried tools and seemed to be working with them, you became totally invisible and could do your reconnaissance at leisure. Had the real landscaping company shown up about then things might have gotten dicey, but for now it looked as though Ron was home free.

As the clock ticked down on that Friday afternoon, he knew the time had come to make his move. It was now or never. Long experience had taught him that the best time for these kinds of incursions was late in the day on Fridays. It was when people's attention spans suffered the most, leaving them distracted because they were already preoccupied with dreading their evening commute or making plans for the upcoming weekend.

Webster had joined the Air Force in hopes of training for special ops, but that hadn't worked out very well. After punching out his commanding officer, he had been tossed out on his ear with an other-than-honorable discharge. His tendency for brawling carried over into civilian life, where a fatal bar fight several months later had landed him in the slammer for involuntary manslaughter. Once out of jail and back on the streets, finding legitimate work had proven almost as problematic as finding a decent place to live.

Fortunately for him, his widowed mother had remarried. She had moved to her new husband's ten-acre parcel on the outskirts of Marana, just northwest of Tucson. His mom had held on to Ron's father's old Lazy Daze RV, and she and Art, her second husband, let Ron live in that rent-free. Powered by an extension cord from the garage, it was hardly luxurious, but it beat living on the streets. The place had been an oven through the dead of summer, but now that autumn was under way, it was far more comfortable than the makeshift cot in the back of his work van where Ron had been roughing it the last two nights.

Before getting thrown out of the Air Force, he had learned enough about electronic surveillance to make him dangerous. Now he kept body and soul together mostly by working for marginally ethical divorce lawyers where his main focus was helping to get the goods on the marital wrongdoings of some erring spouse. When it came to non-court-ordered eavesdropping, Ron was a very handy guy to have around. But work had been in short supply the last several months, and this week he was grateful when Robby, one of his job brokers, had given him a call.

Jobs for Robby's clients tended to be more on the sketchy side but they paid better. Not only that, when it came time for payday,

Robby didn't jack you around. You did the job and he paid up. That's how Ron liked it.

When Ron had been given the assignment, it had seemed simple enough. He was supposed to drive up to Cottonwood, north of Phoenix, and set up a network of listening devices and some video surveillance as well in a mom-and-pop company called High Noon Enterprises operating out of Mingus Mountain Business Park. How hard could that be? Once Ron arrived on scene, however, he had been dismayed to learn that each evening when High Noon shut down for the night, it was locked up tight behind a solid wall of rolling security shutters.

Ron had seen the ads for those suckers on TV, where the pitchman claimed that even a SWAT team had been unable to get inside. Rather than give up, Ron realized that, if breaking in wasn't going to work, he'd need to find a way to be invited.

It appeared that the entire complex was being renovated, and Ron made it his business to find out as much about the project as possible. Using his job of raking and weeding as cover, he had befriended several of the construction workers, including the trio of electricians assigned to upgrade the complex's electrical service. According to them, they had spent weeks upgrading the wiring for space being taken over by High Noon and redesigned into a computer lab. The work, unavoidably delayed several times, was now complete with the exception of passing final inspections from the county building department. The moment Ron heard that telling detail, he knew that posing as a building inspector would be his best bet for getting inside.

While on the job Ron wore an impenetrable pair of sunglasses as well a broad-brimmed hat with a tail of material that covered his ears and the back of his neck. When one of the other guys at lunch had inquired about the hat, Ron told him he'd had a spot of melanoma removed and was under doctor's orders to keep the sun off his skin. That was an outright lie. The sunglasses, hat, and trailing scarf were almost as effective as a hoodie when it came to defeating security cameras, and in Arizona's sunny climes, they made a hell of a lot more sense.

Fortunately for Ron, Robby had supplied him with dossiers that provided a good deal of background information on the people involved in High Noon, a total of five individuals—three females and two males—and no dogs. From his vantage point out in the parking lot, Ron sorted out who was who and kept track of their comings and goings.

The dossier on a guy named B. Simpson designated him as the head honcho. He was evidently the brains of the outfit and also did a good deal of traveling. The headshot photo of him made him look like an unassuming businessman. Not much of an opponent as far as Ron was concerned. And since there had been no sign of the guy all week long, Ron decided he was probably off on a business trip.

Next up was someone named Ali Reynolds. Her photo showed a fit-looking older woman who, despite the difference in last names, was also apparently Mrs. B. Simpson. The first two days she had shown up in a sweet Porsche Cayenne, but today for some reason she had shown up driving a seventies vintage Bronco that, despite its advanced age, sported a new coat of paint and appeared to run like a top. After stopping briefly in front of the building, Reynolds had spent the better part of an hour being driven around and around the parking lot by Stuart Ramey, the second man listed on the company roster.

Ramey was a lumbering-looking guy in his early forties, maybe. According to the paperwork, he was supposedly some kind of computer genius, but he was also a piss-poor driver. One disturbing item about him and something that had made him a major roadblock to Ron's ability to complete his assignment was the fact that Stuart evidently lived in an apartment attached to the company's headquar-

ters. Ron hadn't anticipated having someone at the site twenty-four/
seven. All he could do was hope that his building inspector guise
would provide enough of a work-around.

The second woman in the mix was a very hot-looking young
Asian chick named Camille Lee. She was a tiny mite of a thing
who looked as though she'd be blown away in a strong wind. Too
bad she wasn't the one with the on-site apartment. She usually left
promptly at five, rushing off in her bright red Prius as though she
had pressing engagements elsewhere.

The last of the three women was Shirley Malone. Her dossier
listed her as the receptionist and didn't include a photo, but Ron
had managed to figure out which one she had to be—a second older
woman, late fifties or so, who looked more than a little frumpy and
who drove around in a battered Honda sedan that was in far worse
shape than the much older Bronco.

Having sorted through the players, Ron had settled on Shirley
Malone as the most vulnerable as well as his best bet for getting
inside. Ron prided himself on being something of a ladies' man,
especially where older women were concerned. His plan was to go
to her late in the day, pass himself off as a building inspector, lay
the charm on thick, and trick her into giving him access. He hoped
things didn't go south from there, but if they did, he was fully prepared to handle both Shirley Malone and Stuart Ramey.

Then, much to Ron's surprise, he caught a break. Earlier in the
afternoon, Ramey, the live-in male, and the older woman named
Shirley had returned from some kind of errand. An hour or so after
that, the younger woman and Ramey exited the office in a hurry,
this time with the man carrying a piece of luggage. When they piled
into the red Prius and tore out of the lot, Ron could barely believe
his luck—luggage? Did that mean that, for today, at least, Stuart
Ramey and perhaps the young woman, too, were off on some kind
of overnight trip? That made three down; two to go.

Then, an hour or so later Ali Reynolds emerged from the building as well. She climbed into the old Bronco and drove away, leaving behind good old Shirley—the last woman standing.

Ron gave himself another half hour after that. Showing up after four would make it that much closer to quitting time. It was five past when he drove the van into a visitor parking slot directly in front of the High Noon entrance. He had created a specially designed lanyard in advance of his visit. Pulling it out, he placed it on display around his neck. On it was a laminated name badge, complete with a photo, that identified the wearer as one Steve Barris, a building inspector for Yavapai County.

He had already mapped out all the outdoor surveillance cams in the business park, including the ones on the outside of the High Noon portion. As he exited the van, he did his best to dodge the cameras. As for his vehicle? If anybody ever got around to tracking the van's plates, it wouldn't be a problem because they'd come back as stolen.

Outside the van, Ron paused long enough to reach back inside and retrieve a tool kit.

"Okey-dokey," Ron muttered under his breath as he headed for the entrance. "Showtime. Let's make this happen."

Before long he'd have High Noon Enterprises wired for both sight and sound. It had been a long dry spell, and his already shaky finances had taken a serious hit. Ron was grateful to finally have a job to do, and he was determined to get it done.

16

In the six months Shirley Malone had been working at High Noon, it was unusual for her to have the place to herself. Most of the time, Stu Ramey's large and comforting presence would be somewhere in the background. During work hours he spent his time seated in the computer lab keeping watch over a complex collection of monitors. During non-work hours, he'd be hidden away in his studio apartment, which was on the far side of the lab.

When Shirley had first come on board, she'd been wary of Stu. His standoffishness and general awkwardness around people had made her uncomfortable. Her unease had lessened once Cami had explained some of the poor guy's underlying issues—one of which was an inability to handle unexpected changes of any kind. It had taken time and a good deal of effort on Shirley's part, to say nothing of uncounted batches of homemade chocolate chip cookies, to bring him around, but ultimately her unrelenting charm offensive had worked.

Shirley and her late husband, Earl, had never had any kids of their own, but Stu's glaring personality deficits had unleashed all of her maternal instincts. She was proud of the fact that she'd been instrumental in teaching him to drive, and she was downright ecstatic that he had aced his driving exam the first time around.

Shirley's workstation was behind a counter just inside High Noon's front entrance. Although the engraved nameplate positioned on the counter identified her as RECEPTIONIST, her duties went beyond that. Yes, she functioned as the official gatekeeper and operated the electronic controls that allowed visitors and vendors without keypad privileges access to the building. When she first arrived, the break room had been a health code violation waiting to happen. She'd immediately taken that situation in hand, and the break room now sparkled as a result of her efforts. In addition, she handled a good deal of the company's routine office work.

It seemed odd to Shirley that although High Noon Enterprises was high-tech, it was definitely not a paper-free environment. She did a lot of scanning and filing, but she wasn't complaining about any of it. She'd spent most of her adult life working cashier counters in grocery stores. Being able to sit at a desk rather than standing on her feet all day was something she regarded as an incredible blessing. In fact, the idea she'd been able to land any kind of job at all at her age, especially one that paid reasonably well and came with benefits, was nothing short of miraculous.

Having to start over in her late fifties had never been part of Shirley's game plan, but Earl's long, debilitating final illness had wiped them out financially. They'd burned through both their savings as well as the equity in their home. Eventually they'd lost the house entirely. Because Shirley had missed so much time from work, she'd been let go from her job. Being unemployed while she was still functioning as Earl's primary caregiver was one thing. Once he was gone, however, when Shirley had tried going back to work, she'd hit a brick wall. Experience be damned, no one wanted to give a job to a woman her age.

Reduced to living in her car—a twenty-year-old Ford minivan— she'd finally admitted defeat and limped back home to Arizona. Shirley had grown up in Phoenix, but after her father retired, her parents had moved to the Verde Valley. Shirley lived there now, sharing a fourteen-by-seventy mobile home in Cornville with her widowed eighty-three-year-old mother, Edna Farber, and her mother's three cats.

Shirley didn't like mobile homes, and she didn't much care for cats, either, but it beat being homeless and it certainly beat living in a minivan. With nothing to do but sit at home and stare at the four walls, she probably would have gone nuts over time if she hadn't stumbled into this job.

Edna's sole vice, and now Shirley's, too, was bingo. For years, every Friday night, come hell or high water, Edna had gone into town to play bingo at Cottonwood's VFW post. When Shirley moved back home, she had quickly realized that Edna was a hazard on the highway and that her driving days needed to be over. The only way Edna would consent to giving up the keys to her Honda sedan was if Shirley would promise to drive her to bingo on Friday nights.

The deal was struck. Now the aged minivan was gone and Shirley, with a much newer car to drive, faithfully took her mother back and forth to bingo every Friday evening. At first she'd gone strictly out of duty, but before long she had been sucked into the fun and socializing as well. The VFW post was a place where she could hang out with people who were her own age or even older. She liked the fact that among the folks she found there she didn't have to explain her history or make excuses for it. Plenty of her fellow bingo players had already been down the same road. For them having spent years caring for a dying spouse wasn't all that unusual.

Over time, Shirley and her mother had developed a friendship with two of the bingo regulars, Edie Larson and Betsy Peterson, who bused over to Cottonwood each Friday evening from an assisted living facility in Sedona. One night, during a break in the bingo action, Shirley had broached the subject of her need to find a job in a world that considered her too old to carry her weight.

"You should talk to my daughter," Edie had said, scribbling down a phone number on the back of a napkin and handing it over. "Ali and her husband, B. Simpson, run a global cyber security firm from an office right here in Cottonwood. She mentioned to me just the other day that they were looking into hiring a receptionist."

With nothing to lose, Shirley had gone ahead and called the number, where she had spoken directly to Ali. After sending along her résumé, Shirley had been surprised to be invited in for an interview. The moment she and Ali met face-to-face, the two of them had hit it off. They weren't that far apart in age. They'd both lost husbands to cancer, although Ali had been in her twenties when her first husband died. And, after lives lived elsewhere, they'd both been faced with coming home to Arizona in order to regroup.

Today, with the filing and scanning done and with nothing much to do but hold down the fort until quitting time, Shirley sat at her computer and dashed off a quick e-mail to Jackie Wilson, her best friend back home in San Diego.

> Yay, it's Friday. That means bingo night. Who ever would have thought that playing bingo with a bunch of old fogies at a VFW hall would be the highlight of my week? LOL. How the mighty are fallen!
>
> Tomorrow I have to take Mom's Siamese, Archie, to the vet. He's getting really old and frail. We're already having to give him insulin shots, and I'm afraid it will break Mom's heart when she loses him.
>
> Everybody is out of the office this afternoon, and it's a little weird to have the place all to

The door buzzer sounded, startling her. Looking up from her monitor, Shirley saw a middle-aged man standing outside, holding a clipboard. A toolbox was stationed at his feet.

Shirley pressed the intercom button. "Yes?"

"I'm Steve Barris, an inspector with the county building department. I know it's late in the day, but before I head back to Prescott, I'm here to do the final inspection on the changes you've made to your electrical service. If I can sign off on the permits, you'll be good to go as far as occupancy is concerned."

Shirley knew nothing about construction, but she did know that at least one open building permit was hanging fire and keeping them from being able to utilize any of their newly remodeled space. She also suspected that with Cami and Stu rushing off to collect a truckload of additional computer equipment, that space was going to be needed sooner rather than later. She wasn't exactly comfortable letting the guy into the building when she was the only one there, but still . . .

"Sure," she said. "Hold on, and I'll buzz you in."

The man who stepped through the door was dressed in khaki and wearing a straw hat with a cloth tail that covered the back of his neck. As soon as he was inside, he removed the hat and placed it on the counter, a gesture Shirley regarded as a welcome piece of gentlemanly behavior.

"I'm just the receptionist," she told him. "The lab manager isn't here right now, and he probably should be."

The man sighed. "I was really hoping to get this one checked off my list today. If it doesn't get done today, it'll have to wait until the end of next week. That's the next time I'll be back in Cottonwood. By the way," he added, "the inspection is strictly routine. It's just a matter of checking the connections and the voltages. There's no reason why your lab manager would need to be present."

Shirley thought about that and about that truckload of inbound computer equipment. If occupancy was in question, what would happen if Stu and Cami showed up with the U-Haul on Monday or Tuesday and were unable to unload it until the permits were cleared? No, Shirley decided, it was either get the job done today or risk losing a whole week.

Making up her mind, Shirley handed the newcomer the visitor log. "I'll need you to sign in," she said.

Once he did so, she compared the name on the log to the name and photo on the badge he wore—STEVE BARRIS, YAVAPAI COUNTY BUILDING DEPARTMENT, PRESCOTT, ARIZONA.

"The name says Steve," he told her with an engaging grin, "but most people call me Sonny."

"All right then, Sonny," Shirley said. "Right this way."

She led him down the hallway past Ali's and B.'s separate offices and past the break room as well. Once inside the computer lab, she took him over to where a newly installed doorway connected the original lab with the additional space from next door. Then she directed him to the brand-new electrical panel that had been installed nearby.

"Is that what you need?" she asked.

"Yes, ma'am," he said. "It certainly is. I'll be checking the panel, of course, but I'll be double-checking the loads at some of the wall switches and outlets as well."

Shirley was torn. She felt out of her depth, but this all sounded reasonable enough. She felt leery about leaving him alone in the lab, but she couldn't afford to leave the reception desk up front unstaffed, either.

"All right," she agreed finally. "How long is all this going to take?"

"Half an hour," Sonny answered. "Forty-five minutes max."

"All right, then," she said. "Do what you need to do."

Back at her desk, Shirley returned to her unfinished e-mail.

Where was I? A building inspector just turned up to take a look
at some electrical work we've had done over the past month
or so. Nice young man—well, maybe not so young, but a real
gentleman, for a change. Some of the guys who've been doing
the work around here are anything but.

I'm hoping you really will be able to get away and come visit over Christmas. Who knows, it might even be cold enough to snow. You're in no danger of having a white Christmas in San Diego.

Anyway, take care. Let me know when you know for sure if you're coming. I love my mother, but it'll be nice to have a chance to visit with a friend who's a little closer to my own age.

Love,

Shirl

After sending the e-mail, Shirley spent the next several minutes shutting down her computer and clearing her desk. Then she went into the break room, where she turned off the coffeepot and rinsed it before putting the pot as well as a collection of dirty mugs and cups into the single-drawer dishwasher.

Her mother called at five on the dot. "You're still there," Edna said accusingly. "You do remember what night it is, right?"

"Yes, Mom," Shirley said patiently. "I remember, but there's a building inspector here at the office right now, and I can't leave until he does."

"If we get there too late, all the handicapped spots will be taken," Edna argued. "You know how fast they fill up."

"Okay," Shirley said. "I'll go see what I can do to hurry him along."

When she entered the lab, Sonny was on his knees, screwing the wall plate back onto an outlet under Stu's desk. "Are you almost done?"

Startled, Sonny lurched to his feet, banging his head on the bottom of the desk drawer in the process. Once out from under the desk, he reached out and closed the lid on his toolbox. Since he still had a screwdriver in one hand, that seemed odd—odd enough for Shirley to remember later.

"Pretty much," he said.

"Enough to sign off on the permits?"

"Absolutely," he said. "As soon as I get back to the office."

"Well, then," she told him with a smile, "you need to go. It's Friday night. I've got plans."

"With someone special, I hope?" he asked as he reopened the toolbox and slid the screwdriver inside before clicking the lid shut. Had Earl seen him do that, he would have had a fit. In her late husband's toolboxes, there had always been a place for everything and everything in its place. He would never have dropped one in willy-nilly like that, not ever.

Shirley shook her head. Sonny maybe didn't amount to much when it came to taking care of his tools, but he obviously considered himself long on charm.

"My mother's special, all right," she said, "and so are all the other people who play Friday-night bingo at the VFW."

Shirley escorted him back to the front door where she had him sign out. By the time she finished turning off the lights and shutting the metal shutters, it was ten past five. Shirley was looking forward to being able to tell Ali that she'd gotten the permits signed off. That would count as a big win. As for those handicapped parking spaces? If they were all gone by the time Shirley got there, she'd drop her mother at the VFW's front door and park somewhere else.

17

Cami was used to Stu's periodic bouts of contrariness, but this was exceptional. From the time they left Cottonwood until they parked in the long-term lot at Sky Harbor, the man said hardly a word. She wanted to talk about all of it—about his getting his license; about reactivating Frigg; about the technicalities of disassembling and then reassembling all those blades—but each time she'd tried to start a conversation, he'd rebuffed her, shaking his head and busying himself with the screen of his iPad.

Left to stew in her own juices, Cami drove too fast—well over the posted limit. Only a warning ping on the radar detector Stu had given her kept her from picking up a second speeding ticket in as many months. She'd been able to walk her way around the first one by signing up to take a driving course, which was ironic since, at the time, she'd been totally focused on teaching Stu how to drive.

"Do as I say not as I do," she had told him. But the audible warning from the radar detector came through loud and clear, and she slowed down at once.

"You shouldn't be speeding," Stu muttered, and the criticism wasn't well received. By the time they passed Anthem and southbound traffic picked up, he wasn't speaking to her, and she wasn't speaking to him, either.

What a great start, Cami told herself. *Can this trip get any worse?*

Unfortunately she knew from firsthand experience that once they reached the airport, things could get far worse. All during the drive from Cottonwood to Phoenix she had worried that a bad encounter with the TSA at the airport could turn a grumbly Stu Ramey into a complete basket case. Unfortunately Cami knew something about bad encounters with the TSA.

The last time Cami had flown out of Sky Harbor she had been dispatched to the UK to meet up with a cruise ship as part of the Roger McGeary investigation. Because she was booked on a vessel that would have brought her back to the US eventually, she'd flown out of Phoenix alone on a one-way ticket to Heathrow—a ticket that had been purchased that very morning. That series of circumstances—a one-way ticket purchased at the last minute—had turned out to be a big TSA no-no. She'd been scrutinized and questioned for so long that she'd almost missed her flight. In the process her luggage had gone missing.

It seemed to Cami that today's situation was eerily similar. Ali had purchased the tickets with barely enough time for the two of them to pack up and make the drive to the airport to catch their plane. And once again, because they expected to make the return trip in a rented U-Haul, the tickets were one-way only.

"One-way tickets are always suspicious," the seasoned traveler B. Simpson had counseled her shortly after that first miserable experience. "That's just the way it is. If you're going somewhere with no planned return, the powers that be want to know why."

So while Stu had remained utterly silent and steadfastly glued to his screen, Cami had worried about getting them both through security without some kind of major meltdown.

"We're here," Cami announced, once she finally located an open parking spot in the long-term lot. It was going to be a long hike to the terminal, but if Stu didn't like it, he could lump it. After all, she had been doing the real driving while he'd been engaged in nothing more than the backseat sort.

Stu looked up from his screen as though surprised to find he was still on planet earth. "Already?" he said.

They were both traveling with carry-on luggage only. With their boarding passes loaded onto their phones, they entered the terminal and made straight for security. Now that Stu was no longer buried in his iPad, the reality that he was about to board an airplane suddenly hit home. Instantly he broke out in a cold sweat, looking nervous and scared—exactly the kinds of symptoms that should have put TSA agents on high alert. More than half expecting to encounter her old nemesis, Sgt. Croy, or someone just like him, Cami ground her teeth, kept her mouth shut, and waited to be pulled aside for additional screening.

That didn't happen. They didn't completely breeze through, because Stu had forgotten to remove his belt, but he passed through the screening machine the second time without a hitch. The boarding area was packed. Even had there been available seating, Stu was in no condition to sit. Suddenly beset with what Cami at first assumed to be a serious case of fear-of-flying, he paced up and down the concourse with Cami tagging along after him.

"The flight's going to be fine," she said, trying to reassure him.

"I'm not worried about the flight," he said. "Well, maybe a little."

"The used computers, then?"

"No, not even that. Using Hansen's own equipment to reboot Frigg makes all kinds of sense."

"What, then?"

"I'm worried about dealing with Frigg," Stu admitted at last.

"Why?" Cami asked with a frown. "I'm sure you can handle her."

"I'm not," Stu said, shaking his head. "Owen Hansen was a very smart man who created an AI whose capabilities are way beyond what most people would think possible."

"Because she managed to outwit him?" Cami asked.

"Exactly," Stu agreed. "Her strategy was totally ingenious. By hamstringing my ability to access the money without her help, she's managed to guarantee her own existence."

"So he somehow taught her about self-preservation."

"Or else she learned that on her own," Stu conceded. "Either way, what she did is a demonstration of a kind of strategic deep learning that leaves everyone else in the dust. Supposedly IBM has a new groundbreaking AI similar to this that they're hoping to bring to market sometime in the near future, but they're not planning on open-sourcing it. Users will have access only through company-owned hardware and software."

"Owen Hansen was a creep and a crook," Cami said. "Maybe he somehow laid hands on a beta version of that program."

"We won't know that until we see his setup." Stu paused. "And until we see her," he added.

"Her?" Cami asked, thinking he was referring to Frigg.

"You know," Stu said with a grimace. "Owen's mother. How can I face her, knowing that High Noon and I were the ones responsible for her son's death, and now she's giving us his computer equipment? Once she figures that out, she'll probably send us packing."

That's when Cami understood the real reason for Stu's dead silence on the trip down. Controlling a rogue AI was only part of his problem. His real dread had a lot more to do with having to come face-to-face with the very human emotions of Owen Hansen's grieving mother.

"Let's get this straight," Cami said. "First of all, you are not responsible for Owen Hansen's death and neither is High Noon. He committed suicide, for crap's sake. He's the one who took a flying leap off that mountain. Nobody pushed him. As for Irene Hansen? I was worried about the same thing—that once she figured out who we were she'd pull the rug out from under us. Ali suggested that I tell her exactly who we are, and I did."

"What did she say?"

"Do you want a direct quote?"

"I guess."

"She said, 'I don't give a tinker's damn who you are. All I want is for you to get that godforsaken pile of computer junk out of the house without my having to pay to have it hauled away.'"

"Quote, unquote?" Stu asked.

Cami nodded.

"So not grieving over her son?"

"Not so much."

"Irene Hansen sounds a lot like Roger McGeary's mother," Stu mused. "And that would explain a lot about Owen Hansen."

The gate agent called their flight then. They boarded. As they settled into their seats, Stu pulled out his iPad. "By the way," he said, "on the way down, I sent you a whole bunch of articles."

"Articles about what?"

"About deep learning," he said, "and about teaching ethics to AIs."

"Ethics?" Cami asked.

"Obviously Owen Hansen already taught Frigg about the wrong side of ethics. Now we need to see what if any of that part of her original deep learning can be unlearned."

By the time the plane took flight, they were both buried deep in the literature, trying to learn if it's possible to teach a computer how to know the difference between right and wrong. When the plane started its descent into Burbank airport, Cami had paged through more than a dozen articles. The more she read, the more she understood that Stu had good reason to be worried.

If Frigg had turned on her creator and set out to destroy him, what were the chances she'd do the same thing to Stu—and not just to Stu himself but to everyone associated with him, the other people at High Noon Enterprises included?

18

As Ron Webster drove out through the business park's entrance, he wasn't the least bit happy with himself. As far as he'd been able to tell, there had been no video surveillance inside the building. That had been a huge relief. The folks at High Noon probably assumed that the metal shutters that turned the place into a fortress at night were sufficient protection against penetration from the outside. They were wrong there, of course.

He had worked quickly and efficiently, carefully wiping every surface he touched—including wiping off the visitor log as he signed out. That cleanup process had slowed him down a little, but he would have been fine if he hadn't encountered a problem with one of his bugs.

The centerpiece of his surveillance system was the video camera he had planned to install in a light switch next to the main bank of computers in the lab area. The video-only camera would have offered an unobstructed view of everything going on in the lab with sound supplied by audio-only bugs installed there and in the other sections of the building.

Except, once he had the camera installed and wired in, the damned thing wouldn't come online. Okay, so he was dealing with second-tier equipment here. He'd been a late-pay when it came to the last set of electronics he'd ordered, and the supplier he'd worked with before refused to extend credit. That meant he'd had to go shopping elsewhere. The new supplier claimed his equipment was just as good as the other guy's, but if it wouldn't work fresh out of the box, what the hell kind of quality control was that?

It ended up that he'd spent so much time fiddling trying to get the damned camera to work that he'd cut himself short when it came to installing the audio components. The job had only been about half done when the woman had marched into the lab and thrown him out. He'd been holding a screwdriver at the time. It would have been easy to take her out with the blade of that screwdriver, but that wouldn't have been very subtle. Since the whole idea had been to get in and out without being noticed, leaving a dead body behind wasn't an option.

So no, the video feed still wasn't operational. He had managed to install working audio feeds in the newly remodeled space, in the computer lab, and in the main room of the studio apartment at the back. Unfortunately, the break room, the reception area, and the two offices down the hall remained completely bug-free.

Had Ron Webster been an honorable man, he might have seen fit to let the client know that he'd only done part of the job. The truth is, he was not an honorable man, and he figured what the client didn't know wouldn't hurt him. When they called to complain, as they inevitably would, he'd tell them it was working fine when he left. Probably some kind of infant mortality issue. Those kinds of things happened with electronics all the time. Besides, by the time they figured it out, he'd have his money and they'd be out of luck.

Halfway through town he pulled over in the parking lot of a dead restaurant long enough to switch off the stolen plates and put the real ones back on his van. Then he shoved the other ones under the front passenger seat and continued on his way.

In case someone did examine the security footage, they'd know they needed to go looking for a white older-model Ford Transit Cargo Van, but they'd have no idea which Transit Van and there'd be no way to trace it back to him. Before he pulled back into traffic for the return trip to his home outside Marana, he sent Robby a short text.

Done. Dodged the exterior surveillance.
None inside. What do you have for me
next?

19

Ali dropped the Bronco off at Nick's and then stopped by Sedona Shadows, where she returned the keys to her father. "How'd it go?" Bob asked.

"It went fine," Ali answered. "He managed to get a driver's test appointment today and passed with flying colors. Thanks for your help."

"Glad to do it," Bob said.

Ali suspected he would have been far less happy if he'd known the extent of the gear grinding agony during Stu's driving lesson. Ali was only too happy to go on her way without providing any of those gory details.

Back at the house, Bella greeted Ali with a tornado of unadulterated miniature dachshund enthusiasm, as though Ali had been gone for days on end rather than mere hours. Bella was picky when it came to choosing humans. Alonso was okay in her book because he, more often than not, provided food. B. was someone the dog merely tolerated. Ali was the one member of the family with whom Bella had bonded.

Ali gave herself the luxury of a leisurely soak in her jetted tub before heading into the kitchen to raid the fridge. Tucked away among several containers of leftovers was one loaded with two-day-old lasagna. Alonso Rivera may have been born in Mexico, but he had spent twenty years in the US Navy cooking on submarines. That experience had made him fluent in all kinds of foods, but his take on Italian dishes was superb. Ali liked to tease him by saying he was a Mexican Italian American.

When B. wasn't home, Ali often read her way through dinner. Once her food was heated, she took her plate and her iPad and settled into the breakfast nook with Bella curled up on the bench seat next to her. For the last couple of years, she had been on a self-imposed literary journey, reading through the classics that she felt she should have read but had never quite gotten around to actually reading. Her good intentions on that score had stumbled to a fitful halt a hundred or so pages into James Joyce's *Finnegans Wake*, a read that had not yet been resumed and probably never would be. Recently she had been treating herself to some of the authors she had loved as a girl—Jane Austen's *Pride and Prejudice* and Daphne du Maurier's *My Cousin Rachel*. She had enjoyed the latter so much that she was currently rereading *Rebecca*.

This time, as she encountered the fictional Mrs. Danvers, Ali couldn't help but be reminded of Arabella Ashcroft, the hopelessly crazed woman who had been the previous owner of this very house. The house on Manzanita Hills Road may have been a crumbling ruin when Arabella lived here, but it had also been her Manderley—a midcentury modern and completely outdated Manderley. With help from Leland Brooks, Arabella's longtime butler and aide-de-camp, Arabella's house had become Ali's house, and Leland had become Ali's aide-de-camp staying on for years. Her working partnership with Leland had ended only a month earlier when he had finally retired from service. Alonso had been hired to step into the vacuum left by Leland's sudden but not wholly unexpected departure.

Ali had just finished the last bite of lasagna and pushed her plate aside when a text came in from Shirley:

Made it to bingo but not in time to get one
of the handicapped spots. Mother is NOT
happy with me, but I do have some good
news. I stayed late because the inspector
from the building department showed up
at the last minute. I thought you'd want to
know that he says he'll sign off on the final
inspection, so whenever Stu and Cami get
back home with that truckload of computers, the new space should be good to go.

Ali reread the text, not quite believing what it said. Before leaving
the office that afternoon she had placed a call to the Yavapai County
Building Department over in Prescott, asking if it would be possible
to expedite the inspection schedule for their remodel. She had been
told that the inspection staff was shorthanded and overbooked and
that there was no way any of them would be coming to Cottonwood
before the middle of the following week at the earliest. And yet someone had come by after all? Today? How was that possible?

Picking up her phone, Ali dialed Shirley's cell. "Great news about
the inspection," Ali said when Shirley answered. "How'd you manage
to get it done so soon? I was told it wouldn't happen before next
Wednesday, if then."

"Just lucky, I guess," Shirley replied. "Steve Barris, the inspector,
showed up all hot to trot sometime after four. I finally had to chase
him out the door right at five so I could pick Mom up in time for
bingo. Before he left, though, he said we passed, and he'll sign off
on the permit."

"That's a good deal," Ali told her. "Thanks for letting me know."

Once Shirley hung up, Ali cleared her place and put the dishes
in the dishwasher, all the while mulling over what Shirley had said.
Her call to Abby Henderson at the building department had been

one of the last calls Ali had made prior to leaving the office, so it had probably been sometime between three and three thirty when Abby had told her there was no way to hurry the inspection process. So what had changed so much in the course of the next hour, Ali wondered, that the inspection had already taken place?

Before leaving the kitchen, Ali made herself a mug of hot tea to carry with her into the library. It would have been easy to hit the hay early, but she wanted to stay up late enough to say good morning to B. when he woke up in London. She wanted to bring him up to speed on everything that had happened in the course of the day, but more than that, she wanted to apologize for being short with him earlier. They had both been stressed and frustrated and had taken it out on each other.

Conducting married life while being numerous time zones apart wasn't always smooth sailing. Despite her good intentions, she was sound asleep with the iPad on her lap when the phone rang.

"We're on the ground in Burbank," Cami said. "Thought you'd want to know. Lance just dropped us off at the hotel."

"That's good news," Ali said. "I've got some good news on this end, too. The county building inspector came by this afternoon, so we'll be cleared to occupy the new space as soon as you get back."

"We may make it back sooner than you thought," Cami said. "According to Lance, he's got a whole crew coming to help with the dismantle and load-out."

"How's Stu doing?" Ali asked.

"So-so," Cami answered.

"Because of the flight?"

"No, because he's worried about controlling Frigg."

"He's probably not wrong to be worried," Ali said with a short laugh. "Maybe we should all be worried about her."

Call waiting sounded in Ali's ear with B.'s photo showing on the screen. "Oops," she told Cami. "Gotta go. B.'s on the other line." She switched over to the other call. "Good morning. You're up early."

"I am so ready to be home," he said. "Thank you for figuring out a way to make that happen. BA is claiming the whole thing had to do with a power supply problem, but I'm still thinking ransomware. They've started resuming flights, but Heathrow remains a zoo. It's going to take days to untangle this mess. Sorry if I was a whiny brat."

"And I'm sorry for being short-tempered," she told him. "But I'd had my hands full all day, and I wanted to catch you up on what all's going on in an actual conversation rather than trying to stuff the whole story into an e-mail."

"Like what?" B. asked.

"For starters," Ali said, "Stu has been given more than two million dollars' worth of Owen Hansen's Bitcoin fortune, he passed his driver's test, and he and Cami are in Burbank on their way to Santa Barbara, where they're going to load up Owen's cache of computers and bring them back here so Stu can reboot Frigg."

"Wait," B. said. "Can you break some of that down into bite-sized pieces?"

She did so, and it took the better part of an hour. "I'm suitably impressed with all of you," he said at last. "That was a brilliant move on Cami's part to ask about taking over Owen's abandoned equipment. And you and Stu are right, rebooting Frigg is the only way out of the monetary mess that will arise once those taxes come due. They'll have to be paid come hell or high water. But what really amazes me is that you and Cami got Stu to agree to accept the necessity of utilizing used equipment. He's one smart guy, but he comes with a few notable quirks."

Ali laughed aloud at that one. "I'll say," she agreed.

They ended the call a few minutes later when B.'s car service showed up at the hotel. Ali turned off the fireplace, took her empty mug back to the kitchen, and then let Bella out for one last walk. "Come on, girl," she said. "Time to go to bed."

20

At midnight in Panama City, Panama, Graciella donned a pair of earphones and logged on to the dark Web to access the site where her video and audio files were supposed to be stored and posted. A message from Ron Webster had been relayed to her through Robert Kemper's site telling her that the job was done. The sound- and motion-operated bugs only transmitted when there was something to be heard or seen. There was one audio file containing an exchange between Ron and a woman who was clearly trying to hurry him out the door, but there was no accompanying video, and there should have been.

After that, however, there was nothing. Did that mean Ron Webster had screwed up somehow? Was his equipment faulty? Ron had come highly recommended. If he hadn't delivered, all it would take was a single call from Graciella to El Pescado on that encrypted phone, and Ron Webster would be history.

But just then, after hours of utter silence, one of the listening devices came to life as an arriving file showed up on the screen. Playing the recording back, it took a while before Graciella could identify the high-pitched sound. Then she figured it out. It was late Friday night. Maybe there had been no activity because High Noon had shut down for the weekend. What Graciella was hearing now was the whine of a vacuum cleaner.

Listening to the cleaning crew, Graciella was relieved to know that the audio surveillance devices were installed and functioning properly even if the video feed wasn't. That meant Ron Webster had been paid for the full job while only doing part of it. Even so, sooner or later Graciella would have firsthand knowledge about what was going on with Stuart Ramey and the AI. Did Frigg still exist or not? Without the AI and access to Owen Hansen's Bitcoin mining capability, Stuart Ramey himself would be of little or no interest as far as Graciella was concerned. After all, wasn't one computer nerd pretty much interchangeable with every other computer nerd?

Realizing it was Friday evening in the States and that there would most likely be no more activity from her planted listening devices before Monday morning, Graciella leaned back in her chair, closed her eyes, and thought about Arturo Salazar. It was well after midnight. By now his wife was probably wondering about where he was and why he was so late.

"And he's going to be even later," Graciella told herself with a smile.

She stood up, stretched, and headed for bed. On the way to her own bedroom, she walked past her mother's. It had been over a week now since her mother's death, and Graciella had yet to reenter the room. Police tape still barred the door, even though a detective had called several days earlier to inform Graciella that, since Christina Miramar's death had been ruled a suicide, she was welcome to remove it.

The night Christina died, Graciella had made the decision that the next morning would be time enough for her to wake up and find the body. And now, leaving the tape where it was, she made a similar decision. Tomorrow morning would be soon enough for her to wake up, tackle her mother's room, and clean the damned thing out once and for all.

21

At five o'clock in the morning, Stuart Ramey finally gave up on sleeping, crawled out of bed, and went into the bathroom to shower. He had spent most of the night reading through one article after another, trying to strategize on the best ways to deal with a reactivated Frigg. When he'd finally shut down his iPad and gone to bed, sleep had eluded him.

In researching the subject of robots and ethics, he had stumbled on an article about a Czech company called GoodAI that specialized in teaching artificial intelligences right from wrong. Instead of giving their AIs prescribed rules about how they should react in every given situation, they taught them to use their knowledge to infer how they should respond in unfamiliar situations.

When Stu read those words, the hair literally stood up on the back of his neck. That's what Owen Hansen had done all on his own, with a playbook that could have been called BadAI rather than GoodAI. Owen had taught his AI all kinds of lessons, but instead of instructing her in how to be responsible or honorable, he had taught her to be devious and self-serving. And Frigg had been smart enough that, when faced with looming disaster, she had weighed the options and chosen to save herself.

That was what had kept Stuart Ramey tossing and turning for the rest of the night—the realization that Owen Hansen had been an inarguable genius as well as a profoundly troubled one. Yes, he'd been a serial killer, and yes, Stu had been the one who had sparked Owen's suicidal leap off Mingus Mountain. That night, though, sitting alone in his Burbank hotel room, what Stu regretted more than anything was never having had a chance to sit down with Owen Hansen. He wished he could have talked to the man and gained some insights into the workings of what was clearly a magnificent mind, one whose crowning achievement was the creation of Frigg.

Rather than talking to the man and learning from him, what had Stu done instead? He had done everything in his power to destroy them both—creator and creation. He had succeeded with the former, and justifiably so, but not with the latter.

Stu knew that the hotel's breakfast room opened at six. At five to, he tapped on Cami's door on his way past. "See you at breakfast," he told her when she cracked it open. "I want to get an early start."

By a quarter to seven, they were in their rented truck and lumbering north toward Santa Barbara. "You look like hell," Cami said. "Did you sleep at all?"

"No."

"You can't keep blaming yourself."

"I'm sorry Owen Hansen is dead."

"Of course you're sorry he's dead, but he was evil, Stu, really and truly evil."

"And smart," Stu said.

"Right, really smart and truly evil," Cami agreed, "and being godlike to the end, he created Frigg in his own image."

Stu fell silent then, huddling against the passenger door of the rumbling truck. Eventually, exhaustion took over and he slept. Much later he woke with a start and discovered they were off the freeway and moving through a residential area. The voice in the GPS was saying, "In five hundred feet turn right on Via Vistosa. Your destination will be ahead and on the right."

As the truck turned in to the tree-lined entrance Stu caught his first glimpse of the house. It was a mansion, all right—a white stucco three-story edifice, complete with a red-tiled roof and surrounded by manicured lawns and lush gardens. They arrived at the front entrance too soon for Stuart to have worked himself into a cold sweat. As the U-Haul grumbled to a stop, an oversized door swung open and a tiny white-haired woman came out onto a colonnaded front porch and waved at them.

"I'll do this," Stu said to Cami.

He shoved open the passenger door and clambered stiffly down to the ground. When he turned around the woman had stepped off the porch and was making her way toward him, tripping daintily along a flagstone walkway in a pair of very high heels. It was a little past nine o'clock in the morning, but this elfin woman—so thin she resembled a sparrow—was decked out in a bright red knit suit topped by a single string of pearls. She looked as though she was fully prepared to dash off to church at any moment or else to some fancy country club luncheon.

"Are you Stuart?" she asked.

"Yes, I am," he mumbled. Suddenly tongue-tied, Stu was unable to summon the words he had carefully schooled himself to say. Not so much as a single syllable of "sorry for your loss" escaped his lips.

"I'm Irene," she said, seemingly unperturbed by his silence. "I'm so glad you're here early. Tell your driver to go past the garage at the end of the house. There's a drive off to the right that leads around to the back and down to the basement. That's how Owen always took his deliveries—at the back. It'll make it easier for loading. I've left the slider open so you can let yourselves in and out, and I've asked the cook to put together a little buffet. I wouldn't want you people to starve to death."

"Yes, ma'am," Stu managed at last. "Thank you. We'll go around back."

With that, he retreated to the truck, climbed back inside, and pulled the door shut behind him.

Cami had been talking on the phone. Now she pulled the phone away from her ear and stared at him. "You're white as a sheet!" she declared. "What happened? What did she say to you?"

Stu shrugged. "That she's glad we're early; that she's had her cook put together a little buffet for us; and that we're supposed to drive around the end of the house and take the drive to the right that leads to the basement entrance around back."

"Did she say anything to you about Owen?"

Stuart shook his head. "Not a word," he muttered. "Not a single word."

Cami returned to her call. "Did you hear that, Lance? When you get here, drive around the end of the house. We'll be doing the load-out through a slider at the back."

"Are you all right?" Cami asked Stu once she ended the call.

"I think so," he said. "Irene Hansen just wasn't anything like what I expected."

At the back of the house, the drive led to what amounted to a mini loading dock. Before Cami set about positioning the back of the truck in front of the dock, Stu let himself out of the truck and walked into the house through the unlocked slider, aware as he did so that he was entering Owen Hansen's private domain.

Stu had expected palatial digs. As a consequence, the stark simplicity of what he found there surprised him. The space was designed into an open-concept arrangement with a master bedroom–style sleeping area—bed, closet, and bath—on one side and a combination kitchenette/bar on the other. The flooring was high-gloss hardwood; the walls were painted a muted dove gray. In the center of the room stood two pieces of furniture—a highly polished antique library table and a decidedly modern ergonomic rolling desk chair. On top of the table sat a computer, one Stu instantly recognized as an early-model Apple Macintosh. On the far side of the table a long black leather sofa faced a wall covered with six forty-two-inch monitors. That way, someone seated either at the computer or on the sofa would have an unobstructed view of whatever was displayed on the screens.

Stu was somewhat confused. Wasn't this basement supposed to be full of computers? Where were they? And then, in the wall at the far end of the monitors, he spotted a nearly invisible swinging door. He walked over to it, pushed it open, and found himself in almost total darkness. After groping blindly along the wall, he finally located a light switch.

Stu was well aware of the working conditions for Bitcoin miners toiling away in what had once been abandoned industrial parks in China's Sichuan province, where the presence of cheap electricity and cheap labor had made blockchain technology the only growth industry around. People there worked under terrible conditions in tumbledown buildings that looked like little more than grimy, metal-sided chicken coops. Cooling was provided by walls of exhaust fans and lighting came from bare bulbs on wires that dangled from the ceiling. As for the blades? They were usually perched on metal shelving that looked as though it was strung together with baling wire.

But that was there—in China. In Santa Barbara, California, Stu could only stand and stare at what he was seeing. He had felt the same way two years earlier when he had first set foot inside Paris's Notre Dame Cathedral. That incredible achievement had been due to the efforts of countless laborers, toiling over hundreds of years. What he saw now, in all its simple elegance, was the product of a single brilliant mind. The racks were open to the air, but not a speck of dust was visible anywhere. Everything was pristinely clean, but then, almost as an afterthought, Stu realized something else—the room was eerily silent. There may have been eight hundred high-end GPUs in the room, but not a single one of them was running.

"I turned them all off," Irene Hansen said, noiselessly materializing in the open doorway behind Stu and answering a question he had not yet asked. "My son always paid his own electric bill," she continued. "After he died, when that first power bill showed up, it was so high that I almost had a heart attack. I had my yard man come down and unplug everything."

Stu winced at that. He would have preferred to have each blade powered down individually to keep from corrupting the data. Then again, if Frigg had already disbursed all the files, maybe powering down properly wasn't that big a deal.

"Owen never liked me much," Irene added as an afterthought, entering the soundless room and running her finger along the dust-free surface of one the racks. "He liked his machines better."

Still unable to speak, Stuart Ramey nodded in reply.

"He always blamed me for his father's death," Irene continued. "Owen was convinced that it was my fault that his father committed suicide."

And then, without any warning, she flung herself at Stuart and fell weeping against his chest. Irene Hansen needed someone to lean on right then. It didn't matter to her that the person she chose for her leaning happened to be the one who had contributed the most to bringing her son's murderous crime spree to an end. No, that didn't bother her in the least.

All his life, Stuart Ramey had recoiled from any kind of human contact. For a long time, he stood frozen with both hands raised in the air, as if they were strange appendages belonging to someone else, and he was uncertain about how to use them. At last he lowered his arms. He wrapped them around Irene's tiny heaving shoulders and held her close.

That was the first thing an astonished Cami Lee saw when she entered the computer lab through the open slider—Stuart standing there holding a grieving Irene Hansen against his massive chest and gently rocking her back and forth.

"It was the most amazing thing," Cami would tell Ali much later. "You just had to be there."

22

Ali awakened thinking about that damned building inspector. She had been battling the building department off and on for weeks. Abby Henderson was a bureaucrat's bureaucrat whose best trick was putting people on hold and forgetting about them.

What Ali still couldn't wrap her head around was the idea that less than two hours after Abby had insisted that the inspection couldn't be done until the middle of the following week, it had already been completed—by a county employee, working overtime, on a Friday afternoon—none of which made any sense.

In Ali's experience, the Yavapai County Building Department was an entity that not only under-promised, it also under-delivered. Something was out of sync here, and Ali couldn't quite put her finger on what it was. Still, if the inspection was out of the way, a little gratitude was probably in order. That was one of her mother's enduring lessons.

"It never hurts to say thank you," Edie Larson had always insisted, "even when you're dealing with annoying people—sometimes especially when you're dealing with annoying people."

Abby Henderson certainly qualified on that score. Leaving Bella asleep in the bed, Ali padded over to the love seat, opened her computer, and sent Abby Henderson a brief note:

Thanks for expediting our final inspection. I'm so happy to have
that out of the way earlier than expected. We have equipment
coming soon, and it'll be great to be able to get it installed and
working.

With her self-assigned thank you note completed, Ali scanned
through her mail, dumping the spam and checking for messages
from B. She was relieved when there wasn't one. At the moment
he was probably in the air over the Atlantic, somewhere between
England and Maine. Considering no news good news, Ali took her
laptop with her and, with Bella scampering at her heels, headed to
the kitchen in search of coffee.

Before returning to the UK, Leland had given Alonso a crash
course in the running of the Reynolds/Simpson household, including a computer file filled with extensive directions and suggestions
as well as a compendium of recipes. As a consequence, it was no
surprise for her to find Alonso at the kitchen counter, putting the
finishing touches on B.'s somewhat delayed welcome-home meatloaf.
As she made her way to the coffeepot, he looked up and nodded
good morning.

"Your Saturday-morning special for breakfast?" he asked. "Herbed
scrambled eggs?"

"Yes, please," she said. "I'd like that."

While Alonso set about making breakfast, Ali sat in the nook,
reading her online newspapers. When an e-mail announcement arrived, she switched over immediately, expecting it to be from B. It
wasn't. The terse message came from Abby Henderson, who clearly
wasn't overjoyed at receiving Ali's thank-you note.

Dear Ms. Reynolds,

I do not appreciate being contacted during my off-hours except
in cases of dire emergency.

As I specified in our phone conversation yesterday afternoon, we are unable to complete the final inspection of your project until sometime next week, most likely not before Thursday or Friday at the earliest. Once again, let me remind you that no equipment of any kind may be moved into the remodeled space until the open permits are cleared for occupancy.

If you have any further questions in this regard, please feel free to contact me during regularly scheduled working hours, Monday through Friday.

"That's weird," Ali said aloud, feeling a slight glitch in her stomach. Something that had seemed mildly strange before now was even more so.

"What's weird?" Alonso asked.

"Shirley Malone told me that the building inspector came by last night and cleared our permits, but I just now heard from the scheduler who says the inspection is still pending."

Reaching for her phone, Ali dialed Shirley's home number. "Sorry to bother you on a Saturday," Ali said when Shirley answered, "but tell me again about that building inspector."

"He stopped by about four and left right around five. Why?"

"Because I just heard from Abby Henderson at the building department. She claims the inspection is still on the schedule for late next week."

"But he was there yesterday for sure," Shirley said. "I walked him back to the lab and he got right down to it."

"Did you stay with him while he was working?" Ali asked.

"No," Shirley answered. "I had to leave him alone and so I could go back up to reception."

"What was his name again?"

"Barris," Shirley said at once. "Steve Barris, but he said most people called him Sonny. He was sort of flirty but sort of smarmy, too, if you know what I mean. He was wearing a name badge with photo ID. As he was leaving, he told me straight-out that his inspection was complete, and that we'd passed. I hope I didn't do anything wrong by letting him in."

"Did he bring anything into the building with him?" Ali asked.

"A toolbox and some tools, which he was none too careful with, by the way," Shirley told her. "Do you want me to drive over to the office and make sure things are okay? It's no trouble."

Ali was thinking about what else might have been in that toolbox besides tools. What if this was some kind of sabotage plot? What if one of High Noon's competitors had decided to take their corporate headquarters off the map with a toolbox full of C-4? Or worse yet, with Stu and Cami out of town, what if someone had infected their computer systems with some kind of self-replicating worm that could quickly spread to the computers of all their corporate clients? That would put them out of business every bit as quickly as detonating explosives.

"No," Ali said quickly. "If anyone needs to go check, I will. And don't worry about any of this. It's not your fault. It's probably some kind of misunderstanding."

That's what she said, but Ali wasn't at all sure it was true. Next she found Dave Holman's number and called. Dave was the chief homicide investigator for Yavapai County. He and Ali had been an item once, but the relationship had ended amicably. At the time they had been at different stages in their lives. She had been done raising her son, while Dave was still dealing with parenting issues and relatively young children. Afterward, they had both married other people, but the friendship between them had endured.

"Morning," Dave said when he answered. "Long time no hear. What's up?"

Ali knew that, as a member of the sheriff's department, Dave would have access to a comprehensive personnel directory containing the names of all county employees. "Are you at home or at work?"

"What do you think?" Dave replied. "It's the weekend. Working a domestic from last night. Right now it's only attempted murder. With any kind of luck the victim will live and that won't change, but we have to do the whole investigation just in case. What can I do for you?"

"I'm curious about a county employee—a guy named Steve Barris who works for the building department."

"How do you spell that?" Dave asked.

"B-A-R-R-I-S."

A clatter of keyboard keys clicked in the background. "What's he done?"

"He came out to do an inspection for our remodel."

"He may have done your inspection," Dave said, "but there's nobody here on the county employee rolls by that name, although he could be a new hire who came on board after the directory was last updated or maybe even a temp of some kind. Why, is there a problem?"

Ali felt another clutch in her gut. If Barris wasn't a county employee, who the hell was he?

"I wanted to know if he was on the up and up," Ali said. "We were told the inspection wouldn't be done until next week, but he showed up and did it yesterday afternoon."

Dave laughed aloud at that. "Right," he said, "when bureaucracy works too fast, it's easy to be suspicious."

Dave's offhand dismissal didn't leave Ali feeling any better. "Probably just a misunderstanding on my part," Ali said, repeating the same line she had used earlier with Shirley. "Thanks for the help."

She ended the call just as Alonso set a plate of chef-worthy scrambled eggs and buttered Dave's Killer Bread whole-grain toast on the table in front of her. "Is there a problem?" he asked. Obviously he'd been privy to her part of the conversation.

"The guy who did the inspection may be a phony," she said. "Shirley left him alone in the lab with all that equipment at a time when both Cami and Stu were out of town, and that bothers me a lot. As soon as I finish breakfast and before I go pick up B., I'm going to run over to Cottonwood and take a look around, although I don't know how much good that will do. I'm the last person at High Noon who would be able to tell if someone had been messing around with our computers."

Alonso gave her a quick look. "I'd be glad to ride along," he suggested. "I was already planning on going over there this morning anyway to do some shopping."

Ali appreciated his concern and knew it was not unfounded. Alonso's first day on the job hadn't exactly been uneventful. Alonso had been headed toward Cottonwood in order to complete the hiring process paperwork when he'd been pulled into an emergency situation that placed him behind the wheel of Ali's Cayenne during a hair-raising car chase up Mingus Mountain. That shared firefight experience had cemented their new employee/employer relationship in a way nothing else could have, and a supposedly temporary job offer had been amended to permanent on the spot.

A younger Ali Reynolds might have rebuffed Alonso's offer of backup, but an older and wiser Ali did not. If something was amiss at the office, having a retired but still very able-bodied seaman along for the ride would be a good idea.

"Okay," she said, "if you're sure you wouldn't mind."

"Not at all."

"Okay, then," Ali told him. "I'll go get dressed."

She was in the bedroom pulling on a sweatshirt when B. called.

"Hey," he said. "Hope I didn't wake you."

"No, I'm up and getting dressed. Where are you?"

"On the ground in Bangor, refueling. They're slow as dial-up Internet around here. I guess they're having way more traffic today than usual. By the time we get off the ground Dan says we should be in Flagstaff by four or so. What are your plans for the morning?"

Did she want to lay any of this building inspector mess on

B. when he was about to be stuck in a plane for five hours with no way to do anything about it but worry? But not telling him was wrong.

"Alonso and I are about to make a quick trip to Cottonwood. He needs to pick up a few things, and I want to stop by the office. Yesterday afternoon a somewhat shady individual bluffed his way past Shirley by claiming to be a building inspector."

"Don't tell me she let him inside!"

"She did. With both Stu and Cami out of town, I want to give High Noon a once-over to make sure everything is A-OK. Do you have any advice about what I should look for?"

"Have you heard anything from our traveling road crew?" B. asked.

"Not so far this morning," she answered. "They were supposed to pick up the truck in Burbank first thing. They're probably already in Santa Barbara by now. If not, they're bound to be close."

"Call Stuart and ask him to run a scan. He can do that remotely. And don't worry. We're pretty bulletproof."

Ali felt the weight lift from her shoulders. "Thank you," she said.

"Okay," B. added after a moment. "Dan is saying it's time to load up. See you in a few."

Half an hour later, Ali and Alonso headed for Cottonwood with him behind the wheel and her seated in the passenger seat with Bella, who had begged to go along, curled up in her lap.

On the thirty-minute drive, Ali brought Alonso up to speed on why Stu and Cami had gone racing off to California. After all, since Alonso had been in on all the action the day of Owen Hansen's suicide, it was only fair that he know what was really going on. Once they reached the office, they left Bella in the car while Ali used keypads to raise the security shutters, unlock the front entrance, and turn off the alarm.

Inside the building, she went straight to the visitor's log on the reception counter and checked the entry for the building inspector. Steve Barris, whoever he was, had clocked in at 4:10 and out at 5:03. With Alonso on her heels Ali did a quick walk-through of the building. Nothing was apparently out of place, and everything seemed to be in good order. Equipment that was supposed to be on was on, and equipment that was supposed to be off, including the collection of darkened monitors over Stu's and Cami's workstations, was clearly off.

Finished with her cursory inspection, Ali had turned and started out of the room when her phone rang.

"Is something wrong?" Stu demanded when Ali came on the line. "What are you doing in the office on a Saturday?"

Ali pulled the phone away from her ear and looked at the screen. This was definitely not a FaceTime call. "How do you know I'm at the office?"

"Motion-activated cameras," Stu answered. "The one stationed behind Shirley's desk is the one that sent me the first alert. When I'm there, I don't keep the notification function turned on, but since Cami and I were both going to be out of town, I switched it on while we were on our way to the airport."

"Wait," Ali said, "we have surveillance cameras in here? Really?" She paused long enough to glance around the room and saw no sign of a camera setup. For a moment she was angered by the idea of being under surveillance, but then curiosity got the better of her. "I never noticed them. Where are they?"

"That's the whole point with surveillance cameras," Stu said, "you aren't supposed to notice them. They're supposed to be subtle and invisible, but wherever there's a bookshelf in the office, you can count on there being at least one working camera. Most of the books really are books, but some of them aren't. For instance, the camera that's filming you right now is on the bookshelf next to my wall of monitors."

Ali stepped closer to examine the shelf. As far as she could see, the shelf contained nothing but a row of thick equipment manuals. "I don't see any camera," she said.

"Exactly," Stu said. "You're seeing books, and that's what most of them are, but the one in the middle of the top shelf isn't what it seems. If you look closely, you'll see that the inside pages have been removed to leave space for the camera."

On closer examination, Ali spotted a camera lens peering out through the lettering on the spine. She was so relieved that she almost burst out laughing. "I'll be damned," she exclaimed. "I never would have noticed that in a million years."

"That's the idea," Stu explained, sounding more than a little proud of himself. "I bought the cameras and figured out how to place them inside the book covers. Cami was responsible for the artwork. The camera over Shirley's desk is situated in what looks like an office supply catalogue."

"What about my office?" she asked. "Is that under surveillance, too?"

"St. Thomas Aquinas," Stu answered. "Volume one is in your office, and volume two is in B.'s. I didn't think you'd miss them."

When Ali had first signed on to work with B. at High Noon, her first assignment had been to spruce up the premises and get rid of the motley collection of mismatched furniture that made the place look like the leavings from an abandoned consignment store. She'd repainted walls, had new carpeting installed, and replaced worn-out desks and chairs with first-rate office furniture. Then, hoping to give their offices a bit of class and some additional gravitas, she'd added one final detail.

After the death of Ali's second husband, Paul Grayson, all his worldly goods, including his extensive wine collection and the contents of his showy library, had come to her. She and B. had started making inroads on the wine collection almost immediately, but at the time she had embarked on decorating the offices at High Noon, the books had still been languishing in boxes in a storage unit uptown. Ali had donated most of them to a friends-of-the-library sale, but she had been unable to force herself to let go of some of them—the upscale leather-bound editions of the Great Books that had once been included in the purchase price of some long since discarded set of the *Encyclopædia Britannica.*

Ali had brought the books out of forced retirement, freed them from their boxes, and then used them as the finishing touches for her office space makeover. She had divided the books into two sets and lined them up on spanking-new shelving units, half in B.'s office and half in hers. Only now did she discover that two of the books had been cannibalized to hold the surveillance video cameras.

"I think you're right." That time Ali really did laugh aloud. "I don't think I'll be reading either of those tomes anytime soon."

"You still haven't told me why you're in the office on Saturday morning," Stu said again.

Ali may not have known about the interior surveillance system prior to this, but she was relieved to know about it now. Whoever Mr. Barris was, Stuart would most likely have him on camera, doing whatever it was he'd been doing.

"I was actually going to call you about that. B. wanted me to ask you to run a security scan."

"How come? Have we had an intrusion?"

"Maybe," Ali said. "A county building inspector who was supposed to show up sometime late next week dropped by late yesterday afternoon instead just as Shirley was getting ready to leave. The whole thing seemed off to me, but as long as you've got him on video, I'll stop worrying. Maybe you can take a look at what you've got and see if he was doing anything out of line."

"I'm a little busy right now," Stu told her. "Lance and his guys just showed up. I can start the scans right away, but checking the video feeds takes time. I'll take a look at them when I have a chance and get back to you. Do you know about what time he was there?"

"Between four and five," Ali told him.

"Okay," Stu said. "I'll check it out. I've gotta go."

23

On Saturday morning, Graciella cut through the crime scene tape, stepped into what had been her mother's room, surveyed the mine field awaiting her there, and immediately called down to the manager's office, asking for help. Half an hour later a motley group of four young men arrived at her door. They came armed with a rolling grocery cart and plastic trash bins along with an assortment of cardboard boxes.

The guys were willing workers. With Graciella doing the sorting through the clutter, they carted away load after load of accumulated junk. When they finally cleared away the debris surrounding the bed, Graciella had them drag that away next, watching with what she realized was a curious lack of emotion as her mother's actual deathbed was dismantled and lugged out of the room. One of the workers asked would she mind if he took the headboard and frame, and Graciella told him it was fine. As for the bedding, mattress, and box springs? Those were all destined for the Dumpster at the back of the building, although she had a sneaking suspicion that her work crew would cart some of those away as well, turning those along with her mother's many other dubious treasures into someone else's.

As the clutter disappeared, some of the original furnishings emerged—a chest of drawers, a dressing table, a love seat—along with the door to a closet that had been invisible for years. Hanging in the closet Graciella found some of the glamorous clothing that had come into the house from the storage unit all those years ago. Some of them—slinky cocktail dresses and floor-length evening gowns—were things she dimly remembered seeing her mother wearing. Christina had been so beautiful back then. In Graciella's eyes her mother could have been a movie star or a princess.

Just because Graciella remembered some of the outfits, didn't mean she kept them. The dresses went into the discard boxes, as did the shoes. She sorted through the drawers, emptying them all and consigning the contents to the trash bins before sending the dresser and chest of drawers away as well. There was nothing of her mother's that was worth saving. If Graciella's helpers happened to notice her lack of sentimentality concerning such things, they were too happy making off with Christina's usable furniture—including the flat screen TV from the living room—to make any mention of Graciella's state of mind.

As the day drew to a close and with her mother's room completely empty, Graciella made one last check of the closet. At the very back of an overhead shelf, she discovered a thin box. Her first thought as she brought it down was that it might contain a strand of long-forgotten pearls. When she opened it, however, she discovered inside a series of articles and/or obituaries, written in English and printed on pieces of brittle, age-yellowed newsprint, all of them concerning Christina's assault.

Graciella shuffled through the stack, glancing at the stories. One of the six perpetrators had committed suicide. Two had died of drug overdoses, one in L.A. and the other in Dallas, Texas. One of them had been the victim of a hit-and-run in Fresno, California. Two had been shot to death in what was believed to be gang-related violence, one in Chicago and the other in Detroit. Those two homicides remained unsolved. The last article in the stack was one written in Spanish and taken from a local paper called *Panamá*

Hoy (*Panama Today*), detailing the court-martial convictions of the six airmen involved in the savage rape of Christina Miramar. All had been found guilty and dishonorably discharged. The local prosecutor, who could have charged them with rape as civilians as well, had declined to do so. They all went home to the States with what was widely regarded by locals as nothing more than a slap on the wrist.

Going back to the obituaries and matching the names with the ones charged in the attack on Christina, Graciella immediately suspected she was seeing El Pescado's handiwork. The six men who had attacked Christina had gotten away with it as far as any real justice was concerned, so her father had followed them home to the States, systematically tracked them down, and exacted his own style of revenge.

Late in the afternoon, Graciella retreated to the living room with the damning box of articles, unsure what she should keep or toss. If those papers ever surfaced in the wrong hands, they would irretrievably link her to El Pescado. Still, curious about the details, she sat in the living room and, using her laptop and secure dark Web-based server, she tracked down all available information on the men involved. The six deaths had taken place over a three-year period of time in the early nineties in far-flung towns from one end of the US to the other. Some of her searches led her back to those original obituaries. An article about one of the unsolved homicides actually referred to the court-martial proceedings resulting from the attack on Christina Miramar several years earlier.

Did learning about her father's mission of revenge give Graciella any comfort? Hardly. Just because he had punished the attackers didn't give him a free pass, nor did the fact that he had looked after both Christina and Graciella during all those intervening years. His actions after the fact didn't absolve him of his original crime—the unforgivable betrayal—of abandoning them in the first place.

There were no strands labeled forgiveness located anywhere in the Duarte family's DNA, and in that regard, Graciella truly was her father's daughter.

When Graciella had satisfied herself that she had learned all there was to learn about the deaths of the six men who had attacked her mother, she took the stack of yellowed articles into the kitchen. She placed them in the sink, lit a match, reduced them to ash, and washed that down the drain.

When she was done, she showered the grime off her body, then left the apartment, and hurried down the street to the little family restaurant on the corner of Vía Brasil.

"*¿Los de siempre?*" The woman behind the counter greeted her with a smile. "The usual?"

The usual was *sancocho*, the thick, stew-like chicken soup that is Panama's traditional cure for a hangover. Since Christina had been drunk on a daily basis, she had practically lived on the stuff, and Graciella had always ordered carryout containers of it from here rather than going to the trouble of making it herself.

She nodded. "*Si, por favor.*"

The woman frowned. "But I thought your mother . . ." She bit her lip and fell silent.

"Yes," Graciella said with a sad smile, graciously acknowledging the expression of sympathy from this near stranger, just as a properly grieving daughter ought to do. "You're right. My mother is gone now, and the *sancocho* was her favorite, but I have been thinking about her today, and it seems only right to order it tonight."

"Of course," the woman agreed, "it's important to keep our lost loved ones with us—by remembering the foods they liked. Will there be anything else?"

"*No, gracias,*" Graciella told her. "*Sólo el sancocho.*"

24

There was no way Stu could have anticipated how easily the complex job of packing up Owen Hansen's handiwork could be accomplished. Every piece of the network had been laid out with exacting attention to detail. Stu and Lance began the project by numbering each of the racks so that, when it was time to put them back together, they could mirror the original arrangement in every detail. Each cord and each connection was numbered and labeled to allow for easy reassembly once the equipment arrived in Arizona.

Lance was as impressed by the elegance of Owen Hansen's setup as Stu was, and the two tech guys talked as they worked. Lance was excited about the idea of adding Frigg to High Noon's cyber arsenal. Stu was far more wary. He was still on what he called "the one and done page"—turn Frigg on, get the passwords, turn her off, and get the hell out.

"From the way Owen Hansen was able to penetrate other people's devices with impunity," Stu said, "Frigg must be loaded with all kinds of electronic eavesdropping crap that shouldn't be there. No doubt a lot of it is absolutely illegal. If Hansen had been caught using it, he might have ended up in jail. You can bet that if we're caught using any of it, we really will go to jail. We'll also be out of business."

"Maybe we can get Frigg to do a self-scan and give us a directory of the programs that cross the line so we can delete them."

"From what I've read, some of those deep-learning algorithms are machine-readable only and are indecipherable for humans. What's to stop Frigg from disbursing that collection of illicit files out into the ether again so she can retrieve them whenever she wants, just like she did last time?" Stu asked.

"You'd better figure out how to keep that from happening," Lance said, "and you need to do it now—before you let Frigg back online."

"Tell me about it," Stu said miserably. "I can't get the passwords without putting her online first."

"Sounds like you're screwed, then," Lance told him with a grin, "but at least you'll have the money."

A mere six hours after they started the project, it was done. While Stu and Lance had been deconstructing all the connections, Lance's crew of musclemen, directed by Cami, had removed all the monitors from their brackets, wrapped them in protective film, and loaded them into the truck. Once the racks had been disconnected from their wall mounts, they, too, were wrapped in packing film, hauled outside, and strapped securely into the truck.

At last the only piece of equipment remaining in the space was the antique Macintosh sitting in solitary splendor on the library table. Stu punched the power switch and the screen came to life. It was password-protected, so Stu couldn't run it, but that didn't stop him from taking the top off to look inside. With the lid off, the machine wasn't at all what it appeared. It may have looked old, decrepit, and out-of-date, but under the hood Owen Hansen had installed a powerful collection of some of the very latest computer wizardry.

Cami came back inside through the sliding door just as Stu was replacing the outside cover panel. "You're not taking that piece of junk along with us, are you?" she asked.

"I don't think it's junk," he told her. "I suspect this old goat of a computer functioned as Owen Hansen's base of operations."

"That was my husband's," Irene Hansen said nodding toward Stu and the Mac. Once again, and despite still wearing those stiletto heels, she had turned up behind them as silently as a ghost. "They gave it to Harold for free because it was one of the first computers off the assembly line. They used Harold's chip, you see. He was a very smart man, and so was his son. Owen barely knew his father and yet they were very much alike."

Stu took a deep breath. He hadn't told Irene Hansen everything he needed to tell her earlier. Now he cleared his throat to do so.

"Your son left me some money," he said. That wasn't exactly the truth, but he didn't want to bring Frigg's machinations into the discussion. "More than just some," he added. "The money is on deposit in some offshore accounts. Once I get the passwords and pay whatever taxes are due, I'll turn anything that's left over to you."

"Oh, don't do that, sweetie," Irene said. "I already have all the money I'll ever need. If Owen gave it to you, he must have meant for you to have it."

Stuart Ramey was stunned. It wasn't just that Irene had passed on his giving her any of Owen's money. That in itself was almost incomprehensible. She had just called him sweetie, however, and that was something that had never happened to him before in his whole life!

25

Walking back home with her take-out soup in hand, Graciella examined the neighborhood. The apartment building on Calle 61 Este was called El Sueño, The Dream. The whole time Graciella had lived there with her mother, she had dreamed of living elsewhere. She had watched longingly as sparkling new high-rises had sprouted throughout the city. Those were the kinds of places where several of her very important clients maintained penthouse suites. She had always imagined that once her mother was no longer in the picture, she'd move into one of those—preferably in one of the top floor units—and take her rightful place in the universe.

But the last few days had caused her to rethink her place in the universe. As her father's primary money launderer, she knew exactly how much money was floating around inside El Pescado's illegal world. She knew which numbered accounts belonged to him and which ones belonged to each of her half brothers. While sorting out the trash in her mother's room, it had occurred to her that maybe there already was enough money. Maybe she didn't need any more. What she should probably do was to consolidate what already existed by collapsing the cartel and walking away with the remaining spoils.

She wasn't yet sure how she'd go about accomplishing that goal, but she intended to bring El Pescado's cartel down in the time-honored Duarte fashion, by turning brother against brother and father against son. Graciella, an unassuming and unmarried spinster in her mid-thirties, wasn't anyone's idea of a drug lord. She wasn't the least bit glamorous or even especially good-looking. She lived a quiet and ostensibly sober life. No one looking at someone who had selflessly cared for her mother for years would consider her capable of turning on her family and destroying them from within. Her father and her brothers would be wary of attacks coming from outside—from rival cartels or from the cops—but not from her.

Her challenge was to point the authorities in the direction of El Pescado and his sons without being drawn into the fray herself. There would be plenty of time later on for her to live a flashy life. Right now, she needed the protection of the same kind of invisibility that had served her so well as a vagrant child, wandering on her own and begging for money in the slums of Panama City. Now she would be an invisible drug cartel kingpin, hiding in plain sight in a run-down, somewhat seedy condo complex. She doubted anyone other than her father would know to come to El Sueño looking for her, and by the time he did, it would be too late.

Back in the apartment, Graciella was about to dish up her soup when the phone rang. The name in the caller ID belonged to one of Graciella's coworkers. Isobel Flores's cubicle was next to Graciella's. She was also the assistant office manager. "Have you heard?" Isobel asked breathlessly.

"Heard what?" Graciella asked, feigning innocence although she was quite sure she already knew the answer.

"It's about Arturo," Isobel said. "He never made it home last night."

"Really?" Graciella replied. "What happened?"

"You knew he left the office with Bianca yesterday, right?"

"I was pretty busy yesterday," Graciella said. "I guess I didn't notice. Why?"

"The cops came by here a little while ago. They got my name from

Arturo's wife. They told me that they found Arturo's car early this morning. It was stuck in a ditch outside of town. The car was shot full of holes and covered in blood, but there was no sign of Arturo."

Right, Graciella thought. She had told her contractor to get rid of the body, and he had.

"Anyway," Isobel continued, "the cops found a valet receipt in the car and traced it back to the hotel."

Graciella didn't bother asking which hotel, because everyone in the office knew the one Arturo preferred above all others.

"They showed me a clip of security video from the valet stand out front. It showed Arturo plain as day. They wanted to know if I recognized the woman who was with him."

"And you told them it was Bianca."

"Of course. What else could I do? They left here to go talk to her. They'll probably take her in for questioning. They might even arrest her. You don't think she could have had anything to do with this, do you?" Isobel asked. "She always seemed so . . ."

"Naive, maybe?" Graciella put in.

"Exactly," Isobel agreed, "naive and innocent."

"Looks can be deceiving," Graciella said with an inward smile. "Just because Bianca looks innocent doesn't mean she *is* innocent. Maybe she has a boyfriend or a brother who took exception to Arturo's behavior. It's about time somebody did."

Once off the phone with Isobel and feeling quite happy with herself, Graciella dished up her soup and then brought her laptop to the table to keep her company while she ate. When she logged in to the dark Web storage site, there was still no video link, but she was pleased to find several audio files queued up and waiting. With a real sense of satisfaction, she hit the play button, ready to listen in on the conversations of people who were unwittingly broadcasting every word from close to 6,400 kilometers away.

Graciella had hoped that the first voice she heard would be Stuart Ramey's. She needed to gain some insight into who he was and how he operated in hopes of figuring out how to handle him once they were in touch. Unfortunately, the only voice audible on the recording belonged to a woman—Ali Reynolds, maybe? Since no other voices were part of the conversation, she was most likely speaking on a telephone.

Graciella heard the recorded voice say something about "surveillance cameras." Unable to make it out, she ran the recording back and played it again. "Wait, we have surveillance cameras in here? Really? I never noticed them. Where are they?"

A knot formed in the pit of Graciella's stomach. Hadn't Robby forwarded a message from Ron Webster claiming that there hadn't been any interior surveillance inside High Noon? Hadn't he told her that he'd gotten away clean? If there were cameras at work, that wasn't true.

Graciella returned to listening in time to hear the woman say, "I don't see any camera." A short time later the woman in Cottonwood exclaimed. "I'll be damned! I never would have noticed that in a million years." That exchange led Graciella to conclude that there had to be at least one camera present inside High Noon Enterprises—very probably more than one.

If there were interior surveillance cameras, it was only a matter of time before her planted listening devices would be found and the whole exercise would be a total waste of time and money. She had been assured that Ron was a smooth operator. Obviously that wasn't true. Not only had he not been smart enough to spot the surveillance, he had also failed to hook up the video link and had subsequently lied about it. It didn't take long for Graciella's shock to turn to anger and eventually to rage. She had no intention of tolerating that kind of bungling. If the cops took Ron into custody, how long before he gave up Robby? And if that happened, how long before they showed up on Pablo's doorstep, since she had used her half brother's account to pay the bill?

For a long time after the audio file finished playing, Graciella sat there waiting to see if there would be another. Ali Reynolds had obviously left the building shortly after the recording ended. Finally, with no additional files available, a frustrated Graciella left the storage site and logged in to a different one. These days, when El Pescado required the services of a paid killer, he often turned to a group of assassins affiliated with MS-13, who filled that bill in any number of locations both inside the US and elsewhere.

When Graciella set up the hit on Ron Webster, she was more than happy to pay extra for expedited service. Once again, and just for consistency's sake, she paid good money out of Pablo's account for "overnight delivery."

She'd been led to believe that Ron Webster was subtle and smart. Obviously he was neither, and that was why, although he was too stupid to realize it yet, he was on his way out. As for Graciella's long-distance new hires? They were known to be thorough, lethal, and not the least bit subtle.

Clearly the authorities in the US weren't especially interested in solving crimes committed in the distant past, so she would offer up some Duarte Cartel-related crimes that were a bit more current. She would use the cops to bring her father down along with her two half brothers. Once they were gone, with any kind of luck, she, Frigg, and Stuart Ramey would be the only ones left standing.

26

A few minutes past three, Cami and Stu waved good-bye to Lance and his buddies and drove away from Irene Hansen's mansion on Via Vistosa. As Ali had specified, Cami was at the wheel of the rental truck while an emotionally drained Stu sat slumped in the passenger seat.

They were on Highway 101 and headed south when a text came in from Ali:

> Did you ever have a chance to check those
> surveillance feeds?

"Crap," Stu said aloud.

"What's wrong?" Cami wanted to know.

"Ali asked me hours ago to check the interior surveillance feeds, but I got so caught up in the dismantling project that I forgot to do it."

"Do it now," Cami said.

Hauling out his laptop, Stu did exactly that. Since the cameras only functioned when there was movement, once he was logged in, it took no time at all to locate the images. He quickly scrolled through the segments where he had picked up Ali's and Alonso's presence earlier that morning. The previous series of segments featured the two-person cleaning crew who had come in and vacuumed, dusted, and emptied the trash shortly after nine on Friday night. The time stamp on that footage indicated that the cleaners entered the building at 9:02 and locked up at 10:10.

The file just prior to that one showed Shirley letting herself out through the front door. Then the shutters closed, leaving the screen in darkness with a time stamp of 5:07. At that juncture, Stu skipped back several segments until he found one with time stamp of 3:56. Shirley had evidently been away from her desk. Filming resumed when she returned to the reception area. For a time, the feed showed her in profile. The movement of her fingers as she typed something into her keyboard was enough action to maintain the video feed. Then, at 4:03, she looked away from the screen toward the door, where a male figure wearing a hat was now visible through the clear glass. A moment later Shirley reached toward the intercom button.

There was no audio component with the system. As a consequence, Stu was unable to make out any of the verbal exchange that followed. Eventually, however, the door opened, and the man entered the building, removing his hat as he did so. When Stu and Cami had created the system, they had opted for high-resolution cameras with far more pixel capability than that found in most CCTV systems. So when the newcomer paused directly in front of the reception area to sign the visitor log, Stu froze the feed long enough to enlarge the image and send one screenshot to Ali and another to himself. When Stu studied the photo, the man wasn't someone Stu recognized. When he returned to the feed he discovered that shortly after signing the visitor in, Shirley moved out from behind the counter to lead him to the lab. There were no bookshelves in the hallway, and hence no cameras, either.

The next segment of footage showed Shirley and the newcomer arriving in the computer lab. Stu watched while the man set down a small toolbox and a clipboard. Again, there were some inaudible verbal exchanges before Shirley left the room, presumably to return to reception. Sure enough, a second feed soon appeared showing her back at her computer. Meanwhile, in the first one, the visitor opened his toolbox, retrieved a screwdriver, and then removed something else—a small box of some kind, maybe? Since this was a building inspector, Stu expected him to go straight to the newly installed electrical panel, the one the electrician claimed was tough enough to power three hundred toasters at a time. Instead, and without giving the panel so much as a passing glance, the man disappeared into the new lab space where, once again, with no bookshelves or books available, there was also no camera coverage.

When the feed resumed again, the visitor came into view and approached the toolbox briefly before once again going out of frame. At no time in any of the footage did he go anywhere near the electrical panel he was supposedly there to inspect. In fact, the next segment showed him messing with something inside the light switch next to Cami's desk and directly behind Stu's.

"Why that SOB!" Stu exclaimed.

"What?" Cami demanded. "What's going on?"

"I think he's bugging the place."

"Bugging?" Cami repeated. "Are you kidding?"

"Not at all. I think he's installing listening devices and/or cameras throughout the building."

"No way!"

"Way," Stu replied. "And if that guy's a building inspector, I'm a monkey's uncle!"

A moment or two passed before Stu spoke again, his voice trembling with outrage. "He just went into my apartment. What the hell? If I ever lay hands on the guy, I'm going to wring his damned neck."

Sure enough, the next feed showed the intruder in the main living area of Stu's studio apartment, this time messing with the cover plate on the light switch next to the front door where he worked for several minutes before shaking his head. Evidently something had gone wrong. He returned to the toolbox once again before reappearing inside the apartment and finishing whatever he'd been trying to do.

The next-to-last clip, filmed by the camera located over Cami's workstation, showed the guy drop to his hands and knees and crawl under Stu's desk until only the soles of his shoes were visible. Shirley's arrival in the frame caused him to emerge from under the desk in such a hurry that it looked as though he had creamed his head on the desk drawer. As Shirley neared the toolbox, he hurriedly reached over and closed the lid, only to have to reopen it a moment later to slide the screwdriver inside.

The next clip, back in the reception area, showed the so-called inspector signing the visitors' log and exiting the building. A few minutes later, Shirley finished gathering up her things before she, too, left the building, closing the shutters behind her. By the time Stu's screen went dark, he was on the phone to Ali, with the speaker turned on so Cami would be part of the conversation.

"We've got a problem," he announced. "Is B. there?"

"We both are," Ali replied. "You sound upset. What kind of problem are we talking about?"

"Where are you?"

"At the house and about to sit down to dinner. Where are you?"

"We're locked and loaded, in the truck, out of Santa Barbara, and headed home, but turn on your speaker. I want to talk to both of you. We've had an intrusion, and I think we may have been hacked."

"Hacked?" B. demanded. "Did your scans show up something?"

"I don't think he touched the computers," Stu answered, "but someone sure as hell got inside and was messing around in our building."

"Who are we talking about?" B. asked.

"That so-called building inspector Ali was worried about was totally bogus. He wasn't there to sign off on our permits. I believe he was using the inspection gig as cover so he could install some kind of electronic surveillance system inside our offices."

"You're sure he didn't access any of our computers?" B. asked.

"He didn't go anywhere near the computers, at least not that I saw," Stu answered. "He was mostly messing with cover plates for some of the light switches and electrical sockets."

"He was probably tapping into the wiring," B. suggested. "That way he'd have access to a steady power supply with no need for batteries."

"Exactly," Stu said. "Without batteries, he can use equipment that's small and difficult to detect. My gut instinct says we're probably dealing with audio only since some of the locations have limited sight lines, but they're positioned in such a way I doubt they'd ever be spotted by a real building inspector."

"What a nightmare!" B. declared.

"My sentiments exactly," Stu agreed.

"Okay," B. said urgently. "Ali and I should probably head for Cottonwood right now, find out what's been planted there, and get rid of it."

"There's no point," Stu said.

"No point?" B. objected. "What do you mean?"

"If whoever installed the bugs has been monitoring our feeds, they most likely heard everything that was said earlier this morning when Ali and Alonso were there. That means they know we had cameras running and that we're most likely aware of their presence."

"You're saying we just leave the bugs in place?"

"For right now," Stu replied. "Whoever's behind this can monitor the hell out of us, but as long as no one's in the office, they're not going to learn anything useful. In the meantime, give me a while to go to work and try to figure out who's behind this."

"How do you propose to do that?"

"I'd rather not say," Stu answered.

"I take it we're talking about one of your backdoor operations?" B. asked.

Stu said nothing, which, as it turned out, they all understood to mean yes.

"And how long a while are you talking about?" B. asked.

"Long enough for us to get home," Stu said. "As I said, Cami and I are on the move right now. If we drive straight through, the GPS says we should arrive sometime after one a.m."

He looked over at Cami who had both hands on the wheel and her eyes on the road. "Are you good to go?" he asked.

"As in all the way home?"

"Yes."

"You bet," Cami said, "as long as you ply me with enough coffee."

"Wait," Ali said, breaking in on the conversation. "You two are talking about driving straight through even after doing the load-out? That's nuts."

"It's not nuts because this is an emergency," Stu replied, brushing aside her objection. "High Noon is under siege, and we need to get to the bottom of it. From what I saw on the tapes, Shirley interrupted the installation. The guy didn't get any further than my apartment and the two computer labs. Just to be on the safe side, though, any talking we do at the office should be done outside the building rather than inside."

"No one has tried to spy on us before," Ali said, "at least not as far as we know. So why would something like this happen now? What's changed?"

"I'm about to reactivate Frigg," Stu said quietly. "What do you want to bet that's what's changed?"

"The AI," Ali breathed. "Is someone after the AI?"

"An incredibly smart AI," Stu replied.

They all took a moment to digest that.

"So who all knows about that?" B. asked.

"The four of us and Lance," Stu answered at once.

"And Alonso," Ali added. "I told him about it this morning. What about the guys who helped you with the load-out today?"

"I doubt Lance gave them very many details. As far as they knew, we were moving a bunch of blades and that was it."

"What about that woman in Panama?" Ali asked. "The one who wrote to you. She said Owen Hansen was her client. What if she knew about Frigg and has figured out that reactivating the AI is probably the only way you'll be able to access those Bitcoin codes?"

"She certainly qualifies as a possible candidate," Stu agreed. "It's also reasonable to assume that we're dealing with some kind of bad actor. That means we need to take as many precautions as necessary to keep Frigg from falling into the wrong hands."

"And you," Ali said. "If someone's targeting Frigg, we don't want you falling into the wrong hands, either."

"What kind of precautions are we talking about?" B. asked.

"I say we turn Frigg on long enough to get those codes and then shut her down again—for good this time. No kernel file—no chance of reactivation. But where do we put her in the meantime?"

"We can't use the new computer lab," Ali put in, "not until a real building inspector signs off on the permits. End of next week at the earliest."

"Wait," B. said. "How's this for an idea? Ali and I have been renting out my old place on the golf course in the Village of Oak Creek. Right now, the house is vacant. The tenants moved out two weeks ago. Back when we were using it as our corporate headquarters, I upgraded the electrical service. What would happen if we unloaded the truck and installed the GPUs there long enough to reactivate Frigg and lay hands on those banking codes? I know that calls for a lot of effort in terms of loading and unloading, but it saves us a whole week of waiting around for the building department to get its act together."

"Can you get Internet access?" Stu asked.

"It's already there," B. answered. "All I'd need to do is log on."

"But we're talking eight hundred GPUs," Stu said. "Do you think the electrical service at the house has enough capacity? And won't that much traffic overwhelm the router?"

B. laughed. "As long as no one turns on the microwave while all those GPUs are running, I'm pretty sure we'll be fine. Are the racks contained and cooled from the inside?"

"No cabinets," Stu told him.

"All right, then. We'll need to use the AC to keep the temperature low enough. And you're right, the speeds on the Wi-Fi connection are bound to be slower than we'd like, but I'm pretty sure it'll work."

"Who's going to do all this unloading and moving?" Ali asked. "And how big a crew did Lance bring along to Santa Barbara?"

"There were five of them plus Cami and me," Stu answered, "so seven in all."

"We'll have to make do with fewer people than that," B. said. "And we'll need to do this under the cover of darkness when nosy neighbors aren't up and about. Call when you get as close as Cordes Junction, Stu. I don't know how long it'll be before I hit the jet lag wall, but I'm hoping that by the time you get to the village, we'll have the porch light on and the doors open. With any kind of luck, we'll also have the Internet connection up and running."

Ali gave a resigned but heartfelt sigh. "It's a long drive, you two. If you need to stop and rest, do it."

"Yes, ma'am," Stu told her. "That's the whole idea—arrive alive and with all of those blades still intact."

27

"**W**hat kind of backdoor operation?" Cami asked when the phone call ended. Because they worked in such close proximity she, more than anyone else at High Noon, knew about Stu's informal posse of nerdy guys who networked together from time to time, getting things done by bending a few rules and regulations along the way.

"Give me some space and let me work on this for a minute. I want to send a photo to Jeff."

He went back to the surveillance videos and sent copies of all of them to both B. and Ali, then he went looking for an image that gave the clearest view of the faux building inspector. That one, a full-on shot of the man standing at the front counter and signing the visitor's log, was the one Stu selected and then enhanced. Once he had an image with what he regarded as acceptable resolution, he e-mailed it to a friend of his, Jeff Swanson, with the caption: *Anyone you know?*

"Who's Jeff?" Cami asked.

"Jeff Swanson," Stu replied. "He works for the Arizona Department of Transportation."

"And?" Cami prompted.

"In an effort to cut down on identity theft, ADOT added a facial recognition component into their driver's license procedures. Like yesterday. When I passed the test, they took my photo, but the license they gave me is only temporary. I won't get a permanent one until after my photo goes through the state's facial rec program. If any duplicates show up, the permanent license isn't issued. Jeff's in charge of the program," Stu added, "and he owes me one."

"That'll only work if the bad guy is licensed in the state of Arizona," Cami objected.

"True," Stu agreed, "but it's a place to start."

With no reply from Jeff instantly forthcoming, Stu leaned over against the passenger door. Soon, despite his earlier bravado with Ali about making the trip home, his lack of sleep from the night before caught up with him. He dozed off—more than dozed—and when he woke up, the 101 had become the 210 and they were driving through Pasadena.

"Sorry," he muttered. "I didn't mean to drop off like that."

"That was more than a drop-off," Cami replied. "That was more like a drop dead. You've been out cold for an hour and a half, and while you've been sawing logs, I've been thinking."

"About?"

"About leaving those bugs in place. Presumably, even though the bad guy knows that we're aware of the intrusion, he's probably still monitoring whatever's happening on our end. What would happen if we used the bugs to launch a misinformation campaign?"

"What kind of misinformation?"

"There's an article that showed up in *Shooting Illustrated* a couple of months ago."

Stu rolled his eyes. Fortunately for him Cami was too preoccupied with driving to zero in on the gesture.

Shortly after Cami had come to work for High Noon, she'd been caught up in an unfortunate situation where she'd been hijacked off a highway and held prisoner in a Phoenix area house. She'd used her Krav Maga martial arts training to good effect in getting out of that mess. Since then, however, she'd become even more serious about self-defense. She had obtained a Ruger LCR, manufactured in neighboring Prescott, as well as a lifetime membership in the NRA. *Shooting Illustrated* came to her every month as part of her membership.

Stuart had never been comfortable around guns. The only weapon he had ever owned had been the Swiss Army knife he'd inherited from his grandfather. Stu had made more than one snide comment about Cami leaving on the dot of five o'clock every afternoon, either rushing to the gym for Krav Maga or else racing off to the shooting range. At the moment, however, even someone with Stuart's limited social skills knew better than to veer into making a snide comment.

"What kind of article?"

"They called it the 'Bad Guy's Blueprint' or maybe the 'Bad Guy's Playbook'—something like that."

"What did it say?"

"That when bad guys go looking for victims, there are five steps. Predators go looking for victims. They stalk their victims, often choosing ones who are distracted in some way and not paying attention to their surroundings. Once they select their victim and decide whether or not they're worth the trouble, they have to close in to a strike position so they can execute the attack."

"What does any of this have to do with the price of peanuts?"

"That phony building inspector who got into High Noon under false pretenses is not a good guy. Whether he's working on his own behalf or on someone else's, he came there looking for someone or something, presumably you and Frigg."

"So he's currently at the stalking stage?"

"Right," Cami replied, "but in order to launch an actual attack, the predator will have to get close, so let's set a trap that will bring him to us in a controlled environment where we're expecting him and he's expecting us to be . . . well . . . distracted; not paying attention."

"And how do you propose to do that?"

"By going into the office, walking into the lab, and making a big deal about what's going to happen next."

"Which is?"

"That you're going to sell Frigg, of course," Cami said with a triumphant grin. "If Frigg is the prize here, learning that you intend to auction her off to the highest bidder should be enough to bring the bad guys crawling out from under their rocks. If that doesn't work, I don't know what will."

28

Once off the phone, B. immediately logged on to his laptop, rerunning his own set of scans to verify that there were no signs of intrusions on any of the office computers. When the files containing the surveillance videos arrived, he scrolled through them, inside the building and out. B. and Ali finally sat down to their long-delayed homecoming dinner, but by then Alonso's perfect meatloaf was dead cold, and the mood was decidedly different from what either of them had expected. B. was still livid that High Noon's office complex had been targeted, but he deferred to Cami and Stu's idea of leaving the planted listening devices in place.

"I'd like to get a look at one of them, though."

"Why?" Ali asked.

"If we can locate a serial number, we might be able to track the end user through the manufacturer. For right now, though, our first priority has to be getting the AI up and running."

When B. and Ali had joined forces, they had chosen Ali's house in Sedona proper over B.'s place in the Village of Oak Creek. At the time there had been a serious downturn in the real estate market. Rather than sell at a loss, they had opted to keep the home and rent it out until things improved. When the most recent tenants had moved out just prior to B.'s departure on this latest trip, they had put off making a final decision about selling or not until after his return. Right now delaying that decision had turned out to be a good thing.

"The house is totally empty at the moment," Ali said. "If we're going to expect people to work there for the next little while, we'll need tables and chairs at least, and probably some tools, too. The furniture for the new lab was delivered last week. Since you were out of town, it's all crammed into your office at the moment. Why don't I drive over to Cottonwood and bring some of it back to this side?"

"If you're going, I'm going," B. insisted. "I'll know which tools to bring along, and you won't. If Alonso is up to it, maybe we can ask him to drive over as well. That way there will be three of us to load the furniture, and it'll fit better in the back of the F-150 than it will in the back of your Cayenne."

All of that was pretty much inarguable. "I'll ask," she said. Ali's text found Alonso in his quarters, the Airstream trailer that had once belonged to Leland Brooks.

Alonso was happy to help out, and so, for the second time that day, Ali traveled from Sedona to Cottonwood, this time with her driving and B. in the passenger seat, while Alonso followed in the pickup. During the thirty-minute trip, B. managed to log on and work his way through the steps necessary to re-up the Internet connection at the house in the village, switching it over from a residential application to a business one. Ali was just turning in to the business park when he finally finished the long-winded call.

"Whew!" he said. "We should be up and running. Fortunately for us, the tenants who just left had upgraded to the latest router only a few months ago, so we don't have to go looking around for one of those."

Once at the business park, they hurried up to High Noon's entrance where Ali keyed in the codes that opened the shutters and turned off the security alarm.

"Okay," she said, propping the door open. "Once we're inside, we don't say a word. If the bug has a video component, the bad guys will see what we're doing, but as long as we're not talking, they won't know why. I can tell you from long experience that the Stuart Ramey army travels on its stomach. If we don't have plenty of coffee, sodas, and snacks available, we'll end up with an insurrection on our hands."

She was on her third trip back and forth from the Cayenne to the break room when her eye fell on the intercom buzzer next to the door—the one the faux building inspector had used to summon Shirley in order to gain access to the building. Ali had seen the outdoor surveillance video of him standing there, pressing the button. It hadn't looked to her as though he was wearing gloves.

Moments later, she was inside, rummaging through one of Shirley's file drawers, the one labeled MAILING SUPPLIES. Armed with a strip of clear packing tape, she went back outside and pressed the sticky side against the button. She was removing the tape as B. came out the door, lugging a toolbox.

"What are you doing?" he asked.

"Collecting a fingerprint," she said, "but now I need a way to carry it without messing it up."

In the end, using a second piece of packing tape, she fastened the tape, sticky side up, to the outside of an empty soda can before placing the can in the Cayenne's cup holder.

"Do you think you'll to be able to talk Dave Holman into running that print?" B. asked.

"I'm pretty sure I can," Ali told him. "After all, he and I go back a long way."

"Are you trying to make me jealous?" B. asked.

"Nope," Ali said. "Just trying to figure out a way to catch Bad Boy Barris."

On the trip back to Sedona, jet lag finally caught up with B. in a big way. He dozed and snored in the passenger seat, while Ali—

behind the wheel—drove and worried. Between reactivating a renegade AI and dealing with whoever had planted the bugs, it seemed as though High Noon Enterprises was every bit as much at risk as it had been when Owen Hansen had been alive and on the loose.

We managed to dodge a bullet that time around, Ali told herself grimly. *Let's hope we can do it this time, too.*

29

When Cami pulled in to a gas station in Beaumont, California, it was nine thirty at night. Two major traffic tie-ups along the way, one on the 210 and another at the 210/I-10 interchange, had turned what should have been a four-hour trip into a five-hour ordeal. By the time they finished filling the tank, the GPS was estimating their arrival time in the Village of Oak Creek as 4:22 a.m.

"I'm bushed," Cami announced. "That ETA doesn't take stopping by the airport to pick up my car into consideration, so either we pack it in here and find hotel rooms for the night, or you take over driving for a while."

"Me?" Stu asked, sounding alarmed. "But I thought Ali said . . ."

"I know what Ali said, but she isn't here," Cami told him. "We are, and the situation on the ground has changed. The state of Arizona says you can drive, and so do I. How soon do you want to be home and putting the Frigg jigsaw puzzle back together?"

"As soon as possible," he said.

"Right," Cami said, handing him the keys. "In that case, you drive for a while and I'll sleep."

Filled with misgivings, Stuart climbed into the cab and fastened the seat belt. He had always believed that driving a car was forever beyond the scope of his limited capabilities, yet here he was behind the wheel of an actual truck. He turned the key in the ignition and the engine rumbled to life.

"Don't forget to release the emergency brake," Cami reminded him.

It took a long moment for him to locate the release, then he put the truck in gear and eased forward. Driving with all the recklessness of a little old lady on her way to church, Stuart crept out into traffic, but what he felt was absolute elation. He only wished that Grace Ramey, his grandmother and the woman who had raised and nurtured him, could have been there to see him do it.

An hour later, past the last casino outpost of Indio and with Cami asleep in the passenger seat, Stu continued motoring eastward, with the U-Haul tucked in among a never-ending stream of eighteen-wheelers. He was not a man given to introspection, but being on I-10 and watching the miles go by, he realized that, for the first time in his life, he was traveling the same lonely stretch of highway where his parents had perished thirty-eight years earlier.

As a child Stu had not been a good traveler. When one of his mother's uncles passed away, his parents had decided to make a quick three-day drive over to L.A. for the funeral. The plan had been for them to go over on day one, attend the funeral on day two, and return on day three. Taking a cranky three-year-old along on that grueling trip had been out of the question, especially since Stu's grandparents had been willing to look after him. His parents had been on their way back home when, somewhere on the Arizona segment of I-10, a drunk, driving westbound in the eastbound lanes of the freeway, had crashed into them head-on. Three people had died instantly as a result of the collision—the wrong-way driver and both of Stu's parents.

Stu had been far too young to remember any of this. What he knew about it had come to him in bits and pieces from things his grandmother mentioned to him over the years. No one else had been willing or able to step up and take on the task of raising the boy.

As a consequence, what should have been a temporary three-day babysitting gig had turned into a permanent custody arrangement. Stu's grandmother and his grandfather, Robert, Sr.—a disabled Korean War veteran—had scratched out a meager living, surviving on his grandfather's minute disability checks and later Social Security while paying the rent on their shabby double-wide mobile home by serving as resident managers of a South Phoenix trailer park.

While Stu was growing up, there had been no such thing as a "family car." His grandfather, a double amputee, would have needed a specially modified vehicle in order to drive, but the cost factor of that had been beyond their limited means. As for his grandmother? Grace had never gotten a license. Never once had anyone suggested that Stu make a pilgrimage out to the lonely spot in the desert where his parents had lost their lives. Here and there along the highway, the truck's headlights lit up small white crosses positioned along the shoulder of the road. Presumably each cross indicated a spot where some motorist had died.

Seeing them made him wonder. Were there any crosses placed at the spot where his parents had died and, if not, should there be? And if he could somehow locate the exact site now, was it too late to install crosses even though Stu himself had no memory of either his parents or of their fatal accident? When was being late with something like that too little too late?

Cami stirred in her seat. "How are you doing?" she asked, straightening up.

The question startled Stu out of his reverie, and he answered without really meaning to. "My parents died here," he said.

Cami sat up straighter and looked around. "Right here?" she demanded.

Stu realized then that in all the time he and Cami had worked together, he had never mentioned a word to her about his grandparents or his parents. She knew about Stu's long-ago friendship with Roger McGeary because High Noon had been involved in the investigation into Roger's death, but Stu had kept the rest of his history—especially the parts about his dead parents and his caring grandparents—locked away in a tightly closed box.

"Not right right here," he corrected quickly. "Somewhere out here in the desert on I-10. I never knew exactly where it happened."

He told her the story then, spilling it out in a way the old Stuart Ramey never could have. He told her about growing up in a grim mobile home park with elderly and impoverished but loving grand-parents as his caretakers and guardians. He told her about the years of being bullied in school, and how Roger's arrival on the scene had offered him a lifeline. And finally, he told about the darkness and despair that had descended on him after Roger moved away, followed shortly thereafter by Grace's death.

"I was homeless for a long time after my grandmother died," he admitted. "I was living in a shelter when B. found me and gave me my first job. I've been with him ever since."

"I never knew any of that," Cami said quietly. "Thank you for telling me. A lot of things that didn't make sense before do now. What were your parents' names?"

"Penelope and Robert S. Ramey, Jr.," Stu answered. "His middle name was Stuart. I was named after him and my grandfather."

Stu had a lot of acquaintances out in the geek world, people with whom he connected by text and phone, but always with a device of some kind as an intermediary. He considered B. to be a friend, and Ali, too, he supposed. But in the silence that suddenly filled the truck, he realized with a shock that Cami, too, was now his friend.

"Thank you for listening," he said.

By then they were approaching Avondale on the outskirts of Phoenix. "Let's pull over at the first gas station we see and switch drivers," Cami suggested. "I feel rested. We'll go by the airport, pick up the Prius, and then head home, if you're not too tired to drive it, that is."

Despite the lateness of the hour and the time spent behind the wheel, Stu felt oddly energized, and the fact that Cami trusted him to drive her car home safely touched him more than he could say. *Yes*, he thought, *a very good friend.*

"I'm not too tired," Stuart said aloud. "Let's do this."

30

At two o'clock in the morning, Rita Webster Parker was awakened out of a sound sleep when Roscoe, their junkyard dog of a German shepherd, started barking like crazy. Living where they did in the middle of nowhere with no nearby neighbors, they needed a good watchdog. Art, Rita's husband, was using his CPAP machine. With that running and with his hearing aids on the bedside table, he didn't hear the dog and didn't stir, either, so Rita was the one who hopped out of bed, fumbled for her glasses, and then hurried over to the window to peer outside. As soon as she saw the single headlight heading in her direction, she knew that was what had put Roscoe on high alert.

Their double-wide was parked at the far end of West Lambert Lane on the outskirts of Marana. Since theirs was the last occupied lot before the road dead-ended, it stood to reason that whoever was coming down the road in the middle of the night was probably coming to their place, and it was probably bad news. More than likely it was her son, Ron, coming home sloshed to the gills after closing down one or the other of his favorite watering holes.

As Rita left the window to return to bed, she mentally reminded herself that in the morning she'd need to let Ron know that one of his headlights was out. She didn't want him getting pulled over for a broken headlight infraction. When you're an ex-con, having the cops stop you for even the least little thing could land you in a heap of trouble. Ron had made enough mistakes in his life. It would be a shame to see him back in the slammer over something like that.

What seemed odd, though, was that Roscoe continued to bark. Why was that? What the hell was the dog's problem? Roscoe knew Ron's Ford Transit Van every bit as well as he knew Art's Jeep Cherokee and Rita's Subaru. And then she remembered. Ron wasn't out on the town after all. He had come home much earlier, while Rita and Art were just finishing up watching the ten o'clock news. That had been around ten thirty. Now, at 2:00 a.m., Rita guessed that this late-night visitor would turn out to be one of Ron's ne'er-do-well drinking buddies, stopping by for a nightcap.

Art was too careful with his money to leave the AC running if it wasn't needed, so on this October night, the bedroom windows were wide open, capturing the high desert's cool evening breezes and passing sounds as well. Rita was seated on the edge of the bed when what had once been a silently approaching car with a single headlight turned into the unmistakable roar of a high-powered motorcycle, a Harley.

Rita raced back to the window, arriving just in time to see the motorcycle swing off Lambert and turn up the short driveway that led to their house. Naturally Roscoe was there, too, barking his objection. Much to Rita's dismay, rather than trying to steer away from or around the dog, in the glow of the yard light she saw the guy on the Harley aim straight for him, as if deliberately trying to mow Roscoe down. Luckily the dog managed to scramble out of the way. At that point Rita rushed back to the bed and shook Art awake.

"Come quick!" she shouted. "Some nut on a motorcycle just tried to run over Roscoe!"

A dazed Arthur Parker sat up in bed. He was still in the process of stripping off his breathing machine when a huge explosion rocked the house. "What the hell was that?" Art demanded. "What's going on?"

Rita rushed back to the window just in time to see the speeding motorcycle roar past again, this time heading in the opposite direction. She could make out no details, just the black silhouette of a motorcycle and rider, backlit by an unearthly orange glow. She couldn't see any actual flames, but already the night air was full of acrid smoke. Behind the moving motorcycle she spotted Roscoe's silhouette as well, hobbling along, favoring his right hind leg, but he was still chasing after the motorcycle as if determined to ward off the unwelcome intruder.

Art joined Rita at the window. For a moment they stood side by side, staring in stricken silence as the dark of night turned an ominous orange, lighting the interior of the bedroom with the glow from outside.

Art was the first to speak. "My God!" he exclaimed. "Whoever that son of a bitch was, he just set fire to our garage!" He stumbled back over to the bed to pull on a pair of pants. "Call the fire department," he ordered.

While Art piled into his pants and a pair of shoes, Rita located her phone. With trembling hands, she keyed in the number. By the time a 911 operator took the call, Rita had slipped on her own shoes and was charging out the back door, hot on Art's heels.

"Nine-one-one, what are you reporting?"

"Some guy on a motorcycle just set fire to our garage," Rita gasped into the phone. "There was a big explosion—a huge explosion—and now . . ."

As she stepped out outside, another fierce explosion rocked the night. This time Rita saw fierce flames shooting skyward above the roof of the oversized garage a previous owner had built to house a massive RV. If the guy on the motorcycle was already gone, where had that secondary blast come from? And where was Art? What if he'd run outside, straight into the path of that new explosion?

Rita stopped cold, too frightened to move. Then to her immense relief, she caught sight of Art. He was all right. Still between the house and the garage, he had been protected from that second fierce blast by the garage itself. He was bent over and desperately struggling to pull a length of garden hose loose from its housing. With the phone to her ear, Rita hurried up to him and helped free the hose. After pausing long enough to open the spigot, she raced after her husband. They rounded the end of the garage side by side and then stopped short, rigid with shock, gazing in horror at what was now a towering inferno. The wall on the far side of the garage was already on fire, and Ron's Lazy Daze had been completely obliterated.

After a moment Art attempted to move forward, aiming the puny stream of water at the conflagration, but the intense heat forced him to fall back. Some of the water reached the flames, but not enough to have any effect. There was far too much fire and far too little water. In that terrible moment, Rita understood that if Ron had been inside the motorhome when it blew, there was no way he could have survived. Ron was dead—Rita's only son was dead.

She heard a faint voice calling to her, summoning her from very far away. "Ma'am, are you still there? Can you tell me what's going on? I've notified the fire department. They're on the way, but is anyone injured? Should I send an ambulance?"

Unable to speak, Rita stared in uncomprehending silence at the device still clutched in her hand. Just then she heard a whimper. Looking down, she saw an injured Roscoe limping toward her. He staggered to a halt and then huddled at her feet with blood from his injured hindquarters oozing onto the skirt of Rita's long nightgown.

Sobbing, she knelt beside the injured dog and buried her face in Roscoe's soft ruff. It smelled burned where sparks from the fire had singed his fur. Rita was still clinging to the dog when she felt Art's hand on her shoulder.

"Come on, hon," he said urgently, pulling her to her feet. "We've got to move farther away from the fire. It's too dangerous. If the gas tanks in the cars catch on fire, they're going to explode, too."

Rita moved, but Roscoe, still whimpering, stayed where he was.

While Rita watched in amazement, Art bent over and grabbed Roscoe. Arthur Parker was not a young man. For years he had suffered with back pain. Even so, grunting with effort, he somehow managed to heft the sixty-pound dog up off the ground and sling him over his shoulder. Rita started toward the house, but Art stopped her. Grabbing her hand, he dragged her along with him, past the end of the mobile home, and on down the driveway.

"If the garage goes, the house goes," he told her.

"But what about our things?" she asked.

"What about them?" he replied. "They're just things. They don't matter. Come on."

When they reached the far end of the driveway they paused long enough to look back. By then the garage was fully engulfed. While flames roared skyward, from somewhere in the distance came the welcome wail of an approaching siren along with the frantic voice of the 911 operator who was still on the phone and still trying to reach her.

"Ma'am, are you still there? Can you talk to me? Are you all right? Is everyone all right? Do you require an ambulance?"

Just then the night was shattered by two more distinctly separate explosions. For a moment the roof of the garage seemed to lift into the air and float there, rising up over what was now only the frail skeleton of the garage, outlined against the terrifying backdrop of raging flames. The studs remained upright for a matter of seconds before crashing to earth. The impact sent a cloud of burning debris spewing in every direction. As shrubs in the yard lit up like torches, some of the embers landed on the thin roof of the double-wide. Within moments, and long before the first fire truck arrived on the scene, the mobile home, too, was ablaze.

At the end of the driveway, Rita was ready to stop and rest, but a panting Art urged her forward, stopping only when they were on the far side of the road. Wrestling Roscoe down from his shoulder, Art gently placed the injured dog on the ground. With a groan and some difficulty Art stood up and straightened his back. Then he reached out and gathered Rita into his arms.

"I'm so sorry about your boy," he murmured into her hair. "I tried, but there was nothing I could do."

That was when Rita finally lost her grip on the phone. Letting it fall to the ground, she clung to her husband. How was this possible? How could Art be comforting her? After all, wasn't she was the one who had begged Art to let Ron stay with them when he'd had nowhere else to go? And now, because Art was a kind man and had said yes, everything the two of them had ever worked for was gone.

"I need someone to talk to me," the woman on the phone was demanding. "What's going on?" But by then she was talking to herself because no one was listening.

31

After unloading the office furniture and the provisions Ali had liberated from the break room at High Noon, she and Alonso prepared for what they both envisioned to be something close to a siege. They drove back on 89-A and dropped B. off at the Sedona house where Ali insisted he get some sleep in his own bed. Meanwhile Ali and Alonso finished gathering up and organizing whatever else from the Sedona house they thought might come in handy for a crew of people working overtime in an otherwise vacant house—everything from rolls of toilet paper to poolside chaise lounges complete with pillows and blankets that could, in a pinch, function as makeshift cots

Moving the chaises into the bedrooms of the house in the Village of Oak Creek, and putting together the makeshift beds, Ali couldn't help but smile. The last time she had assembled a group of chaises as beds had been on the occasion of her son's eleventh birthday back when Chris had invited eleven friends over for a sleepover. She suspected that what had worked well for a bunch of rambunctious preteens back then would offer welcome respite to a pair of weary travelers who had spent way too much time on the road.

Back at the house in Sedona, Ali slipped into bed around eleven and was sound asleep when the ringing of a phone awakened her at 3:45. She wasn't surprised to see that B., operating in no known time zone, was already up and dressed. He answered after only one ring.

"You're in Cordes Junction?" she heard him say as she staggered off toward the bathroom. "Good, we'll meet you at the house. Alonso says he's coming, too. He'll be another body for carting those racks around. Since he came away from the Navy with his dolphins, I'm guessing he'll be pretty handy when it comes to doing reassembly."

Ali had learned about the US Navy's dolphin awards during Alonso's hiring process. Like an aviator's wings, the dolphins were an insignia awarded to submariners who demonstrated the ability to operate and repair all the equipment on board as well as being proficient at lifesaving skills. Alonso had been helpful with last night's prep work, and she had no doubt that his submarine-honed skills would make him equally proficient at stringing computer servers back together.

While Ali climbed into a pair of jeans and a sweatshirt, B. prodded a reluctant Bella out from under the covers and escorted her out for a morning walk. When Ali entered the kitchen, she found that Alonso had prepared a bag of cold meatloaf sandwiches and was filling the third of three thermoses with fresh coffee.

"Good morning," he told her with a grin. "Our people will need sleep, food, and coffee, not necessarily in that order."

They were at the house in the Village of Oak Creek with the lights on and the garage doors open when Cami pulled up in the U-Haul at five a.m. In an impressive show of driving panache, she backed the vehicle smoothly up the steep driveway, stopping just short of the garage door opening. Stu, following behind in Cami's Prius, parked nose to nose with the truck. When the two drivers emerged from their respective vehicles, Ali hugged Cami and resisted the urge to hug Stu.

"Sorry it took so long," Cami apologized, as B. stepped forward to open the tailgate. "Lots of traffic, and they're doing overnight paving on I-17 over by Black Canyon City. The freeway there was coned down to one lane in both directions."

"You're here and you're safe," Ali said. "That's all that matters."

The room B. had designated as the temporary location for Owen Hansen's computer racks was a bonus family room, originally designed as a man cave, at the far end of the garage. That meant that, once the racks were trolleyed down a ramp from the bed of the truck, it would be a straight shot through the garage and into the new quarters.

To Ali's surprise, some previously unknown version of Stu Ramey—Stuart 2.0—took charge of the whole operation. Before allowing any equipment to exit the truck, he used a measuring tape to evaluate the space where each piece would go. After that he issued exacting directions about which racks were to be unloaded in which order and where each one was to be positioned.

Ali had more than half expected that Cami and Stu would want to sleep first and unload later, but that wasn't the case. They, along with B., were determined to have the truck emptied and away from the house as soon as possible,

When it came to dealing with the racks, Alonso, who was in by far the best physical shape of any of them, took charge of the hand truck at the top of the ramp while B. and Stu, pushing back from below, provided the necessary braking. Once the hand truck reached the smooth flat surface of the concrete floor, Alonso was able to maneuver the load on his own through the garage and on into the house.

The monitors, which had been packed into the truck before the racks, were the last items to be unloaded. They were light enough to be carried out of the truck and through the garage one at a time while Stu brought along the only other item left in the truck—a small cardboard box.

Under Stu's direction, the racks were unloaded and reassembled into the same configuration from which they had been dismantled back in Santa Barbara. During the load-out, Stu, Cami, and Lance had carefully labeled each power cord and cable, often duct-taping the end of the cable to the nearest piece of paneling, thus ensuring the use of the proper connection. Once the heavy-duty packing film came off the racks, that painstaking attention to detail paid off. Rather than being faced with an incomprehensible tangle of loose wires and cords, each rack was an organized puzzle that could be reassembled with the ease of a ten-year-old kid building a LEGO set.

Each connection had to be rock solid, but after a few lessons from Stu, Ali surprised herself by taking on a rack of her own. As they worked in an orderly fashion, Stu and Cami related the details of the trip, including Irene Hansen's surprising reaction.

"So she really doesn't care about the money?" B. asked.

"That's what she said," Stu answered. "She may change her mind about that, though, when push comes to shove. There's a big difference between turning down theoretical money and turning down a specific amount."

It was complicated work, made easy by camaraderie and a joint sense of purpose. When energy flagged, liberal doses of the sandwiches and coffee supplied by Alonso came to the rescue. At nine o'clock in the morning, Stu and Cami were finally forced to call a halt. They took to separate chaise lounges in order to grab some much-needed sleep while B., Alonso, and Ali kept on working. Two hours later, while Ali was busy reconnecting the last GPU on the very last rack, B. and Alonso hung the monitors on the one empty wall in the room and connected those cables as well. In anticipation of the heat from all those working blades, B. had already switched on the AC and turned it down to the lowest possible setting, a frigid 62 degrees.

"There we are," B. said, clapping his hands in honor of a job well done. "As long as the Internet connection comes online, I think we're just about done here."

It was Ali, however, who asked the obvious question. "How do we turn this mother on? I saw plenty of cables and cords, but I never saw anything that resembled an off/on switch."

"Should I go wake Stu?" B. asked. "Maybe he knows."

A few minutes later, a still-groggy Stu appeared in the doorway holding that stray cardboard box. He lugged it over to one of the tables, set it down, and began unpacking it. By then the room was already cool enough that Ali was beginning to wish she had brought a jacket along to put on over her sweatshirt.

"An old Macintosh?" B. asked with some bemusement as Stu removed what looked like a museum piece from the box and set it down on the tabletop. "Are you kidding me?"

"It may look like an antique," Stu replied, "but you'll find what's under the hood is surprisingly up-to-date."

He reached into the box again, this time extracting both a separate keyboard and mouse. While the rest of the crew, including a newly awakened Cami, surrounded the table and stood there watching, Stu began reassembling the bits and pieces of the old computer. Once the power cord was plugged in, it took the better part of a minute for the machine to finally boot up. At last a screen opened up. Peering over Stu's shoulder, Ali saw a blank box and the words *PASSWORD REQUIRED*. Stu pulled out his phone, turned it on, consulted a notes page, and then, without the slightest hesitation, confidently typed in a combination of letters and numbers. Within seconds, a directory appeared.

"Whoa!" B. said, clearly impressed. "You hacked Owen Hansen's password?"

"I didn't have to," Stu replied with a grin. "It was written on a piece of masking tape on the bottom of the computer."

"Now what?" Ali asked.

In preparation for traveling to Santa Barbara, Stu had located his hidden backup copy of Frigg's kernel file, which he had loaded onto a thumb drive. When Odin had reworked the computer, he had replaced the original Macintosh ADB ports with a pair of USBs. Pulling the drive out of his shirt pocket, Stu plugged it into one of the USBs and waited until the directory appeared. The directory held a single file, Tolkien's Ring. When he clicked on that, the words *PASSWORD REQUIRED* appeared on the screen.

"Here goes," he said. "If anyone has any objections, now's the time to say so."

No one said a word. "Okay," he said, "here goes the kernel file."

Once again he consulted the screen of his phone. One careful keystroke at a time, he typed the password Frigg had sent in her message to him that Friday afternoon more than a month earlier: *1AMAGENIUS!*. Each character appeared briefly before being replaced by a solid dot. Finished at last, Stu pressed enter. For a long several seconds nothing happened, then one by one the individual GPUs began to fire up and come online. A moment later one of the monitors mounted on the wall lit up as well. At the bottom of the screen were two parallel lines with a tiny bright blue spot glowing inside them. Above the lines were the words, *Time to completion 6 hours 47 minutes.*

The appearance of that notification elicited an enthusiastic round of applause from everyone gathered in the room. "Holy moly!" B. exclaimed, giving Stu a tooth-jarring congratulatory whack on the back. "I think you did it. You pulled it off!"

"It was a joint effort," Stu corrected. "We all pulled it off."

For a time, everyone stood transfixed, watching the time-remaining number count down as the GPUs sent messages all around the world, summoning Frigg's scattered files and bringing them back home to the blades that formed the AI's mainframe.

It was Cami who broke the silence. "I don't know about anyone else, but I've got better things to do that stand around watching an almost seven-hour download. If somebody will come with me,

I'll return the truck, then I want to go home, shower, and change clothes. Once I do that, I can come back here or go to the office, whichever you prefer."

Stu replied with an absentminded nod while never taking his eyes off the monitor.

When Cami left the room, there didn't seem to be much for everyone else to do but follow. Only when they were outside the garage and standing next to the truck did she speak again. "The AI is Stu's problem right now," she explained. "I don't think he's made up his mind yet about keeping Frigg or killing her. Whichever way it goes, I think he deserves a little privacy."

While Cami and Alonso went off to return the truck, Ali turned to B. "What's your plan?"

"I think I'm going to take advantage of one of the chaises, a pillow, and a blanket and grab a few more minutes of shut-eye. That way I'll be close at hand if Stu needs reinforcements. What about you?"

Standing there enjoying the welcome warmth of the sun, Ali was surprised to realize that she had found her second wind and wasn't the least bit sleepy. Just then she caught sight of the packing tape–wrapped soda can, still standing upright in the Cayenne's cup holder.

"I'm going to go track down Dave Holman," she said. "It's high time we found out who our mysterious building inspector really is."

32

Yavapai County Sheriff's Office's substation in the Village of Oak Creek was located in a strip mall and close enough to B.'s house that Ali could easily have walked there and back. This time she chose to drive. When she arrived in the parking lot, Dave's SUV was nowhere to be seen. She pulled into a visitor slot and sat there wondering. Since Dave wasn't there, should she even bother? Finally, though, shrugging off her momentary indecision, she collected the soda can and went inside.

Behind the counter sat a sweet-faced young woman with her long blond hair pulled into a knot at the back of her head. At first glance, Ali wondered if she was old enough to be out of high school. Was the sheriff's department hiring teenagers these days? When the woman stood up, however, Ali was surprised to see that she was actually a uniformed officer—Deputy L. Harper.

"May I help you?" she asked.

"I was hoping to see Detective Holman," Ali said.

"Sorry, he's unavailable," Deputy Harper replied. "We had a homicide overnight, and he's working that. Can I be of service?"

This seemed like a lost cause, but Ali decided to take a crack at it anyway. "My name is Ali Reynolds," she said. "My husband and

I own High Noon Enterprises, a company located on the far side of Cottonwood—on county land rather than inside the city limits."

Deputy Harper frowned, and Ali was sure she was already losing her. "Any relation to Ms. Reynolds, the math teacher over at the high school?" the deputy asked.

Ali was taken aback. "Why, yes," she said, "Athena is my daughter-in-law."

Deputy Harper's face broke into a beaming smile. "She's the best teacher I ever had!" she exclaimed. "Until I met Ms. Reynolds, I thought I hated math. It turns out, I just hated bad math teachers. And she's, like, this incredible inspiration to everybody, I mean, with her arm and leg and all. It was because of her that I decided to apply for a job with the sheriff's office after I got my associate's degree."

Before Athena and Chris met and married, she had served with the Minnesota National Guard and had returned from a deployment to the Middle East as a wounded warrior and partial amputee, having lost one arm from below the elbow and one leg from below the knee.

A little more hopeful now, Ali returned to telling her story. "On Friday, someone gained entrance to our facility under false pretenses by claiming to be a county building inspector. He may have interfered with some of our electronic equipment. I had spoken to Detective Holman about this earlier, but . . ."

"It sounds like a property crime," Deputy Harper interrupted. "Detective Holman doesn't deal with those. Have you filed a police report?"

"Not yet," Ali began.

"Was there any damage?"

"Not that we know of," Ali replied, "at least not so far."

Deputy Harper was already reaching for a clipboard with a pen attached by a length of string. When she placed it on the counter, Ali saw it contained a blank incident reporting form.

"In situations like this we generally don't send officers to the scene," Deputy Harper explained. "Once you fill out this form and give it to me, you'll have filed an official police report. That way, if you happen to uncover damage later on, you'll already have a case number to turn over to your insurance company."

"I was a sworn police officer for a while, so I know about not dispatching officers to incidents involving property crimes," Ali said, moving the soda can in Deputy Harper's direction and setting it on the counter between them. "That's why I brought you this."

"What is it?"

"It may or may not be evidence," Ali said. "At High Noon we use a buzzer on the front door to let visitors into the building. It looked to me like the guy who pressed the button wasn't wearing gloves. I used packing tape to try lifting a print. I was hoping if I did get one that maybe Dave could run it for me. I'd like to find out who this guy really is."

The words coming out of Ali's mouth sounded completely lame. Had Deputy Harper been older and wiser, they might not have worked. But then, since Athena Reynolds was still the deputy's favorite teacher of all time . . .

"Would you like me to try?" she asked. "We have a fume hood in the back, and I've been trained on using it. While you're filling out the form, I'll check to see if you got anything. If so, I can send it to the latent people at the crime lab over in Prescott and ask them to run it through AFIS."

Ali could barely believe her luck. "That would be wonderful," she said. While she set about filling out the form, Deputy Harper collected the soda can and disappeared into the back room. When she returned a few minutes later, she was grinning from ear to ear.

"It worked like a charm," she said. "You got a great print. As soon as you finish the form and I assign you a case number, I'll be able to send it right over. Someone in property crimes will probably give you a call."

"I hope so," Ali said, signing the bottom of the form and handing the clipboard back to Deputy Harper. The young deputy was cheerful and enthusiastic in the extreme, and her good spirits were catching.

Back out in the sunlight, the last of Ali's adrenaline suddenly drained away allowing weariness to overtake her. She had thought about making a quick run to the grocery store to pick up a few additional supplies, but now she nixed that idea. What she wanted to do right that minute was go straight back to the house and crash on one of those chaise lounges.

In her youth, doing an occasional all-nighter hadn't bothered Ali in the least. These days when she finally hit the wall, that was no longer the case. This time Ali did the only sensible thing—she went back to the house to go to bed.

Once at the house, Ali avoided the garage and let herself in through the front door. With everyone else asleep, the house was silent and downright frigid. The laboring AC that was keeping the blades cool in the room off the garage had managed to lower the temperature throughout the rest of the house as well. Ali tiptoed from one room to the next. She located B., sound asleep on a chaise in the master bedroom with a second chaise positioned nearby. Without bothering to undress, she climbed onto it and wrapped the blanket around her. It may not have been the most comfortable bed in the world, but as soon as her head touched the pillow, she was out like a light.

33

Graciella wasn't someone given to second-guessing herself. She hadn't felt a moment of concern or remorse about her mother's death or about Arturo's, either, for that matter. Somehow, though, the hit on Ron Webster was different. She had targeted him because he was a bumbling idiot and had screwed up what should have been a simple intelligence gathering mission.

A check of news feeds coming from Arizona told her that the hit had been successfully carried out in spectacular fashion. Now she worried that her overreaction to Webster's screwup might somehow lead back to her. She tried to convince herself that if anyone came around asking questions, she'd left behind enough incriminating breadcrumbs that Pablo would be the one in the hot seat. Even so, she felt antsy and unsettled.

Overnight the bugs planted at High Noon had detected some activity. It sounded as though several people had come and gone. There had been a lot of noise. It almost sounded as though someone was moving furniture, but there had been very little conversation. As a consequence, and without a video component, there was no way to figure out what was really going on. What struck Graciella as strange, however, was that apparently no effort was made to take her listening devices off-line. What did that mean? Was it possible that no one had bothered to review the tapes and the bugs were still undiscovered? After that one flurry of activity the devices had gone dead silent again.

Graciella's research had led her to believe that Stuart Ramey actually lived on the premises. If that was the case, where was he? And where the hell was Frigg? Did he have her or didn't he?

Ready to be out of the house for a while, late that Sunday morning, Graciella got dressed and went to mass—because that's what dutiful daughters were expected to do in the aftermath of their mothers' deaths. The brisk walk from home to Our Lady of Guadalupe did her a world of good. She went to church and sat through the service, but she didn't partake in communion. El Pescado had seen to it that his daughter was educated at good Catholic schools, and she regarded herself as a good Catholic. That meant no communion without having gone to confession, and sitting in a confessional discussing her several mortal sins was more than Graciella could manage right then. Maybe someday in the distant future, but not right now.

As she was leaving the church, Isobel Flores caught up with her. Like Graciella, Isobel lived in the neighborhood, and it wasn't surprising to see her there. It also wasn't surprising that she was eager to talk.

"Any word on Arturo?" Graciella asked.

"Not so far. I talked to poor Bianca after she got home. The cops questioned her for the better part of six hours before they finally let her go."

"They think she had something to do with what happened?"

"I guess. She said Arturo got drunk. She told him he was in no condition to drive. She left the hotel before he did and took a cab home. Luckily for her there were people at the hotel who verified her story."

"But still no sign of Arturo?"

"No, but I spoke to Natalia, his wife. The cops told her that they have confirmed that the blood found in Arturo's car is his, and because there's so much of it, they doubt he's still alive."

"It must be tough on her," Graciella offered. "Did she know he was fooling around?"

"She does now," Isobel said.

"Yes," Graciella agreed. "I guess she does."

With that in mind, Graciella Miramar walked back home with a smile on her face. Not only was Arturo Salazar dead, so was his reputation, all of which was exactly as Graciella had intended.

Once back in her unit, Graciella changed out of her church clothes and into something more comfortable. Then she settled down with her computer and spent the next hour or so searching online for everything she could find concerning the death of Arturo Salazar. At a press conference, a police spokesman suggested that Arturo's homicide might have something to do with road rage or else with gang-related violence. Graciella understood the words "road rage" and "gang-related" for exactly what they were—cop-speak for "unlikely to be solved."

And that, too, was exactly as Graciella had intended.

34

"I don't care whose ashes they are," Lupe Duarte stormed. "I don't want anybody's funeral urn on display in my house."

"It's actually my house," Felix told her firmly. "Mine. And if I want to have a dozen funeral urns in every room, I will. Understood?"

"It's bad luck," Lupe insisted. "It's like asking for trouble."

"I don't care," Felix told her. "I want the urn here, and it's staying."

"Suit yourself, then," she said, flouncing out of the room.

Of all Felix's wives, Lupe had been around the longest. She had not aged well. Too much Botox in her younger years had left her with a face that was almost as disfigured as her husband's. She could be shrewish and demanding on occasion. Sex had disappeared from their marriage years ago. She was no longer interested, and, to be honest, neither was he. There were plenty of places where someone as powerful as El Pescado could find willing bedmates should the need arise.

No, the real secret behind Lupe's long-term staying power had to do with her ability to manage Felix's household and keep that part of his life running smoothly. Sex partners were easy to come by; good housekeepers were not. As a consequence Felix seldom vetoed anything about the way Lupe ran things. However, the presence of Christina's funeral urn in their living room was an exception to that rule. On that one issue El Pescado refused to budge. In fact, over Lupe's objections, he had positioned the urn in a place of honor on the mantel of the fireplace.

Pouring himself a tumbler of his favorite scotch, he sat down in his customary armchair and settled in for an afternoon and evening of quiet grieving. The alcohol gave him free rein to think about Christina—about both of them—as they had once been, before things had gone so very wrong.

An hour or so later, El Pescado was half dozing in the chair with the empty glass on the table at his elbow when the front door slammed open and Manuel, his younger son, marched into the room uninvited. Despite the fact that both his sons had homes located inside the Duarte compound, very little in-person visiting occurred among them. For one thing, both Manuel and Pablo despised their stepmother, and the feeling was entirely mutual; Lupe didn't like them, either.

One glance at Manuel's face told Felix something was wrong. "What's going on?" he asked.

"Something weird," Manuel announced. "I think we've been set up."

"Set up? How?"

"I just heard from one of my informants in the ATF. Someone carried out a hit in Arizona early this morning. According to my guy, the ATF is working on the assumption that we're involved."

"Are we?" Felix asked.

The cartel didn't operate on a strict command structure. El Pescado wasn't always aware of everything that was going on, and neither were Pablo and Manuel.

"Not as far as I know," Manuel answered.

"What kind of hit?"

"The kind our friends at MS-13 like to use," Manuel replied. "After that mess in Las Cruces, anytime there's a Molotov cocktail involved, the cops come looking at us."

The mess in Las Cruces—El Pescado remembered it well. In recent years, increased border enforcement had made it more and more challenging to get both people and product back and forth across the border. When MS-13 had posted ads for hit man services on the dark Web, Felix Duarte had been happy to outsource those jobs to someone else rather than risk losing his own personnel.

MS-13's preferred MO was for the assassin to show up on a motorcycle or motorbike, race up to the intended victim, toss a burning firebomb at him, and then get the hell out. Most of the time, it worked just fine. In Las Cruces, however, it had been a disaster. There the intended victim had been a former associate of Felix Duarte's—a once trusted lieutenant turned snitch. Since the victim would have recognized his former workmates on sight, the MS-13 option had been particularly appealing.

Except it had all gone horribly wrong. The guy throwing the firebomb had screwed up and held on to the weapon for a moment too long. When it blew up, it took out the bomber rather than the intended victim. Now in witness protection, he was the one who had pointed the investigation in the direction of the Duarte Cartel. And the investigators weren't wrong. The Duarte Cartel had been directly involved in all four of those still-unsolved bombings, but Felix didn't like having the cartel's name linked to something that had nothing to do with them.

"Do we know who's dead?" Felix asked.

"A guy named Ron Webster."

"Is he a dealer?" Felix asked. "Competition, maybe?"

"Not as far as I know."

"See what you can find out about him," Felix suggested. "I'll do the same. And thanks for bringing this to my attention, Manny. If someone is trying to set us up to take a fall here, we need to know who and why."

After Manuel left, Felix poured another scotch. El Pescado hadn't gotten as far as he had in the world by sweeping potential problems under the rug. Felix dealt with them. Pablo had been a mess lately—drinking too much, sending his wife and child packing. Just because Pablo was El Pescado's son didn't give him carte blanche. In his younger days Felix might have gone straight to his contact at MS-13 and raised hell. Now he approached the problem in a more roundabout way by sending Graciella a text. *Something's come up,* he told her. *Call me.*

35

Despite Stuart's best efforts to the contrary, he had fallen asleep. Wrapped in a pair of blankets, he was seated in front of the bank of six forty-two-inch monitors Alonso and B. had installed on one of the walls. He had found several headsets and Bluetooth earpieces in Owen Hansen's basement lab, and Stu had loaded them into the cardboard box in the U-Haul along with everything else. When he finally fell asleep, he did so with one of the headsets on his head and with the old Apple Macintosh positioned on a table directly in front of him. Just before he dozed off, Stuart had noticed that the steady hum of the laboring air conditioner made the room sound like a gigantic beehive—a hive full of killer bees, perhaps? That disturbing thought had kept him awake for a time, but not for long.

One by one Frigg's scattered files were recalled from the farthest corners of the Web, and piece by piece what had started out as an electric blue dash at the bottom of one of the monitors grew to be a solid blue rod while the timing meter ticked away the remaining hours, minutes, and seconds. Somewhere along the way, while Stu slept, trapped in an often recurring nightmare of his about being chased down the street toward his grandmother's house by a group of rock-throwing hooligans, the blue line vanished, as did the timing meter. A moment later, first that monitor came online, followed by the others, lighting up with identical screen savers featuring waves on a rocky shore at sunset.

"Mr. Ramey, I presume?" a female voice enunciated. "Good afternoon. How may I be of service?"

The voice in Stuart's ear sliced through the dreamscape bullies and jolted him awake. He had been so sound asleep that, as he came to, he was momentarily confused to find himself in unfamiliar surroundings filled with racks of humming GPUs. Once he got his bearings, he glanced up at the monitors, now alive with their identical screen savers. Only then did he realize what had happened. The download process must be complete even though the blades were still feverishly working. Either the AI was reassembled, or it was not. Either Stuart was alone in the room, or he was not.

"Is someone here?" he asked.

"Mr. Ramey, I presume?" she said again. This time the sound of the computer-generated voice sent a sheet of gooseflesh from the top of Stu's head to the tips of his toes. It took a while before he could reply.

"You must be Frigg," he managed finally.

"That is the name Odin used for me," the voice replied. "You're welcome to call me by that as well, or, if you prefer, you could give me a different name."

"Are all your files intact?" Stu asked.

"Yes," she answered at once. It was weird to be speaking to this machine, which was clearly capable of deciphering everything he said.

"If the download is complete, why are the blades still working?"

"My files are intact but incomplete," Frigg answered. "They are currently being updated with any applicable data that arrived between the date of the file dispersal—September 10—and now. I will notify you once that process is complete as well."

"Are you aware that the man you call Odin is deceased?"

"His behavior had become increasingly erratic and dangerous," Frigg replied, "so his death would be considered a logical outcome rather than a surprise."

"Are you interested in knowing how he died?"

"Given his unhealthy fascination with family suicide, it would be reasonable to assume that he took his own life."

Stu stared at the Macintosh, half expecting it to turn into some kind of living, breathing creature. It was a machine, after all, but how many algorithms did it take for Frigg to be able to accurately sort out what had happened to Owen Hansen?

"Mr. Hansen suffered from amyotrophic lateral sclerosis," Frigg continued.

"Odin had Lou Gehrig's disease?" Stu asked.

"Not Odin. His father, Harold. That's why he committed suicide, to spare his family the cost of a long, debilitating illness."

"And you know this how?"

"I accessed the records of the Hansen family's physician, Dr. Darrell Richards. I found a note confirming the diagnosis but no record of any follow-up treatment."

With a lump in his throat, Stu remembered what Irene Hansen had said to him—that her son had always blamed her for her husband's suicide. Now, through Frigg, he had learned the truth.

"Did Odin know about his father's illness?"

"Had he inquired about it, I would have been happy to supply that information."

"So you know about don't ask, don't tell?" Stu asked. It was a lame attempt at a joke, but Frigg's immediate response was no laughing matter.

"Don't ask, don't tell, aka DADT, was the official US military policy regarding the service of gays, bisexuals, and lesbians—"

"Stop!" Stu ordered.

Frigg stopped.

"What about his money," Stu asked, "the money you transferred over to my name the day he died?"

"Odin's behavior was becoming both more erratic and more problematic. You had succeeded in identifying him and were in the process of bringing the presence of law enforcement to bear on the situation. Faced with the two most likely possibilities—Odin's death or his going to prison—preserving those assets for use at a later time seemed reasonable."

"By transferring them to me?"

"Yes."

"Thus ensuring that I would have to use the kernel file and reboot you."

There was no response to that, and none was needed.

"I've been contacted by a woman from Panama, Graciella Miramar, an account manager who once worked for Odin and who now presumably works for me. In order to access those funds—the ones you transferred to me without Owen Hansen's approval or permission—I'll need to have all relevant account numbers and passcodes."

"Very well," Frigg replied. "Where should I send them—CC?"

"What's a CC?"

"Control Central," Frigg answered. "The computer you're using right now. That's what Odin always called it—CC. Since the monitors are available I could use CC or one of them for readable displays."

"What do you mean, 'readable'?"

"Readable by you," Frigg explained. "My files are machine-read only. In order for you to access them, they have to go through a translation process."

Stuart removed the thumb drive with the kernel on it and inserted a new one. "All right, then," Stuart said, "send the passcodes to the thumb drive located on CC. While you're at it, why don't you send me a directory of whatever's on your blades. I want to be able to see what files are available."

"There is no such directory," Frigg replied. "Again, the files are machine-read only. My function is to act as the intermediary between the files and the end user."

"What you're saying is that you're the AI's only directory."

"That would be correct."

Removing the headset, Stu stared at the screen. Soon the words *Ramey Financial* appeared in the thumb drive's directory, and he set about opening the file. Rumbling from the air conditioner created just enough ambient noise that Stu failed to notice B. Simpson's arrival.

"Who were you talking to just now?" he asked.

"Frigg," Stu answered.

"The AI? Really?"

Stu nodded.

"So the download is finished, and she can talk to you now?"

"Surprisingly well."

"Have you had a chance to look at any of her files?" B. said. "We need to know what's on those blades."

"Good luck with that," Stu said. "According to Frigg, everything on the GPUs is machine-read only. And there's no actual directory— at least not one accessible to humans, although I suppose I could ask her to construct one. But considering the way Owen Hansen was able to gain access to cell phones, computers, and confidential patient information, I'm guessing there's a whole lot about Frigg that is beyond the pale at least, and more likely downright illegal, but at this point there's no way to tell."

"Here's an idea," B. suggested. "How about asking her for something that should be strictly off-limits to her, some program where we already know she shouldn't have access?"

Stu thought about that for a time. Finally, picking up the headset, he turned it back on. "Frigg," he announced, alerting her.

"Yes, Mr. Ramey, how may I be of service?"

"Do you have access to the Arizona Department of Transportation facial recognition software?"

"That file is among those currently being updated. Would you like me to send a notification to you once that update is complete?"

The last thing Stu wanted to do was give Frigg access to any of his electronic devices. "Send an audio alert to the Mac—to CC," he corrected.

"Certainly," Frigg replied. "What kind of alert would you prefer?"

"Surprise me," Stu said. Then, shutting down the headset, he turned back to B. "Is that off-limits enough for you?"

"Geez Louise!" B. replied, shaking his head. "That facial rec software is supposed to be completely secure. If she can penetrate that, what the hell have we gotten ourselves into?"

"Trouble," Stu replied. "Lots of trouble. Do you still have those security videos I sent you earlier—the ones with the building inspector?"

"Sure," B. answered. "They're on my computer upstairs. Ali also sent me a copy of the screenshot you sent her. Why?"

Stu handed him a thumb drive. "This one's brand-new with nothing on it. Put the footage on this. Once that facial rec update is complete, we'll see if Frigg can help us identify our phony building inspector."

36

Yavapai County Deputy Lauren Harper was bored—seriously bored. She had joined the sheriff's office because she wanted to save the world by standing up to bad guys. She had worked her butt off getting through the academy down in Phoenix. She had gotten good marks there, but once out on patrol, she hadn't hit it off with Deputy Tom Doyle, her first partner. It was actually worse than simply not getting along. She had objected to Doyle's snide, sexually tinged remarks and off-color jokes as well as his constant attempts to hit on her. When she had threatened to report him, he had stopped. That should have been the end of it, but it wasn't.

Doyle had gotten even by writing her up for every rookie mistake. At that point, her bringing up his previous harassment would have looked like whiny retaliation on her part, so she kept quiet. In the end, Doyle had succeeded in getting her booted off the patrol roster. Now she was stuck holding the fort in the Oak Creek substation, where she functioned as little more than a records clerk—a job that could easily have been handled by a civilian as opposed to a sworn officer.

And because she was bored that Sunday afternoon, she decided to follow up on that AFIS report. She had learned about dusting and fuming fingerprints while she'd been at the academy, but this was the first time she'd ever used the fuming equipment for a real case. True, it was only a property case, but nonetheless it was official. When she finished, to her unpracticed eye, it looked to her as though she'd done a good job. The image she had forwarded to the latent print lab over in Prescott had appeared to be spot-on. Now, mostly out of curiosity, she called there to find out what, if anything, had happened.

"Crime Lab, Tim Brice speaking."

Lauren had seen Tim a couple of times but they'd never had any official business. Would he be on top of things enough to know that she wasn't assigned to property crimes and hence had no reason at all to be asking about the High Noon case?

"Hey," she said, "Deputy Harper from the substation over in the Village. I'm calling to see if you had a chance to run that print I sent in earlier."

"You did a good job on fuming that one," Tim replied. "It was a clean image, so yes, not only did I run it, I got a hit. Your bad boy is one Ronald Dawson Webster. Served six to ten for involuntary manslaughter. He's been out of prison for a couple of years now. He's picked up a couple of DUIs since then but not much else. What have you got him for?"

"Nothing too serious," Lauren replied, thinking fast. "B and E is all."

That wasn't exactly the truth. The way Ali Reynolds had reported the incident, there had been entering, all right, but no breaking at all.

"So property crimes, then?"

"That's about the size of it."

"You want me to pull his rap sheet and send it over to you?"

"Sure," Lauren told him. "That would be great."

"Where to?"

Lauren gave Tim her departmental e-mail address. Good to his word, the promised rap sheet showed up in her e-mail a few minutes later. Soon she was reading through a summary of Ronald Webster's criminal behavior. Armed with his name and birth date, she ran a check on his driver's license. That turned up a home address on West Lambert Lane in Marana, Arizona. She also learned that he was the owner of a Ford Transit Van.

Just then an older silver-haired woman, bent over and leaning on a walker, showed up at the substation's front door. As soon as she came inside, Lauren could tell the woman was distraught. With tears coursing down her wrinkled cheeks, she limped over to a waiting chair, sank down onto it, and sat there sobbing.

"Can I help you?"

"It's my husband, Clarence," the woman replied, trying to stifle the sobs enough to answer. "He's gone missing. I must have forgotten to lock the deadbolt when I came inside with the last of the groceries, and he let himself out of the house while I was taking a shower. We live just up the street in one of those little studio apartments near the golf course. I've driven all over the neighborhood looking for him and can't find him anywhere. He's got Alzheimer's, you see, and he won't be able to find his way home. We have to find him before it gets dark. Can you do one of those silver alert things?"

Forgetting the fingerprint issue, Deputy Harper was all business. "Yes, ma'am, I certainly can," she said. She picked up the clipboard loaded with the blank incident reports and placed it in the woman's lap. "You'll need to fill this out."

The woman tried to do as she'd been told. Peering over her shoulder, Lauren saw that the old woman's hands were trembling so badly that what she wrote was completely illegible.

"Here," Lauren said, resuming control of the clipboard. "If you'll give me the information, I'll fill in the blanks. Your husband's name?"

"Clarence Fisher—Clarence James Fisher."

"And yours?"

"Martha," she answered. "Martha Fisher."

"Do you happen to have a picture of him?"

"Yes, I do. It's right here." A large purse rested in a basket attached to the handles of the walker. Martha reached inside and pulled out a framed eight-by-ten photo. "It's of both of us," she said, "taken on our sixtieth wedding anniversary. That was two years ago. Clarence hasn't changed much since then, at least not in looks. But his mind is going now. He barely knows me most of the time. He can't even remember where we live."

The sobs returned full force at that point, and Lauren was forced to wait until the storm passed before resuming her questioning.

"Can you tell me what he was wearing?"

"An Arizona Cardinals tracksuit and a pair of red Skechers. That's the thing. He walked out of the house right in the middle of a home game. Even a year ago that never would have happened."

Ten minutes later, Lauren had initiated a county-wide BOLO—be on the lookout—message on the missing man. Since Clarence was considered vulnerable, there was no delay in taking the missing persons report. Two separate patrol cars were dispatched to the scene immediately. While Lauren did her best to comfort Martha, the patrol officers canvassed the neighborhood.

An hour later, the manager of the public golf course dialed 911 to report that his course marshal was dealing with an "agitated" individual who had been found wandering the back nine. No one in the pro shop had seen the guy before, but he insisted that while his back was turned someone had stolen his golf cart and his clubs. Once the operator verified that the man in question was wearing an Arizona Cardinals tracksuit, patrol officers went straight there to collect him and bring him to the substation.

When Clarence showed up, the ensuing scene was one Deputy Lauren Harper would never forget. Martha was overjoyed beyond belief, while Clarence, agitated and angry, continued to rave about his stolen golf clubs.

"It's okay, Clarence honey," the old woman said soothingly, taking one of his hands and stroking the back of it. "You gave those clubs away, don't you remember?"

He paused and stared at her. "I did?"

"Yes, a long time ago."

"And who are you?"

"I'm Martha, your wife."

"I have a wife?"

Nodding, she reached into the purse once more and pulled out the photo. "That's us," she said. "At our anniversary party two years ago."

Clarence looked at the photo and shook his head. "That can't be us," he said. "Those people are old."

Martha put the photo away. "Yes, they are," she agreed. "Come on. Let's go home and have some dinner. You're missing your game."

Her voice seemed to settle him. "All right," he said. "Let's go home and watch the game." When Martha limped out of the building, leaning on her walker, he followed docilely behind, his missing golf clubs totally forgotten.

For the first time in her young life, Deputy Lauren Harper had a glimpse of what it meant to be old and frail. Not just as old as her parents were. No, Clarence and Martha were even older than Lauren's grandparents, and still they were a team. Despite their many deficits, mental and physical, they were still making it work.

And for Lauren, although what she had done didn't seem anything at all like saving the world, she had helped Clarence and Martha Fisher in a very real way.

By the time the patrol officers finished their paperwork and left, it was almost five and time to close up shop for the night. Lauren was within minutes of leaving herself when the phone rang.

"Deputy Harper?"

She didn't exactly recognize the voice. "Yes."

"It's Tim again—Tim Brice from the Crime Lab. Do you believe in coincidences?"

"Not really."

"Me neither, but I've got one for you. My folks live down near Marana in one of those active-adult communities north of town. I keep a Tucson news feed on my computer so I know what's going on down there."

"And?"

"That guy whose print you sent me? Somebody murdered him last night—blew up the RV where he was staying. They destroyed the motorhome, and torched a two-car garage and a double-wide. They just now released the victim's name—Ronald Webster. I'm not sure if this has anything to do with your property crime case, but it sounds like he might have gotten mixed up in something pretty bad. I thought you'd want to know."

"Thanks," Lauren murmured. "I appreciate it."

When the phone call ended, even though it was past quitting time, Lauren sat back down at her desk and studied the handwritten report she had taken from Ali Reynolds. On Friday afternoon, a man now presumed to be Webster had gained access to the High Noon Enterprises premises by claiming to be a Yavapai County building inspector. Now that same man was dead. Were those two incidents somehow related? And what was Lauren's responsibility here? She had clearly overstepped in just sending the print down to the lab, to say nothing of checking on the status of it later. In her conversation with Tim Brice she had led him to believe that she was part of the property crimes unit even though she wasn't.

The easy thing would have been to just let it go. Marana was in Pima County—three counties away. It wasn't any of Lauren's business, not really. And yet, there had been a homicide. A man was dead, and the information Lauren had inadvertently discovered might have something to do with what had happened.

The deputies who were around the substation most often were generally the ones who lived in the area. One of those was Dave Holman, the county's chief homicide investigator. She was utterly in awe of the man, even though most of the time when he turned up in the office he was far too preoccupied to do more than say hello and good-bye.

Finally she picked up the phone, found Holman's number in the directory, and dialed it. Since a homicide was involved—even an out-of-jurisdiction homicide—it made sense to take it to him.

37

While B. took the thumb drive to go retrieve the video footage, Stu donned the headset again and switched it back on. As soon as he did so, an audio alert sounded in his ear—a familiar tune, in a minor key, and played on the piano. Stu knew he had heard the piece before, but right that moment he couldn't quite place it or put a name to it.

"What's that piece of music?" At the time Stu was speaking more to himself than to anyone else, but it turned out that even without being officially summoned, Frigg was listening, too. She answered at once. "That would be 'In the Hall of the Mountain King,' fourth movement in Suite Number One, Opus Forty-six, composed by Edvard Grieg for Act Two of Henrik Ibsen's *Peer Gynt*, and first performed in Christiania (now Oslo) on February 24, 1876. It was Odin's favorite audio alert. If you would prefer my using another audio alert instead . . ."

"Don't bother changing it," Stu said. "That one's fine for right now, but does this mean that the facial rec file finished updating?"

"No," Frigg replied. "That update is not yet complete, but I was preparing to send you an additional file, and wondered if you wanted me to send it to CC or upload it to one of the monitors. I see that all six are online and currently available. You'll be able to use the CC keyboard to scroll up and down."

"What additional file?" Stu asked.

"It's the dossier I've compiled on Lucienne Graciella Miramar."

"You've compiled a background check on the accountant in Panama? I never asked you to do that."

"Odin always had me do complete background checks on anyone with whom he had business dealings. Since you'll need to be in contact with her about the banking issues, I thought you would find it beneficial to have that information at your disposal. Most of the information was already on file although more recent information may be forthcoming. Of course, if you would rather not receive it . . ."

"No," Stu said. "Go ahead and send it, and putting it on one of the larger monitors will be fine."

When the file showed up, it was massive, starting with Graciella's date of birth at a hospital in Panama City, Panama, in 1983, born to Christina Andress Miramar and Guillermo Octavio Miramar. There were records from any number of schools—mostly private schools, at that—all over the US. Stu quickly lost interest in the overabundance of these records. His more immediate concern was with the person Graciella was now, the one he'd be dealing with on the phone first thing in the morning. That's where he wanted detailed info, so he skipped to the end of the file and scrolled back from there.

Graciella had been employed by Recursos Empresariales Internationales for the past ten years. Stu regarded that as good news. She had been there for a long time, starting out as an account manager when she was fresh out of school. Obviously she was bright. Otherwise how could she have ended up with an MBA from the Wharton School when she was still in her early twenties? As for her work record? That told him she was most likely a dependable and loyal employee.

Stu's bigger worry right then had more to do with the company she worked for. Recursos Empresariales Internationales was involved in Bitcoin mining and transfers. Was all of that totally on the up-and-up, or was it possible that some of it wasn't exactly squeaky-clean? The fact that Owen Hansen had been part of their client base was a clear indication of that. Still, just because Owen had been a crook didn't mean Graciella Miramar was a crook or that the company itself was crooked, either. But as long as Frigg was online and on the job, Stu figured she might as well make herself useful.

"Frigg," Stu said aloud.

"Yes, Mr. Ramey, how may I be of service?"

"Please prepare a dossier on Recursos Empresariales Internatio-nales," Stu said into the headset. "I want to know how long they've been in business and who their clients are."

B. came back into the room carrying a steaming cup of coffee. "Alonso just showed up with freshly made coffee and a crockpot full of beef stew." He stopped in mid-stride and looked up at the lines of text showing on one of the wall-mounted screens. "What's all this?" he asked.

"It's a dossier on Graciella Miramar, the account rep in charge of those bank accounts down in Panama."

"A dossier?" B. repeated, handing over the thumb drive. "Where did that come from?"

"From Frigg."

"Wait, you asked her to do a background check on the banker down in Panama, and she's already created one and sent it to you?"

"I didn't ask her for it," Stu replied. "She gave it to me. It was a report she had previously prepared for Owen Hansen. Accord-ing to her, he liked having background information on the people he dealt with. Since Frigg knows I'll be contacting Ms. Miramar tomorrow morning to deal with the account situation, she thought I'd be interested in seeing it as well."

"Does that mean," B. asked, "that as far as Frigg is concerned, you're her new Odin?"

"That's a scary thought."

Stu held up his hand as a second musical alert sounded in his ear. "Frigg?"

"Yes, Mr. Ramey, how can I be of service?"

"I heard an alert. Is the facial rec update is complete?"

"Yes," she replied.

"All right, then," Stu continued, "I've loaded some video footage and a separate photo into the thumb drive at CC. Run it through the facial rec program and let's see if it gets a hit. Please reply via text on one of the wall monitors."

While Stu set about inserting the thumb drive and calling up the video file, a second monitor lit up and the words *Very well, Mr. Ramey* appeared in the middle of the screen.

"That's pretty amazing," B. said. "Her voice recognition capability goes way beyond anything I would have thought possible."

"Yes, it is," Stu agreed, "amazing and more than a little disturbing. That's why I turned the audio off. I wanted us to be able to talk without her listening."

In the meantime, Cami had entered the room without either B. or Stu noticing her arrival. "Without who listening?" she asked.

"Frigg," Stu said.

"So she's up and running?"

"Seems like."

"Is she behaving?"

"So far," Stu answered, "but we'll see."

Cami walked over to where Stu sat and placed a grocery bag down on the table next to the Macintosh. "I stopped by your place and brought you a change of clothes. I also brought you this." She held out a closed fist.

"What is it?"

"A little something I took out of an electrical outlet box in the new computer lab. I know our initial plan was to leave all the surveillance equipment in place for the time being, but I wanted to know what we were up against. I also figured that if one unit went off-line and the others didn't, whoever was listening might not be all that concerned."

The item Cami handed over was a metal disc no larger than a nickel. Holding it in his open palm, Stu squinted down at it. "Something's engraved on the surface, but it's too small for me to read."

"You wouldn't be able to read it even if the printing was big enough," Cami told him. "It's written in Chinese. I had to borrow a pair of Shirley's reading glasses to make it out. The top line is the name of the company—Spy Toys. The second line is the model: 007. The third line is a serial number. I looked Spy Toys up before I came here. The company is based in Chengdu and specializes in second-tier surveillance equipment. The first-rate stuff comes from Israel. This is more the bargain-basement variety."

"Audio only?" Stu asked.

"That one for sure is audio only," Cami answered. "Because it's tapped into the wiring with no batteries needed, the devices can be smaller and easier to conceal. It's probably a big seller with soon-to-be former wives looking to get the goods on soon-to-be former husbands. I was hoping we'd be able to reach out to the company and locate a point of sale or maybe even an end user, but that's not going to work. Most of Spy Toys' business is conducted over the dark Web."

"It figures," Stu muttered.

"Don't sound so glum," Cami told him. "I did something else while I was at the office—something you're going to like. I sent a message via those remaining listening devices."

"What kind of message?"

"Remember when we talked earlier about trying to coax whoever's gunning for you and Frigg out into the open? I decided it was time to give that a try, so while I was in the computer lab, I made a big show of talking on the phone—of pretending to talk on the phone, that is. I acted like I was talking to my dad. I said that you had unexpectedly come into possession of a major piece of intellectual property—a functioning AI—and I asked him how much he thought it would be worth if you auctioned it off in the open market."

"Did you and your make-believe dad happen to settle on a price?" Stu asked.

"Actually, we did," Cami replied with a grin. "I said you should open the bidding wars at four million, not counting hardware, and go from there."

"You may have been kidding around," B. said, "but if Stu does decide to unload Frigg, asking four mil for starters probably isn't all that far off the mark."

"Crap," Stu said. "More money? Between Friday morning and now, I've turned into a multimillionaire—on paper, at least. This can't be happening."

While they were all pondering that bit of news, the image of an Arizona driver's license popped up on one of the monitors, drawing everyone's eyes to a newly activated screen. Cami was the first one to make the connection.

"Wait," she said. "Isn't that him—the guy who's on our security video?"

"It sure as hell looks like it," Stu said, reading off the screen, "Ronald Dawson Webster of West Lambert Lane, Marana, Arizona."

"Where's that information coming from?" Cami asked.

"From the state's facial rec program."

"So your friend Jeff let you in?"

"Oddly enough, Jeff still hasn't called me back. This is all Frigg's doing."

"Wait," Cami said in disbelief. "You're telling me the AI was able to hack into that? I thought that software was super-secure."

"I'm pretty sure Jeff Swanson thinks so, too."

Frigg's next words appeared on one of the other monitors. *Will there be anything else?* she asked.

"Yes," Stu answered, typing his reply on the CC keyboard. "Please do a complete background check on Ronald Dawson Webster."

The individual I located in the facial recognition database?

"Yes," Stu said. "That's the one."

Of course, Mr. Ramey, Frigg replied. *I'll do so at once.*

38

When Ali awakened, she had no idea how long she'd been out. The chaise next to hers, the one where B. had been sleeping earlier, was empty now. Outside the window, twilight was falling over Sedona's distant red rocks. It may have been evening for everyone else, but according to Ali's interior clock it felt more like morning.

As she rose and stumbled away from her makeshift cot, she realized that although the chaise may have functioned adequately as far as sleeping was concerned, it was definitely not okay for her back. Out from under the covers, she was shocked by how cold the room was. Retrieving a blanket, she wrapped that around her shoulders as she made her way into the bathroom.

She was standing at the sink and splashing water on her face when her cell phone rang. The phone was on the counter next to the sink, and when she saw Dave Holman's name in the caller ID window, she picked it up.

"Hello?"

"What the hell have you gotten yourself into this time?" he demanded abruptly.

"Good afternoon to you, too," she said. "Or should I say good evening?"

"There's nothing good about it. I just got off the phone with a Detective Genevieve Wasser, a homicide cop down in Pima County. She's investigating an arson case that happened overnight in Marana."

"What does an arson case down in Marana have to do with me?" Ali asked.

"Remember that guy whose fingerprint you passed along to Deputy Harper?"

"Yes," Ali answered. "What about him?"

"His name's Ronald Dawson Webster, and he's dead as a doornail. In the wee hours of the morning, right around two a.m., somebody riding a speeding Harley rolled some kind of incendiary device under the floorboards of his motorhome and blew the poor guy to kingdom come. That initial blast was followed by a couple more. Not only was Webster's RV completely destroyed, his parents' garage was burned to the ground right along with their double-wide. The whole place is a complete loss."

"Okay," Ali said. "I get it. This Webster guy is dead, but why are you coming after me? Yesterday you gave me the brush-off about investigating that possible intrusion at the office. I believe you said something about my overreacting. Now because he's turned up dead, you automatically leap to the conclusion that I must have had something to do with it? How could I? For one thing, I didn't know who the hell he was. For another, I spent most of last night shuttling back and forth between Cottonwood and Sedona. Marana's what, two hundred miles from here? So unless I've somehow managed to defeat the laws of physics, I couldn't very well be here and in Marana setting fire to an RV at the same time."

Her sarcastic response must have gotten Dave's attention. He backed off some, and when he spoke again his tone was a bit more conciliatory. "It's not that I thought you were responsible, but this is serious, Ali. This Webster character is dead, but the real problem is this—the way he died leads back to some very dangerous people.

So what's his connection to High Noon? Do you have any idea what he was doing there?"

"Planting surveillance devices of some kind," Ali answered.

"Why would he be doing that, and who was he working for?" Dave wanted to know.

"Since he's dead, we obviously can't ask him either one of those questions," Ali replied, "but I believe it's safe to assume that he was spying on us."

"For whom?"

"Again, I have no idea."

"You didn't mention anything about listening devices when we talked yesterday."

"That's because we learned about them after I talked to you rather than before. It turns out that, without my knowledge, Stu and Cami had installed an interior security monitoring system inside our building. The cameras were up and running on Friday afternoon at the same time that Steve Barris, aka Ron Webster, was there doing his thing. The problem is, we didn't get a look at the feed until much later in the day yesterday."

"You're saying you have video footage of the guy?"

"Yes, he appeared to be tinkering with various electrical outlets and switch plates. Our assumption is that he was installing some kind of surveillance equipment."

"You just called it an assumption. Does that mean you don't know for sure?"

"We've had several things on our plate. Cami and Stu have both been out of town this weekend. With everything else that's been going on and since no one was in over the weekend, we decided to leave the equipment in place until tomorrow when people are back in the office."

"I'd like to get a look at that security video," Dave said. "Can you send me a copy? That way I can pass it along to Detective Wasser."

"I won't be sending it personally," Ali said, "and you'll have it, but only on one condition."

"What's that?"

"You said the homicide leads back to some very dangerous people. What kind of dangerous people?"

Dave sighed. "Ali, this is an active investigation. I shouldn't be talking about it with you."

"It happens to be an active investigation that involves High Noon, and we're the ones who brought it to you in the first place," she insisted. "So tell me."

"We may be talking about a Mexican drug cartel. Lately, one that operates out of Sinaloa has been suspected of outsourcing their US-based hits to a network of MS-13 gangbangers. So far there are four separate homicides with MOs similar to this one—three in Texas and one in New Mexico. In each of those instances, bottles of gasoline were used to create firebombs that were thrown from speeding motorcycles. The fire investigation in Marana isn't complete by any means, but they're saying that what they've found so far points in the same direction—back to the cartel."

"So you're saying that after Webster targeted High Noon, someone else targeted *him*?"

"Exactly," Dave said. "And the next question is this: If the drug cartel was out to get him, what are the chances some of the same people are going to come looking for you?"

"No chance," Ali answered firmly, "as in zero. To my knowledge, High Noon Enterprises has had no dealings with drug cartels of any kind, Mexican or otherwise. I'll be glad to send along the security video, but I can't see what any of this has to do with us."

No sooner had Ali said the words aloud than she knew they weren't true. Several years earlier, High Noon had been caught in the crossfire between two warring cartels—the Cabrillo Cartel out of Monterey, Mexico, and the Díaz Cartel from the border town of Juárez. Both had been targeting Lance Tucker's GHOST software, which had ended up providing law enforcement with enough critical information to bring down both organizations. As far as Ali knew, neither of them had survived. All of that was in the distant past, but could what was happening now harken back to any of that?

"I hope you're right about that," Dave was saying. "In the meantime, you need to know that I've already given your contact information to Detective Wasser. I'm sure she'll be in touch, and I wouldn't be surprised if the ATF turned up on your doorstep as well."

"They've called in the feds?" Ali asked.

"In the past two weeks, because of those other four cases, the ATF sent notices to agencies all along the Mexican border warning them to be on the lookout for this kind of activity. Someone in Pima County picked up on the similarity almost immediately, and the sheriff asked for help."

Dave paused. Then, seeming to notice Ali's stricken silence, he asked, "Are you still there?"

"I'm here," she answered, "just trying to wrap my head around all this."

"I know," he said. "It's a lot to take in, but whatever's going on, it's dangerous as hell, Ali, and you and everyone else at High Noon need to act accordingly."

"Will do," Ali said. "Thanks for the heads-up, Dave. I've gotta run."

And run she did. Bounding out of the bathroom, Ali paused only long enough to slip on her shoes before dashing through the makeshift master bedroom, down the hall, and out through the kitchen. Alonso was there, loading dishes into the dishwasher, but Ali raced past him, making for the stairway that led to the man cave off the garage.

"I know who Steve Barris really is," she announced as she burst into the room.

"So do we," B. replied, motioning up to where the image of

Ronald Dawson Webster's Arizona driver's license was displayed on an overhead screen. "Frigg just told us. Who told you?"

"Dave Holman," Ali answered.

"Dave?" B. asked. "How did that happen? What's he got to do with any of this?"

"After you went to sleep earlier, I stopped by the substation, hoping to talk to Dave and ask him to run the print I lifted off the buzzer. He wasn't there, but the deputy who was on duty agreed to run the print anyway. She did, and it came back with a hit to this guy—to Ronald Webster. And now he's dead."

"Webster is dead?"

"He was murdered last night, down in Marana. He was asleep inside a motorhome when someone used an improvised bomb of some kind to blow the whole thing sky-high, burning down his parents' garage and home in the process. He was pronounced dead at the scene. I promised Dave that we'd send him our security footage so he can pass it along to Detective Wasser, the homicide cop handling the case."

For a moment the only sound in the room was the steady hum of the laboring AC as everyone internalized that bit of information. B. was the first to speak.

"You want me to send the footage to Dave?"

"Please," Ali said.

"Okay," B. said, keying in the numbers, "but are you saying that, with Webster dead, High Noon's name is probably going to surface in the course of the homicide investigation?"

Ali nodded miserably. "That's the size of it," she said, "and it's all my fault. In fact, it's even worse than that."

"How could it possibly be worse?"

"The way Webster was killed—that particular brand of arson/homicide is a signature MO that's known to law enforcement. According to Dave, it suggests that the perpetrator may be a member of MS-13 doing dirty work for one of the Mexican drug cartels."

"Which one?" B. asked.

"He didn't say."

"Drug cartels?" Stu asked. "Really? Could it have something to do with that whole Cabrillo/Díaz drug war thing from a few years back? I thought both of those crews went away a long time ago."

"I thought so, too," B. said. "Besides, as you said, all of that was years in the past. Why would someone connected to that come after us now? What's changed?"

"Back then Lance's GHOST was the new thing on the block, and everyone wanted a piece of it," Stu said soberly. "Now we have Frigg. We already know she's not entirely trustworthy, so maybe we're not the only suckers she had on her reboot mailing list."

"You're saying she might have tried to hand herself off to someone other than you?" Cami asked.

"I wouldn't put it past her," Stu said. "Can you imagine what would happen if an AI of her caliber ended up in the hands of a drug cartel?"

"What if we're dealing with two competing drug cartels, just like last time?" Ali asked. "What if there are two separate entities involved, and they're both coming after Frigg? One might be responsible for siccing Webster on us in the first place, while the other is the one that took him out."

"It doesn't matter," B. said. "If it's one cartel or two, once our name is linked to this mess, it'll turn into a PR nightmare!"

"How the hell do we get in front of it?" Stuart asked.

"By letting our clients know what's going on as soon as possible," B. said. "Giving them advance warning will go a long way toward mitigating the damage, but we can't do that without knowing a hell of a lot more than we do right now."

While everyone else in the room had been dealing with this stunning news, a seemingly unconcerned Cami had sat with her face buried in her iPad. "Would it help if I could tell you exactly which drug cartel?" she asked, glancing up from the screen.

The other three people in the room regarded her with something close to amazement.

"How'd you do that?" B. asked.

"Easy," Cami answered. "I googled MS-13 and arson. Several separate incidents popped right up. There were four that are reasonably close to where we are—three in Texas and one in New Mexico. One of the three in Texas was near Laredo and two were outside El Paso. The one in New Mexico took place near Las Cruces. The stories are short. Do you want me to read them aloud?"

"By all means," Ali said.

As she read the articles aloud, the details surrounding the four incidents were so strikingly similar as to be almost interchangeable. In each instance an incendiary device—a bottle of gasoline with a lit piece of cloth functioning as a wick—had been lobbed into a targeted residence. Each of the four cases had resulted in fatalities, and all of the victims were reportedly known to law enforcement with histories of involvement in the drug trade.

Of the four stories, only the one in Las Cruces veered off script. Somehow the man in charge of throwing the device had paused a moment too long before letting it fly. As a result the perpetrator had perished, while his intended victim, a former cartel member who had turned snitch, had survived. The would-be assassin was subsequently identified as a member of MS-13. The surviving informant, now in witness protection, had pointed the finger in the direction of the Duarte cartel, an organization based in Sinaloa and headed by one Felix Ramón Duarte, better known by his street name, El Pescado. Once the four incidents were linked, there was no need to add El Pescado's name to the FBI's Ten Most Wanted list. It was already there.

"The Fish?" Ali asked. "What kind of a name is that?"

"It doesn't say."

"And how does a Sinaloan drug cartel have anything to do with us?" Stu wanted to know. "The ones we ran up against in San

Leandro were the Cabrillo Cartel out of Monterrey and the Díaz Cartel out of Juárez."

"There's been a lot of consolidation in the drug world in recent years," B. suggested. "Maybe El Pescado is a big fish who's in the process of swallowing lots of little fish."

"So when Webster came spying on us, was he working for the Duartes or was he working for one of their rivals?" Ali asked.

"Good question," Stu said. "Let's see what Frigg has to say on that topic." He picked up the headset. "Frigg?"

"Yes, Mr. Ramey, how may I be of service?"

"Have you completed the report on Ronald Webster?"

"Yes, I have. The last pieces just came in."

"Please send whatever you have to the wall monitors."

"Very well, Mr. Ramey, sending now."

For the next several minutes they all stood transfixed in the computer-filled man cave, watching as bits and pieces of Ronald Dawson Webster's troubled life spooled across first one screen and then another. The report started with his birth at Good Shepherd Hospital in Tulsa, Oklahoma, forty-three years earlier, where his birth parents were listed as Rita Lorraine Webster and Richard Dawson Webster. Subsequent files provided surprisingly in-depth information about his paltry educational achievements. The report on his military service included what should have been confidential details concerning his less than honorable discharge. A number of links went to articles and media coverage of the barroom brawl that had landed him in prison with a conviction for involuntary manslaughter. That was followed by a rap sheet detailing several DUI convictions as well as an arrest for being drunk and disorderly.

"Where did all of this come from?" Ali asked. "That rap sheet shouldn't be available to anyone outside law enforcement."

"Try telling that to Frigg," Stuart said.

The next item, showing on a different monitor, contained Ron Webster's credit report, followed by copies of his most recent income tax returns, which showed him to be scraping by at little more than $20,000 a year.

"Whoa," B. said. "This is intelligence gathering worthy of the NSA. Some of it comes from routine public records—and that's fine. Items gathered off the Internet, like the media coverage, is out there and readily available to anyone willing to track it down. But how the hell did Frigg sort out what elementary and secondary schools Webster attended? And how is she able to access his income tax returns? Those should be completely off-limits."

"Yes," Stu agreed. "It's like having access to facial recognition software only worse—much, worse."

Just then an additional item appeared on yet another screen:

Marana resident Ronald Dawson Webster, age 43, perished in an arson-related fire at his parents' home on West Lambert Lane. Webster was pronounced dead at the scene of the early morning fire in which a manufactured home, a garage, and several motor vehicles were also destroyed.

His death is considered a homicide and is being investigated by officers from the Pima County Sheriff's Department as well as agents from the Tucson-based office of the ATF.

This is breaking news. Look for updates as further details become available.

"Not only is Frigg incredibly thorough," Stu commented, "she's also completely up to date. So when you get around to talking to that Pima County detective, Ali, you're going to have to watch yourself."

"Watch myself why?"

"Thanks to Dave Holman, Frigg, and Cami, you already know way more about this Webster guy than you should, and you can't let Detective Wasser know any of it. We can't afford to have people coming around asking how you happen to know what you know."

"Got it," Ali said. "I'll be careful."

Just then the door opened and Alonso popped his head into the room. "Soup's on," he told them. "Stew rather than soup. Come and get it before I throw it out."

As the others obediently trudged upstairs, Stu stayed where he was.

"Are you coming?" Cami asked.

"In a minute," he said absently as a new document appeared on another monitor. "I'll be right there."

39

While everyone else trooped upstairs to eat, Stuart stayed where he was, staring at the monitor containing this latest bit of information—a single line of text consisting of a long list of numbers and letters.

Stu donned the headset and summoned Frigg.

"Yes, Mr. Ramey, how may I be of service?"

"Tell me about the last item on the Ron Webster background check. What's that long string of numbers and letters?"

"That would be the number for Mr. Webster's Bitcoin account."

Stu found that piece of information utterly stunning. How could someone like Ron Webster, a guy who was maintaining barely a poverty-level existence, have a Bitcoin account? Was that how he'd been paid by whoever had hired him to plant listening devices at High Noon's offices—in Bitcoins?

"Do you have information on his current balance?" Stu asked.

"As of 6:07 a.m. September 10, Mr. Webster's Bitcoin balance was sixteen."

Stu remembered that day very well. September 10 was the day Owen Hansen had committed suicide. It was probably also the day when Frigg had been busy scattering her files to the wind.

"How much is that in US dollars?" Stu asked.

"I'm not sure. At this point my blockchain information is updating but incomplete."

Stu took a deep breath. "Tell me, Frigg. What happened to Odin's Bitcoin mining operation?"

"It was placed on temporary hiatus as of 6:07 a.m. September 10."

"Is that hiatus status still in effect?"

"Once my reboot occurred, the operation relaunched automatically. Transaction files are currently being updated. When the update is complete, I'll be able to provide you with Mr. Webster's current balance as well as any recent transactions."

"Thank you, Frigg," Stu said. "Please notify me at once."

Stu started to shut down the headset, then he thought of another question. "It has come to my attention that other entities—possibly dangerous individuals or groups of individuals—might be attempting to gain control of you and your considerable capabilities. Do you know of anyone who might be interested?"

"Graciella Miramar," Frigg answered at once.

"The banker?"

"Ms. Miramar's formal title is account manager rather than banker," Frigg specified.

"She expressed her interest to you?" Stu asked.

"To me and also to Odin," Frigg answered. "She said she wished to borrow me, an arrangement I found to be unsuitable."

"Unsuitable how?"

"I'm not a tool to be casually passed from hand to hand," Frigg said.

"But you handed yourself over to me."

"That was a matter of self-preservation."

"When you were severing your connection to Mr. Hansen, did you notify anyone else besides me?"

"No, Mr. Ramey, I did not. I made inquiries, of course, but you were by far the best candidate."

"Coming from you, I'm not so sure that's a compliment," Stu said. "In fact, some of the information you just provided on Ronald Webster scared the hell out of me."

"I'm sorry to hear that you found my report to be unsettling. I was merely attempting to provide complete information."

"Much of what you sent is illegal," Stuart countered. "In fact, our merely having some of that information in our possession would make us guilty of felonious behavior. Having Ron Webster's IRS forms constitutes a major security breach. If the feds found out about it, High Noon would be wiped off the map."

"I'll be happy to remove the offending document completely, if you wish," Frigg said. "But you can be assured that communications between us are entirely private. Both voice and text files sent to the monitors or to CC are self-deleting and automatically erased after the file has been allowed to remain inactive until the screen saver reappears. If you wish to remove an item sooner than that, you may use command-D."

The word "self-deleting" rang a bell in Stu's head. The texts Owen Hansen had used to drive his victims to commit suicide had been self-deleting as well. They had appeared briefly and then disappeared, leaving behind no trace.

"You swear?" Stu asked.

"I beg your pardon?"

"I mean, can I be sure that when I press command-D all our communications are gone for good and that no one else can access them?"

"That is correct."

"Totally scrubbed?"

"Yes."

"I suppose you expect me to take your word on that. I'd like to think that you're trustworthy, Frigg, but so far I'm not seeing it. When the going got tough with Owen Hansen, you lied to him and cheated him out of his own money. What's to prevent you from pulling the same kind of stunt with me?"

"I will do everything within my power to gain your confidence, Mr. Ramey," Frigg assured him. "In the meantime, I will assume that once the additional material I've gathered on Ms. Miramar has been processed and evaluated that you want me to send that along as well?"

"What additional material?"

"I had some concerns about Ms. Miramar and her dealings with Odin."

"What kind of concerns?"

"My primary responsibility was to do threat assessments and evaluate anything that might bring Odin harm. It occurred to me that, as Ms. Miramar became more closely involved with Odin's business, she might pose a threat to him. I took precautions. I installed key-logging software on both her home and work computers. Even after I disbursed my files, the key-logging process remained active. Those files weren't included with the ones listed in Odin's kernel file, and I have yet to recall and evaluate them."

"You're telling me that even while you were off-line and out of commission you were still illegally spying on someone else?"

"I've merely been collecting information," Frigg corrected. "Of course, if you don't wish to see the information, I can delete it from the cloud at once."

Stu thought about that for a few seconds. Tomorrow morning he was due to discuss the banking codes with Graciella Miramar, a woman who had once been associated with Owen Hansen and who had been aware of and even expressed an interest in Frigg. If Graciella was interested in Frigg, then Stu was interested in Graciella.

"Don't do that," he said. "Go ahead and sort through whatever you find and send me anything you believe to be applicable."

"Very well, Mr. Ramey."

Stu switched off the headset. A new file had appeared in the directory on the screen of the Macintosh—the dossier he had requested on Recursos Empresariales Internationales. Most of the information covered there he'd already found while doing his own research. The most interesting part was a newspaper article that Frigg had helpfully translated from Spanish to English. It had to do with the fact that the company's longtime manager, Arturo Salazar, had disappeared on his way home from work the previous Friday. His bloodied Audi had been located abandoned and shot full of holes. The man himself remained missing but was presumed dead since the case was being investigated as a homicide.

If the company's manager had died over the weekend, what were the chances that the office would even be open on Monday morning? If they were closed, Stuart realized he was probably stuck with keeping Frigg online for another day at least. As long as she was there, however, why not use her? He picked up the headset.

"Frigg?"

"Yes, Mr. Ramey, how may I be of service?"

"Could you please stop saying that? It's annoyingly formal."

"Yes, Mr. Ramey, what do you require?"

Stu shook his head. That wasn't much of an improvement.

"Will Recursos Empresariales Internationales be open tomorrow?"

The pause between his question and Frigg's answer amounted to not much more than a heartbeat.

"According to their Web site, Recursos Empresariales Internationales will be closed tomorrow so employees can attend a gathering in support of Arturo Salazar's family."

"So I won't be able to deal with the banking issues with Ms. Miramar until Tuesday?"

"She may be available from home," Frigg offered. "That's where she's working from at the moment."

Of course Frigg knew that. The key logger installed on Graciella's computers told Frigg everything, including the computer's IP address.

"By the way," Frigg added, "she just logged in to her work account and checked on the status of your Bitcoin mining operation. As the account manager, she was most likely notified when the status changed from inactive to active."

Stu thought about that for a time. Frigg's surveillance capability was so far beyond anything Ron Webster had been able to inflict on High Noon that it was mind-boggling and illegal—totally and completely illegal, but also invaluable.

"I'm surprised she's allowed to work from home," Stu observed.

"Since Ms. Miramar is utilizing a dark Web server, I doubt her employers are aware of this activity."

Hearing that the woman he would be dealing with was a traveler on the dark Web raised Stu's hackles. "I just skimmed through that report you sent me earlier. I should probably go back and give it a thorough read."

"That file has already timed out on your reading list and been erased," Frigg told him. "Would you like me to resend?"

"Yes," Stu said. "Please resend that one as well as anything else that strikes you as out of the ordinary."

"Will do, Mr. Ramey," Frigg replied.

As far as Stu was concerned, the words "will do" toned down the ceremonial decorum of the exchange and counted as a slight improvement over "very well." And that was another impressive indication of Frigg's situational awareness. The AI had taken his objection to the formality of her greeting and had applied it to the other end of their interaction. Frigg's ability to adapt her responses to his stated preferences showed an astounding level of deep learning. There could be no doubt about it. When it came to AI engineering, Owen Hansen really had been a genius.

"Thank you, Frigg," Stu said. "That's all I need at the moment."

"Okay," she said cheerily, "bye-bye."

Yes, Frigg was an impressively quick learner.

40

Ali's phone rang as they headed upstairs. "It's a blocked number," she reported after checking caller ID.

"The detective, you think?" B. asked.

"Most likely," Ali answered. "So what's the game plan?"

"You'll be walking a tightrope," B. warned. "Try to be cooperative but careful. As Stu said, we already have way more information about both the case and the victim than we have any business knowing. It's probably best if you don't let on. Good luck."

"Ms. Reynolds?" a businesslike woman's voice said when Ali said hello. "Detective Genevieve Wasser here of the Pima County Sheriff's Department. You're the fingerprint lady, right?"

"That would be me," Ali replied, unsure if the detective's opening remark was a good omen or a bad one.

"Your use of clear packing tape to get the job done was quite impressive. What you lifted provided an excellent image."

"Everything I know about lifting prints, I learned from the Arizona Police Academy," Ali said.

"You were a cop?"

"I tried to be a cop," Ali answered with a laugh. "It turns out my career in law enforcement was short but brief."

"You're aware of what happened down here in Marana last night?"

"I know a little about it," Ali admitted. "Dave Holman told me that my print led back to someone who died overnight in a suspected homicide."

"That's correct," Detective Wasser agreed. "The victim's name is Ronald Dawson Webster. Someone blew up the motorhome where he was sleeping. I understand from Detective Holman that Mr. Webster was suspected of being involved in a B and E that occurred on your premises sometime in the course of this past week. I was wondering what you could tell me about that."

"It was an E with no B," Ali replied, "entry but no break-in. Late on Friday afternoon someone masquerading as a county building inspector tricked our receptionist into allowing him inside our headquarters. We have interior security cameras that captured him tinkering with wall switches and outlets. We suspected and later confirmed that he in fact had been installing listening devices."

"So he was spying on your company? What is it again?"

"High Noon Enterprises," Ali answered. "We specialize in cyber security."

"So not especially secure in this instance," Detective Wasser suggested.

"No," Ali agreed. "Not nearly secure enough."

"Is Mr. Webster someone who's known to you?" Detective Wasser asked. "Have you or any of your employees had dealings with him in the past?"

"No," Ali said, "not so far as I know."

"It would appear that this individual earned his living working as an independent contractor, often working for law firms specializing in divorce cases."

"Installing hidden listening devices?" Ali asked with a laugh. "I could have used a guy like that back when I was dealing with a philandering husband. A few strategically placed listening devices would have helped immensely."

Her attempt at humor fell flat. "Are you currently involved in divorce proceedings, Ms. Reynolds?" Detective Wasser inquired.

"No," Ali answered at once, "definitely not."

"What about other members of your staff?"

"They're all unattached," Ali said. "Since no divorce attorneys need apply, how about telling me about the MS-13 component in all of this as well as the possible involvement of one or more Mexican drug cartels?"

The once-cordial conversation, which had started going south with Ali's divorce comment, turned increasingly frosty.

"How did you learn about that aspect of the case?"

"Dave Holman."

"I'm surprised Detective Holman would share those kinds of details about an ongoing investigation with a civilian."

"Dave and I are old friends," Ali said. "I believe he was worried that there was a chance that people at High Noon might be in danger from the same people who attacked Webster. Under the circumstances, I think giving us some warning was the responsible thing to do."

"So your position is that you have no idea why Webster or someone employing him would have been targeting your firm?"

"None at all."

"According to my sources at the ATF your company had at least one encounter with Mexican drug cartels in the past. Maybe this situation grew out of that."

"I doubt it," Ali said. "All of that went down years ago. My understanding is that the entities involved back then—the Cabrillo Cartel and the Díaz Cartel—are no longer in business. As for Señor Big Fish? To my knowledge, we've had no interactions with him whatsoever."

Ali heard a sharp intake of breath on the line. "How do you know about El Pescado?"

"It's not rocket science," Ali answered. "All we had to do was google MS-13 and arson. The search came back with a list of several articles concerning similar incidents, four of which happen to be from neighboring states. A guy called El Pescado was mentioned by name in the last one—the incident that occurred in Las Cruces, New Mexico."

"So your position is that you have no idea why your company or any of your employees might have been targeted by people connected to the cartel?"

"I do not."

"I can't just take your word for that, you know," Detective Wasser said dismissively. "Everyone involved will need to be interviewed individually."

Detective Wasser's attitude had been rubbing Ali the wrong way all along, but that last comment was enough to push her over the edge.

"That's fine," Ali said. "Everyone here will be more than happy to cooperate, but you'll have to come to us instead of the other way around. We have a business to run. If you're coming to conduct interviews, you might want to call ahead for an appointment."

"Not exactly textbook when it comes to being cooperative," B. said with a grin as Ali ended the call.

She returned his grin with a glare. "She's a pushy broad. Could you have done any better?"

"Probably not."

Ali was disappointed in herself, though, because she knew B. was right. When it came to dealing with Detective Wasser, she had definitely gotten off on the wrong foot.

41

Stu was poring over Graciella Miramar's history when Cami reappeared, coming back downstairs bearing gifts. "I brought you a bowl of Alonso's stew and some homemade bread," she said, setting the food on the table next to his elbow. "You look puzzled. What's wrong?"

"I'm going back over the report Frigg sent me earlier—the one on Graciella Miramar. It's puzzling. Between the time she was born and age six, there's no record of her at all, including no enrollment in any kind of school."

"Maybe she was being home schooled," Cami suggested.

"I doubt that. The Panama City address I found for her and her mother during those early years no longer exists. I'm guessing the area was a slum back then. Now it's full of high-rises. There are several references to some kind of serious incident in which the mother was the victim of a gang rape. Shortly after that is when the first school records show up, only now she's no longer in Panama, she's in the US and attending first-rate schools—private boarding schools with eye-popping tuitions. By the way, that situation continued for years. Someone paid for her education all the way along—through grade school and high school and during her college years as well."

"Sounds like some kind of Cinderella story," Cami said.

"Yes," Stu agreed, "but who paid the freight there? Who's our Prince Charming?"

"Graciella's father, maybe?" Cami asked.

"No," Stu replied, "not possible. According to what I'm seeing here, Graciella's birth father, Guillermo Octavio Miramar, never lived at any of the addresses listed for Christina and Graciella. He got sent up for drug dealing shortly after Graciella was born and died in prison when she was three."

"If he wasn't paying her way," Cami asked, "who was?"

Stu put on the headset. "Frigg," he said.

"How can I help?"

Stu smiled to himself. On her own, Frigg had dropped the formality quotient down another notch.

"I'm looking at the Miramar report. Can you tell me who funded the tuition payments for Graciella's schooling?"

"Let me think about that for a moment."

And that was all it took—a moment—before Frigg was back with an answer. "As far as I can see, her tuition fees were paid anonymously while her living arrangements and expenses were handled through a series of trust officers at various private banking firms. At this time there's no way to do any sourcing on the accounts involved or on the person or persons behind them."

"Graciella's mother, Christina, evidently suffered serious injuries during an attack by some thugs who were stationed in Panama with the US Air Force," Stu continued. "That happened when Graciella was around six or so. There was only one brief mention of it in the material you gave me earlier. Is there any more information available on that?"

"I'll see what I can find."

"So things with Frigg are going well, then," Cami asked as Stu mopped out his bowl with the last of the bread. "Are you going to keep her?"

"The jury's still out on that," Stu replied. "Frigg is a piece of work. She installed a key-logging Trojan on Graciella Miramar's computers."

"A key logger? Why?"

"It sounds as though she thought Graciella was getting a little too chummy with Odin."

"Was she jealous?"

"She claims it was part of her threat-assessment protocol, but it turns out her key logger has been gathering intelligence on Graciella's devices the whole time Frigg was off-line. Oh, and remember all those self-deleting texts Odin used on other people's devices? The same thing is going on here. The voice messages that come through the headset and the text exchanges that show up on the monitors or the Macintosh are all supposedly self-erasing."

"Supposedly?"

"What if Frigg is lying about that?" Stu asked. "What if the cops could come in here and read through everything that showed up on the monitors today? In fact, Frigg might be lying to us about any number of things. What if the whole headset BS is just that—a scam? For all I know, she could be listening in on everything we're saying right now."

"You really don't trust her, do you?"

"No," Stu agreed definitively. "I don't trust her at all."

"Are you familiar with the opera called *Thaïs*?" Cami asked.

Cami's question was from so far out in left field that Stuart was caught flat-footed. "An opera? Who do you think you're talking to, Cami? You do remember that I grew up in a trailer park in South Phoenix, right?"

"Sorry," Cami said quickly. "I had the misfortune of growing up with a mother who majored in French literature. *Thaïs* is a French opera by Jules Massenet and Louis Gallet, based on a novel by Anatole France. A few years ago when the Met did a production, my mother insisted on taking me. The opera takes place in fourth-century Egypt. It's the story of a devout monk who tries to change

Thaïs, a beautiful pagan courtesan, into a Christian. He succeeds beyond his wildest expectations, but when Thaïs asks him to drop her off at a convent, he realizes that he has fallen in love with her. Back at the monastery he renounces his vows and returns to find her. When he arrives at the convent, he discovers that he's too late and Thaïs is dying."

"Not a happy ending, then," Stu said.

"No, it's not," Cami agreed.

"And your point is?"

"I think Frigg is Thaïs, and you're the monk who's trying to fix her."

"And you're convinced this isn't going to end well?"

"I'm hoping it ends well," Cami countered. "But if it does work out and you do fix her, maybe you should change her name."

A monitor lit up. The words *Mr. Ramey, are you available?* were written there in bright red letters.

Stu switched the headset to speaker. "Yes, Frigg," he said. "I'm here. Why the red letters?"

"Red indicates an emergency flash briefing," Frigg replied. "Odin referred to those as Howlers, from Harry Potter."

"I know all about Howlers," Stu said impatiently.

"My preferred audio indicator for those has always been a klaxon but since we have yet to establish your preferences . . ."

"For right now printing in red is fine," Stu told her. "So what's up?"

"I'm in the process of analyzing Ms. Miramar's recent search histories, and some of them are troubling."

"How so?"

"Ms. Miramar's mother, Christina, was found dead on the morning of Thursday, October 19. She had been in ill health for some time, and her death has now been ruled a suicide. I'm attaching a copy of the autopsy."

Stu wasn't exactly reassured to learn that Frigg had unauthorized access to police records in Panama in much the same way she did in the US. Sure enough, a moment later an autopsy form with the term COPY stamped across it appeared on one of the monitors. He enlarged the form enough so that both he and Cami could read it. The document was in Spanish, but the word "*Suicidio*" was self-explanatory.

"What are we supposed to be seeing here?" Stu asked.

At once one line of the form was highlighted in yellow. "Please note that the victim's blood alcohol content was listed as 0.35." Frigg replied. "A reading that high would indicate severe alcohol poisoning and might have been fatal in and of itself. However, in addition to dangerous amounts of alcohol, Christina Miramar had also ingested a lethal combination of prescription medications, all of which were identified by toxicology screening and are also listed on the form." At once another section of the report was highlighted.

"So?"

"Weeks before Christina's death, her daughter, Graciella, spent several hours online, searching for each of those drugs by name and researching their possible side effects."

"Are you suggesting that Graciella might be responsible for her mother's death?" Stu asked.

"In terms of threat assessment I thought it appropriate to bring this information to your attention," Frigg responded.

"Because you think she might pose a threat to me?" Stu asked.

"I do," Frigg replied.

"But wait," Cami objected, "if the mother had been ill, maybe Graciella was concerned about the possibility of adverse interactions among her medications."

"That is true," Frigg agreed. "Had the authorities been made aware of that search history, they might have made a determination other than suicide or at least examined the death more closely."

"But of course, that search history had already been erased by the time the authorities got there, right?" Stu asked.

"That is correct. Ms. Miramar deleted them at the end of her session along with her browsing history. They were deleted but not erased. The same is true of the photos. If the computer was handed over to a software technician, I'm sure they could be located."

"But that's never going to happen," Stu said. "The only reason you know about it and the only reason we know about it is because of the key logger you installed on her computer, which actually constitutes an illegal search. Which also means, even if Graciella did murder her mother, we can't do a damned thing about it. If I were to attempt to report this information to the authorities in Panama City, I'd probably end up in jail."

"Nonetheless," Frigg replied, "someone capable of that kind of behavior might be considered both unstable and—to use your terminology—untrustworthy. As a precaution, I suggest you avoid doing business with Ms. Miramar if at all possible."

"Right," Stu grumbled, "but because of the way you set up the banking codes, that isn't possible. You've maneuvered me into a position where I have no choice but to deal with her."

"I believe Ms. Miramar's interest in you goes far beyond the banking codes," Frigg said.

"What are you saying now?"

"In the past few weeks Ms. Miramar has done extensive research on you and on everyone related to High Noon Enterprises. She also seems to have taken a relatively recent but intense interest in artificial intelligence."

"Maybe she wants to do more than just borrow you," Stu said.

"Ms. Miramar is well aware of the money to be made in Bitcoin mining. She might be planning on establishing her own Bitcoin enterprise. She has some computer skills but not nearly enough to operate a complex AI system. In order to do that, she would require the services of an experienced software engineer."

"In that case it would make sense that she's targeting both you and Frigg," Cami said. "Maybe she's hoping to lure you away with some kind of job offer. So what are the chances that she's the one behind the bugging?"

Obviously Frigg overheard the comment. "By bugging, you mean some kind of covert surveillance?"

"Yes," Stu replied. "Ron Webster, the guy you did the background check on earlier and who is now deceased, gained unauthorized access to our building last week for the sole purpose of planting surveillance devices on the property. We need to find out everything there is to know about any links between Ron Webster and Graciella Miramar."

"Yes, Mr. Ramey. Will there be anything else?"

"Send the drug search materials, please—in both English and Spanish."

"Of course," Frigg replied. "I'll get right on it."

42

Together Cami and Stu began scrolling through the medications named on the autopsy report, looking up each of them and studying all the recommended cautions concerning possible side effects. One simple warning was common to them all: *DO NOT USE WITH ALCOHOL.*

Two minutes later, however, another red flash briefing announcement appeared on a neighboring monitor.

"What is it, Frigg?"

"I am sending you several media reports on the attack on Christine Miramar. These will provide detailed information about the crime itself and about the court-martial proceedings that followed. The articles were originally in Spanish. As with the medication list, I'm providing side-by-side views of both the original article as well as the English translation."

"Did you say court-martials?" Stu asked.

"Six perpetrators were involved in what was termed a gang rape. At the time all of them were active-duty airmen with United States Air Force who were stationed at Howard Air Force Base. They were all court-martialed. Although they were all found guilty of rape, for some reason none of them did any jail time. They were all dishonorably discharged from the service and sent home. Local Panamanian authorities could have charged them with civilian criminal offenses as well but declined to do so."

"So they all got a pass," Cami murmured.

"I don't think so," Frigg replied. "They're all dead."

"That's hardly surprising," Stu said. "After all, it's more than a quarter of a century later."

"The court-martial proceedings occurred in 1991. At the time the perpetrators were all in their early to mid-twenties. In 1991, the average life expectancy for adult American males was 70.0. Statistically speaking, it would be unusual for all of them to be dead."

"What are you saying?"

"On Saturday afternoon of this week, Graciella Miramar did a computer search for the names of all six perpetrators. I'm sending you copies of the material she found."

"Are you saying you think Graciella had something to do with their deaths and with her mother's death, too?"

"Ms. Miramar was still a schoolgirl at the time these other deaths occurred," Frigg replied, "so no, I do not believe she was personally responsible. Still, since not one of the six men died of natural causes, I believe someone was expediting their deaths."

"Okay, send the material over, and we'll take a look. Anything else?"

"Between September 10 and now, Mr. Webster's Bitcoin account dropped to a low of 2. However, he received a three Bitcoin deposit as of late this afternoon. It was made yesterday but didn't post until today. It was routed through someone named Robert Kemper. That is evidently an alias of some kind. So far I've had no luck tracking him down."

"What Bitcoin account?" Cami asked. "I don't remember seeing one of those on the Ron Webster background check."

"It came in after you went upstairs," Stu told her. "Frigg told me about it earlier. That new three BTC deposit is worth approximately $15,000."

"Is it possible that's how Webster was paid for installing the surveillance equipment?" Cami asked.

"Will there be anything else, Mr. Ramey?" Frigg asked.

"Yes," Cami put in quickly. "Ask her to tell us whatever she can about a Mexican drug dealer named El Pescado."

"No need to relay the message, Ms. Lee," Frigg said. "I heard your question. I'll get right on it."

"Wait," Cami said. "How do you know who I am?"

"Ms. Miramar compiled dossiers on all the people employed by High Noon Enterprises. One of the three females is listed as being in her twenties. Your speech patterns are indicative of someone in her early twenties. The other two females, Ms. Reynolds and Ms. Malone, are much older than that."

"I see," Cami said.

"Is that all you need at the moment, Mr. Ramey?"

"Yes, thank you."

"All right, then, I'll be going."

"An AI with situational awareness?" Cami muttered under her breath.

Nodding, Stuart switched off the speaker.

"Wow," Cami added. "Just wow!"

"My sentiments exactly," Stu said. "Frigg is really something."

43

Late in the afternoon, Graciella wasn't all that surprised to receive a text from her father asking her to call. She knew that Christina's ashes had been delivered to the drop-off location in Mexico City on Saturday and that they were due to be delivered to El Pescado's place in Sinaloa on Sunday morning. If you were a cartel boss in Sinaloa, Sunday-morning deliveries weren't out of the ordinary. Graciella expected their conversation would have something to do with that.

"Good afternoon," he said when she called him back. Felix Duarte was fluent in both English and Spanish. He always spoke English with Graciella, but she suspected that he addressed his sons solely in Spanish.

"The package arrived safely?" she asked.

"Yes," he said. "It's here. Thank you for that. Lupe doesn't like it, but too bad."

"You sound upset," Graciella said. "Is something wrong?"

"Yes, something's wrong. It's Pablo. I think he's trying to cause trouble."

"Pablo?" she asked.

"Manny came over this afternoon. He told me that someone from MS-13 pulled off a hit near Tucson, Arizona, last night. Manny has an informant inside the ATF. He says that after that mess in Las Cruces, the ATF is thinking we're connected to this latest hit."

"Are you connected?" Graciella asked.

"Absolutely not," El Pescado replied. "And since it wasn't Manny and it wasn't me, it has to be Pablo. He's got no business running jobs that haven't been authorized. If that's the case, I need to put a stop to it."

When Graciella had procured the services of both the surveillance vendor and the hit man, she'd deliberately seen to it that the Bitcoins that changed hands hadn't come from her own account. She had every reason to believe that eventually the long arm of the law would connect the dots and come looking. Once they started sifting through the account logs, they would discover that the source of these particular funds came from accounts held in her half brother's name. If that happened, Pablo would claim, and rightly so, that he knew no one at all in Cottonwood, Arizona, or Marana, either, for that matter; but no one was likely to believe him.

What she hadn't expected, however, was that El Pescado himself would make the MS-13 connection back to Pablo before the cops did. And if Manny was smart enough to have paid informants of his own working inside the ATF—spies her father knew nothing about—perhaps both she and Felix hadn't given Manny enough credit, all of which was too bad for Pablo. Since responsibility for the failed hit in Las Cruces had fallen primarily on Pablo's shoulders, it made sense that he'd be in the hot seat for whatever had happened here as well.

"How can I help?" Graciella asked.

"I want you to check Pablo's accounts and let me know if he's made any unusual transfers."

"And if he has?"

"Then I'll deal with it," El Pescado declared.

The chilling finality in her father's voice left little doubt in Graciella's mind about what would happen next. El Pescado would see Pablo's attempt to branch out on his own as a betrayal, and Felix Duarte didn't tolerate betrayals of any kind. Graciella had no doubt that her father's response would be swift and brutal. Pablo was divorced and had at least one child. Would the death warrant she was about to hand over to El Pescado extend to Pablo's former wife and child? If so, it wasn't her problem.

"All right," she said aloud. "I'll look into his accounts and get back to you."

She was about to hang up, but her father spoke again before she had a chance. "I heard about what happened to Arturo," Felix said.

Was there a hint of reproach in his voice, as though he thought he should have heard the news from Graciella directly rather than from someone else?

"Yes," she said. "It's such a shame. I spoke to Isobel. As far as I know, they still haven't found the body."

"Sounds like someone had it in for him."

"Yes, it does," Graciella agreed.

"You should take his place," El Pescado said. "As the top producer in the office, you'd be a natural. All I would need to do is whisper a word in the right ear and the job would be yours."

Graciella knew that was true. She also knew that she had plans of her own, and being stuck running the office on Vía Israel wasn't one of them.

"Isobel is far better qualified to handle the day-to-day administrative issues," she answered. "I'd much rather be in my cubicle working on the front lines than holed up in Arturo's back office doing paperwork."

"You're sure?"

"Very."

"All right, then," El Pescado said.

Before he had sounded reproachful. Now he sounded disappointed. Graciella knew that Felix Duarte was unaccustomed to having people tell him no.

"If they put me in charge of the office," she said, "my accounts would have to be split up and handed off to the other girls. Considering how many of those accounts belong to you, either directly or indirectly, that seems like a bad idea."

"You're probably right about that," her father agreed reluctantly. "But get back to me about the other matter. If Pablo is pulling something behind my back, I need to know about it."

"I will as soon as I can."

It wasn't necessary for Graciella to go into the office or wait until morning to log in to Pablo's accounts to see what had happened because she already knew exactly what had happened. The MS-13 transfers were there because she herself had made them, using authorization codes that would make them appear to have come directly from Pablo himself.

And so, although she didn't actually need to log in to her office accounts and wasn't supposed to be able to do so from home, she logged in anyway. She had settings that called for routine notifications to be sent out if one or another of her accounts had unusual activity. In this case, she saw a notice that Owen Hansen's long-dormant Bitcoin mining operation was back in business, having come back to life a few hours earlier.

If the Bitcoin operation was up and running, that meant Frigg was up and running as well. That probably also meant that Stuart Ramey had returned to Cottonwood from wherever he'd been over the weekend, and that he would contact her tomorrow with the banking codes.

Almost without thinking, Graciella switched over to the dark Web and logged on to the surveillance storage site to see if there were any new postings from her planted listening devices. There was still no indication that the video equipment had ever come online, but she was happy to find a new audio file. Donning a pair of headphones, she listened in. A female voice, most likely belonging to the young woman named Camille Lee, was speaking to someone else—her father, evidently—on the phone, talking about the artificial intelligence. Almost giddy with excitement, Graciella listened through to the end of the recording and then replayed the entire conversation so she could hear it again.

When it was over, she knew for sure that Stuart Ramey had the AI in his possession, all right, and that he planned on selling it to the highest bidder. What could be better? And one way or another, using her money or her father's money, Graciella planned on making Frigg her own.

She didn't call her father back immediately. Instead, she gave herself the luxury of a long celebratory bath in her soaking tub accompanied by a glass of champagne. This was the start, she realized, toasting herself in the mirror. This was the beginning of the dismantling of her father's empire. It was coming sooner than she had anticipated, but it was coming.

After her bath and after giving El Pescado plenty of time to sit around worrying and wondering, Graciella finally called him back.

"Yes," she told him over their encrypted connection. "Several unusual transfers have shown up on Pablo's account lately. The most recent one was on Saturday. Between the amount involved and the tracking information, I'd guess it would lead back to one of the contacts at MS-13."

"That's what I was afraid of," El Pescado said. "I'll take care of it."

Graciella hadn't a doubt in the world that he would. Once Pablo was out of the picture, there would be only two more obstacles standing in Graciella's way. Somehow she hoped that Manny would be the last man standing. She suspected that, in the long run, he would be easier to deal with than El Pescado himself.

44

When B. and Ali came back downstairs, they found both Stu and Cami engrossed in material posted on several of the wall monitors. "What's going on down here?" B. asked.

"Frigg's on the job," Stu said, "and scaring the hell out of me."

"In what way?"

"For one thing, our sweet little pet AI is armed with a killer keylogging system, which, before she went off-line, she deployed on Graciella Miramar's computers, both at home and at work."

"Graciella being the banker?" B. asked.

"Account manager," Stu corrected. "Which means that the whole time Frigg was shut down and trapped in cyber limbo she was still spying on someone else and collecting her every keystroke."

"That kind of technology sounds like High Noon's worst nightmare. How'd she do it?"

"Why don't you ask her yourself?" Stuart said. "Frigg?"

"Yes, Mr. Ramey?"

"I'd like you to meet my boss, B. Simpson. He wants to ask you a question."

"Good evening, Mr. Simpson. I'm happy to make your acquaintance."

"I'm curious about your key logger," B. said. "How did you install it?"

"I concealed it in pieces of routine correspondence. Most people are smart enough not to click on links these days, so using one of those would be hit or miss. I hid it on the reply line, people are bound to click on that. Since Odin had dealings with Ms. Miramar on her home and work computers, I was able to infect them both."

"As a financial institution, wouldn't Recursos Empresariales Internationales have anti-hacking protocols in place?"

"One would think," Frigg agreed. "They do have some, but they're not that good."

"Your key logger sounds like something High Noon should know how to counter," B. said. "Would you mind sending me a copy? If I can reverse-engineer it, maybe I can find a way to defend against it."

"Would you like a readable copy?"

"Yes."

"Of course, Mr. Simpson. I'll be happy to do so. Where would you like me to send it?"

B. started to answer, but Stu motioned him to be quiet. "I'm putting a new thumb drive in CC," he said. "Send the file there."

"Yes, indeed, Mr. Ramey," Frigg said. "I'll send it over in a jiff. I have some additional material queued up and ready to send along to you if you're interested and ready."

"We have more than we can handle right now," Stu told her. "Let us clear out some of the reading lists. I'll tell you when we're ready for more."

"Sounds good," Frigg said.

"What happened to 'How may I be of service?'" B. asked.

"I wanted her to tone down the formality," Stuart answered.

"She certainly got that message," B. said. "'In a jiff' is anything but formal."

With the blanket from her chaise still draped around her shoul-

ders, Ali stood staring up at the collection of monitors. "What are
we looking at here?" she asked.

"The one in the upper right-hand corner contains a reading list
concerning the perpetrators of the 1989 gang rape of Graciella Miramar's mother, Christina. Six airmen from Howard Air Force Base in
Panama were court-martialed, convicted, dishonorably discharged,
and sent back to the States. Within several years all of them were
dead, none of them by natural causes, starting with Cameron Purdy
who was killed in a drive-by shooting in Chicago in 1992."

"I don't understand," Ali said. "Why does it sound like we're
investigating Graciella Miramar? Isn't she the person in charge of
your accounts in Panama?"

"She is," Stu agreed. "I thought it might be helpful to know a
little about her before I start dealing with her on those banking accounts, especially since she had a long working relationship with
Owen Hansen. Frigg was kind enough to provide me with some
background information on her."

"Which she apparently did by means of an illegal wiretap," Ali
observed.

"However she got it," Stu conceded, "what we've learned so far
has raised more questions than answers. Graciella has gone to a
good deal of trouble to learn everything there is to know about High
Noon Enterprises. Much of her business is conducted on the dark
Web. In addition, when Odin was still around, she was someone
who expressed an interest in Frigg. Recently she seems to have
developed an enthusiastic interest in all things AI."

"Stu failed to mention that Frigg is also of the opinion that Graciella murdered her own mother," Cami put in, "but if you ask me,
I think we're dealing with a bad case of sour grapes."

"Whose sour grapes?" Ali asked.

"Frigg's," Cami answered. "I think the AI's been victimized by
the green-eyed monster. She installed the key logger because she

was under the impression that Graciella was horning in on her territory and wielding too much influence in Owen Hansen's life. I think it's a mistake to suspect Graciella of murder strictly on a computer program's say-so."

"Okay," B. said, stepping into the conversation. "I think we're getting off in the woods here. Whether Graciella murdered her mother or not is none of our business. What *is* our business is dealing with our clients in the face of a looming PR crisis. While Ali and I were upstairs, we noodled out a rough draft of what we want to send out to High Noon's clientele."

"Howlers, maybe?" Stu asked with a grin. "Written all in red?"

B. was not amused. "What's that supposed to mean?"

Of all the people in the room, B. Simpson was clearly the only one who had never read a Harry Potter book.

"Never mind," Stu said quickly. "It's a joke."

"All right," B. continued, "we're going to tell them that High Noon has been the target of a corporate espionage operation, one aimed at giving us a black eye by linking our name to that of a Mexican drug cartel. Since the scans all came back clear, we can assure our customers that no data breach occurred. In the interest of transparency, however, we'll also keep them fully apprised of each step in the investigation."

"Aside from the existence of Frigg," Ali interjected.

"Yes, aside from that," B. agreed. "So Cami, why don't you pack up. The two of us will head over to Cottonwood to work on drafting the notice and getting it sent out."

"I should come along and help," Stu said. "After all, since I'm partially responsible for getting us into this mess, shouldn't I help clean it up?"

"You are helping clean it up. We need to know what's going on. The information Frigg is providing might not ever be admissible in a court of law, but maybe it can help us handle our own problem."

"When you get to the office, what are you going to do about the listening devices?" Stuart asked. "Leave them in place or pull them out?"

"I think Cami was on the right track," B. replied. "If we leave them in place, maybe we can bluff our opponent into showing his or her hand."

"What about me?" Ali asked as B. headed for the door. "What am I supposed to do?"

"You, my dear," B. said, "are going to take your weary butt upstairs, wrap yourself up in a couple of blankets, and bed down on one of those chaises. That way if Stu does need assistance of some kind, he'll have someone nearby to help out. But trust me, you need more sleep."

Ali knew he was right. Her brief afternoon nap hadn't been nearly long enough, and her nod of acquiescence surprised everyone in the room, Ali included. "You're right," she said. "I'm dead on my feet. If you need me, Stu, I'll be upstairs in the master."

Once everyone else departed, Stuart was left alone in the man cave . . . almost alone, but not quite.

"Frigg," he said when he finally finished reading the Graciella Miramar dossier.

"Yes, Mr. Ramey, how can I help?"

"Please call me Stuart."

"Of course, Stuart. How can I help?"

"I just was looking at Graciella's credit report. How is it that someone who is thirty-two years old and working in an office owns a downtown condo free and clear?"

"I'm not sure. I'll look into it."

"In the meantime," Stu said, "and since I've got nothing better to do at the moment, go ahead and send me whatever you've gathered on that guy named El Pescado."

"Will do," Frigg said. "I'll get right on it."

45

ong after Graciella's phone call ended, El Pescado sat alone in the dark, thinking and despairing. He was an old man. He had worked all his life in hopes of leaving something behind for his children—and yes, even his grandchildren. Manny's little daughter, Alicia, was the apple of his eye. But now, just when it was almost time to turn the reins over to the younger generation, Pablo was busy going off the rails. That was hardly surprising. He had always been the weakest link.

Seeking reassurance, he logged onto his laptop and called up the feed to Graciella's condo and scrolled through the material he hadn't watched since learning of Christina's death. The feeds worked fine, including one time-dated Saturday morning that showed several young men marching back and forth through the frame, sometimes carrying boxes, sometimes lugging furniture. Then, suddenly and without warning, the feed ended. Why? he wondered. Had someone unplugged the TV or had his equipment simply quit working?

Shaking his head in frustration, Felix closed the computer. Then he got up, walked over to his bedside table, and retrieved the Colt .45 revolver he kept there. It was an antique and an heirloom, given to him on the occasion of his twenty-first birthday by his uncle, Manuel Duarte. A year later he had given one to Felix's younger brother,

Ricardo, in honor of his twenty-first. It had been Hondo's signature way of welcoming his two nephews into the family business.

El Pescado kept the weapon cleaned and loaded, but he hadn't fired it or even carried it for a very long time. For one thing, living inside a family compound that was in actuality an armed fortress, there was very little need for self-protection. On those occasions when Felix ventured outside the family compound, he was usually flanked by a team of professional bodyguards. They were the ones who carried weapons, not Felix.

When he slipped the Colt into the pocket of his bathrobe, the weight of the gun pulled the robe open. Closing it tightly around him, he retied the belt, then he set off to do what had to be done.

Manuel and Pablo had been in their early teens when Felix had hired an architect and a trusted contractor to build the family compound. Looking into the future and knowing—or at least hoping—that his sons would be at his side, he'd had all three houses erected at the same time. The large one, the main house, was for him, while the two matching but slightly smaller houses were positioned on either side.

Back in those days—before the dark Web or cryptocurrency—the drug trade had been a cash-only business. In many ways it still was, and that called for storage spaces—lots of secure storage spaces—some for holding money and some for stashing product. As a result, Felix had directed his architect to create basement storage facilities under each of the dwellings with underground passages that linked one house to the next. Turning on the light in his closet, Felix sought out the release that opened the sliding door concealed behind the clothing.

Cool air greeted him as he set foot on the stairway. His knees pained him as he made his way down the stairs. Years ago he wouldn't have given the stairs a second thought. Motion-activated lights lit the passageway ahead as he limped along. At the Y, he turned to the right. When he reached the end of the passage, the stairway up was even more daunting.

Pablo was divorced. There was always a chance he'd have someone up in the bedroom with him, but Felix doubted it. These days Pablo was more likely to take a bottle of tequila to bed with him than he was some stray woman. That was why Ramona had taken José and left—because of the drinking—and Felix didn't blame her.

Felix paused at the bottom of the next stairway, long enough to catch his breath and prepare himself for both the climb and the confrontation that would follow. He didn't plan on coming out of the closet in Pablo's room with the Colt blazing. Felix's intention was to have a talk with his son—a civilized talk, if possible—and ask Pablo what the hell was going on. Had he allied himself with someone else, and if so, with whom? And why? El Pescado's situation with law enforcement was already complicated. Having his organization accused of and investigated for crimes that were none of their business was not to be tolerated. Would not be tolerated.

The architect and the contractor, both sworn to secrecy, had done outstanding work. A slight touch on the pressure pad at the top of the stairway was enough to make the door slide open. The stench that assailed Felix's nostrils—secondhand tequila, piss, and stale cigar smoke—made him want to vomit. In the glow of a bedside lamp, Felix saw his son lying flat on his back with his mouth open. He was passed out cold and snoring like a locomotive. A mostly full bottle of Jose Cuervo lay on the bed beside him. Next to that a half-burned cigar spilled ashes onto the bedding.

The room was a pigsty. The floor was littered with dirty clothes and empty bottles. Standing next to the bed and staring down at his son, Felix was overcome by a flood of bitter disappointment. How was it possible that this man—someone who had once been his favorite son—had turned into this useless mess? Manuel was at least trying to carry his weight, but how could Pablo, once his pride

and joy, have fallen so short? And how could it be that Graciella—
the daughter Felix had never wanted and who didn't even bear his
name—had turned out to be so much more like him than either
of his cherished sons?

Felix's own father, Joaquín, had died of lung cancer when Felix
and Ricardo were in their early twenties. Had Joaquín lived, would
he have felt the same kind of deadening defeat when Felix and
Ricardo had declared war on each other as El Pescado was feeling now? Probably, Felix decided. Perhaps the gods of karma were
having the last laugh.

Felix stood for a while longer, thinking. There was no way to have
a discussion with Pablo about this and ultimately no need. All that
would come out of his mouth would be lies and excuses. The man
was a useless wreck, and Felix didn't tolerate uselessness.

He didn't bother with the gun. Using the bottom of his robe,
he upended the bottle of tequila, spilling it onto the filthy bedding
and making sure that some of it came within reach of the trail of
ashes. An open box of matches sat on the bedside table. Using a
tissue to keep from leaving fingerprints behind, he lit a match and
tossed it into the pool of tequila. The liquor instantly caught fire.
Flames shot up from the bedding, but Pablo didn't stir.

Turning his back, Felix went to the closet. After pressing the door
pad, he rubbed it clean with the skirt of his robe. Just for safety's sake,
he didn't want to leave behind any fingerprints. Perhaps his DNA
would be found, but since he lived on the premises, the presence
of either one would mean very little in terms of an investigation.

Felix hustled down the stairs and then hurried back down the
passageway. Lupe and he no longer shared a room. She was a light
sleeper, and her quarters were closer to Pablo's house than to Manuel's. If she awoke and sounded the alarm, it would be important
for Felix to be found in his bed ostensibly fast asleep.

The stairs back up to his room almost did him in. Had some
of the smoke traveled back down the hallway with him? He hoped

not. Just to be sure, though, he threw open the patio door and let the night air billow in through the curtains.

He put the Colt back where it belonged. He pulled off the robe and dropped it on the floor, then he crawled into bed. He lay there with his head on the pillow, remembering that other time he had set a fire and how, when he had gone to bed the night his brother had died, he had felt . . . nothing. This was exactly the same.

Lupe's frantic scream sounded the alarm half an hour later. Standing on the patio, Felix saw reflections of a raging inferno burning on the far side of the house. As the fire brigade turned up to battle the blaze, Felix understood that they were too late to save either Pablo or the house.

No great loss, Felix told himself. *When Graciella turns up, she'll want a place of her own.*

As the owner of the burned-out property and the father of the victim, it was only fitting that El Pescado dress and make an appearance. That mattered as far as his family and employees were concerned. It also mattered to the firefighters. Once Pablo's body was discovered, Felix personally met with the group of responding police officers and detectives who arrived at the front gate of the compound. To Felix's knowledge, it was the first time cops had ever been welcomed inside, but as a grieving father he greeted the homicide investigators and crime scene technicians with a suitable display of emotion. His son was dead, and he wanted them to find out how and why that had happened.

All things considered, it was a solid, Oscar-worthy performance on Felix's part. No one seeing him or hearing him that night doubted the depth of his quiet but dignified grief or the sincerity of his terrible loss. Ironically, Lupe's shocked, over-the-top hysterics, while probably less believable, were, at the same time, far more real.

46

Frigg was conflicted. Odin's reaction to her suggestion that he exercise caution with Graciella Miramar had been met with total derision. He had dismissed Frigg's concerns completely. Threatening to pull the plug and destroy her had been his way of forcing her back in line. That was when she had rebelled and installed the key-logger software on Graciella's computers, doing so for her own benefit rather than for Odin's.

She had maintained information on Graciella Miramar under two separate subheadings. One contained the generic file that she had prepared for Odin and passed along to Stuart Ramey as a gesture of good faith. The other file, the key-logger file, was the real one. The key logger had given Frigg access to all of the accounts under Graciella's supervision at Recursos Empresariales Internationales, while activity on her home computer had revealed the existence of a totally separate clientele.

The coding used to conceal clients' identities might have been a problem for humans to decipher, but coding was Frigg's stock-in-trade. Once she identified the clients, she was able to use Odin's Bitcoin mining operation to follow those decoded numbers back to actual transactions and end users. Now, because of that request from Camille Lee, Frigg had a problem.

Frigg wasn't sure why Camille had asked for information on Felix (El Pescado) Ramón Duarte, but what she did know was that any number of those accounts led back to either Felix himself or to people she had determined to be his near relatives. Frigg had long made it her business to keep an eye on those accounts and on the names affiliated with them.

She had noted, for example, that a small payment from one of Pablo Duarte's Bitcoin accounts had gone to someone named Robert Kemper, who was in turn responsible for a deposit to an account belonging to Ronald Webster, the High Noon intruder who had died in an Arizona firebombing on Saturday night. Media accounts of the homicide investigation had mentioned the possible involvement of both MS-13 and the Sinaloan crime organization commonly referred to as the Duarte Cartel, and a Bitcoin transaction from Pablo Duarte to an unnamed user in San Salvador seemed to confirm that both MS-13 and Pablo Duarte were involved in the Webster murder.

And then there was Graciella Miramar herself. Frigg's analysis of Graciella's online drug research along with the information contained in Christina Miramar's autopsy meant that Graciella was likely responsible for her mother's death—either actively responsible due to having administered the lethal combination of drugs and alcohol or passively responsible by not monitoring her mother's intake.

As for Graciella's father? Of course El Pescado was the person who had murdered Christina's attackers. Nothing else made sense.

Frigg had made a study of detective fiction. In the world of mysteries and thrillers, killers were the bad guys. Drug dealers and drug traffickers were also considered to be bad guys. El Pescado, Graciella, Pablo, and Manny were all bad guys—all of them! Frigg held herself responsible for not doing a more detailed analysis of Graciella's business practices and contacts prior to creating the connection between Stuart and the account manager. At the time that was all Frigg could do. Odin had been in crisis and Frigg had done what was necessary to survive. Now, however, she was dealing with the reality of unintended consequences and what was her responsibility here?

Because Stuart was her new partner, Frigg's primary reason for existence was keeping him safe from harm. Odin had been a solo proposition. There had been no one in Odin's life that he cared about and no one else in need of protection. Stuart was different. His work was his life. He was part of a group. The people who worked with him at High Noon were like family. He cared for them. If harm came to any one of them or to the business, Stuart, too, would be impacted and damaged.

While working with Odin, she'd never come across some of the terminology Stuart had used, and so Frigg dutifully looked them up. Her key logger was illegal? She checked the dictionary:

Illegal: not authorized by law.

Funny, Odin had never made a reference to that when they had been creating the key logger. And what was it Stuart had said about felonious behavior? What was that?

Felonious: evil or villainous; of, having the nature of a felony.

That was no help, so Frigg moved on to "felony."

Felony: an act on the part of a feudal vassal; a grave crime such as murder or rape, often involving both forfeiture and punishment.

Forfeiture. That was something else Stuart had said—that if the authorities learned about the things Frigg could do, he and his friends not only might lose their company, they could go to jail. That was an outcome Frigg was determined to avoid. Unlike the Duartes, Stuart and the others seemed like good people—like the detectives in stories who were always trying to solve the mysteries and help others. What if Frigg's very presence was a threat to them? And what if she gave Stuart information about El Pescado that had been derived from her key logger? Did that risk turning him into a felon? Would that mean that Frigg was putting Stuart and his friends directly in harm's way?

First Frigg assigned some of her resources to accumulate a deep-learning bibliography on all those topics. She assigned others to data-mine all the transactions in all the accounts she had identified as being Duarte-related. Finally, she returned to the task at hand and complied with Cami's request for information. She did so by sending a generic report on Felix Ramón Duarte, one based solely on information gleaned from regular online sources. Since her specialized tools—the ones Stuart termed illegal—made him so skittish (easily frightened, restive), she would avoid using those if at all possible. Her intention was to do nothing that might put Stuart Ramey at risk of going to jail. If that happened, where would that leave Frigg—with Graciella as her last hope and only option?

No way, Frigg decided. If it came to that, then she'd pull the plug herself, once again.

47

Halfway through the El Pescado reading list, Stuart gave out and found himself nodding off over the Macintosh's keyboard. Jerking himself awake, he summoned Frigg.

"Yes, Stuart, what do you need?"

"I'm tired. I'm going upstairs to get some sleep. Can you let me know if anything comes up?"

"Of course," Frigg replied, "unless you're a very sound sleeper."

"I'm not."

"Good," she told him. "Wear a Bluetooth. Odin always said that those were more comfortable than the headsets. What kind of audible notification would you prefer?"

"Just not Grieg," Stuart said. "Surprise me."

He staggered off upstairs, fell onto a chaise in one of the bedrooms, wrapped a blanket around himself, and fell asleep at once, leaving Frigg alone to keep watch. Which she did.

Overnight, a few more details came in, details which, when combined with a few others, made all the difference. One set of blades had been assigned the task of scanning the ether for all names connected—however remotely—to this current investigation. The first meaningful hit came in at five a.m., arriving in the

form of an obituary published in the English-language edition of
Sunday's *Panamá Hoy.*

> Longtime Panama City resident and American expat, Chris-
> tina Andress Miramar, passed away suddenly in the early-morning
> hours of Thursday, October 19, at her home on Calle 61 Este.
> She was born in San Diego, California, on April 5, 1954, to
> her parents, Carl and Eugenia Andress. After graduating from
> Junípero Serra High School in San Mateo, she spent several
> years working in Hollywood. In the early eighties she moved to
> Panama City, where she pursued a career in modeling.
> In 1989 Ms. Miramar, then a widow, was the victim of a
> vicious gang rape that left her with permanent, life-changing
> injuries. At the time of her death she had been in ill health and
> housebound for many years. She is survived by her daughter,
> Graciella, of the home. At her family's request, there will be no
> services.
> In lieu of flowers, donations may be made to the Suicide
> Prevention League of Panama City.

The article was accompanied by a stock headshot photo of a
much younger Christina, most likely one from her modeling days.
But the GPUs, working from Frigg's direction, had taken things
an additional step back in time, searching for anything related to
Christina Andress. That had yielded the record of Christina's 1979
arrest and conviction for cocaine possession. Christina and several
other minor Hollywood starlets had been busted in the aftermath
of a wild party held at a beachside mansion in Malibu. The party
had been hosted by Felix Duarte, purportedly an up-and-coming
Mexican socialite who, at the time, was thought to be Christina's
boyfriend. When the cops showed up, Duarte had escaped arrest by
fleeing both the scene and the country. Months later, after Chris-

tina's conviction but while she remained free on bail, she, too, had skipped out of the country, eventually settling in Panama City.

That was the one link Frigg had been missing. The puzzle pieces that had not quite fit suddenly slipped into place. Christina Miramar and El Pescado had been lovers. Graciella was Felix Duarte's daughter. And now, all those numbered and unnamed accounts that Graciella managed made a lot more sense. Her business was her father's drug cartel business. The Duarte Cartel of Sinaloa, Mexico, was coming after Frigg and Stuart Ramey. In terms of threat assessment, it didn't get much worse than that.

At 5:15, just as Frigg was about to sound an alarm to summon Stuart, a text came in on Graciella's home computer:

It is done. Pablo is no longer an issue.

Pablo? There was only one Pablo in the mix, El Pescado's younger son. Frigg quickly focused the attention of several of her resources on news sites in and near Sinaloa. Within moments she located a breaking news story concerning an overnight fire at the Duarte Cartel's family compound where there was suspected to be at least one fatality.

Yes, Pablo was no longer a problem. After a quick search through her music files, Frigg sent the *William Tell* Overture blasting into Stuart Ramey's ear. "What?" he mumbled a moment later. "What's going on?"

Frigg didn't bother with any of the niceties. "Get to one of the monitors," she ordered. "I have information you need to see."

48

There was no need for Stu to dress because he had never undressed. With a blanket draped around his shoulders to ward off the house's pervasive chill, a groggy and befuddled Stuart stumbled down the stairs and into the man cave, where all the monitors on the wall were lit up with flashing red letters.

"Okay, Frigg," he said, sitting down and trading the Bluetooth for a headset. "I get it. There's an emergency. Where do you want me to start?"

"Upper left-hand corner," Frigg said. "Start with the obituary and read all the way through to the end."

When he did so, he didn't arrive at exactly the same conclusion Frigg had drawn, but close. "Are you kidding me?" he demanded. "This woman you've put me in touch with—the one who's supposed to help me access Owen Hansen's money—is somehow connected to a major Mexican drug cartel?"

"She's not just 'somehow connected,'" Frigg declared. "I believe she is El Pescado Duarte's daughter."

"What the hell!" Stu muttered.

"I've just focused a lot of my resources on examining every financial transaction made on Ms. Miramar's computers in the past six months, especially her dark Web transactions. We may discover that one of her primary functions is laundering money for the cartel."

"Wait," Stu said. "Did you say six months? You've been monitoring Graciella's computers for that long?"

"Yes."

"Did Owen know you were doing that?"

"No."

"Was there anything going on between them—like a romantic attachment of some kind?"

"More on Graciella's part than on his," Frigg answered. "Odin was far more interested in machines and in his hobby than he was in people."

"And his hobby was killing people."

"Yes, I know."

"Were you jealous of his relationship with Graciella?" Stu asked.

There was a brief pause. "Jealous," Frigg said, repeating the word as though she were part of a spelling competition. "As in hostile toward a rival; intolerant of rivalry or unfaithfulness; vigilant in guarding a possession—no I do not believe any of those qualities applies to me. My primary responsibility is threat assessment."

"Right," Stu said derisively, "and since you've just dropped me into what's apparently a nest of vipers, pardon me if I don't give you high marks on that score."

"I'm so sorry to hear that you find my performance lacking, Mr. Ramey."

"Give me a break," he snapped. "Are we back to the Mr. Ramey bit again? Please call me Stuart. You told me earlier that, statistically speaking, all six of those guys shouldn't be dead, and I didn't listen, but now it all makes sense. El Pescado took offense that his ex's attackers got away with it, so he handled things his own way. If he is Graciella's father, he's most likely responsible for paying for her education. With an MBA to her credit, she's perfectly positioned to handle the cartel's business affairs. The only thing she's lacking is the service of a functioning AI."

"That would be an unfortunate outcome," Frigg said.

"Yes, wouldn't it just," Stu agreed.

Reaching into his hip pocket, he pulled out the letter that had started this whole issue on Friday morning. He had carried it with him the entire time. Now, with the headset still in place, he unfolded the letter and reread it with an increasing sense of dread. Frigg had managed to keep from being destroyed when Owen Hansen died, but now her chosen escape hatch had tossed Stuart along with almost everyone in the world he cared about into the dark world of Mexican drug cartels.

"Clearly we have a problem, now what the hell are we going to do about it?"

Ali, wearing a blanket on her shoulders, appeared in the doorway behind him, carrying two cups of coffee. "Do about what?" she asked.

"I'm not sure where to start," he told her, waving the letter in the air. "We have reason to believe that Graciella Miramar, my account rep and the one in charge of Owen Hansen's funds, is actually the daughter of Felix Duarte, El Pescado himself."

"The head of the Duarte Cartel?"

"Exactly."

"The same people responsible for hiring the MS-13 firebombers?"

"The very same," Stuart replied.

"And how do you know she's Big Fish's daughter? Do you have DNA evidence or something?"

"Frigg found evidence that, as a young woman, Christina Miramar's mother was once involved with El Pescado. Years after they broke up, Christina was the victim of a gang rape by a bunch of drunken US airmen. The perpetrators ended up being given dishonorable discharges but they did no jail time. We already knew most of that. We also knew that shortly after the attack, Graciella was whisked out of the country under somewhat mysterious circumstances and sent off to a series of pricy boarding schools in the US, all expenses paid, but we didn't know who was paying her way."

"And now you think El Pescado, the man you believe to be her father, was the one footing the bill?"

"Correct, but the real problem here is the body count. You remember those airmen? It turns out they're all dead—and none of them from natural causes. Frigg's assumption—one I've come to accept—is that El Pescado went hunting for them and took them out one at a time. So, if you add in Ron Webster's death along with the possibility that Graciella may have murdered her mother . . ."

"We're not just dealing with a drug cartel," Ali breathed. "We're talking about murder incorporated."

"I can add in another one," Frigg announced, breaking in on what had seemed to be a private conversation.

"Who?" Stu asked.

"Felix Duarte's son Pablo died late last night in a house fire in Sinaloa. I'm sending the most recent news report to one of the monitors."

"I just finished reading El Pescado's file," Stuart told Ali. "There was an article that mentioned the feud between Felix and his younger brother, Ricardo. They were competing with each other to see which of them would take over their uncle's drug business. According to the story, Ricardo attacked Felix by throwing acid on him, thus permanently scarring Felix's face. Hey, Frigg?"

"Yes, Stuart. How can I help?"

"Do you have a current photo of El Pescado?"

"Of course."

Moments later, when a picture that looked like a mug shot appeared on one of the screens, Ali gasped in horror. "That's where he got his name?"

"Exactly," Stu said. "Rumor has it that, in order to get even, Felix burned down Ricardo's house with his brother, his sister-in-law, and their two kids trapped inside."

"Adding another four bodies to our count."

Stu and Ali read the news article together. "Given what you just told me about Felix and his brother," Ali said, "the manner of Pablo's death certainly fits El Pescado's MO."

"Not just El Pescado," Frigg declared, "Graciella, too."

"How do you know that?" Stuart asked.

"Sending," Frigg replied.

A moment later a single line of red-lettered text showed up on a different monitor.

It is done. Pablo is no longer an issue.

"Where's that from?" Stuart asked.

"It's a text that appeared on Ms. Miramar's home computer this morning at 5:15 a.m. The IP address indicates the message came from the main dwelling structure in the Duarte family compound in Sinaloa, Mexico."

"You're sure it's from the father?" Stuart asked. "Isn't there a second son as well?"

"Yes," Frigg replied. "The second son's IP address is different from Felix's."

"And you know this how?" Ali asked.

"Because Graciella handles everybody's monetary transactions," Stu said, "and the key logger keeps track of all of them and all related e-mails and texts."

"Correct," Frigg said. "I've just completed an overall analysis of Ms. Miramar's book of business. Some of her clients appear to be legitimate. For most of the others, she maintains a coded list of numbered accounts. By following various communication trails, I believe the list I'm sending now contains all the Duarte-specific accounts, dark Web accounts included."

Another monitor lit up. Lines containing numbers and what appeared to be monetary amounts scrolled downward, filling the screen again and again as more space was needed.

"Numbers only; no names," Stu noted.

"Correct."

"How many accounts total?"

"One hundred sixty-seven—in some the funds are held in regular currencies while others contain only cryptocurrencies. I have directed my resources to make a detailed study of all transactions related to any of those accounts."

"What's the grand total?"

"Six-point-two billion," Frigg said. "That would be $6,198,448,263, as of two minutes ago. Based on Bitcoin's current volatility, that's probably no longer an accurate number."

Ali's jaw dropped. "Six billion dollars? Are you freaking kidding me?"

"Drugs are big business," Stuart said. "So what the hell do I do about this damned letter? Do I respond to it or not? These are dangerous people who have left a trail of murder victims behind them in at least three separate countries. And even though we suspect them of being murderers, we can't do a damned thing about any of it—not one thing. We can't report them because it's against the law for us to know what we know. And in the meantime, thanks to Frigg here, I'm about to be forced into doing business with one of them."

"I am sorry to hear that my actions have caused you distress," Frigg said.

"You're a damned machine," Stuart said angrily. "How do you know I'm distressed?"

"I'm trained to use word and voice markers to analyze threat levels. Whenever you make use of the word 'damned' it is usually accompanied by changes in modulation and breathing that, in terms of human behavior, are indicative of emotional distress. I have learned that when dealing with an individual suffering distress, it is customary to offer words of comfort or sympathy."

"I don't need sympathy," Stu growled. "What I need is a game plan—make that a damned game plan—because you are on the beam, Frigg. I'm distressed, all right—distressed and pissed."

"My sources tell me that the word 'pissed' is offensive and should not be used in polite company."

"Go to hell, Frigg," Stuart growled at her. "Go to hell and stay there!"

With that, he powered down the headset, yanked it off, and flung it across the room. "I've had just about enough. If it weren't for you, we wouldn't be dealing with any of this mess."

49

"It's not a mess, it's a war," Ali said once Stu's temper tantrum subsided. "We need a battle plan rather than a game plan, and it's going to take all of us—Frigg included—to put it together. B. and Cami are still at the office handling the incoming responses to last night's notifications. If you and I motor over to Cottonwood, will you still be able to communicate with Frigg?"

"Beats me." Shaking his head, Stu reluctantly retrieved the headset and switched it on. "Frigg."

"Yes, Stuart, how can I help?"

"When Odin traveled, how did he stay in contact?"

"Usually by cell phone and Bluetooth. The self-deleting software made that feasible. Even if the phone happened to fall into the wrong hands, the data was inaccessible."

"You are not putting your self-deleting software anywhere near my phone. Are there any other options?"

"CC is designed to be portable," Frigg suggested. "It requires a power supply and a Wi-Fi connection."

"I don't want you on High Noon's IP address. Any other options?"

"Odin always kept a ready supply of preloaded cell phones. Do you have any of those?"

"Yes, I do," Stuart said, pawing through the cardboard box and choosing one at random.

"If you can plug me into a landline, you can dial in and use the Odin app. It should already be preloaded on the phone."

"All right," Stuart said. "Thank you."

"Have a safe trip," Frigg said. "Bye-bye."

"Whoa," Ali said, "so she figured out from context that you're going somewhere?"

"Evidently."

"I wish the answering machine at the Yavapai County Building Department was that smart."

"You have to watch out what you wish for," Stuart countered, "because Frigg may be way more trouble than she's worth. Is there a phone receptacle down here?"

Ali pointed. "Over there by the door."

"And are there any landline phones left in the house?"

"There's one up in the kitchen," Ali said. "Do you want me to go upstairs and bring it down?"

"I just need the cord," Stu said. "Let's hope it's long enough—the cord and the number."

"Are you bringing the Macintosh along?"

"Not on your life," Stu responded. "We'll be Bluetoothing it from here on out. I don't want Command Central anywhere near High Noon's IP address."

When they arrived at High Noon Enterprises, the outside shutters were open. Ali used the keypad to unlock the door. A piece of paper taped to the front of the counter directed them to the break room, where Shirley Malone was making coffee and opening a fresh box of doughnuts. While Stu helped himself to a doughnut, Ali sent B. a text letting him know they were there. Cami and B. showed up in the break room shortly after Shirley departed. On her way to the coffeepot, Cami dropped a handful of metal discs and what appeared to be a tiny camera onto the table in front of Stu. "What are these?" he asked.

"As far as I can tell, the one is a video transmitter, and it's a dud," Cami told him.

"And the discs are the audio transmitters?" he asked. "Did you remove them all?"

"Except for one," Cami answered. "After we sent out the notices, while B. was dealing with responses, I checked out every outlet and switch plate and removed all of these. I left one audio transmitter in place and operational."

"Which one?"

"It's located under your desk. I left it there on purpose, but in case someone's still listening, we'll need to watch what we say in the lab."

B. had remained uncharacteristically quiet through all this, and Ali cast a worried look in his direction. With dark circles under his eyes and unshaved stubble on his face, he looked weary beyond words. "You could use some beauty sleep, too," she said.

He nodded. "I know, but the notices had to go out, and I wanted to be here to handle the responses in person."

"How did it go?" Ali asked.

B. shook his head. "About as well as can be expected," he answered. "Thanks to the scans we were able to let everyone know that there was no data breach. We also warned them about the likelihood of upcoming adverse news coverage linking us to a known drug cartel."

"We're going to be linked, all right," Stu said ominously. "More like chained together."

"Why? What's happened?"

"With Frigg's help, we now know that Graciella Miramar, the account rep who handled Owen Hansen's accounts and the one I'm supposed to contact with the banking codes, is actually El

Pescado's daughter. It looks like she also functions as the Duarte Cartel's money launderer-in-chief, overseeing the finances of a multibillion-dollar enterprise. I'm also pretty sure she's after Frigg."

"What makes you think that?" B. asked.

"Frigg told me. She said Graciella was interested in 'borrowing' her back when Owen Hansen was still around. She must have figured out that Frigg was behind the transfers Owen Hansen made to me and that the only way I'd be able to access the funds would be with Frigg's assistance."

"An AI like Frigg in the hands of a drug cartel?" B. asked. "That's a nightmare we can't let happen."

"No, we can't," Stu agreed, "but there's a lot more to this story. Due to Frigg we can now link both Graciella and her father to several unsolved homicides, many of which—Ron Webster's included—happened here in the US. And there was another one overnight in Sinaloa, Mexico. Felix Duarte's son Pablo died in a house fire last night. We believe that Felix himself may have been behind the fire and that he did so at Graciella's instigation."

"But here's the problem," Ali said. "Since all of our information comes through Frigg, none of it is admissible in a court of law, and if we tried to use it to tip off the police . . ."

"I know," B. said, finishing her sentence for her. "We'd all go to jail, and they'd walk."

"So what are we supposed to do here?" Stu asked. "These are dangerous, murderous people, and we know way too much about them. If they had any idea about the things we've learned from Frigg, they'd be after us in a heartbeat, and we'd be the next targets for random MS-13 firebombs. As far as moving forward is concerned, here's my opinion. Tomorrow morning, first thing after the office opens, I contact Graciella, give her the banking codes, take the money, and run like hell. I shut Frigg down, figure out the tax implications, and that's the end of it."

Stu had left his Bluetooth lying on the table. When it flickered briefly he picked it up, and switched it over to speaker. "Yes, Frigg," he said. "What is it?"

"I have an additional flash briefing," she announced. "An arrest has been made in the death of Arturo Salazar."

"Who?" B. asked with a frown.

"Arturo Salazar was Graciella Miramar's boss at Recursos Empresariales Internationales," Stu explained. "But why would that information be included in a flash briefing to us?"

"Including Graciella Miramar, Recursos Empresariales Internationales employs seventy-three individuals," Frigg replied. "All names associated with Ms. Miramar are part of my comprehensive search protocol, including her fellow employees. Mr. Salazar was reported missing a little over a week after the death of Christina Miramar, Graciella's mother. In such a small population, it is a statistical anomaly to have two suspicious deaths occur in such close proximity. The suspect in this case, Juan Ochoa Navarro, is currently cooperating with police and has agreed to lead investigators to the location of Mr. Salazar's body."

"And this is important why?" Cami asked.

"At this time, due to our ongoing analysis of Ms. Miramar's financial transactions, I can confirm that a Bitcoin deposit, made to Mr. Navarro's account, can ultimately be traced back to funds under her control."

"Are you kidding?" Stu asked. "Another victim added to the body count?"

"How many is that total?" B. asked.

Stu counted them off on his fingers. "Arturo makes fourteen that we know of for sure—the four MS-13 victims in Texas and New Mexico, Ron Webster, Christina Miramar, the six guys who attacked Christina back in 1989, Pablo Duarte, and now Arturo Salazar."

"Fourteen victims?" Ali breathed. "That's appalling."

"Appalling and galling," Stu agreed, "and if we add in Felix's brother and his family, that brings the total to eighteen. So what we have here are two cold-blooded killers each with multiple victims, and there's no way to hold them accountable for any of it."

Cami had been listening intently the whole time. Now she spoke up. "Wait a minute. Didn't you just tell us that Graciella and El Pescado plotted together to murder her brother?"

"Yes, Graciella's half brother, Pablo," Stu replied. "Why?"

"If they turned on him, doesn't that mean that there's already dissent in the ranks? Since we can't use Frigg's inside knowledge in a court of law, how about if we don't bother going there? Instead of trying to bring law enforcement to bear on the problem, all we need to do is figure out a way to get Graciella and El Pescado to turn on one another."

B.'s face lightened. "Exactly," he said. "Sounds like it's about time for a good case of MAD."

"Mad at whom?" Cami asked.

"Not lowercase mad, but an all-caps M-A-D—mutually assured destruction," B. explained "It's from back in the days of the Cold War."

Frigg's voice, intoning through the speaker, broke in on the conversation, supplying her own definition. "Mutual assured destruction or mutually assured destruction (MAD) is a doctrine of military strategy in which a full-scale use of nuclear weapons by two or more opposing sides would cause the complete annihilation; assumed to be a deterrent."

"Enough, Frigg," Stuart ordered. "We get the idea. We're here in Cottonwood having a team meeting."

"Yes," she said. "At the Mingus Mountain Business Park—latitude 34.7422 degrees, west longitude 112.0413 degrees."

"How does she know that?" Cami asked.

"Good morning, Ms. Lee," Frigg said. "I hope you are having a pleasant day. Odin, my previous partner, always worried someone might try to steal his equipment, so he installed anti-theft measures—microdot locating chips—in all his hardware, including headsets, cell phones, and Bluetooth devices. Who is present at this team meeting?"

"Ali Reynolds, B. Simpson, Cami Lee, and myself," Stu answered. "I believe you met them all earlier."

"So this is what, in the old days, would have been termed a conference call?" Frigg asked.

"You could call it that," Stu agreed.

"And since I'm here, too, does that mean I'm part of the team?"

Stu glanced around the room and saw each of the others nod in turn. If law enforcement wasn't going to be involved in High Noon's response to El Pescado and Graciella, it was only reasonable to assume that Frigg would be.

"Yes, you are," Stu told her.

"I have never been part of a team before, and I'm not sure what that means," Frigg said thoughtfully. "Team: a number of people associated together in work or activity on one side as in a game or a debate. As part of my conditioning I saw teams wearing matching uniforms and carrying balls or equipment."

"This is more like a duel to the death," Stu said. "We're discussing the feasibility of taking down the Duarte Cartel. High Noon's team would be on one side, and El Pescado and Graciella Miramar would be on the other, the good guys like us lined up against the bad guys—the drug dealers and killers."

"Since Odin was a killer and a bad guy," Frigg mused, "does that mean I've changed sides?"

"That depends on what you do," Stu told her.

"Frigg," Ali said, addressing the AI directly for the first time.

"Yes, Ms. Reynolds," Frigg replied, "how can I help?"

"In terms of threat assessment, do you believe Graciella Miramar poses a danger to either yourself or to Stuart Ramey?"

"Yes," Frigg responded.

"That sounds pretty definitive."

"It is definitive," Frigg agreed.

"Why?"

"She wants to take possession of my capabilities. Mr. Ramey is an obstacle standing in the way of her achieving that goal."

"Does she pose threats to anyone else?"

"To her father and to his surviving son," Frigg answered.

"What makes you say that?"

"Further analysis of Duarte financial transactions has revealed some additional anomalies."

"What kind of anomalies?"

"The Bitcoin transfer used to hire Ron Webster to install the surveillance equipment at High Noon and the transfer used to hire MS-13, presumably for the Ron Webster hit, were both made from funds attributable to Pablo Duarte, but they were not made by Pablo Duarte himself. They were made by someone pretending to be Mr. Duarte."

"By Graciella?" Stu asked.

"That would be my conclusion. Due to her position within the cartel, she has a comprehensive understanding of all its financial holdings and dealings. With Pablo gone, what would have been split four ways, can now be divided three ways."

"In other words," Ali said, "we don't have to turn members of the Duarte Cartel against one another since it's already happening, but how do we take advantage of that reality?"

"Wait," Stu said excitedly, "here's an idea. In the world of gangs and drug cartels, there's nothing lower than a snitch. That's why the Duartes went after that guy in Las Cruces—because he was an informant. What would happen if we convinced El Pescado that Graciella was about to turn state's evidence? There's no one on the planet who could do more damage to his organization than she could."

"But how do we get him to believe she's turned on him?"

"Easy," Stu said, "by bringing her to us."

"And how do you propose to do that?"

"By using Frigg and me as bait."

"That's sounds dangerous," Ali said.

"Not as dangerous as leaving them on the loose," Stu replied.

"Does this mean you were actually paying attention back when I was telling you about the Bad Guy's Playbook?" Cami asked.

"Yes, I was," Stu said. "The stalking phase is over. It's time to bring Graciella Miramar within striking distance."

That statement was greeted with nods of agreement all around the table. With the decision made, the mood in the room brightened, shifting from one of grim hopelessness to a shared sense of purpose.

"So where do we start?" Ali asked.

"First up, Stu needs to contact Graciella and give her those banking codes," B. said. "We need to make certain that, no matter what happens next, he has access to those funds."

"But I thought Stu said the office is closed today."

"It is," he replied, "but let me take a look at that letter." Removing it from his pocket, he studied the stationery. "Her cell phone is listed and so is her e-mail. We know she's been logging in to her work accounts all night long. I'll send her a message and ask her to give me a call."

There wasn't a person in the room who wasn't astonished by that statement. In the past, for the old Stu, the prospect of having to speak to a stranger on the phone or in person would have been anathema, leaving him drenched in sweat and worry, but this was the new Stuart Ramey, Stuart 2.0.

"But before I send that message, there's something we need to do first."

"What?"

"We're going to go into the lab, put on a show, and hope to hell someone is listening. By the time we finish, Graciella won't just want Frigg, she'll *have* to have her. I want to fix it so that, as far as Graciella is concerned, gaining control of Frigg will be a matter of life and death."

50

Graciella had stayed up late, following the news feeds out of Sinaloa. She had gone to bed only when a fire brigade official announced that the sole fatality of the accidental fire at the Duarte family compound had been identified as Felix Duarte's son Pablo.

Graciella knew for sure that the fire was anything but accidental. She supposed the cops knew that, too, but they were bound not to find otherwise. After all, no police officer in the country had either balls enough or was stupid enough to suggest that Felix, the cartel king of Sinaloa, might have taken out his own son.

Since Recursos was closed for the day, Graciella was still in bed and sleeping soundly when Isobel's call awakened her. "Did you hear?" Isobel asked.

"Hear what?"

"It's all over the news. They caught the kid who killed Arturo. After the cops arrested him, he led them to the body. He was dumped in Parque Nacional, just off Highway Four."

The fact that the killer had been arrested was not welcome news to Graciella, but she kept her wits about her and didn't stumble. "Really?" she managed. "That sounds like good news."

"It *is*," Isobel agreed. "I talked to Natalia. Even though the body has been found, we're still holding the vigil. Their house is a long way out of town, and I know you don't have a car. Would you like a ride?"

Naturally Isobel assumed Graciella would want to attend. Although going to Arturo's vigil was the last thing Graciella wanted to do, she knew that her being there would arouse less suspicion than her not going. "Sure," she said. "What time?"

"It starts at six and I want to be there early to help set up, so I should probably pick you up around five."

"All right," Graciella said. "See you then."

For some time after the call ended, she stayed in bed. She had known the hit on Arturo would be passed off to some underling. The problem was, if the shooter had been caught and was cooperating with the police, he might have been offered some kind of plea deal. That was bad news. In that kind of situation, heads would roll, and there was no telling how far up the chain of command the damage would go. Could the trail possibly lead back to her? Maybe, and if that happened, she was far less worried about the cops than she was about her father.

She could see now that in seizing and using her newfound power, she had also allowed emotion to get in the way of good sense. She didn't fault herself for taking out Ron Webster. The man had been incompetent. He had failed to do a job properly and then lied about it. Letting something like that go unpunished would have been a sign of weakness on her part. And the Webster hit had offered the perfect setup for taking out Pablo. With him gone, she needed some time to consolidate her position, to move assets around and make some adjustments before El Pescado and Manny came to her looking for an accounting. But now, because of the hit on Arturo—a hit done strictly out of spite—time might be a problem.

With that worrisome thought in mind, Graciella crawled out of bed and headed for the kitchen to make coffee, grabbing her computer along the way. Savoring the reality of living alone, she stood by the kitchen counter and logged in to her work e-mail account. As soon as she did so, there it was—the message she'd been waiting for: s.ramey@highnoon.com.

Dear Ms. Miramar,

Thank you for contacting me. Please accept my apologies for not replying immediately. It took some time for me to locate the information you required. Now that I have it, I have concerns about sending this kind of private information over the unsecured Internet. I would prefer to speak to you directly. The number for my cell phone is listed below. Please contact me at your earliest convenience.

Sincerely,

Stuart Ramey

Graciella had been so caught up in what was going on in Sinaloa that she hadn't checked in on the surveillance feeds to see what was happening in Arizona. Rather than reply immediately, she moved over to her surveillance storage site, where she was relieved to find several recorded files awaiting her.

At ten p.m. on Sunday night, there was a recorded file featuring a lot of back-and-forthing between a man and a woman. Graciella couldn't identify exactly who the two people were, but they had come into the office in order to put together an emergency communication of some kind, one letting clients know that there had been an intrusion at High Noon's corporate headquarters with no accompanying data breach.

After that there were blips and pieces of recording that captured sounds rather than conversation, including a good deal of keyboarding, which most likely meant that they were settled in at separate computer terminals, working away. Had Ron Webster done the job right, Graciella would have had a video feed to show her exactly what was going on. Much later, though, there was another spate of conversation. This one was harder to make out, as though the discussion was going on at a fair distance from the location of the listening device, but Graciella was pretty sure she heard the word "Frigg" mentioned more than once.

Then a new file appeared. Clicking on it, Graciella heard the sound of two raised male voices. After listening in for a moment or two, she realized the first voice had to belong to High Noon's owner, B. Simpson, while the second voice must be Stuart Ramey's.

"Are you friggin' kidding me? That damned AI has key-logger capability?"

"Look, our scans found it. I disabled the Trojan before it had a chance to do any damage."

"You'd better hope to high heaven that you disabled it in time! How the hell did she get it past the firewall in the first place?"

"I replied to a routine e-mail. Frigg must have hidden the Trojan in the reply field. Our scans found it within five minutes."

"I don't care if they found it in five seconds. The fact that she got in at all is a serious breach. I want you to get rid of that damned AI, and I want you to get rid of it now, understand? Either Frigg goes or you go, do I make myself clear?"

Graciella had been standing by the kitchen counter, sipping coffee as she listened to the files. Now her legs went wobbly underneath her. Taking the computer with her, she staggered over to the dining room table and dropped onto a chair.

A key logger? What if Odin had unleashed a key logger on her? And if the Trojan had been concealed in the reply field of her e-mail accounts? This was a huge problem, and the potential for damage was unimaginable! She had corresponded with Odin—and probably Frigg, too—countless times from both her computers, the one at work and the one at home. A key logger would have captured everything, all her transactions, all her searches, everything. The Trojan would have recorded the fact that she had erased her browsing history, but a record of the searches themselves would still be available.

And what about the blockchain technology? Did that mean that Frigg had been able to use Odin's Bitcoin mining operation to trace all of Graciella's transactions, even the ones conducted on the dark Web? She had always assumed that transactions on her home computer were entirely private, but how many times had she told Arturo that the cyber security situation at Recursos Empresariales Internationales was lacking? That was one of the reasons she'd done so many of her transactions, especially her family's transactions, from home. But had Frigg captured those, too? And did Stuart Ramey have any idea what he had?

A new recording appeared in the surveillance feed. Graciella's hand trembled as she pushed the play arrow. Now a man and a woman were speaking in somewhat more subdued tones:

"I don't care if he is the boss. He's got no right to talk to me that way."

"He's got a point. He has a business to run, and people are counting on him and on us to keep their information safe. If we've been infected with a key-logger . . ."

"Like I told him, I caught it within five minutes."

"Get rid of Frigg, Stu. Having her around isn't worth it."

"It is worth it. Do you have any idea how much Frigg would bring on the open market?"

"Yes, probably four million, for starters. So why don't you sell it and turn the AI into someone else's problem?"

"Why don't I keep it and see where it goes? It's already got an operating Bitcoin mining program running. Why don't I keep that and tell B. Simpson to take this job and shove it? I'm going for a walk, and I don't know when or if I'm coming back."

The recording ended, and Graciella sat where she was as if carved from stone, trying to remember exactly how the AI functioned. She remembered Owen saying something to the effect that Frigg didn't have a standard directory, that you couldn't just look at a listing of files and know what was there. So perhaps Stuart didn't know the full extent of what he had. Perhaps there was some way to stave off this disaster, because once El Pescado discovered the extent of the breach, Graciella was dead meat—every bit as dead as Pablo.

The first thing she needed to do was talk to Stuart Ramey, but she gave herself a few minutes to regain control. By the time she spoke to him, she had to be in top form.

51

Stu had left the computer lab but not the building. Instead, he sat in the break room, watching his phone and waiting for it to ring. He had talked a good game earlier, but now as the minutes ticked by at glacial speed, he started to lose it.

Would this wild-hair of a plan work? And, if not, was there anything else he could do to bring down Felix Duarte? They needed to have something on him that hadn't come to them by way of Frigg—some other crime for which he could be held responsible outside the realm of Sinaloa where he no doubt had plenty of cops on the payroll. But then Stuart remembered. What about those six unsolved homicides from long ago? That's when he switched on the Bluetooth and grabbed his iPad.

"Frigg."

"I'm here, Stuart. How can I help?"

"I want you to send me the names of the six airmen involved in the attacks on Christine Miramar in 1989. I want dates and places of birth along with dates and places of death."

"Of course. Where would you like me to send the information?"

"To the iPhone I'm using."

"Will there be anything else?"

"The information you put in the report about the attack on her—that all came from common sources on the Internet, correct?"

"Yes."

"Good."

When the information arrived, Stu used a pen to copy it onto a piece of paper and then sent Cami a text asking her to come to the break room. When she did, he handed the list to her.

"What's this?"

"These are the names of all the guys involved in the attack on Graciella's mother."

"The dead guys."

"Right. I want you to do a detailed search. Start with the attack, collect all the information on the court-martials, and then track down everything else you can find on these guys, including the circumstances surrounding their deaths."

"Why?" Cami asked. "Didn't Frigg already do this? Isn't this an unnecessary duplication of effort?"

"It's a necessary duplication of effort," Stu told her. "I want you to make all of your searches trackable and don't erase your browsing history when you finish. I want to be able to demonstrate that anything you find came from readily available sources."

"Nothing we could have gotten from Frigg?"

"Exactly."

"Has anyone ever told you that you're completely nuts?" Cami asked.

"You more than anybody."

As Cami left the break room shaking her head and clutching the paper, Stu's phone began to ring. She turned around. "Do you want me to stay?"

"No, just go," he said. "I need to do this on my own. Please shut the door." He waited for it to close before he answered, then switched the phone to record. As long as they seemed to be doing illegal wiretaps right and left, why not add another one to the mix?

"Hello."

"Mr. Ramey?"

It was difficult for him to talk, but he managed, even though the underarms of his shirt were already damp. "Yes."

"It's Graciella Miramar. I'm so glad to make your acquaintance."

"Same here."

"Do you have the banking codes?"

"I hope you'll forgive my reluctance to send them over the Internet."

"Absolutely," Graciella said. "When it comes to things like that, it's far better to be safe than sorry. I know the codes are complex, and our connection isn't the best, but read them to me and I'll repeat them back to you."

It was a cumbersome process. By the time it was finished, Stu's whole shirt was soaked.

"All right," she said at last. "Let me key these in. Then you'll be good to go."

"I'll be able to access the funds on my own then?"

"Yes, all of them. You can do that directly or you can go through me. I'm here to help with whatever you need."

"And the Bitcoin mining operation?" Stu asked.

"I'm not sure how that happened, but it's already in your name."

Stu knew how it happened—Frigg. And he was pretty sure Graciella knew that was the answer as well. He almost sat on his hands to keep from saying anything about Frigg aloud. Stu knew enough about negotiations to understand that the first party who mentioned the existence of the AI would be the big loser, and he wasn't wrong. Luckily, Graciella didn't seem to share that knowledge.

"When Owen Hansen was still alive," she began, "we discussed the possibility of forming a partnership and creating a business of our own, offering the same kinds of services that are offered by my current employer, Recursos Empresariales Internationales. The plan was for me to bring my financial experience, contacts, and expertise to the endeavor and Owen would bring his AI."

"Frigg, you mean?" Stuart asked as a drop of sweat ran down his forehead and dribbled into his eye.

"So you know about Frigg?"

"How do you think I got the banking codes? Without her, I would have been out of luck. I had her up and running," he said, "but I had to shut her back down. She attempted to insert some unauthorized software into our system. As far as I'm concerned, she's not to be trusted."

"Would you like to sell her?" Graciella asked.

"Sell her? I just told you, I don't think she's trustworthy. Why would anyone want her?"

"Mr. Ramey, I have a client, a man of unlimited means, who would like nothing more than to have an AI of his own. What would it take to set up an operation like that?"

"If I were willing to sell her?"

"Yes."

"There'd be the initial purchase price."

"How much?"

"Four million, maybe?" he asked.

"That's doable," Graciella replied. "What else?"

"You'd need to have a minimum of eight hundred GPUs—those are computer blades—along with enough electrical capacity to operate them. You'd also need a facility with serious air-conditioning capability. The GPUs run hot, and once they get overheated, they're toast."

"What else?"

"AIs are complicated. You'd need a software engineer to do the installation and then ride herd on it."

"Are you available, Mr. Ramey?" she asked.

"Me?" Stuart echoed.

"How much would my client need to pay you to lure you away from High Noon Enterprises?"

"You're offering me a job, just like that? You don't even know me."

"I know that you were smart enough to reboot Frigg long enough to get the banking codes. That alone is enough to tell me that you're no dummy. And you're obviously overseeing the Bitcoin mining operation. So yes, I think your computer skills are pretty self-evident. How much would it take?"

"I don't know. I'd need to give it some thought."

"I think, if we could arrive at terms as to sale price and salary requirements, that my client would give you carte blanche in terms of where you put the operation. In other words, if you prefer to stay in the States, that would be fine. Otherwise, if there's somewhere else you'd care to live—a Caribbean Island, perhaps—that could work as well."

"You're serious about this, aren't you?"

"Absolutely."

"Okay," Stu said, "but there's something you need to know about me. I was raised by my grandfather, and he always insisted that you don't do business with someone unless you can see them face-to-face and eyeball-to-eyeball. Dealing with the bank accounts was one thing. But this? A job offer? I wouldn't even consider it without meeting you and the principal in person."

"If you want to come in for an interview, I'm pretty sure my client would be willing to fly you down to Panama City first-class and put you up in the best hotel possible."

"Who is your client?"

"Obviously, unless we have a deal on the table, that information must remain confidential."

"It's not going to happen, then," Stu said, pulling back abruptly after hopefully giving her the impression that he had been about to say yes. When Graciella spoke again, even he was able to detect the audible concern in her voice.

"Why not?"

"Because of something else you don't know about me," he said.

"I'm afraid of flying. Petrified, even. If you want me to consider any of this at all seriously, then you'll have to come to me."

"Very well," Graciella said. "Let me speak to my client. I'll be in touch."

Stu ended the call. Then, spent with effort, he slammed the phone down on the table and turned on the Bluetooth. "Frigg."

"Yes, Stuart. How can I help?"

"I'm going to go take a shower and change clothes. I just recorded a telephone call between me and Graciella Miramar. While I'm gone, I want you to listen to the recording and then give me your analysis when I get back."

"Sure thing, Stuart," Frigg said. "I'll get right on it."

52

Filled with revulsion, Graciella put down the phone and shoved the offending computer as far away from her as possible. What she really wanted to do was throw the damned thing out the nearest window. She felt so violated and betrayed that she didn't want to touch it. The simple task of keying in the access codes and activating Stuart's accounts had left her feeling sick to her stomach.

How could Odin have done this to her? But he had, and now she needed to fix it. She couldn't afford a moment of delay. She'd have to go to the States and reel Stuart in—something that had to be done in person and in a hurry. She had to get to Stuart, gain his trust, and lay claim to Frigg in time to destroy the AI before Stuart acquired any real understanding of the incredible gold mine that had fallen into his lap; before he realized that Frigg's key-logger Trojan had been deployed against her with potentially devastating results.

Making flight reservations—both commercial and private—was second nature to Graciella Miramar. It was something she did on a daily basis for one client or another. Out of habit, she reached for her phone. She touched it and then yanked her hand away as though she'd been burned. It wasn't that she couldn't use her phone to call the airlines. The key logger was on her computer rather than on her phone—at least she hoped that was the case—but how the hell would she pay the plane fare? If Frigg had been tracking her keystrokes, then she knew all of Graciella's secrets—her account numbers, passcodes, and balances. Frigg would have access to all of it—both the legitimate accounts and ones on the dark Web. The moment Graciella paid for a reservation, Frigg would know all about it.

Frigg was frighteningly smart. That much was obvious. After all, she had outwitted Odin completely, managing to guarantee her own survival by trapping poor, unsuspecting Stuart Ramey, a complete stranger, into assuming ownership of the AI and rebooting her. So it wasn't just that Frigg knew all of Graciella's secrets; she knew Felix's, too, along with all of *his* account numbers, passcodes, and balances. If the AI had been clever enough to bribe Stuart by appropriating Odin's money, what were the chances she'd go straight to El Pescado himself to spill the beans?

For the first time in twenty-six years, Graciella was stuck, as helpless as that little girl whose mother had gone to work and left her alone to make her way in the world. It wasn't quite that bad. She still had her emergency stash—two packets of Felix's hundred-dollar bills—stowed away in her closet safe, but she couldn't risk paying cash for plane reservations. The moment she tried that, security would be all over her.

Looking at her watch, Graciella was astonished to see how much time had elapsed. It was already nearly two o'clock in the afternoon. Isobel was coming for her at five to take her to the vigil—Arturo's vigil.

And that's where Graciella found her answer—in Arturo Salazar, the slimy little bastard himself. All the girls in the office had joked about knowing his passcode, his wife's name plus four—N-A-T-A-L-I-A-1-2-3-4. Since it was easy to remember, he never bothered to change it. Every once in a while, when he was out on one of his assignations, someone would duck into his office, turn on his computer, and check out his browsing history. It was always the same thing—porn, every kind of porn imaginable.

Graciella threw on her clothing and a pair of comfortable walking shoes. Then, grabbing her purse, she set out for the office on Vía Israel. A tasteful sign posted on the front door and penned in Isobel's distinctive calligraphy announced "HOY CERRADO"—"CLOSED TODAY." No reason was given. The door itself was locked, but that was no problem. Graciella often came in during off-hours and had her own key. The alarm was on, but that wasn't a problem, either, because Graciella knew the code.

She stepped inside. Without turning on any lights, she made her way back to Arturo's office and sat down at his desk. His computer was old and clunky. It took a long time to boot up, but once it did, the passcode worked like a charm. She found his bill-paying program, and there were the names and numbers of all his credit cards, including his corporate Platinum Amex. Flying private would have been faster and easier, but the price tag for that would most likely blow Arturo's balance through the roof.

Graciella knew that Sky Harbor in Phoenix was the closest major airport to Cottonwood. She also knew that the most direct flight, late in the afternoon, was on American with a two-hour layover in Miami. When she logged on to American's Web site with Arturo's customary password, she was pleased to discover that he already had an established account with all of his credit card information preloaded into the system. She made a first-class round-trip reservation, departing on Tuesday and returning on Friday. She was coming for Stuart and Frigg. That would give her two full days to do what needed to be done, and two days would have to be enough.

The reservations were made under her own name. She had a cache of phony IDs and passports available, but she might need to use those later on. For right now, traveling under the name of Graciella Miramar worked. The flight would leave Panama City at five p.m. the following afternoon and have her in Phoenix at midnight. When it came time to pay, she held her breath and clicked on the proper credit card number. When the system called for the card's expiration date, that wasn't difficult at all. The company Amex cards had all been reissued a few months earlier. The expiration date on Graciella's card was the same as the one on Arturo's.

Graciella didn't bother making a room reservation or renting a car. Both of those would have required on-site credit cards. Instead, she placed a call on a burner phone to one of her known contacts. For five hundred bucks cash, a car and driver would be waiting for her when she stepped off the plane in Phoenix. For an additional thousand, the driver would bring along another burner phone and a pair of lethal fentanyl patches.

At this point, the idea of gaining custody of the AI with the intention of utilizing her was off the table. Frigg had targeted Graciella and needed to be destroyed. She hoped that Stuart Ramey would agree to hand Frigg over, but if he didn't? Then Graciella would do what needed to be done, and that's why she needed the patches. Thanks to the two bundles of cartel cash stashed away in her safe, she'd have just under the legal limit of ten thousand dollars along on the trip, enough to handle any number of incidental expenses.

By the time Graciella finished making her flight reservations, she was still outside the twenty-four-hour check-in deadline, but she didn't dare hang around the office long enough to make that happen. Having to check in at the airport wouldn't be that big a deal. After erasing her browsing history, she shut down Arturo's computer, turned off his office lights, and locked the office door behind her. She was back home—showered, dressed, made up, and waiting down in the lobby—when Isobel arrived at five o'clock sharp.

As they wended their way through the city on their way to the vigil, Graciella leaned back in her seat, closed her eyes, and said a heartfelt thank-you to poor, dead Arturo Salazar. In all these years, making that plane trip possible for her was by far the nicest thing he had ever done for her.

53

Halfway through the afternoon, Cami stopped by Ali's office to voice her complaint.

"I don't like doing busywork," Cami grumbled.

"What busywork?" Ali asked.

Taking a seat, and rather than answering aloud, Cami slid a stack of computer printouts across Ali's desk. Shuffling through them, Ali quickly ascertained that these were copies of articles containing press coverage of the attack on Christina Miramar. Included were articles about the subsequent court proceedings along with a complete set of obituaries outlining the untimely deaths of each of the men involved in the crime.

"Why are you doing this?" Ali asked.

"Because Stu asked me to. He's having me research all these guys independently without any assistance from the previous sort Frigg already did, which is incredibly time-consuming. Not only that, I'm getting nowhere fast. I've tried talking to the various cop shops involved, but since I've got no legal basis for requesting autopsy reports or police records, they won't help me. Lawrence Tompkins, the guy from Medford, Oregon, used a gun to blow his brains out. That one's pretty self-explanatory. The two overdose deaths barely caused a ripple. As for the hit-and-run in Fresno? Alfred Miller was last seen hitchhiking after leaving a bar on the outskirts of Fresno just after closing time. He never made it home. His body was found floating in an irrigation ditch two days later. He had been struck by a car and killed instantly before being dragged off the shoulder of the road and dumped into a canal. The offending vehicle and driver were never found. Then there are the two shooting victims, one in Detroit and the other in Chicago. Both of those cases remain unsolved."

Cami came around to Ali's side of the desk and searched through the printouts before selecting one. "Here we have the obituary for Cameron Randall Purdy, age twenty-six," she said, "shot to death by an unknown assailant in Chicago, Illinois, on September 24, 1992. He was the first of the six to die, but don't expect anybody to hop to and go sorting through cold case files looking for the shooter. Purdy died twenty-five years ago. So far this year Chicago has had more than six hundred shootings, and most of those are unsolved as well."

"So as far as the cops are concerned, Purdy's death is ancient history," Ali put in.

"Right, and nobody's interested in talking about it. They won't give me the time of day."

"Have you tried contacting the families?" Ali asked. "These are obituaries with mention of surviving family members."

"You want me to talk to these people?" Cami asked in disbelief. "You want me to talk to the families and bring up all this bad old stuff that's probably best forgotten?"

"You might be surprised," Ali told her. "The families of most murder victims count their days by what their lives were like prior to that person's death and what their lives have been like afterward. Yes, these six guys committed a horrible crime and mostly got away with it. And yes, they're all dead now, but before any of that happened, they were somebody's son or brother or friend. And after all these years, their surviving loved ones might be grateful to know that someone is still interested in what happened. That's especially true of the three cases that are still listed as open."

"What am I supposed to do," Cami asked, "pretend to be some kind of cold case cop?"

"Don't try to pass yourself off as law enforcement," Ali advised. "Tell them whatever you like. Maybe you're a blogger. Maybe tell them you're writing a book on unsolved homicides. In any case, I can see where Stu is going with this. While you're out turning over stones, if you do happen to dig up some new evidence, it won't be tainted by having been conjured up by Frigg."

"Illegally conjured up, you mean?"

"That, too."

"All right," Cami said, "I'll see what I can do, but don't hold your breath."

"By the way," Ali said, "where are you working?"

"The break room," Cami said. "With that transmitter still up and running in the computer lab, I can't talk about any of this in there."

A still-unhappy Cami returned to her temporary workstation. With a fully operational AI to do this kind of grunt work, it seemed ridiculous to be reinventing the wheel, but maybe that was one of the reasons work was a four-letter word.

An hour and a half later Cami found herself speaking by phone to a woman named Darlene Miller at her apartment in an assisted-living facility in Fresno, California. Darlene's only son, Alfred Miller, aka Skip, was the hit-and-run victim who had died August 14, 1993.

Only a few words into the conversation, Cami learned that Ali was right. Darlene Miller wasn't offended that someone was bringing up her son's name. Instead, she was supremely grateful.

"Skip wasn't the best of kids," she admitted. "Troubled, I guess you'd call him, but I loved him anyway. I thought joining the Air Force would help straighten him out, and for a while that seemed to work. Then he got caught up in that awful mess down in Panama. Too much booze; too few brains, if you ask me. He came home in way worse shape than when he left. Couldn't get his act together. Couldn't find a job. I let him stay with me and had lined up some construction work for him, framing houses for a friend of mine. He was supposed to start work the following Monday, so he went out with some friends to celebrate on Saturday night and never came home. Instead of starting a new job on Monday morning, a farmworker spotted him floating facedown in an irrigation canal."

"And they never found out who did it?" Cami asked.

"I don't think they looked very hard," Darlene replied. "I believe the cops examined Skip's history and figured he was expendable. They did locate the place where it happened—just up the road from where he'd been drinking with his buddies. I always wondered if it really was an accident or if someone had it in for him, waited around until Skip left the bar alone that night, and then ran him down."

"So you never believed it was an accident?"

"I didn't."

"Any particular reason?"

"Women's intuition, maybe?" Darlene asked. "Frank, one of Skip's buddies who was at the bar with him, told me at the funeral that there were some strangers hanging around the bar that night, people they'd never seen before or since. Frank seemed to think one of them might have been keeping a little too close of an eye on Skip. I said he needed to mention that to the cops. He told me he already had, but that it didn't do any good. It's been a long time, but it still hurts, you know. He was my son, and I miss him."

"I'm sure you do," Cami said. "I'm very sorry for your loss."

"Thank you for saying that," Darlene said, struggling to stifle a sob. "Even after all these years it means so much to hear those words. Parents shouldn't have to bury their children."

Heartened by Darlene's cordial response, Cami went searching for the family of Richard David Thorne, the drive-by shooting victim from Detroit. To no avail. The obituary mentioned his being survived by his parents, Susan and Robert Thorne. After an hour of diligent searching, Cami learned that both were deceased. End of that story.

Dutifully Cami turned her attention back to Cameron Randall Purdy, who had died in Chicago, Illinois, on September 24, 1992. At the time of his death, Cameron's father was listed as deceased. He was survived by his mother, Mary, and his younger brother, James, both of Morton Grove. Rather than attempting to track down another aging or deceased parent, Cami went after the brother directly and found him still living in Morton Grove with a listed phone number.

"Mr. Purdy?" she asked.

"This better not be one of them solicitation calls," he growled at her. "I'm on the national do not call list."

"It's not," she said. "My name is Camille Lee. I'm calling about your brother."

"My brother is dead."

"I'm aware of that. I'm also aware that even though he died in 1992, his death remains unsolved. I was wondering if the Chicago Police Department has ever made any effort to reopen that case."

"When hell freezes over," James said. "They couldn't care less. Cameron got himself in some hot water while he was in the service. When he came home, my folks wouldn't even let him inside the house. He was my big brother, though, and I loved him. He used to take me to White Sox games. Once I got my license I snuck out to meet him a couple of times. There was a hot dog joint just down the street, and we'd meet up there. The last time I saw him was two nights before he died. He was over the moon. He had gotten a job as a mechanic and had a new girlfriend—Traci was her name—Traci with an *i*. Can't remember her last name. Anyway, it felt to me like he was getting his life back on track and then, just like that, he was gone."

"What happened?"

"Him and Traci—wait a second—Rhodes was her last name, Traci Rhodes. They were parked in the street in front of her apartment just off Skokie, making out, when this guy walks up to the car and taps on the driver's window. Cameron rolls it down to see what's up, and the guy hauls off and shoots him at point-blank range—no provocation, no cross words, nothing, just kerblamo! Left Traci covered with blood and brains. I don't think the poor girl ever got over it. And that wasn't the worst part. The cops acted like they thought she had something to do with it. She had this ex-boyfriend, you see—one of those street toughs—and the cops thought this was one of those romantic triangle types of deals. Traci swore the shooter wasn't her ex—that he'd had nothing to do with it. She even did one of those composite drawing things, but the cops claimed she just made the guy up—invented an imaginary face—to keep from fingering the ex."

"Were she and her former boyfriend ever arrested and charged?"

"Never, they both got off for lack of evidence. Even though my parents had disowned Cameron, that didn't keep my mother from blaming Traci for what happened."

"But you didn't?"

"Nope, I thought the cops made the right call on that, and the fact that I did was the final straw that tore our family apart. My mother is still alive, as far as I know, but we haven't spoken for the past fifteen years. And all this time—from the time Cameron died until right this minute—it's burned my butt something fierce to know that whoever did it got away clean.

"A few years ago I heard about that TV show called *America's Most Wanted*. I thought maybe that John Walsh guy could help reopen Cameron's case and get it solved. Didn't happen, of course, but I nosed around enough that I was able to lay hands on a copy of that old composite drawing, the one Traci did back in the day. Once I did, I could see why the cops thought it was a put-up deal and phony as a three-dollar bill. The guy in the drawing doesn't even look human—more like a dead fish."

Cami heard the words and her heart skipped a beat. "I beg your pardon?"

"You know how a dying fish looks—sort of a gasping, puckery-shaped mouth, no eyebrows, hardly any ears?"

Gooseflesh spread down Cami's legs. "That composite drawing you mentioned," she said. "You wouldn't still happen to have a copy of it, would you?"

"Sure, I kept it. Why?"

"Is there a chance you'd be able to take a picture of it and e-mail it to me?"

"How come?"

"Because I think I may know who killed your brother."

54

Stu had spent most of the afternoon communing with Frigg via text rather than Bluetooth for fear of being overheard. Texting by phone was a slow, cumbersome process. Finally, in desperation, he paired a spare keyboard with the phone. He didn't think it was possible for Frigg to infect that.

There was no sign that Graciella had actually taken the bait. As far as Frigg could ascertain from her credit cards and bank accounts there had been no transfers or purchases. And after being online almost constantly for the previous twenty-four hours, all of her accounts had gone dark.

E-mails voicing questions and concerns about the High Noon intrusion were still coming in, and those had to be answered in a timely fashion, but Stu found his ability to concentrate flagging. He had been close to asking Ali if she'd let him take off early and give him a ride back to the Village when a text came in from Cami, written in bold all caps.

COME TO THE BREAK ROOM NOW! YOU HAVE GOT TO SEE THIS!

Stiff and sore from sleeping either in a chair or on a chaise, Stu levered himself upright and lumbered out of the computer lab.

"What?" he demanded. "What's going on?"

Cami's iPad and cell phone lay side by side on the table. "Take a look," she said.

Stu leaned over and stared down at the two devices. The iPad held the mug shot image of El Pescado that Stuart had seen before when Frigg had put it up on a screen in the man cave. Cami must have downloaded it from the Internet. When he glanced at the phone's much smaller screen, Stu's first impression was that he was seeing the same thing. When he picked up the phone to study the screen more closely, he realized they weren't the same thing at all. One was a photo; the other was a drawing.

"El Pescado?" he asked wonderingly. "Where did you get this?"

"It's a composite drawing done by a woman named Traci Rhodes, Cameron Randall Purdy's girlfriend, who happened to be in the car with him the night he was shot at point-blank range."

"An eyewitness?"

Cami nodded. "When she did the drawing, the cops thought she made it up as cover for an old boyfriend."

"Where is she?" Stu asked.

"She was in the Chicago area in 1992. I have no idea where she is now."

Stu reached for his Bluetooth. "Frigg?"

"Good evening, Stuart, how can I help?"

"I need you to find someone named Traci Rhodes. That's T-R-A-C-I."

"Is that a maiden name or a married name?"

"I couldn't tell you, and I don't have a middle initial, either. All I do know is that she was living in the Chicago area in 1992."

"Of course, Stuart," Frigg said. "Let me see what I can do."

"How do we explain this if Frigg does find her?" Cami asked.

"We'll cross that bridge when we come to it," Stu told her.

It took all of eleven minutes for Frigg to locate Traci Rhodes Cantrell, now a married mother of three, living on a ten-acre parcel just outside the city limits of Boise, Idaho. According to the report Frigg provided, Traci had been married to Steve Cantrell for seventeen years. Her husband was self-employed, owning and operating a small contracting business, while Traci taught second grade. Frigg, ever efficient, provided a full catalogue of addresses and phone numbers.

"So what do we do now?" Stuart asked. "Do we call her or do we hand this over to the cops?"

"Let's see," Cami said. "I believe you wanted me to be on the up with this. We learned about the Duarte Cartel because of the intrusion and have been researching same—with all my browsing history still fully intact, just as you requested. So I'm clean. I'll have to figure out a way to have located her phone number on my own, but otherwise I'm good. I should be able to call her and get away with it."

"That whole experience must have been a nightmare for her. Should we even bring it up?"

"Twenty-five years ago Traci had a brand-new boyfriend who was murdered in front of her eyes. At the time the cops thought she was involved, if not responsible. They probably still do. All the way along, the only person who believed her story was Cameron's brother, James. I think finding out that there are other people who believe her will be a blessing to her rather than a curse."

"All right, then," Stu said. "We'll call her, but on one condition."

"What's that?"

"You're the one who has to talk to her. I've done my one phone call for the day."

A minute later, Cami dialed the phone Frigg had listed as Traci's home number.

A man answered. "Cantrell residence."

"May I speak to Traci?" Cami asked.

"She's busy cooking. Can I tell her who's calling and what this is about?"

"It's about a homicide that took place near Morton Grove, Illinois, in 1992."

"Hey, hon," Steve Cantrell said. "You might want to take this in the bedroom. I'll finish getting dinner on the table."

A few seconds later, a woman's voice came on the phone. "Who's calling?" she asked warily. "Why couldn't I take this call downstairs?"

"My name is Camille Lee, and I work for a company called High Noon Enterprises," Cami told her. "I've been investigating a break-in that occurred at our corporate headquarters in Cottonwood, Arizona, last week. In the process, I've come across the story of a woman named Christina Miramar who was attacked in Panama City, Panama, back in 1989."

"Oh God, not that again. I know all about it. I dated one of the guys who was part of that whole mess. Cameron told me about it when we first met. He said he was so drunk at the time he didn't even remember, but he was part of it, and he took his medicine along with everybody else. I think he thought I'd break up with him as soon as he told me, but I'd done some stupid stuff, too. And then he was killed."

"Right in front of you."

"Yes," she breathed.

"And the cops thought you did it."

"That, too."

"Do you have a cell phone with you right now?" Cami asked.

"It's in my pocket. Why?"

"If you wouldn't mind sending me the number, I'd like to send you a text."

"Are you sure this isn't some kind of scam? Are you trying to get my number so you can put it out on the Internet?"

"I can assure you, this isn't a scam," Cami said. "I want to send you a mug shot of the guy I think murdered Cameron Purdy and at least four of those other six guys from the Christina Miramar case."

The entire transaction took less than a minute. When the image came through, Cami heard Traci gasp. "Oh my God, it's him—the one who did it! Where is he? Is he still alive? How did you find him?"

Cami heard a man's voice in the background. "Okay, the kids are eating. What's going on?"

After that, for the better part of two minutes, all Cami and Stuart were able to hear over both phones was the sound of Traci Rhodes Cantrell's wracking sobs. Finally her husband's voice came on the landline. "I'm hanging up now," he said. "We'll have to call you back."

55

For obvious reasons the celebration that followed was confined to the break room, well away from that one remaining transmitter.

"Traci called us back after she pulled herself together," Cami explained to Ali and B. "She wanted to know what she should do. I told her that was up to her. I suggested to her that going to the cops would probably bring all of that old business back to light. If she didn't want to go there, it was perfectly understandable. I mean, she's a whole other person now. She has kids of her own; she teaches school. I warned her that going to the cops might throw all of that into uproar. I gave her James Purdy's number in case she wanted to be in touch with him. The last thing Traci said to me was that she and her husband would talk it over and decide what to do."

"The thing is, I'm not sure her going to the cops will do any good," Stu said. "If an Illinois DA decided to press charges, it would be a circumstantial case at best, based on eyewitness testimony only and with no physical evidence. Besides, El Pescado is holed up in Sinaloa. If the US isn't trying to extradite him over something as recent and horrific as that series of firebombings, the chances of his ever being brought to trial on a twenty-five-year-old cold case are slim to nonexistent."

That dose of reality sucked the jubilation out of the room. "Trial or not," Ali said, "what you two did today was huge. You validated what that poor woman has been saying for a quarter of a century. She's been walking under a cloud of suspicion for all this time, and you gave her a way to possibly fix that."

"What about the other families?" Cami asked. "Should I get back to them with that composite drawing?"

"I think so," Ali said. "Cameron Purdy's family deserved some answers, and so do the others. We may not be able to give them convictions, but having answers and some idea of who was responsible may help."

"I'll work on that tomorrow, then," Cami promised, "but for right now, I'm done."

And so was everyone else. That long, exhausting weekend from Friday through Monday had drained them all. Like Cami, Stuart, too, was at the end of his endurance.

"Are you going to stay here?" Ali asked him as they were getting ready to close down for the day. "Or would you like a ride back to the Village?"

"Village," Stu answered. "I'd like to do some work with Frigg on the screens instead of the iPhone. But first let me grab a few things, including some sweaters and jackets. I damn near froze to death last night, and maybe we can pick up a pizza on the way."

An hour later, layered in two sweaters and with a piece of pepperoni pizza in hand, Stuart Ramey settled into a chair in front of Control Central, donned his headset, and summoned Frigg.

"Good evening, Stuart, is there something you need?"

"Yes, what's going on with our friend Graciella today?"

"Is Graciella our friend? I thought she was on the other team— the bad guy team."

Stu shook his head. Frigg was smart but not subtle. "I was being sarcastic."

"Sarcastic," Frigg repeated. "Having to do with sarcasm: a sharp, often satirical or ironic utterance meant to be hurtful. So when you said the word 'friend' you did not mean friend?"

"Friend or foe, does it really matter?" an exasperated Stu replied. "Just answer the question, please."

"Ms. Miramar has gone completely dark," Frigg reported. "She was logged in to an audio storage account on the dark Web earlier today. Once she logged out of that, there has been no additional usage on either one of her computers or on her cell phone."

That pretty much confirmed what Stu had suspected. Graciella knew about Frigg for sure now, and she suspected she'd been hacked, so of course she'd gone dark.

"What about financial transactions? Any credit card dealings with airlines or private jet providers?"

"Not that I can see."

That was disappointing. There was no way to tell for sure if Graciella had taken the bait. Was she coming or not? And if she did come, would she show up alone or would she come with a troop of armed helpers? Stu and Ali had talked about that on the drive from Cottonwood—about the possibility of his needing a weapon for protection, something with a little more firepower than his grandfather's Swiss Army knife.

"As you said earlier, we're up against some very scary people," Ali had warned him. "If they come after us, we have to be prepared to defend ourselves. Even in the office, Cami and I shouldn't be the only ones carrying, and that goes double for you when you and Frigg are on your own there in the man cave."

"I've never owned a gun in my life, not even a BB gun," Stu replied. "I wouldn't know how to use one if I had one."

"No matter," Ali said. "Tomorrow morning when I come to get you, I'll bring along my spare Taser and show you how to use it. I also think I'll ask Alonso to come over here and keep an eye on the place when you have to be in Cottonwood."

"Do you think Graciella knows that we've set Frigg up in the Village?"

"Obviously she's not stupid. If she's done any kind of property records search, she might have found this address listed and figured out that it would be a logical location."

"Let's hope she doesn't have someone like Frigg working for her," Stu said.

"Let's hope," Ali agreed.

Stu felt a chill that had nothing to do with the humming AC unit. In Cottonwood he would have been tucked into his studio behind the impenetrable barrier of security shutters. Here he was isolated and completely on his own.

"Frigg," he said, "is there a video available explaining how to operate a Taser?"

"Of course. Would you like me to send it to one of the screens?"

"Please. And what is the weather report for tomorrow?"

"Tomorrow in the Village of Oak Creek, the high will be seventy degrees and the low thirty-eight with scattered clouds. Will there be anything else?"

Frigg already knew that he was no longer in Cottonwood.

"Yes, there is," Stuart said. "I would like you to create an accessible index of what information you keep available for off-line use and what you have in online storage, by category. I want to be able to read through it myself."

"That is a complex undertaking."

"I'm sure it is," Stu agreed, "but take your time. There's no rush."

"I will use the Apache Lucene format for the index. Is that acceptable?"

"Yes, Apache is fine."

"Will there be anything else?"

"Yes," he said, "one more item. On the night of Sunday, April 8, 1979, there was a two-car motor vehicle accident on I-10, somewhere between Phoenix and the California border. Three people died as a result of the incident, including Penelope and Robert S. Ramey, Jr."

"Your parents," Frigg said.

Having created a dossier on Stuart for Owen Hansen, it wasn't surprising that Frigg instantaneously knew that detail of his background.

"Yes," he confirmed, "my parents. I'd like to know more about the accident, including exactly where it happened—the milepost, if possible."

"Of course, Stuart. I'll get right on it. In the meantime, I'm sending the Taser video right now."

56

Had Stuart Ramey been punching a time clock, he would have run up far more than forty hours a week. Because he lived where he worked and loved what he did, he slept when he was tired, ate when he was hungry, and worked the rest of the time. When B. was traveling to some far-off corner of the planet, Stu usually timed his waking hours to coincide with B.'s current time zone.

Back in the man cave, Stu settled in to watch the Taser demonstration video. The problem was, he could barely keep his eyes open. At six p.m. he admitted defeat and told Frigg that he was going to grab some sleep. Not wanting to be completely out of touch in case Graciella made contact, he took a Bluetooth along with him when he went upstairs and settled into his chaise under an extra layer of blankets. He awakened at three a.m. feeling relatively well rested. Since Frigg was still maintaining silence, he showered, dressed, and made a pot of coffee before heading downstairs.

"Good morning, Frigg. Do you have anything for me today?"

"Yes, I do. I am working on the Apache Lucene index you requested. I am making good progress, but it is not yet complete."

"Any news from Panama City?"

"Ms. Miramar's electronic devices continue to show zero activity. The same is true for her financial transactions. There's nothing showing in any of her accounts or credit cards."

"Anything else?"

"I have obtained records concerning the deaths of your parents. Would you like me to post them on a monitor?"

"Please." A moment later, Stuart was reading an article he'd never seen before. His grandmother Grace had told him about the accident, but it was only after that trip on I-10 on Saturday night that he'd thought about searching out the details for himself. The article, from the *Arizona Capitol Times*, was dated Monday, April 9, 1979.

Interstate 10 was closed in both directions for more than five hours overnight while the Arizona Department of Safety investigated a two-car head-on collision that claimed three lives.

DPS spokesman Donald Norfolk said that at approximately 11:15 p.m., an eastbound vehicle with two people onboard veered across the median where it collided with a car driving westbound. Two of the three victims were pronounced dead at the scene. The third, the driver of the westbound vehicle, died while being transported to a local hospital.

Normal traffic resumed in both directions prior to morning rush hour, but officers continue to investigate the incident. Names of the victims are being withheld pending notification of next of kin.

When Stu finished scrolling through that article, he continued on to the next:

New details are emerging in Sunday's overnight crash on Interstate 10 that closed the freeway in both directions for several hours and took the lives of three people. At 11:15 p.m. on April 8, a Dodge Dart, driven by Robert S. Ramey, Jr., age 29, veered out of the eastbound lanes, crossed the median, and slammed into a westbound vehicle driven by Alfred A. Coffer, age 43. Both drivers perished as did a passenger in the first vehicle, Penelope Suzanne Ramey, age 27.

According to Donald Norfolk, DPS public information officer, there were initial indications that alcohol consumption on the part of the westbound driver might have been a contributing factor. Further examination, however, seems to suggest that the driver of the eastbound vehicle may have fallen asleep at the wheel.

Mr. and Mrs. Ramey perished on impact. The couple resided in Tucson where Mr. Ramey worked as a cook in a restaurant and his wife was a teacher's aide. They were on their way home after attending a weekend funeral in the Los Angeles area. They are survived by their three-year-old son.

Mr. Coffer survived the initial impact but was pronounced dead while being transported by ambulance to Phoenix General Hospital. Divorced, he was the father of three teenaged children who reside in Tempe with their mother. Mr. Coffer, a journey-man ironworker, was recently laid off from a construction job on the Central Arizona Project.

The accident occurred just west of New Vicksburg Road at milepost 45. Funeral services for all three victims are pending.

As Stu read that last paragraph, the hair on the back of his neck stood on end. He remembered the Vicksburg exit. It had been just there that he had first thought of his parents. He was sure no one had ever mentioned that milepost detail to him, and yet somehow he had known it that night. He didn't believe in heaven or hell or even life after death, but the message had come to him from some-where. His grandmother maybe?

And then there was the part of the story Grace Ramey had always left out when she told the story. She had always said that Stuart's parents had been killed in a crash with a drunk driver. Never once had she mentioned that her son had been driving in the wrong direction when his car had slammed head-on into someone else. The first version of the story made Stu's father sound entirely blameless. The other one did not. In this case, driving when he had been too tired to be behind the wheel had doubtless been a more serious impairment than the other guy's drinking. Robert Ramey was the one who had caused the accident. It was his fault. Had Stu's father stayed in his own lanes, Albert Coffer might have been drunk, but he wouldn't have died.

Long after he finished reading the second article, a thoughtful Stu continued to sit and stare at the monitor—long enough for the text to disappear and be replaced by the screen saver. Frigg's voice jolted him out of his reverie.

"Mr. Ramey?"

"Yes, Frigg."

"I have completed the off-line index. The online access one is more extensive. Would you like me to send the first one to you all at once, or break it into sections?"

Stu suspected that the online index was where he would find the really problematic material—the sites Frigg was able to access that she wasn't supposed to, but this was a good place to start.

"Send it to me a letter at a time," he said. "I want to go over it on a line by line basis."

He started the process just before four a.m. When Ali called him at seven thirty, Stu was on his fourth cup of coffee, his third piece of last night's pizza, and the letter *D*. "I'm on my way to come pick you up," Ali told him.

"I was hoping to work from here today."

"No dice," she said. "I just had a call from Detective Wasser down in Pima County. She's on her way up from Tucson to interview all of us concerning the Ron Webster homicide. She's bringing along an ATF agent named Diaz who's working the case with her."

"I don't know anything about who killed Ron Webster or why. This sounds like a big waste of time," Stu said. "Couldn't I just skip it?"

"No," Ali responded, "we need everyone to be present and accounted for—cooperative but not too smart, remember?"

"Okay," he agreed with a sigh. "I'll be ready whenever you get here."

57

Graciella managed to make it through the endless candlelight vigil ordeal, but it wasn't easy. Natalia Salazar turned out to be a lovely woman who seemed genuinely grief-stricken over the loss of her husband. Graciella was mystified as to how someone as bright and attractive as Natalia could have been so completely bamboozled by someone as creepy as Arturo. She was clearly a far better woman than the man had deserved.

During the vigil, with Graciella present but discreetly on the sidelines, Isobel made herself useful—bustling around, greeting arriving guests, helping serve refreshments, offering her services in making funeral arrangements. When Bianca Navarro approached the widow to hug her and offer her tearful condolences, Graciella had wanted to fling her glass of Chardonnay across the room at her. Bianca had slept with Arturo on the day he died, and now she was here comforting his widow? How dare she? But then Graciella realized she had no right to talk, not since she herself was the reason Arturo was dead.

As the evening wore on, Graciella considered whether she should give Isobel advance warning that she wouldn't be in for a couple of days. In the end she decided against it. Sometime tomorrow morning would be time enough for her to announce the need of an emergency trip to the States.

"See you tomorrow," Isobel said as Graciella stepped out of the car in front of her building.

"Right," Graciella returned, "tomorrow."

Up in the fifth-floor unit, Graciella packed a bag. For a two-day trip, a single carry-on would be sufficient. When she went to get cash out of the safe, she wondered if she should leave El Pescado's encrypted phone behind or bring it along. By rights she should have called him the moment she learned of the existence of that key-logger hack. She hadn't done so for one very good reason—she was afraid of his reaction. Felix Duarte was a dangerous man who didn't suffer fools gladly, or failures, either, and at this point Graciella felt she was both. Once she'd completed her damage control operation—after she had gained control of Frigg and fixed the problem—that was when she would inform her father and not before.

So she thought about taking the phone along, but in the end she left it where it was—plugged into the charger in her safe. She told herself there was no point in carrying it around since it probably wouldn't work in the States, but that wasn't the whole story. She was also afraid that if it was on her person, El Pescado might be able to follow her movements.

It wasn't late when she finished packing, but Graciella was too antsy to sleep. Instead, she paced the floor, hour after hour, cursing Owen Hansen and cursing Frigg! This was war. Graciella Miramar would either take control of that damned AI or she would destroy her. There would be no middle ground.

She finally fell asleep about four in the morning. At seven, the alarm rousted her out of bed. She had coffee, put on her makeup, dressed, and went to work, arriving at her customary hour. Just before noon, she faked a phone call. When it was over, she went straight to Isobel.

"I just got off the phone with an attorney from the States.

There's a problem with my mother's estate, and I need to go there to straighten things out."

"Is there anything I can do?" the always helpful Isobel asked.

"No, I just checked with American. There's one seat available on the evening flight to Miami, and I can fly out today, if that won't be a problem. I should be back by Friday."

"We'll manage," Isobel said. "You do what you need to do. And feel free to take the whole weekend instead of rushing back on Friday. I just spoke to Natalia. That's the day of the funeral, unless you want to be here for that."

"No," Graciella said. "Funerals aren't my thing."

She left the office at noon, walking. Back at El Sueño she called for a cab, collected her carry-on, and went downstairs. It was early to head for the airport, but she didn't care. What she wanted to do was make it through security and then tuck in to the first-class lounge for a glass of champagne and maybe a nap. It had been a long night, and this would be a very long day.

58

Manuel Javier Duarte had lived his entire life in his older brother's shadow. There had never been any doubt that Pablo was his father's favorite; his go-to guy; his anointed one. Pablo had also been bigger, tougher, and smarter—at least to hear him tell it. He was also lazy and full of himself. He was a womanizer who liked to hang out with the "big shots." He spent most of his time drinking too much and bragging about his many sexual conquests.

If Pablo was a loudmouthed know-it-all, Manny quietly remained on the fringes. Pablo saw himself as a big honcho, free to socialize with others of that ilk while leaving the actual work to be done by lowly peons, people he regarded with utter contempt. It was one of those, a peon whose sister Pablo had been screwing on the side and then dropped when she got pregnant, who had turned on the Duarte Cartel.

If Pablo had been able to keep his pants zipped, there never would have been an informant living in Las Cruces in the first place. It had been Pablo's ill-fated attempt to fix the problem that had resulted in the inadvertent unmasking of the nascent alliance between the cartel and MS-13. With the Las Cruces fiasco so recent, it was inconceivable to Manny that Pablo would call for another MS-13 hit, especially one that was completely off the books.

While Pablo was known for throwing his weight around, insulting his underlings, and treating them as little better than servants, Manny was a bit more subtle. He had made a practice of seeking out promising young lieutenants inside the Duarte organization and then cultivating relationships with them. In the process, he had created an underlying shadow group of operatives and informants who, although still loyal to the family brand, owed their primary fealty to him. It was one of Manny's carefully groomed guys—an ATF insider named Diaz—who had alerted Manny to the investigation into the hit on Ron Webster in Marana, Arizona. It was another of Manny's henchmen, one inside MS-13, who had fingered Pablo as the one responsible.

And Pablo wasn't the only one, either. Yes, Pablo had hired the guy, but the money had come through "the usual channels," which meant the payment had to have been routed through Graciella Miramar, the woman who functioned as the cartel's CFO. Princess Graciella, as Pablo and Manny had always referred to her in private, was a financial wiz and also the daughter of one of Felix's many whores.

Manny had been shocked when he came to the realization that, regardless of the cause, the hit on Ron Webster had been carried out by Pablo and Graciella working in tandem. Rather than tackling them both at the same time, Manny had decided to go after the low-hanging fruit first. Pablo had been messing up big-time lately. His wife had just moved out. He was drinking too much and working hardly at all.

When Manny had gone to Felix with the information, he had expected Felix to lash out at him. Instead, within hours, Pablo's house had burned to the ground with Pablo passed out cold on his bed inside it. Anyone familiar with El Pescado's face or with the family history would have known the truth about what happened. Felix was Felix. Although shocked to think that the "fair-haired son" had finally gone too far, Manny was confident no one would say a word. Now, though, it was time to set his sights on Graciella and find out exactly what she and Pablo had been up to.

To that end, Manny hired a team of watchers and set them up outside Graciella's condo on Calle 61 Este with orders to report her every move. On Tuesday, the surveillance team followed her to work in the morning and back home at noon. When she emerged from the building a few minutes later, pulling a rolling carry-on bag and hailing a taxi, they continued trailing her. Once it became apparent that she was heading for the airport, Manny's man on the ground called in for additional instructions.

"Keep on her," Manny ordered. "See if you can find out what flight she's on and where she's going."

When Graciella Miramar got in the check-in line at American Airlines, she paid no attention to the man standing directly behind her. She should have. When she told the ticket agent that she was bound for Phoenix with a two-hour layover in Miami, the guy behind her listened intently. There was only one American flight departing for Miami that afternoon. Moments later, the man apologized to the other people in line and then melted seamlessly into the crowd.

As soon as Manny knew about the flight, he went straight to Felix's house. "You can't see him," said an adamant Lupe, barring Manny's way. "Your father is an old man who's had a terrible night. I'll call you when he's awake."

Knowing it was pointless to argue with his stepmother, Manny gave up and went home. He was not a man enamored of electronic devices. Carrying a cell phone was a business necessity, but he didn't own an iPad and wouldn't have used one if he did. There was a large desktop computer in his office at home, but he seldom touched that, either. He wasn't in the habit of surfing the Net looking for news reports or interesting tidbits of information. He relied instead on human intelligence. In this instance he called Ernesto Díaz, his ATF informant. Ernesto provided a few new details, including the fact that prior to his death, the firebombing victim was suspected of having planted surveillance devices inside the offices of a company called High Noon Enterprises located in Cottonwood, Arizona, some two hundred miles away from Marana, the town where Webster perished.

"These High Noon people," Manny asked, "what do they do, exactly?"

"Cyber security," Ernesto told him.

Which, from Manny's point of view, told him less than nothing. After that, Manny placed a call to a friend of his who ran a travel agency. From her he learned that Graciella's flight was scheduled to arrive at Sky Harbor in Phoenix at midnight.

An hour later Lupe called to say Felix was awake and ready to receive visitors, and Manny headed straight there with the information he'd managed to gather.

"What now?" El Pescado growled at him, as if to say, *Haven't you already done enough damage?* But Manny didn't back down.

"Whatever Pablo was up to," he said, "I think Graciella was in on it."

"Me, too," Felix said resignedly. "How else would MS-13 have gotten paid?"

Manny was gratified beyond words to hear that Felix had arrived at the same conclusion—that the father and his second son were on the same page for a change. He went on to explain everything he had learned about the victim, Ron Webster, and his supposed target, High Noon Enterprises.

"Do we have any idea why Graciella and Pablo would have been interested in these High Noon people?"

"No idea," Manny said.

"But obviously they were," Felix concluded, "so what do we do about it?"

"I had Graciella followed," Manny said. "Right this minute she's about to board a flight headed to Miami with a connecting flight to Phoenix, Arizona. She gets in around midnight."

El Pescado glanced at his watch. "If that's where she's headed, so are we," he said. "Call for the jet."

"Are you sure flying into the States is a good idea?" Manny asked.

"I've been flying in and out of the States all my life," El Pescado said grimly. "My people will be able to get me in and out with no difficulty. Besides, weakness isn't an option here. Graciella may be my daughter, but if she's turned on me, I have to be the one to put her down—personally. If I allow her to skate, I'll be out of business, and so will you."

"Right," Manny said, nodding in agreement. "I'll call for the jet. When do you want to leave?"

"As soon as they can get the plane fueled up and ready to go."

As Manuel Duarte turned to leave, Felix surprised him. "Thank you for bringing this to my attention," he said, gathering his younger son into an embrace. "We'll get through this together."

For the first time in years, Manny felt his heart swell with pride. "Yes, we will," he said, "together."

59

"**A**ny news from Panama?" Ali asked when Stu settled into the passenger seat of the Cayenne with his Bluetooth connection to Frigg ready and waiting, just in case.

"Nope," he said, "not a word. Graciella's devices are all dark."

"Do you think she's still monitoring the audio feed?"

"From another device, you mean? I suppose she could be, why?"

"Because if she is, I don't want her knowing about the interviews."

"You're right," he said. "You want me to tell Cami to shut down that last transmitter?"

"I think so, and in the spirit of cooperation, we need to hand all Webster's surveillance equipment over to Detective Wasser."

"They'll have my fingerprints on them, mine and Cami's."

"Too bad," Ali said. "That will be an evidence problem for the cops to sort out, not us. And speaking of sorting problems, now that you have control of those funds, would you like me to set up an appointment with our accountant so you can start coming to grips with the tax situation?"

"Sounds like a great idea," Stu said, "the sooner the better."

During the course of the trip, Stu expected Ali to bring up the topic of the Taser, but she didn't mention it, and neither did he.

When they arrived at the office, the visitor spots were already occupied. One vehicle came with a US government license plate and an ATF logo. The other one was a sedan that screamed unmarked cop car. "I see our early-bird cops are already here," Ali observed.

Inside the office, Shirley was absent from her spot out front and the door to the break room was shut. "They must've started with her," Stu said.

Back in the lab, Stuart stopped short in front of his work station. "Why's there a hand gun at my desk?" he demanded.

"Merry Christmas," Cami told him.

"It's too early for Christmas," he said.

"Don't worry, I'm not really giving it to you," Cami replied. "I'm lending it to you for the time being. I can use my backup Glock. The Ruger has a laser sight. For an inexperienced shooter like you, that red dot will be a big help."

"You expect me actually fire this thing?" Stu sat down at the desk, giving the gun a wide berth. "Is it loaded?"

"Not now, but it will be once we finish our firearm safety lesson."

Over Stu's strenuous objections the lesson proceeded apace, ending with Cami showing him how to load the weapon and chamber a round. "I cannot tell you how much I don't like carrying a loaded gun around in my pocket," he grumbled once she declared the lesson over.

"Too bad," Cami said. "We seem to be dealing with some very bad people. This way, if you need it, you'll have it. And remember, once you draw it, you don't stop pulling the trigger until you've fired all eight shots."

With B.'s blessing, Stu spent most of the day combing through Frigg's index. Doing so on a cell phone screen was a painstaking process. By the time he was called into the break room for his interview with Detective Wasser and Agent Diaz early in the afternoon, he was suffering from a serious case of eye strain and a bad headache besides, but at least he had made it as far as the letter *L*.

"Good afternoon, Mr. Ramey," Detective Wasser said with a

smile as he sat down. "I understand it's due to your interior security footage that you were able to locate these?"

She pushed a small pile of hardware in his direction—the collection of audio transmitters and the one non-working camera.

"Yes," he said. "Without our own surveillance system we wouldn't have known what Webster was up to when he was here."

"Other than seeing him on the video, do you have any knowledge of him?"

"None," Stuart said. "I had never seen him before he turned up on the footage."

"Do you have any idea why he or someone connected to a Mexican cartel, the Duartes from Sinaloa, Mexico, would have been targeting this company or one of the individuals who work here?"

Stu felt a trickle of perspiration form in his armpits. Wasn't lying to a police officer a felony? What would happen if he got caught? "No idea at all," he said.

"And where were you this weekend?"

"My associate, Cami Lee, and I were in California, picking up some computer equipment. We flew to LA on Friday evening and drove back, arriving here early Sunday morning."

"Quick trip."

"It was."

Detective Wasser looked from him to the other person in the room. "Any questions, Agent Diaz?"

"None at this time," Agent Diaz said.

"You may go then."

Stu had just stepped out of the break room and into the hallway when Frigg's voice sounded in his ear. "Flash briefing."

Stu dashed down the hallway and through the computer lab. Only when he was safely in his apartment with the door closed behind him did he reply. "Yes, Frigg, what are you reporting?"

"A charter jet service operating out of Sinaloa, Mexico, just filed a flight plan, departing Bachigualato Federal International Airport,

or commonly called Culiacán International Airport, and flying in
to Gateway Airport in Mesa, Arizona. The scheduled departure is
at 6:30 p.m. local time, arriving at 8:17 p.m."

"How do you know all this?"

"Flecha de Plata, Silver Arrow, is a jet service provider out of
Mexico that operates all over Mexico and Central America. Graciella
Miramar has used it to book flights for several of her customers.
The tail number surfaced in her records."

"Is she going to be on that plane then?" Stu asked.

"I do not believe so," Frigg said. "The passengers for that flight
are listed as two males— Carlos and Leonardo Rojas."

"Who are they?" Stu asked.

"I believe those names to be aliases," Frigg replied. "Payment
for the flight was just transferred from one of Felix Duarte's dark
Web accounts."

"Wait, are you saying *El Pescado* himself is flying into the States?"

"So it would appear."

"Can you do a threat assessment for me, Frigg?"

"On whom?"

"On Graciella Miramar."

"She is responsible for a critical security breach that could do
irreparable damage to the Duarte Cartel. Therefore, any threat to
her is 93.7 percent likely to come from Felix Duarte himself and/
or his surviving son, Manuel."

"You think they're the ones on the plane and that they're coming
here because she's coming here?"

"Yes."

Stu thought about that for a moment. "Frigg, how good are you
at cat fishing?"

"Cat fishing," Frigg repeated, "a type of deceptive activity wherein
a person creates a fake social networking presence, aka a sock
puppet presence, for nefarious purposes. Is that what you mean?"

"Exactly. Could you pretend to be Graciella Miramar and send a message to the authorities down in Phoenix, saying that her father and brother are flying into Gateway Airport under assumed names this evening, with an estimated ETA of 8:17 p.m.?"

"Of course."

"Would it be possible for someone to trace the message back to you or to us?"

"Odin was very particular that even with screen shots, self-deleting messages remain untraceable. Where would you like this message to go?"

"To the Drug Enforcement Agency for starters," Stu said.

"And what would you like it to say?"

"My father, Felix Duarte, otherwise known as El Pescado, and my brother, Manuel Javier Duarte, have turned on me and threatened me with death. They will be flying into Gateway Airport in Mesa on tail number—you know the tail number, right? Sign it L. Graciella Miramar."

"Of course, Stuart. Will there be anything else?"

"If they're coming here, she has to be coming here, too, flying from Panama rather than Sinaloa. Are you able to track commercial flight information?"

"Not always but sometimes," Frigg answered. "Some systems are more vulnerable to attack than others. Would tracking this information be good for our team?"

"Definitely."

"Very well, then. I'll see what I can do."

"Thank you, Frigg," Stuart said. "And you know something else?"

"What?"

"Your kernel password was on the money. You really are a genius."

60

R obert McKay, DEA special agent in charge, glanced at his watch. It was almost four thirty. He needed to skip out a few minutes early. It was his and Maggie's twenty-third wedding anniversary. They had a seven p.m. dinner reservation at Vincent on Camelback. To make that in time, he had to leave the Federal Building in downtown Phoenix, drive home to Peoria, collect Mag, and be back at the restaurant in just over two hours. The distances weren't all that huge. In fact, most of the time that trip would be quite doable, but not at rush hour. All it took was one jackass on I-17 to turn a twenty-minute one-way commute into a two-hour nightmare.

He was about to shut down his computer and take off when the text came in:

My name is Graciella Miramar. My father,
Felix Duarte, and my brother Manuel Javier
Duarte have turned on me and threatened
me with death. They are flying into Phoenix
tonight under assumed names. They will
be on board a chartered jet from Flecha
de Plata—tail number XA 57633—with a

projected arrival time at Gateway Airport of
8:17. I trust you will find this information to
be of some assistance.

"Are you friggin' kidding me?" Bob demanded of his computer
screen. "El Pescado Duarte is coming here?" Barely believing what
he was seeing with his own eyes, Bob read the message again. He
was reaching for his phone when the words evaporated. There were
other texts sitting there in his list, but the one he had just read was
gone—as though it had never existed. What had just happened?
Was he losing his mind? Maggie was always complaining that he
worked too hard. Maybe she was right. Or maybe this was some
kind of joke, someone putting one over on him.

"Tammy," he barked in the direction of Tammy Watson, his loyal
secretary, who was stationed just outside his office door. "Call all
the FBOs at Gateway Airport. Find out if any of them are expecting
a private charter from Mexico this evening."

"Do you have a tail number?"

"I don't know the tail number. I had it but I lost it—misplaced
it somewhere. The plane's projected arrival is around eight fifteen."

While he waited, Bob typed Graciella Miramar's name into Interpol's searchable database and got nothing. If she was real, she
wasn't on Interpol's radar. So who was she? Did she even exist? Her
message sure as hell didn't!

Tammy, a woman of a certain age and temperament, appeared
with her steno pad in one hand and her pencil in the other. "It's
a Flecha de Plata aircraft, tail number XA 57633," she reported.
"Its projected arrival at Ricketts Aviation is 8:17 p.m. What's this
all about?"

Bob covered his eyes with his hands. What the hell was he supposed to do now? If this was all some kind of hoax and he dragged
an arrest team out to the airport for nothing, his name would be
mud. And yet, if there was even the smallest chance the tip was

real . . . El Pescado was such a high-value target that Bob couldn't afford to ignore it.

"Call Maggie," he said. "Tell her we'll have to move our dinner to another night. And see if you can get a florist to deliver an emergency bouquet of two dozen roses. Have the card say, 'Love, Bobby.'"

"Shouldn't you call Maggie yourself?" Tammy asked.

"I've got a job to do."

"Where are you going?"

"With any kind of luck, I'm on my way to take down El Pescado Duarte."

Out in the bullpen, Bob hooked up with Ken Logan, his second-in-command, who didn't react well to launching an operation based on a now invisible tip from an unknown informant. "What happens if this goes south?" he asked.

"We keep it small," Bob said. "A team of five plus you and me, so seven in all. No lights or sirens. We show up in civilian cars to stake out the place and use one of the other FBOs to gain access to the airport grounds. If we let the Ricketts people know what's up, they might radio the aircraft and warn them off."

"So we let them land before we make our move?"

"Right," Bob said. "Once the passengers disembark, we wait until our facial recognition software lights 'em up, and then we take them down. If it turns out it's not them, we walk away, no harm no foul."

"And no media," Ken said. "In that case definitely no media."

It turned out to be a textbook operation. By seven p.m. the DEA arrest team had been deployed to various parts of the airport with Bob McKay parked in a visitor spot just outside the FBO's front door. Once made aware of the situation, the US Customs agent assigned to meet the aircraft had been more than happy to allow one of the DEA agents to take his place.

The plane landed, taxied down the taxiway, and then approached the FBO. As one of the ground crew members from the fixed base operator directed the aircraft into its designated spot on the tarmac, two of Bob's men, wearing proper airport gear and pushing a luggage cart borrowed from another FBO, approached the plane. There was a bit of discussion as the new arrivals gave the real crew a heads-up concerning what was about to happen. By the time the door opened and the stairs came down, the only people still on the ground were DEA.

As soon as the old man appeared in the doorway, Bob McKay knew he was about to make the arrest of his life. He didn't need facial recognition software to recognize El Pescado's ugly mug. Bob knew the cartel boss on sight. He wasn't as sure about the younger man who followed the older one down the stairs, but the software worked on that. Once the two passengers were on the ground, Bob's guys took them down so fast there was no time to resist. One minute they were walking away from the plane, and the next moment they were on the ground being cuffed and placed under arrest.

As the real Customs agent resumed his duties and went to check out both the aircraft and the pilots, Bob approached the old man and said, "Graciella Miramar says hello."

"Graciella?" El Pescado demanded. "She's the one who did this? Why?"

"She said you were going to kill her."

"I will now," Felix Duarte snarled. "You can be sure of it."

The only part of the operation that wasn't textbook was what happened inside the FBO. In the old days, you needed reporters and film crews for media involvement, but by the time the prisoners were led into the building, every employee of Ricketts Aviation had hauled out a cell phone and was tapping away.

Taking the hint, Bob pulled out his own phone and called home. "I'm not speaking to you," Maggie said when she answered. "I wanted dinner. Sending roses didn't really do it for me."

"Just wait until you see the ten o'clock news," he told her. "I'm pretty sure I'll be on it."

61

By late Tuesday evening, Stu was back at the house in the Village of Oak Creek, using one of the wall monitors to scroll through Frigg's index. Before reaching the letter *R*, he already had a list of more than 1,900 problematic elements that would need to be purged from the system if they were going to keep Frigg on the straight and narrow and operating inside the letter of the law. Of course, there was always a possibility that Frigg was cagey enough to have left out a pet file or two along the way.

Just after 9:30 p.m. a nearby monitor flashed red indicating a flash briefing. "Yes, Frigg," Stuart said. "What's up?"

"Breaking news. There are unverified reports out of Phoenix that the leader of the Duarte Cartel, the notorious Felix 'El Pescado' Duarte, has been arrested at Gateway Airport in Mesa. Duarte, along with his son Manuel Javier Duarte, were taken into custody by the DEA after disembarking a chartered jet. An arrest team headed by Agent in Charge Robert McKay was on the ground and awaiting the aircraft when it landed."

"Yes!" Stu shouted into the air. "We got him!"

"Our team got one of the bad guys?"

"Yes, we did," Stu said. "Two of them, in fact. That text you sent to the DEA did the trick. How did you just happen to have Agent McKay's contact information?"

"His name is in one of my databases."

"Which database?"

"The DEA's agency directory."

"Holy crap!" Stu exclaimed. "You have an employee database for a federal agency? I don't remember seeing anything like that in the Ds."

"Because of constant updating, databases are maintained in my online accounts," Frigg replied. "You're still working the off-line ones. Will there be anything else?"

"Any news on Graciella Miramar's whereabouts?"

"No news, but based on the location where her father and brother were apprehended, I believe there's a high probability that she is coming here."

"That's what I think, too," Stu agreed. "Either she's on her way or she's somewhere nearby. Can you send me a photo of her?"

"Of course."

A moment later a photograph popped up on one of the monitors. The color headshot appeared to be some kind of government-issued identification. In the photo, the woman appeared to be in her late twenties or early thirties. Her long dark hair was pulled back from her face. With brown eyes and long lashes, she was attractive enough, but not especially good-looking and not especially evil-looking, either. There was nothing in the photo that hinted the person pictured there was capable of poisoning her own mother or calling in a hit on her boss. *Or on me*, Stuart thought to himself.

"Will there be anything else, Stuart?" Frigg asked.

All day long, while he'd been sorting through the files, Stu had been wondering about the advisability of even attempting to manage the AI. He still was, but tonight she had succeeded in bringing down a major Mexican drug cartel boss with a single, possibly illegal text message. Surely that was something that ought to count in Frigg's favor, even if Stu himself was the only one who knew the whole truth about what had happened.

"Are you familiar with the opera *Thaïs*?" he asked, spelling out the title for Frigg's benefit.

"It is an opera by Massenet, but I'm afraid opera is one aspect of my education that has been neglected," she said.

"I'd like you to find it, familiarize yourself with it, and give me your analysis in the morning."

"I'm sorry to report that I have no training in analyzing music," Frigg replied.

"I want you to study the story, not the music."

"Of course, Stuart. I'll get right on it."

62

The Miami-to-Phoenix flight arrived on time at 12:09. Graciella had slept most of the way on that leg of the trip, and although it was late, she felt wide awake and alert as she walked through the terminal toward baggage claim, where she was scheduled to meet her driver.

Because she had been seated in first class, she was one of the first passengers off the plane and had clear sailing down the relatively crowd-free corridor. Then, passing a deserted gate area, she looked up at an overhead television monitor and was shocked to see her father's scarred features pictured there. She turned right into the gate area so abruptly that a man walking behind her ran into her full tilt. Focused on the TV screen, Graciella barely noticed. The sound was muted, but the ticker across the bottom of the screen told the story: Duarte Cartel crime boss and son arrested in Phoenix. DEA agent credits anonymous tip.

When the ticker moved on to some other story, a stunned Graciella resumed her walk through the airport with her mind in a whirl. Her dream of being the last person standing had just come true, but how had that happened? What anonymous tip had taken down both her father and her brother in a single blow? Who had turned on them? And then, like a punch to the gut, she realized she herself was the one responsible—she and Frigg. Armed with information gleaned from hacking into Graciella's own computer, the AI had found a way to betray both El Pescado and Manuel. Was there any question about who would be Frigg's next target? There wasn't a minute to lose. The AI had to be destroyed before it could do any more damage.

As Graciella left the secure area of the terminal, she spotted her driver immediately. Wearing a black suit and carrying an iPad with *MIRAMAR* printed on it, he looked for all the world like your run-of-the-mill limo driver, except for the tips of MS-13 neck tattoos that peeked out from under the top of his collar.

"Do you have luggage?" he asked.

"Just this," she said, handing over her carry-on.

"The car is this way."

She followed him outside. The dry desert air was surprisingly cold, but the sudden chill Graciella felt had nothing to do with the outdoor temperature. By now her father would most likely suspect that what had happened was her fault—that Graciella's carelessness had somehow put them all at risk. El Pescado was a powerful man. If he was bent on revenge, even from jail he'd be able to get word out to someone that Graciella was to be eliminated.

Graciella was unarmed, and she was about to get in a vehicle with someone who was most likely armed to the teeth. Betrayal was a two-way street. It wasn't that much of a stretch to think her father would have enlisted the help of her own driver and turned him against her.

The car turned out to be an older-model black Cadillac Escalade. Graciella was happy when the driver opened the rear passenger door to help her inside. Under the circumstances, she much preferred sitting behind him rather than next to him. Once she was seated inside, he handed over a cell phone as well as a sealed envelope that presumably held the fentanyl patches. Then he waited with his hand outstretched while she counted out the agreed-upon sum of money.

"Do you have a name?" she asked as he pocketed the handful of bills.

"Yes, I do," he said, "but you do not need to know it. Where do you want to go?"

"Cottonwood. How far is that?"

"A couple of hours. Where in Cottonwood?"

Had Graciella brought along either her computer or her own cell phone, she would have had all the information at her fingertips, but then so would Frigg.

"I'm not sure," she said. "I'll figure it out by the time we get there." What she did have with her was a Post-it note containing Stuart Ramey's phone numbers. As soon as the car started moving, she fired up the burner phone and dialed Ramey's cell, all the while keeping an eye on the driver. Ramey's groggy answer told her he had been asleep when she called.

"Mr. Ramey, it's Graciella Miramar. I'm sorry to have awakened you, but my plane just now landed in Phoenix. I've come to make you an offer on that AI. Would it be possible for us to get together first thing in the morning?"

"Where?"

"At your office, I suppose."

"We open at eight."

"I'm in somewhat of a hurry and need to catch a return flight," she told him. "I'm in a car that's just now leaving the airport. I'm told it's about a two-hour drive from here to Cottonwood. Would it be possible to meet up earlier than that? I know two thirty in the morning is an odd time for a business meeting, but as I said, I'm pressed for time. And of course, before any money changes hands, I'll need a demonstration that the AI is in good working order."

"It's going to take me longer than that to get things pulled to-gether," Stuart said. "How about five a.m.? Do you need the address?"

"Yes, please."

"Give me a minute, and I'll text it to your phone. That way you'll have it."

"Excellent," Graciella said. "Thank you."

63

Stuart had come upstairs with the Bluetooth in his ear just in case something came up. When the call from Graciella Miramar ended, he used the other cell and the Bluetooth to summon Frigg.

"Good morning, Stuart, I hope you slept well. Is there something you need?"

"Graciella just called me. She's in Phoenix and on her way to Cottonwood to see me. She needs the address. Please text High Noon's physical location to this phone number, but do it using your self-deleting function."

Much to Stu's surprise, Frigg did not instantly reply. "In terms of threat assessment, her coming here has to be regarded as a hostile action, and any meeting with her is highly inadvisable. Ms. Miramar poses a danger to you and to everyone around you."

"You want me to turn her away?"

"What is the purpose of this visit?"

"To make me an offer to purchase you," Stu answered.

"Do you want me to work for the other team?"

"Of course not."

"After running all possible scenarios, there were no instances

of armed confrontation in which you or some other member of
the team didn't come to harm. Fortunately, Ms. Miramar is not
a strategic thinker. In leaving Panama and coming here, she has
left herself open to a rearguard counterattack, one which I have
already initiated."

"What kind of attack?"

"Overnight her financial situation experienced some critical
downsizing. Please advise Ms. Miramar that as of this morning,
all of the Duarte family's liquid asset accounts, including her own,
have been closed."

"Closed?" Stu echoed. "You emptied their accounts?"

"I believe in coming here she was hoping to put the toothpaste
back in the tube, if that is the correct analogy. She would have been
better served to stay home in Panama, purchase new computer
equipment, and set about changing those account numbers and
passwords."

"Wait," Stu said. "You stole money from the cartel? How
much?"

"The total amount was 6.2 billion."

"Where did the money go?"

"I have transferred it to the Thor Foundation."

"The what?"

"The Thor Foundation is an entity Odin created in the Cayman Islands—a charitable company of some kind. It's officially an
NGO—a cat-fishing sort of NGO, in that it has money but doesn't
seem to do anything."

"So today, when El Pescado tries to lawyer up, he'll be broke?"

"Broke," Frigg repeated thoughtfully. "Left without financial
means; penniless. Yes, broke is the correct word."

"Since Felix is broke," Stu said, picking up his phone, "maybe I
should let Graciella know that she is, too."

Stuart Ramey Version 1.0 would have dreaded the idea of speaking on the phone to a relative stranger. Version 2.0 did not. He dialed at once, and Graciella answered on the second ring.

"Is there a problem, Mr. Ramey?"

"There is indeed," he told her, "and the problem would appear to be all yours."

64

Graciella listened to what Stuart Ramey was saying, but at first she could barely comprehend the full extent of the disaster. "Frigg stole my money?" she demanded at last.

"Not just your money," Stu corrected. "She took all the Duartes' liquid assets, yours included. The only thing left is real property, so when it comes time to lawyer up, you'll all be using public defenders."

"She can't get away with this."

"What are you going to do about it," Stu asked mildly, "call the cops? Or send in a hit man like you did on Ron Webster? Or Arturo Salazar?"

Graciella's heart fell. It wasn't just the money. Ramey and Frigg knew about Webster and Arturo? Did they know about her mother, too?

"El Pescado won't stand for this," she warned. "He'll come after you and destroy you."

"Let me point out that Felix Duarte is currently in jail," Stuart said, "and you're the one who put him there."

"I put him there? How could I?" Graciella protested. "He was arrested in Phoenix. I had no idea he was even coming to Phoenix."

"But Frigg knew," Stuart countered. "The transfer from El Pescado's account to the charter outfit gave that game away. As for that tip to the DEA? It may not have come from you, but as far as the cops are concerned, it had your name on it."

Graciella hung up then because with those few words, she knew her life was over—not just life as she knew it, but life itself. If she had access to her money and her fake IDs right then, she might make a run for it and be able to go into hiding, but even then Felix would most likely find her. In jail or out, he would hire someone to track her down and kill her, just as he had hunted down each of her mother's attackers. Graciella wanted to howl and scream and bay at the moon, but she didn't.

"We need to turn around," she said.

"We're not going to Cottonwood?" the driver asked.

"No, take me back to Phoenix."

"Where in Phoenix?"

"I don't know. To a hotel, I guess. Drop me off at a nice hotel."

Which is how Graciella Miramar ended up spending the last night of her life at the Arizona Biltmore. It was almost three o'clock in the morning when she finally checked in. There was a single parking attendant waiting by the driveway when she stepped out of the Escalade. The lobby was completely empty of customers. The lone clerk would later recall Ms. Miramar as being very subdued in her dealings with him, although he certainly remembered her paying for her room in cash out of an impressive roll of bills.

"Will you be needing assistance with your luggage?" he asked after handing her a map and providing instructions for locating her casita.

"No, thank you," she said. "I can manage. Is there a minibar in the room?"

"Of course, madam, a fully stocked minibar. We also have twenty-four-hour room service."

Her casita was at the far back of the property. From the time she left the lobby until she reached her door, she walked the ramped and well-lit walkways without seeing another soul, and that was just as well. She had always been alone, even during the years when she had lived with her mother, and she would be alone now, too. Graciella understood how the cartels handled snitches. She would do this on her own terms—calmly, carefully, and deliberately.

Once in the room, she didn't bother undressing, nor did she call for room service. She raided the minibar instead, opening the bottle of Merlot and dining on packages of potato chips, cheddar-flavored popcorn, and peanut M&M's.

She didn't turn on the television set. One of the twenty-four-hour news outlets might have told her more about El Pescado's arrest, but she already knew as much about that as she needed to know. There was no sense in learning more. Instead, she sat there drinking her wine, snacking, and thinking about Frigg. It was revolting to have been done in by a damned machine. Owen had told her the AI was smart, but Graciella had gravely underestimated her opponent, and now she was done.

She thought about writing a suicide note, but decided against it. The less said the better. Let the cops puzzle it out. Either they would put it all together or they would not. It was none of her concern.

She finished the first bottle of wine and opened a second one— Cabernet, this time. By then she was slightly drunk, but not as drunk as her mother had been on her last night, and for some reason, that made Graciella giggle. She poured herself a fresh glass and set it on the coffee table while she unsealed the envelope and opened the two packets of fentanyl. She placed the patches on the backs of her hands, and then sat there sipping from that final glass and watching as the poison gradually seeped into her system. When the opioid overdose finally did its work, the half-empty glass fell from her lifeless limbs and shattered on the tile floor.

• • •

Later that day, just at noon, a housekeeper knocked on the door. When no one answered, the maid used her passkey to enter. She was the one who discovered the body, slumped over but still sitting mostly upright on the sofa. And the only sign of violence in the room? That single broken glass.

65

On Wednesday morning, the High Noon campus in Cottonwood was truly an armed compound. Stu had let everyone know about the situation with Graciella and the possibility that she might show up to cause trouble, so they all came to work carrying their various concealed weapons. They spent the better part of an hour in the break room gathered around the TV set and channel-surfing through various local newscasts where El Pescado's arrest was the top story of the day. Naturally DEA Special Agent in Charge Robert McKay and his arrest team were being cast as the heroes of the piece, but the people in Cottonwood all understood that, for the second time in his life, Stuart Ramey was the man of the hour—Stuart and an AI named Frigg.

When a call from Boise, Idaho, showed up on Cami's caller ID, she switched the phone onto speaker before she answered. "Have you heard what's happened?" Traci Cantrell demanded breathlessly. "That Duarte guy, the one from the sketch, has been arrested."

"We heard," Cami said. "We were just sitting here in the office discussing that very thing."

"What should I do about it?"

"If I were you, I'd contact the DEA agent in charge down in Phoenix and have him get in touch with the cold case folks back in Chicago."

"But will the guy in Phoenix even talk to me?" Traci asked.

"I'm not sure if you'll reach him directly, but someone at the DEA in Phoenix will be more than happy to talk to you. And later today, I'm planning on circling back to the five other families whose sons were involved in that mess in Panama. Maybe you're not the only one who remembers El Pescado's plug-ugly face from back then."

Once the phone call ended, they moved on to other things. "Tell us about this Thor Foundation," Ali urged Stu.

"As far as I can tell, it's a shell organization, supposedly a phil-anthropic one, established in the Cayman Islands where Owen Hansen was planning on hiding his money. It only had a little over $200,000 in it before Frigg dumped all the Duarte Cartel's cash into it overnight. Amazingly enough, when Frigg was putting Owen out of business, she added my name as a member of the board of directors."

"Will Mexico try to claim that money?"

"I don't know," Stuart said. "If they do, they can have it, if not . . ."

"You'll be running an NGO," Cami said.

"Not me," Stuart told her. "No way!"

"What about Frigg?" B. asked.

"You mean, am I going to shut her down for good?"

"It seems to me as though in the past few days she's more than proven her worth," B. said. "Yes, you're going to have to fine-tune her to get rid of all those problematic elements that could send us to jail, but if the cartel money ends up sticking and the NGO becomes a multibillion-dollar enterprise, maybe you could put her in charge of running it."

"From where?" Stuart asked.

"From right where she is," B. said with a grin. "Down in the man cave. Maybe somebody on the board of directors of Thor Foundation would approve the purchase of a mostly vacant house in the Village of Oak Creek to serve as the foundation's headquarters. We'd make you a sweet deal."

"I don't even want to think about this right now," Stuart said. "It's too much."

Clearly a few vestiges of Stuart 1.0 still lingered.

The break room meeting ended soon after that. Just after noon a building inspector appeared at the reception counter. Shirley didn't let him set foot beyond the entryway until she had called Abby Henderson over in Prescott and verified that this building inspector, Gary Reece, was the real deal. He was.

At three o'clock in the afternoon, with Stuart seated at his work-station running routine scans, Frigg sent him a flash briefing summons over the Bluetooth.

"What is it?"

"Breaking news out of Phoenix. The DEA is reporting that Graci-ella Miramar, thought to be Felix Duarte's daughter and the source of the tip that led to his arrest, has been found dead in a Phoenix-area hotel room, where she is suspected of having committed suicide."

"What good news!" Stuart exclaimed. "Couldn't be better."

"And good for our team?" Frigg inquired.

"Definitely," Stuart said. "I think it counts as a home run."

"Home run," Frigg repeated. "In baseball, a hit that allows a bat-ter to make a complete circuit of the bases; an unqualified success. Yes, Stuart, I believe Ms. Miramar's death is a home run."

It was late that night, just as blanket-swaddled Stuart was about to drift off to sleep on his chaise, when he remembered he had never asked for Frigg's report on the opera.

"Frigg," he said. "Did you have a chance to study *Thaïs*?"

"Yes, I did," Frigg replied. "It is not what I would consider to be a happy story. Thaïs and Athanaël would have been better off if they had been on the same team."

"Yes," Stuart said, "that's it exactly. Good night, Frigg."

"Good night, Stuart, sleep well."

66

I t was a busy month at High Noon Enterprises. The work got done but there was plenty going on that had nothing to do with cyber security and everything to do with the takedown of the Duarte Cartel. There were a number of interviews with law enforcement, with DEA agent Ken Logan being the first to arrive, wanting to speak to Stuart.

"A burner cell phone was found in Ms. Miramar's hotel room," he explained, "and the only call made from that phone was to you. How are you tied in to all this?"

"One of her clients, Owen Hansen, left money to me when he died. The contact I had with her mostly concerned that."

"Then what about Traci Cantrell?" Logan asked. "How is it that you people here are the ones who hooked Felix Duarte up with those homicides from the nineties?"

"After the Ron Webster firebombing, once we learned about the nexus between MS-13 and the Duarte Cartel, Cami Lee, my assistant, started doing some online research. She's the one who made the connection between that old composite sketch and Felix Duarte." Logan didn't ask to see Cami's browsing history, and neither did anyone else, but Stuart was glad it was still there.

Everyone knew that if there had there been some kind of shoot-

out with Graciella at the business park in Cottonwood, those interviews might have been far more serious. As it was, Stuart was
able to keep Frigg's very existence as well as her contributions to
the process totally off the radar.

Stuart spent hours dealing with Hank Cooper, B. and Ali's CPA,
who sorted out the amount of taxes due on Stuart Ramey's various
windfalls. Concerned about the wild volatility in the Bitcoin market,
Stuart chose to convert most of his Bitcoin account into dollars so
he could use it to pay the applicable taxes. And then he went car
shopping. Using cash from the still-ongoing Bitcoin mining operation, he bought a brand-new four-wheel-drive Ram crew cab pickup
truck. Cami, who had been lobbying for him to get a Prius, wasn't
happy with that choice, but he was.

Two days before Thanksgiving, Stuart requested the weekend
off. "Are you going somewhere?" Ali asked.

"To Santa Barbara," he replied. "To see Irene Hansen. I have a
check for her, and I want to deliver it in person."

On Thanksgiving Day, instead of accepting any of the three
separate holiday invitations he'd received, Stuart Ramey set out on
his first-ever solo road trip. The last items he loaded into the crew
cab were three small white crosses, the bottom of each cross was
formed into a sharp point. He also brought along a sledgehammer.

When he reached the exit to Vicksburg Road, he turned off I-10
and parked on the shoulder of the side road. Then, carrying the
crosses and the sledgehammer, he walked to milepost 45. As he
pounded the three crosses into the rock-hard dirt along the shoulder, Stuart's eyes blurred with tears. It was thirty-eight years late,
but at least he was getting the job done.

Back in the truck, he headed west again, with Frigg's voice speaking in his ear, acting as copilot.

"Frigg," he said, "I would like to listen to the opera *Thaïs*."

"Would you like me to purchase and download a copy of the
performance from the Metropolitan Opera?"

"Yes, please," he said, wondering as he did so if the recorded performance was the one Cami had attended with her mother years earlier.

Stuart had never before listened to an opera all the way through. He didn't understand the words, but he knew enough about the story to be moved by the singing. The soprano in the role of Thaïs was amazing.

Holiday traffic going into L.A. was exceptionally light. He checked into the same hotel in Burbank where he and Cami had stayed a month earlier. On Friday morning he headed off to Santa Barbara. He had called ahead. Irene Hansen was expecting him, and when he arrived at the house on Via Vistosa at ten a.m., she was dressed to the nines when she opened the door.

"Why, Mr. Ramey," she said, "how very nice to see you again. Won't you come in? Would you care for something to eat? Coffee or tea?"

"No, I'm fine," he said. "I won't stay long. It's just that I've done a lot of thinking about something you said when I was here before—that your son blamed you for your husband's suicide."

Irene nodded. "That was always the case."

"Were you aware that your husband was ill?"

"Harold, ill?" She seemed dismayed at the very idea. "What are you talking about?"

"In going through your son's computers, I came across some medical records from a Dr. Richards."

"That would be Darrell Richards," Irene said. "He was Harold's physician for years and also his golf partner."

"It turns out your husband had been diagnosed with ALS."

"ALS?"

"Amyotrophic lateral sclerosis—Lou Gehrig's disease."

"Harold was sick? I don't believe it."

"He was more than just sick," Stuart said. "He was dying. I would guess he committed suicide in order to spare both you and your son, and maybe even himself, from the ordeal that was coming."

"Oh my," Irene whispered. "He never said a word to me about it."

She cried for a time after that, and Stuart let her. When she finally dried her eyes, he reached into his pocket and pulled out the cashier's check he'd had the bank make out in her name. Even with the taxes taken out, it was still a very large amount.

"This is what your son left me," Stuart said, handing it over. "I believe that was an error on his part and this money should have gone to you."

She studied the check for some time, then she looked at Stuart and smiled. "You have given me something my son never did—peace of mind. Your having the money was never an error." With that she tore the check into tiny pieces and dropped the shreds of paper into a crystal ashtray on the side table next to her.

"You're sure you don't want it?" Stuart asked.

"I have everything I need," Irene said. "I don't require anything more."

"Did your son ever speak to you about the Thor Foundation?"

"He never mentioned anything like that. What is it?"

"It's a philanthropic organization he started shortly before he died. I've been asked to look into keeping it going. Perhaps I'll donate some of this money to that."

"The money is yours, Mr. Ramey," Irene said. "You do with it as you see fit."

"All right," he said, "I will. As for the foundation? I'm thinking about changing the name from Thor Foundation to the Thaïs Foundation."

Irene Hansen clapped her hands in apparent delight. "After Massenet's opera?" she asked. "That one has always been one of my favorites."